Winthrop Mackworth Praed

Essays

Collected and arranged by Sir George Young, with an introd. by Henry Morley

Winthrop Mackworth Praed

Essays

Collected and arranged by Sir George Young, with an introd. by Henry Morley

ISBN/EAN: 9783337217976

Printed in Europe, USA, Canada, Australia, Japan

Cover: Foto ©Andreas Hilbeck / pixelio.de

More available books at **www.hansebooks.com**

ESSAYS

BY

WINTHROP MACKWORTH PRAED

COLLECTED AND ARRANGED BY

SIR GEORGE YOUNG, BART., M.A.

WITH AN INTRODUCTION BY HENRY MORLEY

LL.D., PROFESSOR OF ENGLISH LITERATURE AT
UNIVERSITY COLLEGE, LONDON

LONDON

GEORGE ROUTLEDGE AND SONS

BROADWAY, LUDGATE HILL

GLASGOW AND NEW YORK

1887

INTRODUCTION.

The readers of our Library are greatly indebted to Sir George Young for his kindness in presenting them with this first collected edition of the prose writings of his uncle, Winthrop Mackworth Praed. He little knows the charm of the bright regions of Literature who cannot yield himself to full enjoyment of their infinite variety. As we pass from book to book, it is a long leap from Euripides to the brilliant young Etonian who brought all the grace of happy youth into such work as we have here. Happy the old who can grow young again with this book in their hands. If we all came into the world mature, and there were no childhood and youth about us, what a dull world it would be! Any book is a prize that brings the fresh and cheerful voice of youth into the region of true Literature. Of Praed's work in this way none can speak better than Sir George Young in his Preface.

Of his life, these are a few dry facts. He was born in 1802, lost his mother early, and went to Eton at the age of twelve.   He was still at Eton when, at the age of eighteen, in 1820, he and his friend Walter Blount edited the *Etonian,* which began its course in October 1820 and ended in July 1821.   In the following October Praed went to Trinity College, Cambridge, where he obtained a Fellowship.   He obtained medals for Greek odes and epigrams, a medal for English verse, and he was still full of the old grace of playfulness.   He was called to the Bar in 1829.   An elder sister died in 1830, and his love for her is shown in tender touches of his later verse.   The *vers de société* which he wrote, and which no man wrote better than Praed, retain their charm because their playfulness is on the surface of a manly earnest nature, from the depth of which a tone now and then rises that comes straight into our hearts. Praed was in Parliament from November 1830 until after the passing of the Reform Bill, and again in 1834, when he was Secretary to the Board of Control under Sir Robert Peel. His father died in 1835 ; in the same year Praed married ; and in July 1839 he died, aged thirty-seven.

H. M.

October 1887.

PREFACE.

—◦◦◦—

THE prose pieces of Winthrop Mackworth Praed have never before been presented in a collected form. They are worthy of preservation, in a degree hardly less than his verse; though by the latter he has hitherto been best known, and will probably be longest remembered. At the time when the high quality of his literary work obtained for the *Etonian* the honour, unprecedented in the case of a school magazine, of a complimentary notice in the *Quarterly Review*, it was to the merit of his prose, as much as to that of his poetry, that attention was called by the reviewer. It is not, however, as the phenomenally precocious work of a schoolboy that these papers have been thought worthy of reproduction in the UNIVERSAL LIBRARY. The circumstance that they were, most of them, written at Eton, is only to be accounted of as adding to their interest, by giving the reader a point of view from which to sympathize with the writer's humour. It would, however, be a mistake to consider the senior Etonian of 1820 as corresponding to any reasonable description of what is generally denoted by the word "schoolboy." At

the age of eighteen or nineteen, when his grandfathers had
already taken their first degrees, subjected to a discipline
as light as that of a modern University, more free to study
in the way the spirit moved him, or not to study at all, than
the undergraduate of a " good " college now, the pupil of
Goodall, Keate, or Plumptre was of a maturer sort than is
now to be found among the denizens of Sixth Forms. He
came between two ages in the history of our Public
Schools, in neither of which could such literary work as
here follows have been produced by a " schoolboy." There
preceded him the age in which a youth went early to the
University, and early into life. There has followed the day
in which "boys" at school, when no longer boys, but men
in years, are held fast by discipline to boyish studies, or at
any rate to boyish amusements. The circumstance that a
few individuals, of great and early matured literary gifts,
were assembled together under these conditions at a single
school, on two several occasions, in two successive generations, at an interval of about thirty years, operated to
enrich English Literature with two graceful and unique
volumes. Of the *Microcosm*, the best pieces are due to
Canning and Frere; in the *Etonian*, the share of Praed
surpasses and eclipses that of his contemporaries. From
his University friends, indeed, he derived powerful help;
there are a few lines of poetry, by William Sidney Walker,
better than any of his own; and there are a few pages of
prose, by Henry Nelson Coleridge, which are also better ;
but for sustained excellence, and for an energy and variety
in production, truly extraordinary under the circumstances,
Praed, and Praed only, is the hero of the *Etonian ;* the over-

praised and ambitiously constructed efforts of his friend
Moultrie not excepted.

After Praed left Eton, his bent led him to verse, rather
than to prose, as his appropriate vehicle of expression; and
it was only occasionally that he sent a prose contribution,
either to *Knight's Quarterly Magazine*, or to the *London
Magazine*, or to the ephemeral pages of the *Brazen Head*.
Two speeches of his in Parliament were "reprinted by
request;" but they seem to have owed this distinction
rather to the special interest, at the time, of their subject-
matter, than to any exceptional finish in their literary form.
They were speeches in Committee on the Reform Bills of
1831 and 1832, the one on moving as an amendment what
was afterwards known as the "three-cornered constituency"
arrangement; the other on moving, similarly, that freeholds
within the limits of boroughs should confer votes for the
borough and not for the county. His partly versified squib,
"The Union Club," in which he parodied the style and
matter of the principal speakers among Cambridge under-
graduates in 1822, has been included in this collection, for
the sake especially of the comical imitations of Lord
Macaulay and Lord Lytton. It was written, as Macaulay
himself informed me, "for Cookesley to recite at supper-
parties." The late Rev. William Gifford Cookesley, long an
assistant master at Eton, who acted as Lord Beaconsfield's
cicerone when he came down to the spot to make studies
for "Coningsby," is gratefully remembered by many of his
scholars for his genuine, if somewhat irregular, love of
literature, and for his hearty sympathy with boyish good-
fellowship. He was a contemporary of Praed's both at

Eton and Cambridge, and long preserved, in maturer years, his admirable faculty of mimicry.

Among the characteristics of these pieces will be found an almost unfailing good taste; a polished style, exhibiting a sparkle, as of finely constructed verse; a strong love of sheer fun, not ungracefully indulged; a dash of affectation, inoffensive, and such as is natural in a new-comer, upon whom the eyes of his circle have, by no fault of his, been drawn; a healthy, breezy spirit, redolent of the playing-fields; and a hearty appreciation of the pleasures arising from a first fresh plunge into the waters of literature. Powers of observation are shown of no mean order, and powers, also, of putting in a strong light, whether attractive or ridiculous, the more obvious features of everyday characters. These powers afterwards ripened into a truly admirable skill of political and social verse-writing; and they showed signs of deepening into a more forcible satiric power, tempered with humour, as his too short career drew towards its end.

Praed is moreover especially to be commended in that he is never dull. Although free from "sensationalism," he is not forgetful that the first business of a writer is—to be read. There are gentle lessons of good manners, of unselfishness, and of chivalry, to be read in his pages; they are not loudly trumpeted, but there they are; there is also a sincere respect for great minds and for good work in literature, enlivened, not neutralized, by unfailing high spirits. One could dispense, certainly, with some of his antithesis; perhaps with all his punning; but life is not so short, or so lively in itself, as to leave us no time to be amused, and no ground for gratitude to the writers who amuse us.

The only omissions from this collection are, besides the speeches above mentioned, the prefaces contributed, in the taste of the day, to the several numbers of the *Etonian*, under the title "The King of Clubs," and to *Knight's Quarterly Magazine*, under the title "Castle Vernon." These are lively in their way, but unequal, and full of allusions which would require notes to make them intelligible. Occasionally, too, they are padded out with contributory matter by other hands. One rather ambitious failure, to be found in the *Etonian*, "On Silent Sorrow," has also been omitted, and will not be missed.

It should be added, that the leading articles of the *Morning Post* newpaper, from August 1832 to some time in the autumn of 1834, were for the most part of Praed's writing. Many of them are exceedingly well written ; but their contents are, of necessity, too ephemeral for reproduction in these pages.

GEORGE YOUNG.

October 1887.

Praed's Essays.

———•◆•———

RHYME AND REASON.

" Non eadem est ætas, non mens."—Horace.

He whose life has not been one continued monotony ; he who has been susceptible of different passions, opposite in their origins and effects, needs not to be told that the same objects, the same scenes, the same incidents, strike us in a variety of lights, according to the temper and inclination with which we survey them. To borrow an illustration from external scenes,—if we are situated in the centre of a shady valley, our view is confined and our prospect bounded ; but if we ascend the topmost heights of the mountain by which that valley is overshadowed, the eye wanders luxuriantly over a perpetual succession of beautiful objects, until the mental faculties appear to catch new freedom from the extension of the sight ; we breathe a purer air, and are inspired with purer emotions.

Thus it is with men who differ from each other in their tastes, their studies, or their professions. They look on the same external objects with a different internal perception, and the view which they take of surrounding scenes is beautified or distorted, according to their predominant pursuit or their prevailing inclination.

We were led into this train of ideas by a visit which we lately paid to an old friend, who, from a strong taste for agricultural pursuits, has abandoned the splendour and absurdity of a town life, and devoted to the cultivation of a large farming establishment, in a picturesque part of England, all the advantages of a strong judgment and a good education. His brother, on the contrary, who was a resident at the farm during our visit, has less of sound understanding than of ardent genius, and is more remarkable for the warmth of his heart than the soundness of his head. In short, to describe them in a word, Jonathan sees with the eye of a merchant, and Charles with that of an enthusiast ; Jonathan is a man of business, and Charles is a poet. The contrast between their tempers is frequently the theme of conversation at the social meetings of the neighbourhood ; and it is always found that the old and the grave shake their heads at the almost boyish enthusiasm of Charles, while the young and the imprudent indulge in severe sarcasms at the mercenary and uninspired moderation of his brother. All parties, however, concur in admiring the uninterrupted cordiality which subsists between them, and in laughing good-humouredly at the various whims and foibles of these opposite characters, who are known throughout the country by the titles of Rhyme and Reason.

We arrived at the farm as Jonathan was sitting down to his substantial breakfast. We were delighted to see our old friend, now in the decline of life, answering so exactly the description of Cowper—

> An honest man close-buttoned to the chin,
> Broadcloth without, and a warm heart within.

We felt an inward satisfaction in contemplating his frieze coat, whose *début* we remember to have witnessed five years ago, and in speculating upon the snows which five additional winters had left upon his head since our last interview. It was some time before we recovered sufficiently from our reverie to inquire after the well-being of our younger companion, who had not yet made his appearance at the board. "Oh !" said Jonathan, " Charles is in his heyday years ; we must indulge him for the present ; we can't expect such regularity from five-and-twenty as from six-and-fifty." He had hardly done speaking when a loud halloo sounded as an avant-courier of Charles's approach, and in less than a minute he presented himself before us. "Ten thousand pardons!" he cried. "One's enough," said his brother. "I've seen the finest sunrise," said Charles. "You're wet through," said Jonathan. "I'm all over rapture," said Rhyme. "You're all over dirt," said Reason.

With some difficulty Charles was persuaded to retire for the re-adjustment of his dress, while the old man continued his meal with a composure which proved he was not unused to the morning excursions of his volatile yoke-fellow. By the time he had got through his beefsteak, and three columns of the *Courier*, Charles re-entered, and despatched the business of eating with a rapidity in which many a modern half-starved rhymer would be glad to emulate him. A walk was immediately proposed ; but the one had scarcely reached an umbrella, and the other prepared his manuscript book, when a slight shower of rain prevented our design. "Provoking," said Rhyme. "Good for the crop," said Reason.

The shower, however, soon ceased, and a fine clear sun encouraged us to resume our intentions, without fear of a second disappointment. As we walked over the estate, we were struck with the improvements made by our friend, both as regarded the comfort and the value of the property ; while now and then we could not suppress a smile on observing the rustic arbour which Charles had designed, or the verses which he had inscribed on our favourite old oak.

It was determined that we should ascend a neighbouring hill, which was dear to us from its having been the principal scene of our boyhood's amusements. "We must make haste," said Charles, "or we shall miss the view." "We must make haste," said Jonathan, "or we shall catch cold on our return." Their actions seemed always to amalgamate, though their motives were always different. We observed a tenant of our friend ploughing a small field, and stopped a short time to regard the contented appearance of the man, and the cheerful whistle with which he called to his cattle. "Beatus ille qui procul negotiis," said the poet. " A poor team, though," said his brother.

Our attention was next excited by a level meadow,

whose green hue, set off by the mixture of the white fleeces of a beautiful flock of sheep, was, to the observer of Nature, a more enviable sight than the most studied landscape of Gainsborough's pencil. "Lovely colours!" ejaculated Charles. "Fine mutton," observed Jonathan. "Delightful scene for a rustic hop!" cried the enthusiast. "I am thinking of planting hops," said the farmer.

We reached the summit of the hill, and remained for some moments in silent admiration of one of the most variegated prospects that ever the country presented to the contemplation of its most ardent admirer. The mellow verdure of the meadows, intermingled here and there with the sombre appearance of ploughed land, the cattle reclining in the shade, the cottage of the rustic peeping from behind the screen of a luxuriant hedge, formed a *tout·ensemble* which every eye must admire, but which few pens can describe. "A delightful landscape!" said Charles. "A rich soil," said Jonathan. "What scope for description!" cried the first. "What scope for improvement!" returned the second.

As we returned we passed the cottage of the peasant whom we had seen at his plough in the morning. The family were busily engaged in their several domestic occupations. One little chubby-faced rogue was conducting Dobbin to his stable, another was helping his sister to coop up the poultry, and a third was incarcerating the swine, who made a vigorous resistance against their youthful antagonist. "Tender!" cried Rhyme—he was listening to the nightingale. "Very tender!" replied Reason—he was looking at the pigs.

As we drew near home, we met an old gentleman walking with his daughter, between whom and Charles a reciprocal attachment was said to exist. The lateness of the evening prevented much conversation, but the few words which were spoken again brought into contrast the opposite tempers of my friends. "A fine evening, Madam," said the man of sense, and bowed. "I shall see you to-morrow, Mary!" said the lover, and pressed her hand. We looked back upon her as she left us. After a pause: "She is an angel!" sighed Charles. "She is an heiress," observed Jonathan. "She has ten thousand perfections," cried Rhyme. "She has ten thousand pounds," said Reason.

We left them the next morning, and spent some days in speculations on the causes which enabled such union of affections to exist with such diversities of taste. For ourselves, we must confess that, while Reason has secured our esteem, Rhyme has run away with our hearts; we have sometimes thought with Jonathan, but we have always felt with Charles.

ON THE PRACTICAL BATHOS.

" To sink the deeper—rose the higher."—POPE.

ALTHOUGH many learned scholars have laboured with much diligence in the illustration of the Bathos in poetry, we do not remember to have seen any essay calculated to point out the beauties and advantages of this figure when applied to actual life. Surely there is no one who will not allow that the want of such an essay is a desideratum which ought, as soon as possible, to be supplied. Conscious as we are that our feeble powers are not properly qualified to fill up this vacuum in scholastic literature; yet, since the learned commentators of the present day have their hands full either of Greek or politics, we, an unlearned, but we trust a harmless, body of quacks, will endeavour to supply the place of those who kill by rule, and will accordingly offer, for the advantage of our fellow-citizens, a few brief remarks on the Practical Bathos.

We will first lay it down as a principle that the ἀπροσδόκητον, as well in life as in poetry, is a figure, the beauties of which are innumerable and incontrovertible. For the benefit of my fair readers (for Phœbus and Bentley forbid that an Etonian should here need a Lexicon) I will state that the figure ἀπροσδόκητον is "that which produceth things unexpected." Take a few examples. In poetry there is a notable instance of this figure in the " Œdipus

Tyrannus" of Sophocles, where the messenger who discloses to Œdipus his mistake in supposing Polybus to be his father, believing that the intelligence he brings is of the most agreeable nature, plants a dagger in the heart of his hearer by every word he utters. But Sophocles, although he must be acknowledged a great master of the dramatic art, is infinitely surpassed in the use of this figure by our good friend Mr. Farley of Covent Garden. When we sit in mute astonishment to survey the various pictures which he conjures up, as it were by the wand of a sorcerer, in a moment—when columns and coal-holes, palaces and pigsties, summer and winter, succeed each other with such perpetually diversified images; we are continually exclaiming, "Mr. Farley, what next?" Every minute presents us with a new and more perfect specimen of this figure. Far be it from us to speak disrespectfully of Sophocles, for whom, as in duty bound, we entertain a most sincere veneration; but he certainly must rank beneath Mr. Farley as a manager of the ἀπροσδόκητον. One of the most striking examples in the present day, which we can recommend to those who wish to apply this figure to the purposes of actual life, is (may we say it without being accused of a political allusion?) her Majesty Queen Caroline. That illustrious personage in one beautiful passage (we mean her passage from Calais to Dover) has certainly proved herself a perfect mistress of the ἀπροσδόκητον.

Of this figure the Bathos must be considered a most elegant species. Again, for the benefit of our fair readers, we will observe, that the usual signification of the Bathos is —the Art of Sinking in Poetry; but what we here propose to discuss is "the Art of Sinking in Life"—an art of which it may be truly said that those who practise it skilfully only stoop to conquer.

It must be evident to every person who is at all conversant with the motives and origin of human opinions, that man is accustomed to regard with a feeling of animosity those who are pre-eminent in any science or virtue—

> Urit enim fulgore suo qui præegravat artes
> Infra se positas.

But this invidious and hostile feeling vanishes at once,

when we behold the object of it sinking suddenly from the dazzling sphere he originally occupied, and reducing himself to a level with ordinary mortals. The divine and incomparable Clarissa would never have been considered divine and incomparable, had she never been betrayed into a *faux pas;* and I question whether Bonaparte was ever looked upon with so favourable an eye as when he afforded a specimen of the Bathos, in his descent from "the Emperor of France" to "the Captive of St. Helena."

But the strongest argument that can be used in recommendation of this science is, that we are by Nature herself compelled to make use of it. Whatever riches we may amass, whatever age we may attain, whatever honours we may enjoy, we are continually looking forward to one certain and universal Bathos, "Death." From learning, from wealth, from power, our descent is swift and inevitable. We look upon the graves of our kindred, and say with Hamlet, "To this must we come at last."

This doctrine is so beautifully illustrated by a passage in Holy Writ, that we cannot refrain from laying it before our readers :—

"Alexander, son of Philip the Macedonian, made many wars, and won many strongholds, and slew the kings of the earth. And he gathered a mighty strong host, and ruled over countries and nations and kings, who became tributaries to him. And after these things he fell sick, and perceived that he should—*die.*" *

A more beautiful instance of this figure cannot be imagined. It needs no comment. But we fear we are growing too serious, and shall therefore pursue this branch of our dissertation no further.

We hope our readers are by this time thoroughly convinced of the beauty and utility of this figure; we will proceed to exhort them most earnestly to apply themselves immediately to the study of "the Art of Sinking in Life."

The art may be divided into a great number of species ; but all, we believe, may be comprehended under two heads —the *Bathos Gradual* and the *Bathos Precipitate.* We will offer a few concise remarks upon both, without pre-

---

* Maccabees, ch. i.

tending to decide between the various merits of each. Indeed, the opinion of the world appears pretty much divided between them; as there are some bathers, who stand for a time shivering on the brink, and at last totter into the stream with a tardy and reluctant step, while there are others who boldly plunge into the tide with a hasty and impetuous leap.

The Bathos Gradual is principally practised by poets and by coquettes. Of its use by the former we have frequent examples in our own day. A gentleman publishes a book: it is bought, read, and admired. He publishes another, and his career of sinking immediately commences. First he sinks into a book-maker; next he sinks into absurdity; next he sinks into mediocrity; next he sinks into oblivion; and, as it is impossible for him to sink much lower, he may then begin to think of rising to a garret.

The life of Chloe affords an admirable instance of the effect with which this species of the art may be exercised by coquettes. At twenty-four, Chloe was a fashionable beauty; at twenty-six she began to paint; at twenty-eight she was—not what she had been; and at thirty she was voted a maiden lady! Or, to use the slang of the loungers of the day: at twenty-four she was bang-up; at twenty-six she was a made-up thing; at twenty-eight was done up; and at thirty it was—all up with her.

The Bathos Precipitate is adapted to the capacities of great generals, substantial merchants, dashing bloods, and young ladies who are in haste to be married.* For examples of it in the first we must refer you to Juvenal's Tenth Satire, as this part of our subject is hackneyed, and we despair of saying anything new upon it.

---

* We might have added stage managers. Their genius for the Bathos Precipitate is frequently displayed in notices of the following kind:—

"Monday, January 7.

"The new drama, entitled ——, has been received with uninterrup'ed bursts of applause, and will be repeated every evening till farther notice."

"Tuesday, January 8.

"In obedience to the wishes of the public, the new drama, entitled ——, is withdrawn."

For examples of the Bathos Precipitate in trade, you must make inquiries among the Dulls and Bears on the Stock Exchange; they can instruct you much better than ourselves by what method you may be a *good* man at twelve o'clock, and a bankrupt at one.

Upon referring to our memoranda, we find some inimitable examples of this species of the Bathos among the two latter classes of its practitioners. Some of these we will extract for the amusement of our readers :—

Sir Edmund Gulley.—Became possessed of a handsome property by the death of his uncle, February 7, 1818. Sat down to Rouge et Noir, February 14, 1818, 12 o'clock P.M. Shot himself through the head, February 15, 1818, 2 o'clock A.M.

Lord F. Maple.—Acquired great *éclat* in an affair of honour, March 2, 1818. Horsewhipped for a scoundrel at the Second Newmarket Meeting, 1818.

Mr. G. Bungay.—September 1819—Four-in-hand, blood horses, shag coat, pearl buttons. October 1819—Plain chaise and pair.

Miss Lydia Dormer.—May 1820—Great beauty, manifold accomplishments, £4000 a-year. June 1820—*Chère amie* of Sir J. Falkland.

The Hon. Miss Amelia Tempest.—(From a daily paper of July 1820.) —"Marriage in High Life.—The beautiful Miss Amelia Tempest will shortly be led to the hymeneal altar by the Marquis of Looney."

(From the same paper of August 1820.)—"Elopement in High Life.— Last week the Hon. Miss Am-l-a T-mp-st eloped with her father's footman."

Reader,—When we inform you that we ourselves had long entertained a sneaking kindness for the amiable Amelia, you will image to yourself the emotion with which we read the above paragraph. We jumped from the table in a paroxysm of indignation, and committed to the flames the obnoxious chronicler of our disappointment; but the next moment composed our feelings with a truly stoic firmness, and, with a steady hand, we wrote down the name of the Hon. Miss Amelia Tempest as an admirable proficient in the Bathos Precipitate.

NICKNAMES.

" Lusco qui possit dicere 'lusce.'"

THE invention and appropriation of Nicknames are studies which, from want of proper cultivation, have of late years very much decayed.   Since these arts contribute so much to the well-being and satisfaction of our Etonian witlings—since the younger part of our community could hardly exist if they were denied the pleasure of affixing a ludicrous addition to the names of their seniors—we hope that the consideration of this art in all its branches and bearings will be to many an amusing, and to some an improving, disquisition.

The different species of nicknames may be divided and subdivided into an endless variety.   There is the nickname direct, the nickname oblique, the nickname κατ' ἐξοχὴν, the nickname κατ' ἀντιφράσιν, and a multitude of others, which it is unnecessary here to particularize.   We shall attempt a few remarks upon these four principal classes.

The nickname direct, as might be expected, is by far more ancient than any other we have enumerated.   Much has been argued upon the elegance or inelegance of Homer's perpetually repeated epithets; for our part we imagine Homer thought very little upon the elegance or inelegance of the expressions to which we allude, since we cannot but regard his Ξανθὸς Μενέλαος—πόδας ὠκὺς Αχιλλεὺς— ἄναξ ἄνδρων Αγαμέμνων, and other passages of the same kind, not even excepting the thundering cognomen which is tacked on to his Jupiter, Ζεὺς ὑψιβρεμέτης, as so many ancient and therefore inimitable specimens of the nickname direct.   This class is with propriety divided into two smaller descriptions; the nickname personal and the nickname descriptive.   The first of these is derived from some bodily defect in its object; the latter from some excellence or infirmity of the mind.

The nicknames which were applied to our early British kings generally fell under one of these denominations.

William Rufus and Edward Longshanks are examples of the first, while Henry Beauclerc and Richard Cœur de Lion afford us instances of the second. We cannot depart from this part of our subject without adverting to the extreme liberty which the French have been accustomed to take with the names of their kings. With that volatile nation, "the Cruel," "the Bald," and "the Fat" seem as constantly the insignia of royalty as the sceptre and the crown. We must confess that, were it not for the venerable antiquity of the species, we should be glad to see the nickname personal totally discontinued, as in our opinion the most able proficient in this branch of the science evinces a great portion of ill-nature, and very little ingenuity.

The merit of the nickname oblique consists principally in its incomprehensibility. It is frequently derived, like the former, from some real or imaginary personal defect; but the illusion is generally so twisted and distorted in its formation, that even the object to whom it is applied is unable to trace its origin or to be offended by its use. The discovery of the actual fountain from whence so many ingenious windings and intricacies proceed is really a puzzling study for one who wishes to make himself acquainted with the elementary principles of things. In short, the nickname oblique resembles the great river, the Nile: its meanders are equally extensive, its source is equally concealed. We have a specimen of this species in the appellation of our worthy secretary. Mr. Golightly made a pleasant, though a sufficiently obvious hit, when he addressed Mr. Richard Hodgson by the familiar abbreviation of Pam. We should recommend to the professors of the nickname oblique, two material, though much neglected, requisites—simplicity and perspicuity; for, in spite of the long and attentive study which we have devoted to this branch of the art, we ourselves have been frequently puzzled by unauthorized corruptions both of sound and sense, and lost amidst the circuitous labyrinth of a far-fetched prænomen. We were much embarrassed by hearing our good friend, Mr. Peter Snaggs, addressed by the style of "Fried Soles," until we remembered that his grandfather had figured as a violent Methodist declaimer in the metropolis: nor could we conceive by what means our old associate, Mr. Matthew Dunstan, had obtained his classical title of "Forceps," until we recollected the miraculous attack made by the tongs of his prototype upon the nasal orifices of his Satanic antagonist.

The third species is derived from an implied excellence in any one specified study. It is known by the sign "The." Thus, "*The* Whistler," in "Tales of My Landlord," is so called from his having excelled all others in the polished and fashionable art of whistling. When we call Mr. Ouzel "*the* blockhead," we are far from asserting that he is the only blockhead among our well-beloved companions, but merely that he holds that title from undisputed superlative merit; and, when we distinguish Sampson Noll by the honourable designation of "*The* Nose," we mean not to allege that Mr. Noll is the only person who challenges admiration, from the extraordinary dimensions of that feature, but simply, that Sampson's nose exceeds, by several degrees of longitude, the noses of his less distinguished competitors.

We know not, however, whether the species which we are discussing is not rather to be considered a ramification of the first, than a separate class in itself; for it unavoidably happens that the two kinds are frequently confused, and that we know not under which head to arrange a name which is of an ambiguous nature, and may be referred with equal propriety to either definition.

The fourth and last kind is promiscuously derived from sources similar to those of the three preceding; but in its formation it entirely reverses their provisions. We all know that a grove was called by the Latins "lucus;" *a non lucendo*, that the Præses of the Lower House of Parliament is called by us, "Speaker," because he is not allowed to speak. Such is the system of the nickname which is at present under consideration; it is applied to its object, not from the qualities which he possesses, but from those which he does not; not from the actions which he has performed, but from those which he has not: in short, contrariety is its distinguishing character, and absurdity its principal merit. Antiquity will supply us with several admirable specimens. Ptolemy murdered his brother, and was called "Philadelphus." The Furies, to say the best of them, were spiteful old maids, and they were nicknamed "The Benevolent." In our times it is certainly in more general use than any other class ; nor is this to be wondered at, when we consider the extraordinary neatness of irony which is with great facility couched under it. It has been well observed by some French author, whose name has escaped our memory, that if you call Vice by her own name, she laughs at you ; but if you address her by the name of Virtue, she blushes. To give a plainer illustration : if you say to Ouzel "Blockhead," it is an unregarded truth ; if you cry out to him, "Genius," it is a biting sarcasm. Nothing, indeed, can be imagined more malignantly severe than this weapon of irony, exercised with skill, and pointed with malevolence ; no satire is more easy to the assailant, and more painful to the assailed, than that which gives to deformity the praise of beauty, and designates absurdity by the title of absolute wisdom.

We lately had the honour of reckoning among our nearest and dearest friends Dr. Simon Colley, a gentleman who was as estimable for the excellent qualities of his mind as he was ridiculous from the whimsical proportions of his body. Must we give a description of our much lamented friend? If the reader will collect together the various personal defects of all his acquaintance—if he will add the lameness of one to the diminutive stature of another—if he will unite the cast of the eye which designates a third to the departure from the rectilineal line which beautifies the back of a fourth, he will then have some faint idea of the bodily perfections of Dr. Simon Colley. The Doctor was perfectly conscious of his peculiarities, and was frequently in the habit of choosing his corporal appearance as the theme of a hearty laugh or the subject of jocular lamentation ; yet the sound sense and cultivated philosophy of our respected friend was not proof against the unexpected vociferation of a well-applied nickname ; and, although his favourite topic of conversation was the personal resemblance he bore to the renowned Æsop, he flew into the most violent paroxysms of rage when he was pointed at by some little impertinents as the Apollo Belvidere.

But this sort of nickname is not used merely as the instrument of wit or the weapon of ill-nature: it assumes occasionally a more serious garb, and becomes the language of flattery or the adulation of hypocrisy. In this form it is of great service in dedicatory epistles and professions of love. When Vapid entreats Lord —— to prefix his name to a list of subscribers, he whines out the praises of his "Mæcenas" with all the mournful earnestness with which a criminal exalts the clemency of his judge; but the manner in which he chuckles at the munificence of his patron over a beefsteak at the Crown and Cushion proves very evidently that Vapid is a hypocrite, and that "Mæcenas" is a nickname. And when Miss Pimpkinson, a maiden lady with £40,000, smiles upon the adoration of Sir Horace Conway, a fashionable without a farthing, she little dreams that "Venus," which is her title in the boudoir, is only her nickname at the club.

Having now presented our friends with a cursory sketch of these four principal classes, we shall sum up the whole by offering to the reader a specimen in which we lately heard the four kinds admirably blended together. "Toup," cried "All the Talents," "tell 'Swab' that I have a thrashing in store for 'The Poet.'" "Toup" is the nickname oblique, borne by its possessor in consequence of some supposed relation between the longitude of his physiognomy and the Longinus of the erudite Toupius; "Swab" is the nickname direct, applied to a rotund gentleman; "*The* Poet" is κατ' ἐξοχὴν—"*the* poet," because he is super-eminently poetical; and "All the Talents" is κατ' ἀντιφράσιν—"All the Talents," because he is the veriest blockhead upon the face of our Etonian hemisphere.

It will be needless to enumerate the many minor classes of this important subject; it will be needless to dwell upon the nickname classical, the nickname clerical, the nickname military, and the nickname bargee; as we believe that no specimen of these is to be found which may not be ranked under one of the preceding descriptions. There is, however, one great and extensive species remaining, to which we shall here give only a brief notice, as we may possibly, at some future period, devote a leading article to its consideration—we mean the nickname general. This last-mentioned class claims our attention, from the comprehensive range of its operation. It is not applied to the mental foibles or personal defects of a single object, it does not attack the failings of a solitary individual, it wastes not the lash of censure on an isolated instance of absurdity; but it inflicts a wound upon thousands in a moment, and stamps the mark of ridicule upon numberless victims. The Quizzes, the Prigs, the Marines, the Chaises are, amongst our *alumni*, well-known examples of the nickname general.

But we have too long lost sight of the main object of our present lucubration, which was the recommendation of this art to our fellow-citizens, as a commendable, though much neglected, study. When we say much neglected, we mean not that nicknames have ceased to be the rage, and are falling into disuse (for certainly there never was an age in which they spread more luxuriantly); but we allude to the lamentable decay of imagination and ingenuity in their formation. If we look back to ancient times, we shall find that, in those days, nicknames were derived from the same sources as in the present age; they had their origin from natural defects, from personal deformities; yet how amazingly do the *cognomina* of antiquity exceed in elegance and taste the nicknames of more modern date. How wonderfully are the "Chicken," the "Shanks," the "Nosey," of Etonian celebrity surpassed by the "Pullus," the "Scaurus," the "Cicero," of Roman literature. It is a disgrace upon the genius of our generation, that, at a time when other arts have arrived at such a high perfection that our age may almost be considered the Augustan age of the world, the art of nicknames should have totally lost the classical polish for which it was in the olden time so eminently remarkable, until it has sunk into the vehicle of vulgar abuse, neither adorned by wit nor chastened by urbanity.

These considerations have induced us to give our most serious attention to the advancement and improvement of the art. We are confident that our researches in this line of literature have not been misapplied; and our readers will surely agree with us, when they reflect on the manifold utility of the study, when properly cultivated. There is so little variety in English Christian names, that, where friends are in the habit of using them, great mistakes must naturally take place. A surname, as Charles Surface observes, "is too formal to be registered in Love's calendar." A nickname avoids alike the ambiguity of one, and the stiffness of the other; it unites all the familiarity of the first with all the utility of the second. Besides this, the nickname is a brief description of its object: it saves a million of questions, and an hour of explanation: it is in itself a species of biography. Homer, when he gives to his Juno the nickname of "Bull-eyed," expresses in a word what a modern rhymer would dilate into a canto.

For the rescuing of nicknames from the obloquy into which they have fallen, we have collected a large assortment of them, which we are ready to dispose of to applicants at a very low price. We have in our stock appellations of every descriptions—the Classical, the Familiar, the Theatrical, the Absurd, the Complimentary, the Abusive, and the Composite. By an application at our publisher's, new nicknames may be had at a moment's notice. The wit and the blockhead, the sap and the idler, shall be fitted with denominations which shall be alike appropriate and flattering, so that they shall neither outrage propriety nor offend self-conceit. The dandy shall be suited with a name which shall bear no allusion to stays, and the coquette with one which shall in no way reflect upon rouge. In short, we have a collection of novelties adapted to both sexes, and proper for all ages. In one thing only is our stock deficient; and that, we are confident, will be supplied previous to the appearance of our second number. We have no doubt that some obligingly sarcastic associate will favour us with a new and an ingenious nickname for the *Etonian.*

YES AND NO.

"We came into the world like brother and brother,
And now let's go hand in hand, not one before another."
SHAKESPEARE.

MR. LOZELL'S TREATISE ON THE ART OF SAYING "YES."	MR. OAKLEY'S TREATISE ON THE ART OF SAYING "NO."
" He humbly answered 'Yea! Bob.'" ANON.	" My son—learn betimes to say No." MISS EDGEWORTH.

OUR opinion is very much strengthened by the belief that many of our friends will assent to it, when we assert that no art requires in a greater degree the attention of a young man, on his entrance into life, than that of saying "Yes." A man who deigns not to use this little word is a bulldog in society; he studies his own gratification rather than that of his friends, and of course accomplishes neither: in short, he deserves not to be called a civilized being, and is totally unworthy of the place which he holds in the creation.

Is not it right to believe the possible fallacy of one's own opinion?—Yes. Is not it proper to have a due consideration for the opinion of others?—Yes! Is not it truly praiseworthy to sacri-

OUR opinion is not a jot weakened by the probability that many of our friends will dissent from it, when we assert that no art requires in a greater degree the attention of a young man, on his entrance into life, than that of saying " No." A man who is afraid to use this little word is a spaniel in society; he studies to please others rather than to benefit himself, and of course fails in both objects: in short, he deserves not to be called a man, and is totally unworthy of the place which he holds in the creation.

Is he a rational being who has not an opinion of his own?—No. Is he in the possession of his five senses who sees with the eyes, who hears with the ears, of other men?—No!

fice our conviction, our argument, our obstinacy upon the shrine of politeness?—Again and again we answer —Yes! yes! yes! ·

Nothing indeed is to us more gratifying than to behold a man modestly diffident of the powers which Nature has bestowed upon him, and assenting, with a proper sense of his own fallibility, to the opinions of those who kindly endeavour to remedy his faults or to supply his deficiencies. Nothing is to us more gratifying than to hear from the lips of such a man that true test of a complying disposition—that sure prevention of all animosity —that immediate stop to all quarrels—that sweet, civil, complacent, inoffensive monosyllable—Yes!

Yet, alas! how many do we find who, from an affectation of singularity, or a foolish love of argument, do as it were expunge this admirable expression from their vocabularies. How many do we see around us, who are in the daily habit of losing the most advantageous offers, of quarrelling with strangers, and of offending their best friends,

Does he act upon principle who sacrifices truth, honour, and independence, on the shrine of servility?—Again and again we reply—No! no! no!

Nothing indeed is to us more gratifying than to behold a man relying boldly on the powers which Nature has bestowed upon him, and spurning, with a proper consciousness of independence, the suggestions of those who would reduce him from the rank he holds as a reasonable creature to the level of a courtier and a time-server. Nothing is to us more gratifying than to hear from the lips of such a man that decided test of a free spirit —that finisher to all dispute— that knock-down blow in all arguments —that strong, forcible, expressive, incontrovertible monosyllable— No!

Yet, alas! how many do we find who are either unable or unwilling to pronounce this most useful, most necessary response! How many do we see around us, who are in the daily habit of professing to know things of which they are altogether ignorant, of making promises which it is impossible for them to perform, of saying (to use for solely because they obstinately refuse to call to their assistance the infallible remedy for all these evils, which is to be found in the three letters upon which we are offering a brief comment.

We are sure we are only chiming in with the opinion of other people, when we lament the manifold and appalling evils which are the sure consequences of this disinclination to affirmatives. To us it is really melancholy to look upon the disposition to contradiction by which some of our friends are characterized, to observe the manifest pride of some, the unreasonable pertinacity of others. Of a surety, if we are doomed at any future season to put on the yoke of wedlock, Mrs. L. and all the Masters and Misses L. shall be early instructed in the art of saying "Yes."

Look into the pages of history! You will find there innumerable examples in support of our opinion. When the Greeks begged Achilles to pocket his affronts and make an end of Hector, he refused. Very well, we have no doubt he did all for the best; but we are morally sure that Patroclus would

once a soft expression) the thing which *is not*, solely because they will not call to their assistance the infallible remedy for all these evils, which is to be found in the two letters upon which we are offering a brief comment.

It is dreadful to reflect upon the evils which this neglect must infallibly produce. It is dreadful to look round upon the friends and relatives whom we see suffering the most appalling calamities from no other misconduct than a blind aversion to negatives. It is disgusting to observe the flexible indecision of some, the cringing servility of others. Forgive us, reader, but we cannot help soliloquizing: "God save the King of Clubs, and may the Princes of the Blood Royal be early instructed in the art of saying 'No.'"

Look into the pages of history! You will find there innumerable examples in support of our opinion. Pompey was importuned to give battle to Cæsar: he complied. Poor devil! He would never have been licked at Pharsalia if he had learned from us the art of saying "No." Look at the conduct of his rival and not have been slain if Achilles had known how to say "Yes." We all know how he cried about it when it was too late. To draw another illustration from the same epoch, how disastrous was the ignorance which Priam displayed of this art when a treaty was on foot for the restoration of Helen. Nothing was easier than to finish all disputes, to step out of all difficulties, by one civil, obliging, gentlemanly "Yes." But he refused— and Troy was burned. What glorious results would a contrary conduct have produced! It would have prevented a peck of troubles both to the Greeks and the Etonians. It would have saved the Ancients ten years, and the Moderns twelve books, of bloodshed. It is almost unnecessary to allude to the imprudent, the luckless Hippolytus: he never would have been murdered by a marine monster if he could but have said "Yes;" but the word stuck in his throat, and he certainly paid rather dear for his ignorance.

"Yes," cries a critic, "I agree with all this, but it's all so old." We assent to your opinion, my good friend, and will endeavour conqueror, Cæsar! You remember the words of Casca, "I saw Mark Antony offer him a crown and he put it by once; but for all that, to my thinking, he would fain have had it!" Now this placid "putting by" was not the thing for the Romans: we are confident Julius Cæsar would never have died by cold steel in the Senate if he had given them a good decisive insuperable "No!" Whatever epoch we examine, we find the same reluctance to say "No" to the allurements of pleasure and the mandates of ambition, and alas! we find it productive of the same consequences. Juvenal tells us of an unfortunate young man, one Caius Silius, who was unlucky enough to be smiled upon by the Empress Messalina. The poor boy knew the danger he ran — he saw the death which awaited him; but an Empress sued, and he had not the heart to say "No!" He lost his heart first, and his head shortly afterwards.

"Dam'me," says a blood, "all that happened a hundred years ago." An Etonian has occasionally great difficulty in carrying to benefit by your suggestion. Come, then, we will look for illustrations among the characters of our own age.

There's Lord Duretête, the misanthrope. He has a tolerable fortune, tolerable talents, and tolerable person. He plays a tolerable accompaniment on the flute, and a tolerable hand at whist. Yet, with all these tolerable qualifications, he is considered a most intolerable man. What is the reason of this seemingly anomalous circumstance? The reason is obvious—His Lordship can't say "Yes." This abominable ignorance of our favourite art interferes in the most trivial incidents of life; it renders him alike miserable and disagreable. "Will your Lordship allow me to prefix your name to a dedication?" says Bill Attic, the satirist. "I must go mad first," says his Lordship. "Duretête! lend me a couple of hundreds!" says Sir Harry. "Can't, 'pon honour!" says his Lordship. "You dear creature, you'll open my ball this evening!" says Lady Germain. "I'll be d—d if I do!" says his Lordship. See the catastrophe. Bill Attic lampoons him, Sir

his ideas a hundred years back. Well, then, we will go example-hunting nearer home.

There's Sir Philip Plausible, the Parliament man. He can make a speech of nine hours and a calculation of nine pages; nobody is a better hand at getting up a majority, or palavering a refractory Oppositionist; he proffers an argument and a bribe with equal dexterity, and converts by place and pension when he is unable to convince by alliteration and antithesis. What a pity it is he can't say "No!" "Sir Philip," says an envoy, "you'll remember my little business at the Foreign Office!" "Depend upon my friendship," says the Minister. "Sir Philip!" says a fat citizen, with two votes and two dozen children, "you will remember Billy's place in the Customs!" "Rely on my promise!" says the Minister. "Sir Philip!" says a lady of rank, "Ensign Roebuck is an officer most deserving promotion!" "He shall be a colonel! I swear by Venus!" says the Minister. *Exitus ergo quis est?* He has outraged his friendship, he has forgotten his

B

Harry spits in his face, and Lady Germain votes him a bore. How unlucky that he cannot say "Yes!"

Look at young Eustace, the man of honour! He came up to town last year with a good dress, a good address, and letters of introduction to half a dozen great men. He made his bow to each of them, spent a week with each of them, offended each of them, and is now starving in a garret upon independence and cold mutton. What is the meaning of all this? Eustace never learned how to say "Yes!" "*Virtus post nummos!* Eh! young man?" says old Discount, the usurer. "I can't say I think so," said Eustace. "Here! Eustace, boy," says Lord Fanny, "read over these scenes, and let me have your opinion! Fit for the boards, I think! Eh?" "You'll excuse me if I don't think they are," says Eustace. "Well! my young friend," cries Mr. Pliant, "we must have you in Parliament I suppose; make an orator of you! You're on the right side, I hope?" "I should vote with my conscience, Sir," says Eustace. See the finale. Eustace is

promise, he has falsified his oath. Had he ever an idea of performing what he spoke? Quite the reverse! How unlucky that he cannot say "No!"

Look at Bob Lily! There lives no finer poet! Epic, elegiac, satiric, Pindaric—it is all one to him! He is patronized by all the first people in town. Everybody compliments him, everybody asks him to dinner. Nay! there are a few who read him. He excels alike in tragedy and farce, and is without a rival in amphibious dramas, which may be called either the one or the other; but he is a sad bungler in negatives. "Mr. Lily," says the Duchess, his patroness, "you will be sure to bring that dear epithalamium to my conversazione this evening!" "There is no denying your Grace," says the poet. "I say, Lily," says the Duke, his patron, "you will dine with us at seven?" "Your Grace does me honour," says the poet. "Bob," says the young Marquis, "you are for Brookes's to-night?" "Dam'me! to be sure," says the poet. Mark the result. He is gone to eat tripe with his tyrannical bookseller; he has disappointed his patroness, he has offended his enlisted for life in the Grub Street Corps, where he learns by sad experience how dangerous it is to say "No" to the avarice of a usurer, the vanity of a rhymer, or the party spirit of a politician. How unlucky that he cannot say "Yes."

Godfrey is a lover, and he has every qualification for the office except one. He cannot say "Yes." Nobody, without this talent, should presume to be in love. "Mr. Godfrey," says Chloe, "don't you think this feather pretty?" "Absurd!" says Godfrey. "Mr. Godfrey!" says the lady, "don't you think this necklace becoming?" "Never saw anything less so!" says Godfrey. "Mr. Godfrey," says the coquette, "don't you think I'm divine to-night?" "You never looked worse, by Jove!" says the gentleman. Godfrey is a man of fashion, a man of fortune, and a man of talent, but he will die a bachelor. What a pity! We can never look on such a man without a smile for his caprice and a tear for its consequences. How unlucky that he cannot say "Yes!"

In the position we are next going to advance we know everybody will agree with us, and this consideration very

patron, he has cut the Club! How unlucky that he cannot say "No."

Jack Shuttle was a dashing young fellow, who, to use his own expression, was "above denying a thing;" in plainer terms, he could not say "No." "Sir!" says an enraged Tory, "you are the author of this pamphlet!" Jack never saw the work, but he was "above denying a thing," and was horsewhipped for a libeller. "Sir!" says an unfortunate pigeon, "you hid the king in your sleeve last night!" Jack never saw the pigeon before, but he was "above denying a thing," and was cut for a blackleg. "Sir!" says a hot Hibernian, "you insulted my sister in the Park!" Jack never saw the lady or her champion before, but he was "above denying a thing," and was shot through the head the next morning. Poor fellow! How unlucky that he could not say "No!"

In the position we are next going to advance we know everybody will differ from us; but this only much strengthens our opinion. Nothing is so becoming to a female mouth as a civil and flattering "Yes." It is impossible, indeed, but that our fellow-citizens should here agree with us, when they reflect that they never can be husbands until their inamorata shall have learnt the art of saying "Yes." For the most part, indeed, civility and good-nature are the characteristics of our British fair, and this natural inclination to the affirmative renders it unnecessary for us to point out to our fair countrywomen the beauties and advantages of a word which they love as dearly as they do flattery. While we are on the subject of flattery, let us *obiter* advise all Etonians to say nothing but "Yes" to a lady. But as a thoughtless coquette or a haughty prude does occasionally forget the necessity and the beauty of the word we are discussing, we cannot but recommend to our fair readers to consider attentively the evils which this forgetfulness infallibly entails. Laurelia would never have been cut by her twenty-first adorer; Charlotte, with £4000 a year at fifteen, would never have been an old maid at fifty; Lucy, with a good face and not a farthing,

strengthens our opinion. Nothing is so becoming to a female mouth as the power —ay, and the inclination—to say "No." So firmly, indeed, are we attached to this doctrine, that we never will marry a woman who cannot say "No." For the most part, indeed, the sex are pretty tolerably actuated by what the world calls a spirit of contradiction, but what we should rather designate as a spirit of independence. This natural inclination to negatives renders it unnecessary for us to point out to our fair countrywomen the beauties and advantages of a word which they use as constantly as their looking-glass. Nevertheless, they do occasionally forget the love of opposition, which is the distinguishing ornament of their sex; and alas! they too frequently render themselves miserable by neglecting our conclusive monosyllable. We most earnestly entreat those belles who honour with their notice the humble efforts of the *Etonian*, to derive a timely warning from the examples of those ladies who have lived to regret a hasty and unthinking assent. Anna would never have been the mistress of a colonel; Martha would

would never have refused a carriage, white liveries, and a peerage, if these unfortunate victims had studied in early youth the art of saying "Yes."

Sweet — light — gay — quaint monosyllable! Tender, obliging, inoffensive, affectionate "Yes!" How we delight in thy delicate sound! We love to hear the enamoured swain petitioning for his mistress's picture, till the lady, or overcome by affection, or wearied by importunity, changes the "No" of coy reluctance for the "Yes" of final approbation. We love to hear the belle of Holborn Hill supplicating for Greenwich and the one-horse shay, till her surly parent alters the shake of unconvinced obduracy for the nod of unwilling consent. We love to see the hen-pecked husband humbly kneeling for his Sunday coat and the "Star and Garter," till Madam, conscious that the Captain is secreted in the closet, transmutes the "No" of authoritative detention into the "Yes" of immediate dismissal. We love—but it is time to bring our treatise to a conclusion, and we will merely observe, that whenever we see Beauty without

never have been the wife of a cornet; Lydia would never have been tied to age, ugliness, and gout, if these unfortunate victims had studied in early youth the art of saying "No."

Short — strong — sharp — quaint monosyllable! Forcible, convincing, argumentative, indisputable "No!" How we delight in thy expressive sound! We love to hear the Miss of fifteen plaguing her uncle for her Christmas ball, till Square-toes, finding vain the excuses of affection, finishes the negotiation with the "No" of authority. We love to hear the enamoured swain pouring forth his raptures at the feet of an inexorable mistress, till the lady changes her key from the quiet hint of indifference to the decided "No" of aversion. We love to hear the schoolboy supplicating a remission of his sentence, until his sable judge alters the "I can't" of sorrowful necessity, to the "No" of inflexible indignation. We love—but it is time for us to bring our treatise to a conclusion, and we will merely observe, that whenever we see a man engaged in a duel against his will or in a debauch against his conscience; whenever a husband or Talent without a place; whenever we hear a lady considered an old maid, or a gentleman voted a bore, we turn from the sight in melancholy mood, and whisper to ourselves: " This comes of not being able to say 'Yes.'"

we see a patriot accepting of a place, or a beauty united to a blockhead, we turn from the sight in disgust, and mutter to ourselves: " This comes of not being able to say 'No.'"

THOUGHTS ON THE WORDS "TURN OUT."

" We all, in our turns, turn out."—Song.

TURN OUT! There are in the English language no two words which act so forcibly in exciting sympathy and compassion. There is in them a melancholy cadence, beautifully corresponding with the sadness of the idea which they express: they awaken in a moment the tenderest recollections and the most anxious forebodings: there is in them a talismanic charm which influences alike all ages and all dispositions; the Church, the Bar, and the Senate are all comprised in the range of its operation: indeed, we believe that in no profession, in no rank of life, we shall find the man who can meditate, without an inward feeling of mental depression, on the simple, the unstudied, the unaffected pathos of the words "Turn out."

Is it not extraordinary, that when the idea is in itself so tragic, and gives birth to such sombre sensations, Melpomene should have altogether neglected the illustration of it? Is it not still more extraordinary that her sportive sister Thalia should have dared indecorously to jest with a subject so entirely unsuited to her pen? To take our

meaning from its veil of metaphor, is it not extraordinary
that Mr. Kenney should have writtten a farce on the words
" Turn Out?"   We regard Mr. Kenney's farce as a sacrilege,
a profanation, a burlesque of the best feelings of our nature ;
and in spite of the ingenuity of the writer, and the talents
of the performers, humanity and its attendant prejudices
revolt in disgust from the scene which endeavours to raise
a laugh by a parody of so melancholy a topic.

It is not difficult to account for the pensive feelings
which are excited by these words : they recall forcibly to
our mind the uncertainty of all human concerns; they bid
us think on the sad truth, that from power, from affluence,
from happiness, we may be "turned out" at a minute's
warning ; they whisper to us that the lease of life is held on
a precarious tenure, subject to the will of a Providence
which we can neither control nor foresee ; they oblige us to
look forward to that undiscovered country, from whose
dark limits we would fain avert our eyes ; they convince us
of the truth of the desponding expression of the Psalmist,
" Man is but a thing of nought, his time passeth away like
a shadow."

Are not these the reflections of every thinking mind ?   If
they are not, we must entreat the indulgence of our readers
for the melancholy pleasure we take in the discussion of the
subject.   The words may indeed be more than ordinarily
affecting to us, inasmuch as they remind us of a friend who
in his life was "turned out" from every thing that life can
bestow, but who in his death shall never be "turned out"
from that consolatory tribute to his Manes—the recollection of a sincere friend.   Poor Gilbert !   The occurrences of
his eventful existence would indeed furnish materials for the
poet or the moralist, for a tragedy of five acts, or a homily
of fifty heads.   His father always prophesied he would turn
out a great man ; and yet the poor fellow did nothing but
turn out, and never became a great man.   At fourteen he
turned out with a bargeman, and lost an eye ; at seventeen
he was turned out from Eton, and lost King's ; at three-
and-twenty he was turned out of his father's will, and lost a
thousand a-year ; at four-and-twenty he was turned out of a
tandem, and lost the long odds ; at five-and-twenty he was
turned out of a place, and lost all patience ; at six-and-

twenty he was turned out of the affections of his mistress, and lost his last hope; at seven-and-twenty he was turned out of a gaming-house, where he lost his last farthing. Gilbert died about a year ago, after existing for some time in a miserable state of dependence upon a rich uncle. To the last he was fond of narrating to his friends the vicissitudes of his life, which he constantly concluded in the following manner:—"So, gentlemen, I have been turning out during my whole life; you now see me on the brink of the grave, and I don't care how soon I turn in."

We had not heard from him for a considerable space of time, and were beginning to wonder at his protracted silence, when a friend who was studying the *Morning Post* apprised us of his decease by the following exclamation:—"My God! Old Gilbert's dead! Here's a quaint turn out!"

Alas! how often does it happen that we are not aware of the value of the blessings we enjoy until chance or destiny has taken them from us. This has been the case in our acquaintance with our lamented companion. How bitterly do we now regret that we did not, while his life was spared, make use of his inestimable experience to collect some instructions on the art of turning out, both in the active and the neuter signification of the words. For surely no two things are more difficult than the giving or receiving of a dismissal. To go through the one with civility, and the other with firmness, is indeed a rare talent, which every man of the world should study to attain.

When we consider the various chances and vicissitudes which await the citizens of our little commonwealth in their progress through life; when we recollect that some of them will enter into political life, in order to be turned out of their places; others will enjoy the titular distinction of M.P., that they may be turned out of their seats the next election; while others again, by an attachment to Chancery expedition, will endeavour to get turned out of their estates; —it is surely worth while to bestow a little attention upon the most proper mode of behaving under these unfortunate circumstances.

Mr. Monxton receives a turn out better than any political man of our acquaintance. It was of him that Sir Andrew Freeman, a Hertfordshire Independent, who, to do him justice, would be witty if he could, broached the celebrated remark—" He has turned out so often, that I should think he's turned wrong side out by this time." Mr. Monxton is indeed a phenomenon in his way. The smile he wears on coming into office differs in no respect from that which he assumes on resigning all his employments. He departs from the enjoyment of place and power, not with the gravity of a disappointed Minister, but with the self-satisfied air of a successful courtier. The tact with which he conceals the inward vexation of spirit beneath an outward serenity of countenance is to us a matter of astonishment. When we have heard him discussing his resignation with a simper on his face, and a jest on his lip, we have often fancied that Mr. Kemble would appear to us in the same light were he to deliver Wolsey's soliloquy with the attitudes and the gestures of a harlequin in a pantomime. Juvenile politicians cannot propose to themselves, in this line of their profession, a better model than Mr. Monxton.

Nor is this art less worthy the attention of the fair sex. There are very few ladies who have the talent of dismissing a lover in proper style. There are many who reject with so authoritative a demeanour, that they lose him, as an acquaintance, whom they only wish to cast off as a dangler; there are many again who study civility to such an extent that we know not whether they reject or receive, and have no small difficulty in distinguishing their smile from their frown. The deep and sincere interest which we feel in all matters relating to the advantage or improvement of the fair sex induces us to suggest that an academy, or a seminary, or an establishment should be forthwith instituted for the instruction of young ladies not exceeding thirty years of age, in the most approved method of saying "Turn Out." So far indeed has our zeal in this laudable undertaking carried us, that we have actually communicated our ideas upon the subject to a lady, who, to quote from her own advertisement, " enjoys the advantages of an excellent education, an unblemished character, and an amiable disposition." We are happy to inform our friends and the public in general that Mrs. Simkins has promised to devote her attention to this branch of female education. By the end of next month she hopes to be quite competent to the instruction of pupils in every mode of expressing "Turn Out"—the Distant Hint, the Silent Bow, the Positive Cut, the Courteous Repulse, and the Absolute Rejection. We trust that due encouragement will be given to a scheme of such general utility.

In the meantime, until such academy, or seminary, or establishment shall be opened, we invite our fair readers to the study of an excellent model in the person of Caroline Mowbray. Caroline has now seven-and-twenty lovers, all of whom have successively been in favour, and have been successively turned out. Yet so skilfully has she modified her severity, that in most cases she has destroyed hope without extinguishing love: the victims of her caprice continue her slaves, and are proud of her hand in the dance, although they despair of obtaining it at the altar. The twenty-seventh name was added to the list of her admirers last week, and was (with the most heartfelt regret we state it) no less a personage than the Hon. Gerard Montgomery. Alas! unfortunate Gerard!

> Quantâ laboras in Charybdi,
> Digne puer meliore flammâ.

He had entertained us for some time with accounts of the preference with which he was honoured by this miracle of obduracy, and at last, by dint of long and earnest entreaty, prevailed upon us to be ourselves witness to the power he had obtained over her affections. We set out therefore, not without a considerable suspicion of the manner in which our expedition would terminate, and inwardly anticipated the jests which "The King of Clubs" would infallibly broach upon the subject of Gerard's "Turn Out."

Nothing occurred of any importance during our ride. Gerard talked much of Cupids, and Hymen; but, inasmuch as we were not partakers of his passion, we could not reasonably be expected to partake of his inspiration.

Upon our arrival at Mowbray Lodge we were shown into a room so crowded with company that we almost fancied we had been ushered into the Earl's levee instead of his daughter's drawing-room. The eye of a lover, however, was more keen. Gerard soon perceived the Goddess of the Shrine receiving the incense of adulation from a crowd

of votaries. Amongst these he immediately enrolled himself, while we, apprehensive that our company might be
troublesome to him, hung back, and became imperceptibly
engaged in conversation with some gentlemen of our
acquaintance. To speak the truth, on our way to the
Lodge these "Thoughts on Turn Out" had been the
subject of our reveries, and whatever expressions or
opinions we heard around us appeared to coincide with the
cogitations with which we were occupied. We first became
much interested in the laments of an old gentleman who
was bewailing the "Turn Out" of a friend at the last
election for the county of ——. Next we listened to an
episode from a dandy, who was discussing the extraordinary coat "turned out" by Mr. Michael Oakley at the
last county ball. Finally, we were engaged in a desperate
argument with a Wykehamist, upon the comparative degree
of talent "turned out" from each of the public schools
during the last ten years. Of course we proceeded to
advocate the cause of our foster-mother against the
pretensions of our numerous and illustrious rivals. Alas!
we felt our unworthiness to stand forward as Etona's
panegyrist, but we made up in enthusiasm what we wanted
in ability. We ran over with volubility the names of those
thrice-honoured models, whose deserved success is constantly the theme of applause and the life-spring of
emulation among their successors. We had just brought
our catalogue down to the names of our more immediate
forerunners, and were dwelling with much complacency on
the abilities which have during the last few years so nobly
supported the fair fame of Eton at the Universities, when
our eye was caught by the countenance of our hon. friend,
which at this moment wore an appearance of such unusual
despondence, that we hastened immediately to investigate
the cause. Upon inquiry, we learned that Montgomery
was most romantically displeased, because Caroline had
refused to sing an air of which he was passionately fond.
We found we had just arrived in time for the finale of the
dispute. "And so you can't sing this to oblige me?" said
Gerard. Caroline looked refusal. "I shall know better than
to expect such a condescension again," said Gerard, with a
low sigh. "Tant mieux!" said Caroline, with a low

curtsey. The audience were unanimous in an unfeeling laugh, in the midst of which Gerard made a precipitate retreat, or, as O'Connor expresses it, " ran away like mad," and we followed him as well as we could, though certainly not *passibus æquis.* As we moved to the door we could hear sundry criticisms on the scene. " Articles of eject-ment !" said a limb of the law. " The favourite distanced !" cried a Newmarket squire. " I did not think the breach practicable !" observed a gentleman in regimentals. We overtook the unfortunate object of all these comments about a hundred yards from the house. His wobegone countenance might well have stopped our malicious disposi-tion to jocularity; nevertheless we could not refrain from whispering in his ear, " Gerard! a decided *turn out !'* " I beg your pardon," said the poor fellow, mingling a smile' for his pun with a tear for his disappointment, " I beg your pardon ; I consider it a decided *take in."*

SOLITUDE IN A CROWD.

" This is to be alone ; this, this is solitude."—BYRON. .

READER ! Were you ever alone in a crowd? If not, thank your stars, and bestow a grain of pity upon those who must return a different response to the question. A crowded solitude, if we may use such a strange expression, is, in sober sadness, as melancholy a sensation as human nature is capable of enduring.

A crowded solitude ! If you are young, thoughtless, and talkative, you will be astonished at the idea ; and there will be nothing extraordinary in your surprise. The ancient poets—poor ignorant souls !—have given us a very different description of being alone. They have defined various kinds of solitude, suited to various descriptions of men ; but all of them are alike founded on mistaken notions

and groundless prejudice. Were we to follow their
opinions, we should place the solitude of the lover in
whispering groves, purling rills, and moonlight; that of
the sage in a library or an observatory; that of the poet
in a dish of vegetables and a Sabine farm; and *à fortiori*,
that of the Etonian in an uncarpeted domicile, with a
fractured window on the one side and a smoking fire on
the other. Is this solitude? Far from it! We must
most strenuously contend that true solitude is to be found
in a multitude.

We are aware that the solitude we are now discussing
is not that which is generally understood by the term.
Many persons have probably never heard of any but a
corporeal solitude; that which we are describing is mental.
The one is to be found in caves and Caucasus; the other
in theatres and Almack's. The former delights in moonshine—the latter in candelabras; the first sets a great value
upon the silence and pure air of the country—the second
gives the preference to the noise and squeeze of the
fashionable world; and which of these is real solitude—
the corporeal, which is removed from the sight and hearing
of all objects; or the mental, which both hears and sees
a variety of things, and is utterly unconscious that it does
either?

We are distrustful of our powers of description, and
will therefore endeavour to illustrate our meaning by
examples. We are provided with plenty, for we have still
in our recollection Lady Mordaunt's last "At Home."
All the world was there. Whist, music, dancing, and
last, not least, eating, were all going on in the usual style
at the same time; the squeeze in the rooms was beyond
parallel in the annals of *ton;* and of course we found
more solitude in that evening than we had done throughout
the whole season. We made our *entrée* when her ladyship
was in her highest glory: she was bowing to one, smiling
to another, and curtseying to a third, and straining every
nerve and feature to *do the proper* to all her guests: this,
however, was as impossible as the number of her satellites
was innumerable; the tumult was tremendous; and there
was so much bowing, and begging pardon, and getting out
of the way, that it was quite impracticable to advance or

recede a step. Good breeding and bare elbows were thrust in our faces alternately; we with difficulty preserved our toes from the frequent attacks made on them by kid slippers, and with still greater difficulty preserved our hearts from the sweet smiles that said "I beg ten thousand pardons." It was a vortex of delight, and we were hurried so rapidly in its eddies, that much time elapsed ere we were able to collect our editorial serenity, in order to make a few observations on the scene before us.

The multitude at length began very slowly to diminish; and, having lodged ourselves in an unperceived corner of the music-room, we proceeded, according to our ancient custom, to speculate upon character. Our attention was first attracted by a tall gentleman of a very noble appearance, who was leaning against a pillar, in an attitude of profound meditation. His dress was after the English fashion, but the cast of his features, and his short curling hair, sufficiently denoted him to be a foreigner. His eyes were fixed directly upon us, but we satisfied our curiosity by an attentive survey, without fear of detection, as his mind was evidently some furlongs distant. Upon inquiry we heard that he was an Indian chieftain, by name Teioninhokarawn (we have doubts as to the correctness of our orthography). He had done considerable services to the British arms in the American war, and had now been invited by her ladyship as the lion of the evening. He had been surrounded without intermission by a tribe of quizzers, loungers, and laughers, but one glance was sufficient to convince us that Teioninhokarawn was— alone.

We observed Lady Georgiana Wilmot standing at the other side of the room, the very picture of fatigue. She had been singing much, and was evidently quite exhausted. A young star of fashion was moving towards her with a languishing step; and, as we had a strong curiosity to hear his address, we changed our station for that purpose. "'Pon my soul," the gentleman began with a bow, "you are divine to-night." "Am I?" said the lady, with a vacant gaze. "Never heard you in better voice," returned her assailant. Her ladyship knew it was the tone of flattery, so she smiled, but she had neither spirits nor sense sufficient to attempt an answer. We immediately decided that Lady Georgiana was—alone.

We next proceeded to the card-room. At first the din, and the disputing, and the quarrelling was so loud, that we doubted whether we should find any solitude there; but another look convinced us of our mistake. Lord Mowbray was evidently—alone. He was walking up and down, deliberating whether he should sacrifice his conscience or his place at to-morrow's division. Not less apparent was the solitude of the Duchess of Codille; although her Grace was busily engaged at cassino with a select party of right honourables. She had been for a long time alone in the contemplation of her new brocade, and was recalled into company by the vociferation of her partner, " Rat me if I ever saw your Grace play so ill!"

We were about to retire to the ball-room, when we remarked our noble hostess reclining on an ottoman, seemingly quite exhausted with fashionable fatigue. She was still, however, exerting herself to do the *agréable*, and was talking with appalling rapidity to every one who approached her, although utterly unconscious of what she heard or said. We advanced to pay our respects, and were saluted with "Ah, my lord! what has kept you away so long? And there's Ellen, poor thing, dying to see you! Ellen, love!" With some difficulty we explained to her ladyship that she was mistaken as to our rank. "Eh! Mon Dieu! Sir Charles," she exclaimed. "Pardonnez— but I'm really dead with ennui." We allowed ourselves to be knighted without further explanation, and made a precipitate retreat, for we perceived that her ladyship, after the labour of the evening, would be very glad to be—alone.

The first survey we took of the ball-room presented us with nothing but cheerful faces and laughing eyes; at the second, we discovered even here much and melancholy loneliness. There were moralists without sense, and country squires without acquaintance; beaux without a thought, and belles without a partner. We hastened to make a closer study of the various characters which presented themselves.

We first addressed ourselves to Mr. Morris, a respectable Member of Parliament, with whom we had become acquainted the year before in Norfolk. "What! you're not a dancer, Mr. Morris?" we began. "By the Lord, sir," he returned, "if this Bill passes——" We passed on, much vexed that we had intruded on our worthy friend's solitude.

We were hastening to accost Maria Kelly, a very interesting girl, whose lover had lately left this country for Minorca, when we were attracted by a conversation between an exquisite and our old acquaintance, General Brose. "Ah! General," said the dandy, "how long have you ceased to foot it?" "Foot!" interrupted the General, "by Jupiter! their cavalry was ten thousand strong." The old man was decidedly—alone.

Before we could reach the recess in which Maria was sitting, she had been assailed by an impertinent. "May I have the honour and felicity——" he began. The poor girl started from her reverie with a sort of vacant gaze, and replied, "He sailed last Tuesday, sir!" "Sola in siccâ," said the impertinent, and lounged on. We had not the barbarity to speak to her.

Old Tom Morley, the misanthrope, had been admiring a wax taper in an unthinking sort of way ever since we entered the room. We went up, prepared to be witty upon him; but we had hardly opened our mouth when he cut us short with "For God's sake leave me alone!" and we left him—alone. We were proceeding in our observations, when we saw Ellen Mordaunt, the beautiful daughter of our hostess, surrounded by a set of dashing young officers, at the other end of the room. We had just began to examine the features of one of them, who was somewhat smitten, and appeared prodigiously alone, when the idol herself turned upon us that bright and fascinating eye,

> Which but to see is to admire,
> And—oh! forgive the word—to love!

We had originally inserted here a rhapsody on Ellen's glance, which would have occupied, as our printer assures us, three pages and a half; but, in mercy to our friends, we have erased this, and shall content ourselves with stating that we were alone for at least ten minutes, before we recollected that it was five o'clock, and that we ought to think of retiring from the solitude of Lady Mordaunt's "At Home."

POLITENESS AND POLITESSE.

" I cannot bear a French metropolis."—JOHNSON.

WE have headed our article with two words which are very often, and certainly very improperly, confounded together. Nobody needs to be told that the one is from the English, the other from the French vocabulary ; but there may perhaps be some who will be surprised to hear that the one expresses an English, the other a French quality.

Frown if you will, Monsieur Duclos, we must maintain that the English are the only people who have a true idea of politeness. If we are wrong, our error may be excused for the feeling which prompts it ; but we believe we are right, and we will try to make our readers believe so.

The English are kind in their politeness—the French are officious in their *politesse ;* the politeness of the English is shown in actions—the *politesse* of the French evaporates in sound ; English politeness is always disinterested—French *politesse* is too often prompted by selfishness.

When we consider the various forms of these qualities, we appear to be discriminating between the rival merits of two contending beauties, who reign with equal dominion, and divide the admiration of an adoring world. There are many who prefer the ingenious delicacy of politeness, and we congratulate them on their truly English feeling ; there are perhaps more who are attracted by the coquettish vivacity of *politesse*, and we do not envy them their French taste.

A variety of instances of both these traits must have occurred to everybody, but as everybody does not behold the shades of character through the exact medium of an editorial microscope, we will endeavour to bring out more distinctly those examples which seem to us to bear immediately on the subject.

When you dine with old Tom Hardy, he gives you little more than a joint of meat, a bottle of excellent port, and a hearty welcome ; when Lord Urban "requests the honour" of your company, you are greeted with every delicacy the season can afford; you are pampered with every wine, "from humble port to imperial tokay," and you are put to the blush by every form of adulation that a wish to be civil can devise. Yet we had rather dine once with Tom Hardy than a hundred times with Lord Urban; for the mutton of the one is cooked by politeness, and the turtle of the other is dressed by *politesse*.

About a month ago, as we were shooting in the north of England with the son of a celebrated Tory baronet, we were encountered by Mr. Ayscott, a landed proprietor notorious for his Whig principles. We were somewhat surprised to see the latter divest himself of all prejudices in a moment; he came up to our companion with the greatest appearance of cordiality, shook him by the hand, reminded him that politics ought not to interfere among friends, knew he was fond of dancing, and hoped to see him frequently at Ayscott. Now this really looked like politeness; for politeness is that feeling which prompts us to make others happy and pleased with themselves, and which for this purpose puts off all dislike, all party spirit, all affectation of superiority. But when we were informed the next day that Mr. Ayscott had seven marriageable daughters, we decided that his behaviour was not politeness, but *politesse*.

We remember, shortly after Mrs. C. Nugent eloped with an officer in the dragoons, we were riding in Hyde Park with poor Charles, who endeavoured to bear his loss unconcernedly, and betrayed not, except to a close observer, the canker that preyed upon his heart. We were met in the Park by Sir Harry Soulis, an intimate acquaintance of our friend. He was riding at a brisk pace, but the moment he observed us he pulled up, and his flexible features immediately assumed the appearance of unfeigned sympathy. He came up to us, and began, "Ah Charles! How are you? How is this unfortunate business to end? I feel for you, Charles! Upon my soul, I feel for you! You know you may command me in anything"—and he rode on with the same air of nonchalance that he had first worn. Immediately afterwards we met Colonel Stanhope, who also halted, and entered into conversation. He inquired after our friend's health, addressed a few indifferent remarks to us on the weather, bowed, and passed on. We are sure Nugent felt, as we should have felt under such circumstances : Soulis had wounded his feelings—Stanhope had spared them. The officiousness of the former was *politesse*—the silence of the latter was politeness.

But their distinct shades were never so fully impressed upon our minds as upon a visit which we lately paid to two gentlemen, during a short tour. The first specimen of their dissimilarity is to be found in the letters by which we were invited to partake of their hospitality. They were as follows :—

"As Mr. P. Courtenay will in the course of his tour be within a few miles of Melville Lodge, Mr. Melville hopes that he will not turn southward without allowing him, for one day at least, the gratification of his company.

"Melville Lòdge, August 1820."

"DEAR PEREGRINE,—You'll pass within eyeshot of my windows on your way to Eastbourne. I am sure you'll stop a moment to ask your old friend how he does, and we will try to detain you for the night.

"Yours, as sincerely as ever,

"MARMADUKE WARREN.

"P.S. The girls would send love if I'd let 'em.

"Hastings, August 1820."

Our first visit was paid at Melville Lodge. We have known Mr. Melville long, and we know him to be one who is generally actuated by good motives ; and when he is swayed by interested ones is himself unconscious of the fact. On the whole, his character is such that when he is absent we feel the strongest inclination to like him, and when we are in his company we feel an equally strong inclination to say, "Mr. Melville, you are a fool." We arrived at the Lodge in good time to prepare for dinner, with its usual accompaniments of bows from our host, compliments from our hostess, and smiles from their daughters. A small party was invited to meet us, which somewhat diminished the frequency of the compliments we were doomed to undergo, while it rendered those

which were actually forced upon us infinitely more distressing. We pass over the civilities we received at dinner,
the care taken to force upon us the choicest morsels of
fish, flesh, and fowl; the attention with which Mr. Melville
assured us that we were drinking his very best champagne.
We hasten to take notice of the far more perplexing
instances of *politesse* which rendered miserable the evening.
When tea and coffee had been disposed of, the Misses
Melville sat down to the piano ; and, as we are passionately fond of music, and the ladies excel in it, we should
have been perfectly happy if we had been allowed to
enjoy that happiness unmolested. *Diis aliter visum est.*
Our sisters were known to be tolerable singers ; *à fortiori*,
we must be downright nightingales ourselves. Upon the
word of an editor, we never committed any further outrage
upon harmony than what takes place when we join in the
chorus of our witty associate Mr. Golightly or our well-
meaning friend Mr. O'Connor, and we were now required
to assist the Misses Melville in "La mia Dorabella."
Horrible idea! Peregrine Courtenay warbling Italian!
His Majesty of Clubs sinking into an opera-singer!
Politesse was sure he could sing—*politesse* knew he had
a sweet voice—*politesse* knew we only refused from
modesty. *Politesse* was disappointed, however, for we
were immovably determined not to be made a fool.
Nevertheless we felt somewhat uncomfortable at being the
subject of general observation, and this feeling was not
diminished by what followed. *Politesse*, in the shape of
Mrs. Melville, whispered it about that the fat silent young
gentleman in the black coat was a great writer, who had
published an extraordinary quantity of learning, and was
likely to publish an extraordinary quantity more. This was
all intended to flatter our vanity, and the consequence was
that we were bored throughout the remainder of the
evening by hearing whispers around us, "Is that the
gentleman Mrs. Melville was speaking of?" "I guessed
who he was by the family likeness!" "I knew he was an
author directly!" "How odd that he should be so
reserved!" At the suggestion of *politesse* Mrs. Melville
next discovered that we were precisely a year older than
Kitty, and Mr. Melville hinted in a loud whisper that the

girl would have ten thousand pounds. Finally, *politesse* prepared for us the great state bedroom ; and, when we retired, insisted upon it that we had spent a most miserable evening. Alas ! Politeness had hardly the grace to contradict *politesse* upon this point.

How different was the reception we received on the following day ! Our old friend Mr. Warren rose from his armchair as we entered, with a look that set formality at defiance ; Mrs. Warren put by her work to observe how much we were grown ; and their two daughters greeted with a smile, beautiful because it was unaffected, the scarce-remembered playmate of their childhood. The flowers which Elizabeth was painting, the landscape which Susan was designing, were not hastily concealed at the approach of their guest ; nor was our old acquaintance Shock, who was our favourite puppy ten years ago, driven in his old age from the parlour rug at the appearance of an idler dog than himself. The few friends who met us at dinner were not prepared to annoy us by accounts of our abilities and attainments. The conversation was general and entertaining ; and on reconsideration we perceived that Mr. Warren took pains to draw out what talent we possessed, although we could not at the same time perceive that such was the object of his attention. In the evening Elizabeth entertained us with Handel and Mozart, and Susan sung us some simple airs, in a voice perhaps the more engaging because it was uncultivated. We were allowed to enjoy the "melody of sweet sounds" unmolested and unobserved. The quadrille which followed was not danced with the less spirit because the Brussels carpet supplied the place of a chalked floor, and a single pianoforte was substituted for the formality of a band. We were happy—because we were permitted to enjoy our happiness in our own way ; we were amused—because we did not perceive the efforts which were made for our amusement. "This," we exclaimed, as we buttoned our coat, and proceeded on our journey the next morning—"this is real politeness."

In spite of the endeavours of those who would dress our native manners in a Parisian costume, *politesse* will never be the motive by which England as a nation will be

characterized. As long as France shall be the mother of
light heads, and Britain of warm hearts, the Frenchman will
show his *politesse* by the profundity of his bow, and the
Englishman will prove his politeness by the cordiality of his
welcome. Who is not content that it should be so?

A WINDSOR BALL.

WE have often thought that the endeavours of a dancing
master go but a very little way to prepare a lady for a ball.
Were it possible to procure such an acquisition, we should
recommend to our sisters not only a *maître à danser*, but
a *maître à parler*, inasmuch as it is usually much easier to
dance than to talk. One does not immediately see why it
should be so; dancing and talking are in a ball-room
equally mechanical qualifications; they differ indeed in
this, that the former requires a "light fantastic toe," and
the other a light fantastic tongue. But for mind—seriously
speaking, there is no more mind developed in small-talk
than there is in *chassez à droit.*

We do not admire the taste of Etonians who dislike
dancing; we are not of the number of those who go to a
ball for the purpose of eating ice. On the contrary, we
adore waltzing, and feel our English aversion for the
French much diminished when we recollect that we derive
from them Vestris and quadrilles. Nevertheless, if anything could diminish the attachment we feel for this our
favourite amusement, it would be that we must occasionally submit to dangle at the heels of an icy partner, as
beautiful, and, alas! as cold as the Venus de' Medicis;
whose look is torpor, whose speech is monosyllables; who
repulses all efforts at conversation, until the austerity, or
the backwardness of her demeanour, awes her would-be
adorer into a silence as deep as her own. Now all this
gravity of demeanour, in the opinion of some people, is a

proof of wisdom : we know not how this may be, but for
our own part we think with the old song, " 'Tis good to
be merry and wise," and if we cannot have both—why, then
the merry without the wise.

These are the ideas which occur to us upon looking back
to the last time that we heard " *Voulez vous danser ?*"
played at the Town Hall. Start not, fair reader! do not
throw us into the fire ; we will not be very libellous ; and if
you shall erroneously suppose that your own defects have
afforded matter for our malicious pen, we are sure your
indignation will forthwith subside when you recollect that
you may possibly have listened to the colloquial raptures of
Gerard Montgomery, or been honoured with an editorial
tête-à-tête by the condescension of Peregrine Courtenay.
Think over your favourite partners. Did any one ask your
opinion of the Bill of Pains and Penalties? It could be no
one but Sir Francis Wentworth. Did any one hold
forth upon the beauties of a Scotch reel? Of a surety it
was Mr. Alexander M'Farlane. Did any one observe to
you that a quadrille was a "strange cross-road, and very
hilly?" Doubt not but it was the all-accomplished Robert
Musgrave. Did any one remark upon the immorality of
waltzing? Thrice-honoured fair one! You have danced
with Martin Sterling.

Alas! we intended, as Mr. Musgrave would say, to drive
straight to the Town Hall, and we have got out of our road
a full page. It is indeed a cruel delay in us, for we know,
reader, say what you will, you have been all the time
turning over the leaf to meet with a spice of scandal. Well,
then, suppose all preliminaries adjusted ; suppose us fairly
lodged in the ball-room, with no other damage than a ruined
Cavendish and a dirtied pump ; and suppose us immediately struck dumb by the intelligence that the beautiful,
the fascinating Louisa had left the room the moment before
we entered it. It was easy to perceive that something of the
kind had occurred, for the ladies were all looking happy.
We bore our disappointment as well as we could, and were
introduced to Theodosia——No! we will refrain from sur-
names——Theodosia is a woman of sense (we are told so,
and we are willing to believe it), but she is very unwilling
that any one should find it out. As in duty bound, we

commenced, or endeavoured to commerce, a conversation by general observations upon the room and the music. By-the-by, we strongly recommend these generalities to our friends in all conversations with strangers; they are quite safe, and can give no offence. In our case, however, they were unavailing—no reply was elicited. A long pause. We inquired whether the lady was fond of "The Lancers?" To our utter astonishment we were answered with a blush and a frown which would have put to silence a much more pertinacious querist than the Etonian—we ventured not another word. Upon after-consideration, we are sure that the lady was thinking of a set of dashing young officers instead of a set of quadrilles.

We were next honoured by the hand of Emily. When we have said that she is backward, beautiful, and seventeen, we have said all we know of the enchanting Emily. Far be it from us to attack with unwarrantable severity the unfortunate victim of *mauvaise honte;* we merely wish to suggest to one for whose welfare we have a real regard, that modesty does not necessarily imply taciturnity, and that the actual inconvenience of a silent tongue is not altogether compensated by the poetical loquacity of a speaking eye.

Being again left to ourselves, we sunk by degrees into a profound fit of authorship, and were in imminent danger of becoming misanthropic, when we were roused from our reverie by a tap on the shoulder from George Hardy, and an inquiry, "what were our dreams?" We explained to him our calamities, and assured him that, had it not been for his timely intervention, we should certainly have died of silence. "Died of silence!" reiterated our friend; "God forbid! when Corinna is in the room!" And so saying, he half-led, half-dragged us to the other end of the room, and compelled us to make our bow to a girl of lively manners, whom he described to us in a whisper as "a perfect antidote for the sullens." Our first impression was, "she is a fool;" our second, "she is a wit;" our third, "she is something between both!" Oh! that it were possible for us to commit to paper one-half of what was uttered by Corinna! Our recollection of our *tête-à-tête* is like the recollection of a dream. In dreams we remember that we were at one

moment in a mud-built cottage, and were the next transported to a Gothic chapel, but by what means the trans-
mutation of place was effected our waking thoughts are
unable to conceive. Thus it was when we listened to
Corinna. We were hurried from one topic to another with
an unaccountable velocity, but by what chain one idea was
connected with its predecessor we cannot imagine. The
conversation (if conversation it may be called, where the
duty of talking devolves upon one person) set out with
some mention of fresco; from hence it turned off to Hercu-
laneum, and then passed with inconceivable rapidity through
the following stages :—Rome—the Parthenon—National
Monument at Edinburgh—*Edinburgh Review*—*Blackwood*
—Ebony bracelets—Fashion of short sleeves—Fashion in
general dress in Queen Elizabeth's time—" The Abbot "—
Walter Scott—Highland scenery. In the Highlands we
lost our route for some minutes, and soon afterwards found
ourselves (we know not how) at Joannina, in company with
Ali Pasha. By this time we were thoroughly wearied, and
were unable to keep up regularly with our unfeeling con-
ductress, so that we have but a very faint idea of the places
we visited. We remember being dragged to the Giant at
the Windsor Fair, from whence we paid a flying visit to
the Colossus of Rhodes ; we attended Cato, the lady's
favourite pug, during a severe illness, and were shortly after
present at the Cato Street conspiracy. We have some idea
that after making the tour of the Lakes, we set out to
discover the source of the Nile. In our way thither we
took a brief survey of the Lake of Como, and were finally
for some time immersed in the Red Sea. This put the
finishing stroke to our already fatigued senses. We resigned
ourselves, without another struggle, to the will and disposal
of our sovereign mistress, and for the next half-hour knew
not to what quarter of the globe we were conveyed. At
the close of that period we awoke from our trance, and
found that Corinna had brought us into the Club-room, and
was discussing the characters of the members with a most
unwarrantable freedom of speech. Before we had time to
remonstrate against this manifest breach of privilege, we
found ourselves in the gallery of the House of Lords, and
began to think we never should make our escape from this

amusing torture. Fortunately, at this moment a freeholder of —— entered the room. One of the candidates was a friend of Corinna's, and she hurried from us, after a thousand apologies, to learn the state of the poll.

Sic nos servavit Apollo.*

Our next companion was Sappho the Blue-stocking. We enjoyed a literary confabulation for some time, for which we beg our readers to understand we are in every way qualified. The deep stores of our reading, enlivened by the pungent readiness of our wit, are *bonâ fide* the admiration of London as well as of Windsor belles ; we beg our friends to have this in mind whenever they sit down to peruse us. But to proceed. We very shortly perceived that Sappho was enchanted with our erudition, and the manner in which we displayed it. She was particularly pleased with our critiques on "Zimmerman upon Solitude," and was delighted by the praise we bestowed (for the first time in our life) on Southey's "Thalaba." We had evidently made considerable progress in her affections, when we ruined ourselves by a piece of imprudence which we have since deeply regretted. We were satirical—this satire is the devil!—we were satirical upon German literature. The lady turned up her nose, turned down her eyes, bit her lip, and looked—we cannot explain how she looked, but it was very terrific. We have since heard she is engaged in translating Klopstock's "Messiah" into the Sanskrit.

We were next introduced to one of those ladies who are celebrated for the extraordinary tact which they display in the discovery of the faults of their sex. Catherine is indeed one of the leaders of the tribe. She has the extraordinary talent which conveys the most sarcastic remarks in a tone of the greatest kindness. In her the language of hatred assumes the garb of affection, and the observation which is prompted by envy appears to be dictated by compassion. If in her presence you bestow commendation upon a rival, she assents most warmly to your opinion, and immediately destroys its effect by a seemingly extorted "but." We were

* Sir Francis Wentworth points our quotation thus :
Sic nos servavit A—Poll—O !—Hor.

admiring Sophia's beautiful hair. "Very beautiful!" said Catherine, "but she dresses it so ill!" We made some allusion to Georgiana's charming spirits. "She has ever-lasting vivacity," said Catherine, "but it's a pity she is so indiscreet." Then followed something in a whisper which we do not feel ourselves at liberty to repeat. We next were unguarded enough to find something very fascinating in Amelia's eyes. "Yes," replied Catherine, "but then she has such an unfortunate nose between them." Finally, in a moment of imprudent enthusiasm, we declared that we thought Maria the most interesting girl in the room. We shall never (although we live, like our predecessors, Griffin and Grildrig, to the good old age of forty numbers), we shall never, we repeat, forget the "Some people think so!" with which our amiable auditress replied to our exclamation. We saw we were disgraced, and, to say the truth, were not a little pleased that we were no longer of Catherine's Privy Council.

Now all these ladies are foolish in their way. Theo-dosia is a silent fool, Emily is a timid fool, Corinna is a talkative fool, Sappho is a learned fool, and Catherine is a malicious fool. With their comparative degrees of moral merit we have nothing to do; but in point of the agreeable, we hesitate not to affirm that the silent fool is to us the more insupportable creature of the five.

We lately were present at a large party, where an Etonian, for whom we have a great esteem, was terribly abused by a witty Marchioness for his inflexible taciturnity. Without entering upon the merits of this particular case, let us be allowed to plead in behalf of our sex, that a gentleman may be silent when a lady is silly, and that it is needless for a beau to be entertaining where a belle is decidedly imprac-ticable.

LOVERS' VOWS.

" What grace hast thou, thus to reprove
These worms for loving?" SHAKESPEARE.

WE were engaged the other day in making some pur-
chases at Flint's, when Lady Honoria Saville entered,
attended by the Hon. George Comyn. As the lady is a
professed coquette, and the gentleman a professed dangler,
we conceived it by no means improper to play the listener;
for the conversation of these characters is seldom such as
to require much secrecy. We therefore placed ourselves in
a convenient situation for hearing whatever was said by the
beau, the belle, and the milliner, which last I consider the
most rational person of the three. The questions which
were put to her by her ladyship escaped us; they seemed
to be conveyed, not in the language of common mortals,
but in signs which were to us incomprehensible. Without
exposing ourselves to the notice of either party, we were
beyond measure amused at the timely aid which the
milliner's descriptions of her wares afforded to the lover's
description of his passion; for whenever the latter was at a
loss for words, the former stepped in to finish his sentence,
and occasionally gave a point to it, in which lovers' vows
are generally deficient.

When they first made their appearance, the gentleman
was deposing upon oath to the truth of something of which
his companion seemed to entertain doubts. He had run
through some of the usual forms of adjuration, such as Sun,
Moon, Stars, Venus, and Blue Eyes, when he was stopped
by "Lovers' vows, Comyn! lovers' vows! Where do they
come from?" "Where?" repeated the gentleman, in a
theatrical attitude; "they come from a sincere affection,
from a passionate heart; from a devoted adoration, from——"
"From Paris, I assure you, madam," said the milliner, who
was turning over some silks. "But I wonder, Comyn!"
resumed her ladyship, "I wonder you can continue to
bore me with this nonsense! Lovers' vows have given me

the vapours these last five years, and, after all, what are they worth?" "Worth!" reiterated the fop; "they are worth the mines of Peru, the diamonds of Golconda, the sands of Pactolus!" "They are worth five shillings a pair, madam," said the milliner, "and it's really throwing them away." She was talking of some kid gloves.

"You gentlemen," said her ladyship, "must think us very weak creatures, if you fancy that we are to be imposed upon by any folly you choose to utter. Lovers' vows have been proverbial since the days of Queen Bess, and it would be strange if, in 1820, we should not have found out what they are made of." "In my case," said the exquisite, "your ladyship is cruel in supposing them to be made of anything but the purest sincerity." "They are made of the finest materials," said the milliner, "and your ladyship can see through them like glass." She was holding up to the window some stuff with a hard name, which we know nothing about. "Say what you will, Comyn," said her ladyship,

> Men were deceivers ever;
> One foot on sea, and one on shore,
> To one thing constant never.

"Lovers' vows are never intended to last beyond a day!' "Your ladyship is unjust!" replied the dandy; "they will last when all other ties shall be broken; they will last when the bond of relationship shall be cancelled, and the link of friendship riven; they will last——" "They will last for ever, madam, and wash afterwards!" said the milliner. She was speaking of some scarfs.

"Really, George," observed her ladyship, "you would think me an egregious fool if I were to believe one quarter of what you say to me. Speak the truth, George, for once, if it is in your nature—should I not be *folle—folle* beyond measure?" "You love to trifle with my passion," sighed the Honourable; "but this is what we must all expect! Fascinating as you are, you feel not for the woes of your victims; you are more insensible than flints— nothing is dear to you." "Flint's will make nothing dear to your ladyship," said the milliner, wrapping up the parcel.

"In this age of invention," said Lady Honoria, "it is surprising to me that no one has invented a thermometer to try the temperature of lovers' vows. What a price would a boarding-school miss give for such an invention! I certainly will make the suggestion to young Montgomery, that writes the sonnets!" "Good God!" cried the worshipper, "where shall I send for such a test of sincerity? I would send to the suns of India, to the snows of Tobolsk; I would send to the little-toed ladies of China, and the great-hatted chieftains of Loo-Choo; I would send——" "Shall I send it to your ladyship's house?" said the milliner, holding up the parcel.

"Well," said her ladyship, rising to leave the shop, "I shall contend no more with so subtle a disputant; my opinion of lovers' vows remains unchanged, and I desire you won't pester me with them at the Opera this evening, or I shall positively die of ennui." We saw that this was meant as an assignation, and the Honourable George Comyn saw things in the same light. "How," he cried, "how shall I thank your ladyship for this condescension? How shall I express the feelings of the heart you have rescued from despair? Language is too poor, utterance is too weak, for the emotion which I feel; what can I say?" "Much obliged to your ladyship," said the milliner.

ON THE PRACTICAL ASYNDETON.

"Nil fuit unquam
Tam dispar sibi." HOR.

THE treatise on the Practical Bathos which appeared in our first number, and which we have the vanity to hope is not entirely blotted out from the recollection of our readers, was intended as the first of a series of dissertations, in which we design to apply the beauties of the figures of the grammarians to the purposes of real life. We are very strongly tempted to pursue this design, when we reflect upon the advantages which have already been the result of the above-mentioned treatise. We are assured, from the most indisputable authority, that the number of the specimens of that most admirable figure exhibited by our schoolfellows in the exercises of the ensuing week was without precedent in the annals of Etonian literature. We have no doubt but those apt scholars who have so readily profited by our recommendation of the Bathos, as far as regards *com*position, will, at no very distant period, make the same use of this inestimable figure in the regulation of their *dis*position. But it is time to quit this topic, and to enter upon the second of our proposed series : " A Treatise on the Practical Asyndeton."

First, then, as in duty and in gallantry bound, we must construe this hard word. The figure Asyndeton, in grammar, is that by which conjunctions are omitted, and an unconnected appearance given to the sentence; which is frequently inexpressibly beautiful. Who is there of our rising orators who has not glowed with all the inspiration of a Roman, when fancy echoes in his ears the brief, the unconnected, and energetic thunders of the Consul, " Abiit, excessit, evasit, erupit ?" What reader of tragedy does not sympathize with the Orosmane of Voltaire, when, upon the receipt of the billet from Zayre, his anxiety bursts out in those beautifully unconnected expressions—

Donne !—qui la porte ?—donne !

The use of connecting particles in either of these cases would have ruined everything. They would have destroyed the majesty of Cicero, and reduced to the level of an every-day novelist the simple tenderness of Orosmane.

The use of this figure, however, is not confined to particular sentences or expressions. It sometimes pervades the five acts of what is miscalled a regular drama, or spreads an uncertain transparent gleam over the otherwise insupportable sameness of some inexplicable epic. Numberless are the writers who have been indebted to its assistance ; but our own, our immortal countryman, Shakespeare, preserves an undisputed station at the head of the list. Fettered by no imitation, but the imitation of Nature; bound down to no rules but the vivid conceptions of an untutored, self-working genius, he hurries us from place to place with the velocity of a torrent; we appear to be carried on by a rushing stream, which conveys our boat so rapidly in its eddies, that we pass through a thousand scenes, and are unable to observe for a moment the abruptness with which the changes are effected.

Our modern farce-writers have, with laudable emulation, followed the example of this great master of the stage; but as in their use of this figure they possess the audacity without the genius of the bard they imitate, they cannot prevent us from perceiving the frequent Asyndeton in place, in plot, or in character. The beauty of the countries to which they introduce us is not such as to withdraw us from the contemplation of the outrageously miraculous manner in which we were transported to them.

We have delayed the reader quite long enough with this preliminary discussion, and will now enter at once upon our main subject : the Asyndeton in life.

We should imagine that few of our readers are ignorant of the charms of novelty; few have lived through their boyhood and their youth without experiencing the disgust which a too frequent repetition of the same pleasure infallibly produces. There is in novelty a charm, the want of which no other qualification can in any degree compensate. The most studied viands for the gratification of the appetite please us when first we enjoy them, but the enjoyment becomes tasteless by repetition, and the *crambe repetita* of satiety provokes nausea instead of exciting desire. Thus it is in other and weightier matters. The pleasures which we first devoured with avidity lose much of their relish when they recur a second time, and are mere gall and wormwood to us when their sweets have become familiar to our taste. A common every-day character, although its possessor may enjoy abundance of worth and good sense, makes no impression on our minds; but the novelty of capricious beauty or uncultivated genius finds a sure road to our hearts.

This is something too long for a digression; but novelty

is a very pretty theme, and must be our excuse. We will
return forthwith to our subject.

Since novelty then has so much weight in influencing the
judgment, or at least the prejudices of mankind, it is right
that this most desirable qualification should not be neglected by young persons on their *début* upon the stage of
life; we must be masters of this excellence before we can
expect to shine in any other; we must be new before we
can hope to be amusing.

Now the figure which we have been discussing, or
rather the figure which we ought to have been discussing,
is the very essence and quintessence of novelty. It is
perpetually bringing before our eyes old scenes in a new
form, old friends in a new dress, old recollections in a new
imagery: it is the cayenne of life; and from it the dishes,
which would without it cloy and disgust, derive a perpetual
variety of taste and pungency. It takes from the scenes we
so often witness their unpleasing uniformity, and gives to
our mortal career an air of romance which is inexpressibly
amusing. All ranks of persons may alike derive benefit
from it. By its use the charms of the beauty become more
irresistible, the exploits of the general more astonishing, the
character of the rake more excusable. It gives in an equal
degree pleasure to those who behold, and advantage to
those who practise it.

How then is it to be practised? The manner and the
method are sufficiently obvious. Never wear to-morrow
the same character, or the same dress, that you wore to-
day. Be, if you can, *puncto mobilis horæ*. Be red one hour,
and pale the next; vary your temper, your appearance,
your language, your manners, unceasingly. Let not your
studies or your amusements continue the same for a week
together. Skim over the surface of everything, and be
deep in nothing; you may think a little, read a little,
gamble a little: but you must not think deep, read deep, or
play deep. In short, be everything and nothing; the
butterfly in life, tasting every flower, and tasting only to
leave it.

Do you think too much is required? Far from it.
Antiquity has handed down to us a character possessed, in
a most transcendent degree, of all the qualifications we

c

have exacted. We always like to get an example or two from antiquity, because it looks learned. Alcibiades then we can safely propose as a model for all juvenile practitioners in the Asyndeton. Was he grave one day? He laughed the next. Was he an orator one day? He was a buffoon the next. Was he a Greek one day? He was a Persian the next. To sum up his character: he was skilled in every profession; an amateur in every fashion; adorned by every virtue; made infamous by every vice. He moralized like a philosopher, jested like a mountebank, fought like a hero, lied like a scoundrel, lived like a knowing one, and died like a fool.

We assert, and we defy the soundest sophist in the world to contradict us, that these mixed characters obtain and preserve a greater portion of the admiration of the world, than more consistent and less interesting personages. We wonder not at the uniformity of the fixed star, but our imagination is actively employed upon the unusual appearance of the comet. Thus the man of firm and unchangeable steadiness of principle receives our esteem, and is forgotten; while the meteoric appearance of inconsistent eccentricity takes instant hold of our admiration, and is decorated with ten thousand indescribable attractions by the proper exercise of the Asyndeton.

But why do we dilate so much upon the authority of Alcibiades? It has been the almost invariable practice of all great men, in all ages, to pay particular attention to the cultivation of this figure. What a prodigy of the Asyndeton was Alexander! His father Philip may have had more science, perhaps more bottom; but the eccentricities of Alexander, the extraordinary rapidity with which he changed the ring for the gin-shop, and laid down the thunderbolt of Ammon to assume the quart-pot of Hercules, have given, and will preserve to him, the first leaf in the good books of the young and the hasty.

Are we not more delighted by the capricious mutability of Queen Bess than by the moral uniformity of Queen Anne? Is it not a pleasing marvel, and a marvellous pleasure, to look at the last days of Oliver Cromwell, when the usurper, perpetually stretched upon the tenter-hooks of conscience, dared not travel the same road twice, nor sleep two nights following in the same bed? Spirit of mutability, what pranks must thou have played with the Protector!

Since these are the charms of the Asyndeton, it is not surprising that the poets should have so frequently thrown a spice of it into the characters of their heroes. Putting Fingal and Æneas out of the way, we have no hero of any importance who can make pretensions to a consistency in perfection; and even the latter of these trips occasionally into the Asyndeton; especially when he puts off his usual denominations of *pius* or *pater*, in order to be simply *Dux Trojanus* at the court of Queen Dido. As for Achilles, his whole life, *magno si quicquam credis Homero*, is an Asyndeton. He is equally a warrior and a ballad-singer, a prince and a cook. To-day he cuts up oxen, and to-morrow he cuts up Trojans. In battle he is as stout a glutton as ever peeled at Moulsey Hurst. At supper he is as hungry a glutton as ever sat down to a turtle. Homer has been blamed for the faults of his hero. For our part we think, with his defenders, that the character which aims with success at perfection, aims in vain at interest; and the feats of Achilles appear to us to derive much of their lustre from the Asyndeton which pervades them. Aware of the charm which a character receives from the use of this figure, modern writers have followed, in this point, the example of their great forerunner, and have thrown into the characters of most of their heroes a particle of this fascinating inconsistency. Hence we have the soldier of Flodden Field, something between a freebooter and a knight—

> Now forging scrolls, now foremost in the fight,
> Not quite a felon, yet but half a knight.

Hence we trace the unconnected wanderings of a noble but ruined spirit in Manfred; and hence we wonder at the mysterious union of virtue and vice in the gloomy Corsair, who

> Leaves a name to other times,
> Linked with one virtue and a thousand crimes.

Now, for the instruction of our readers in this elegant,

nay, necessary accomplishment, we must begin by observing that the Asyndeton may be practised in various manners and matters. There is the Asyndeton in actions, the Asyndeton in dress, and the Asyndeton in conversation. The first of these is adapted to the capacities of promising young men, who have some talent, some wit, and just sufficient vanity to render both of no service. The second is very proper to be used by the lady with little beauty, who wishes to be *brillante;* and the third is equally suitable to the lady with little wit, who wishes to be *piquante.* We have made our treatise so prolix, and indulged in such frequent digressions, that we fear our description will be considered a specimen of the figure we are describing; we will therefore briefly conclude this, as we concluded our former essay, by throwing together a few promiscuous specimens of the Asyndeton, in the above classes of its professors :—

William Mutable.—Jan. 31, 1820, left Cambridge a wrangler.— Feb. 12, studied "Fancy" with Jackson.—March 10, entered the "Bachelors' Club."—April 1, married ! the day was ominous.

Charles Random.—Feb. 20, 1820, bought a commission.—26th ditto, entered himself of the Temple.—March 1, entered the Church, and sported a wig.—March 6, left off the wig and fell in love.— March 20, despaired, and turned Quaker.—March 30, caught a fever by dancing.—Feb. 1, quite recovered.—Feb. 2, died.

Sophia Mellon —First Masquerade in the season, a Venus.—2nd, a Vesta.—3rd, a Georgian.—4th, a Gipsy.

Laura Voluble.—Seven o'clock, talking morality with the Doctor.— Eight, nonsense with the Captain.—Nine, Greek with the pedant. —Ten, love with the Poet.—Eleven,—Silent !—This was the most marvellous change of all, and Laura is without a rival in the Practical Asyndeton.

ON HAIR-DRESSING.

"Jamque à tonsore magistro
Pecteris." Juv.

We intend, with the permission of Mr. John Smith, to present our readers with a few observations upon Hair-dressing. Before we enter upon this topic, which we shall certainly treat *capitally*, we must assure the respectable individual above alluded to, that it is our intention in no respect to assume to ourselves the shears which he has so long and so successfully wielded. We should be sorry to encroach upon the privileges, or to step into the shoes, of so respectable a member of the community. We have a real veneration for his pointed scissors, and his no less pointed narratives, although our ears are occasionally outraged by both, since the first deal occasionally in the *Tmesis*, and the latter more frequently in the *hyperbole*. Long may he continue in the undisturbed possession of those rights which he so deservedly enjoys ; long may he continue to restore its youthful polish to the whiskered lip, and to prune with tonsoric scythe the luxuriance of our capillary excrescences.

The last paragraph is from the pen of Allen Le Blanc. We must pull him down from his high horse, and remount our ambling hobby. As we observed, it is not our intention to provoke any competition or comparison with Mr. J. Smith in the science of hair-dressing. We shall treat of a branch of the profession totally distinct from that which is exercised by the worthy tortor, or *dis*tortor of curls. We propose to discuss hair-dressing as a test of character, and to show how you may guess at the contents of the inside of the head by an inspection of the cultivation of the outside of it.

The difficulty we experience in reading the hearts of men is a trite subject of declamation. We find some men celebrated for their discrimination of character, while others are in the same proportion blamed for their want of it.

The country maiden has no means of looking into the intentions of her adorer until she has been unfeelingly deserted; and the town pigeon has no means of scrutinizing the honour of his Greek until he has been bit for a thousand. These are lamentable, and, alas! frequent cases. The prescriptions of the regular philosophers have had but little effect in the prevention of them. The idea of Horace, *torquere mero quem perspexisse laborant,* has but little influence, since the illiterate, who are most frequently in want of assistance, have seldom the cash requisite to procure the necessary *merum.* Allow us then to recommend our nostrum.

Think of the trouble we shall save if our proposal is adopted! We doubt not but it might be carried into execution to so great an extent that one might find a sharp genius in a sharp comb, and trace the intricacies of a distorted imagination through the intricacies of a distorted curl. Perfumes and manners might be studied together, and a Cavendish and a character might be scrutinized by one and the same glance.

Do not be alarmed at the importance we attach to a head of hair; Homer would never have attributed to one of his warriors the perpetual epithet of Yellow-haired, if he had not seen in the expression something more than a mere external ornament; nor would Pope have

> Weighed the men's wits against the ladies' hair,

if he had not discerned on the heads of his belles something worthy of so exalted a comparison. The attention which is paid by certain of our companions to this part of the outward man, will with them be a sufficient excuse for the weight which we attach to the subject.

We might go back to the ages of antiquity, and traverse distant countries, in order to prove how constantly the manners of nations are designated by their hair-dressing. We will omit, however, this superfluous voyage, concluding that our schoolfellows need not to be informed of the varieties of the ornaments for the poll, in which the Persian, the Greek, and the Roman character evinced itself. We shall find sufficient illustration of our position in the annals of English manners. In the days of our ancestors the flowered wig was the decoration of the gentlemen; and the hair, raised by cushions, stiffened with powder, and fastened with wires, formed the most becoming insignia of the lady. The behaviour of both sexes was the counterpart of their occipital distinctions; among the gentlemen the formal gallantry of those days was denoted by a no less formal peruke, and among the ladies the lover was prepared to expect a stiffness of decorum by the warning he received from so rigid a stiffness of *tête.* In our days the case is altered—altered, we think, for the better; unshackled politeness and innocent gaiety have by degrees succeeded to haughty repulsiveness and affected condescension ; and, in the same proportion, the wig of one sex, and the tower of the other, have been gradually superseded by fashions less appalling and more becoming. The harmless freedom, which is the prevailing characteristic of the manners of the present age, is shown in no particular more strikingly than in the cultivation of the head ; and the various shades by which the habits and dispositions of men are diversified, are not more distinct from each other than the various modes and tastes in which their heads are made up.

This, we believe, is the substance of a series of observations which we heard from a stranger the last time we were at Covent Garden Theatre. We were seated in the pit (in the fifth row from the orchestra—a situation which we recommend to our readers) ; our companion was a middle-aged man, of a tolerable person, but marked by no peculiarity except that ease of deportment, and that ready conversational power, which are invariably the characteristics of a man of the world. We were imperceptibly engaged in a conversation with him, which finally turned upon the subject of this paper. We are aware we have not done justice to his ideas. He expressed them with all the ease and perspicuity, mingled with playful humour, which denote a powerful mind employing its energies upon trivial pursuits. Then, pointing as he spoke with a curiously knotted cane which he held in his hand, he proceeded in the following manner to exemplify his doctrines :—

"Cast your eye for a moment upon the pair of figures who are leaning towards each other in the stage-box. The gentleman wears his hair cut somewhat of the shortest,

thrown up negligently in front, so as to discover a full high
forehead ; I fancy he must be a naval officer—open, bold,
thoughtless.   The character of the lady is equally legible.
Her long auburn hair, erected by the most assiduous attention into an artificial cone, has a bold and imposing appearance, and denotes that the lady is a beauty, and—knows it.

"There are three old gentlemen in the next box, who
are worth a moment's notice.   I mean the three in the
second row, who are discussing some question with no little
vehemence of action and attitude.   The first of them, who
has his hair so sprucely trimmed, and fitted to the sides of
his head with such scrupulous exactness, appears to be a
sinecure holder, who receives yearly a large salary, and finds
his only occupation in his brush ; the second, whose hair
seems to have been too much neglected by the scissors,
although it is powdered for the occasion, and tied behind
en queue, is, I should conceive, a disappointed and dis-
affected military officer ; the third, whose locks seem to
have a natural tendency to what was the newest fashion ten
years ago, must be a country gentleman come up to town to
benefit his constituents and ruin his heirs.   By the earnest
manner in which they are speaking, their topic is probably
some political change ; and the fat old gentleman, in the
close wig, who is listening to them in the third row, is
reflecting upon the influence which such an event would
have on the five per cents.

"In the centre box there are a large body of fashionables,
with some of whom I have a trifling acquaintance.   Let us
see how far they comply with my wishes in making the
head an index of the heart.   Look at the young man on
the right.   His locks are composed into a studied negligence by the labour of two hours ; they are glossy with all
the invention of Delcroix, fragrant with a *mélange* of rose,
jasmin, and jonquil.   You need not proceed to the inspection of his neckcloth or his waist, in order to be convinced
that such a being is an exquisite.

"The lady next to him is a *languissante.*   You might,
with no great effort of ingenuity, divine it from the state of
her head.   Its curls hang over the ivory surface of her neck
in a sort of artful listlessness, which is admirably adapted to
her torpid style of beauty, and her yet more torpid style of

mind. The other lady, in the front row, is her sister. She has more fashion than beauty, more vivacity than fashion, and more malice than either. With such qualifications, the course of conquest she was to pursue was obvious. She studies singularity, dresses her hair *à la grecque*, and sets up for a Spirituelle. The success of these light troops is frequently more brilliant than that of the Regulars. The fop with whom she is coquetting is a young author striving to be known. His character is written legibly on his forehead. The spruceness with which every hair is bound down in its proper station, and the stiff pertness with which the topknot is forced up, as if disdainful of the compression of the hat, plainly show that he is, at least in his own estimation, a favourite of Apollo.

"There is a gentleman in the next box, of whom it was once remarked that his countenance bore some resemblance to that of Lord Byron. Since this luckless expression the poor man has studied much to make himself ridiculous by imitating his lordship in his eccentricity, since to copy his genius is out of the question. Without looking at the eye, which takes great pains to be 'fixed in vacancy,' or the lip, which endeavours to quiver with an expression of moroseness, you may tell, from the wild and foreign costume of his tresses, that Lord Fanny is a would-be Furioso.

"It is needless to multiply examples. You will see them at every glance which you throw around you. Aurelia shows her reigning passion for rule or misrule by the circlet of gold with which her head is encompassed ; and her husband, by the lank and dejected condition of his scanty forelock, gives room for a conjecture that the principal feature of his character is submission. Old Golding, the usurer, shows his aversion for extravagance by the paucity of his visits to the barber; and his young bride, Chloe, takes care to evince a contrary taste by the diamonds which are so bountifully scattered amidst her profusion of dark ringlets. Anna, by the unvaried sameness of her head-dress, gives you a warning of the unvaried sameness of her disposition ; and Matilda, by the diversity of modes which her forehead assumes, gives you to understand that her temper and character are diversified as often. It is not surprising that this should be the case. Look to the stage, from which, indeed, our attention has been too long withdrawn. Would you not smile if Juliet were to soliloquize in Mrs. Hardcastle's *tête*, or the Royal Dane to moralize in the peruke of Sir Peter Teazle?"

Here the stranger paused, and we shortly became interested to such a degree in the sorrows of Belvidera, that we know not what further remarks he communicated, nor at what time he ceased to be our companion. As the curtain fell we looked round, and he was no longer by our side.

ON A CERTAIN AGE.

" Tempora certa."—HOR.

WE happened the other day to be present at a small party, where, being almost entire strangers ourselves, we had little to do but to listen to and reflect upon what was said by others. While we were engaged in this occupation, we heard one expression repeated several times, which made a strong impression upon us, and induced us to draw up the following treatise.

We first heard some gentlemen observing that it was quite proper for Mrs. —— to withdraw from the stage in time, for that she was now of a " certain age." Immediately afterwards we heard it remarked by Mrs. Racket, that it was lucky for Maria the Nabob had proposed in time, for the lady must be of a " certain age." Now, as the former of these objects had seen fifty winters, of which the latter fell short by at least twenty, it was natural for us to exert ourselves to discover what this " certain age " might be, the limits of which were so extensive. We accordingly commenced an investigation into the subject with great alacrity, and carried it on for some time with great perseverance. We regret to add that our success has not been proportionate to our exertions; and that, by the most

indefatigable research, we can only ascertain that nothing
in life is involved in such uncertainty as this "certain age."

Our first hope was, that by inquiries from some lady of
our acquaintance, who had the fortune or the misfortune
to come under this definition, we might be able to
ascertain the precise boundaries of the period. But here
we met with a difficulty, as it were on the threshold of our
project. Out of all the young beauties of whom we made
inquiries; out of all the fashionable belles in high life, and
the vulgar belles in low life, and the languishing belles
who have no life at all, we could find no one to return
a satisfactory answer to this mysterious, unanswerable,
insupportable question, "Are you of a certain age?" One
laughed naturally, and another laughed artificially; one
looked amazed, and another looked chagrined; one
"left it to us to decide," another left the room; one
professed utter ignorance, and another tapped us with
her fan, and wondered how we could have the impertinence. But plain "Yes" or "No" was not forthcoming.
The ladies had not studied our second number, or they
would doubtless have learnt from Messrs. Lozell and
Oakley the absolute necessity of these little monosyllables.

But to proceed. Finding this method ineffectual, we
changed our battery, and carried on the siege in another
quarter. We now applied to the same ladies for the names
of such of their acquaintances as they considered were
liable to this imputation (for a terrible imputation the
witnesses appeared to consider it). Our difficulties were
forthwith redoubled. We are not acquainted with a single
girl with good eyes, good hair, good complexion, good
fortune, or good character, whose name was not given
to us as verging upon a "certain age." And it seemed
to us extraordinary that middle-aged fair ones, whose
charms were manifestly in their autumn, were seldom
honoured with this appellation; it appeared to be exclu-
sively reserved for those who were young, beautiful, and new
to a fashionable life. Far be it from us to insinuate that
envy had any influence in making this appropriation.

Finding that the study which we had already bestowed
upon this subject had tended rather to perplex than to

elucidate the matter, we found it necessary to pursue the investigation a step farther. We now applied for information to the middle-aged matrons, the sober wives, the mothers of families. "Here," said we to ourselves, "prejudice will have ceased to influence, vanity to mislead, envy to embitter; here we shall learn the real, the whole truth, from lips unsoured by petty peevishness or violent passion." But the event disappointed our expectations: there appeared to be a strange disagreement upon this topic, for we found no two opinions to coincide. Mrs. Cranstoun, who has two daughters, and is in her twenty-ninth year, is of opinion that a "certain age" commences at thirty-four: but Mrs. Argent, who, according to our guess, is just entering her thirty-fourth year, is inclined to put off the dreaded period to forty. Lady Evergreen, again, who, to do her justice, paints as well at forty as she did at fourteen, disapproves of the impertinent notions of these "girls," and thinks that ten more years are wanting to give any one a just and proper claim to this enviable distinction. Fifty is with Lady Evergreen the precise period, the golden number, the "certain age." Still dissatisfied with the result of our examination, we betook ourselves as a last hope to the dowagers. "They," we thought, "as they must have long passed the boundaries of this dreaded space, can have no object or interest in withholding from us the truth." Alas! we were again lamentably deceived. Some of their ladyships had daughters whom they were anxious to preserve from this abominable imputation. Others had particular friends whom they were anxious to bring under it. Lady Megrim begged we would not interrupt her; she really never held good cards when any one looked over her hand; and Mrs. Volatile assured us that she had made it a rule never to think after she was married. She never would have married if she had thought before.

Finding ourselves quite at a loss to connect or reconcile with each other these several sentiments, we shall throw together a few observations which occur to us on the subject, and then leave it to wiser heads to determine the day, the hour, the minute, at which the unconscious fair one enters upon—"A certain age!"

And first, we must notice a peculiarity in the words which we do not well know how to account for—viz., that their use appears to be almost entirely confined to the fair sex. They are but seldom applied to a gentleman. We have certainly been ear-witnesses to some exceptions upon this rule : for instance, we heard old Cleaver the butcher, who has lived nearly seventy years, and amassed nearly seventy thousand pounds, advised by his friend Gibbie, the tobacconist, to leave off business, as he was now of a "certain age." And in like manner did we hear Mrs. Solander, when inclined for a solitary walk, admonish her husband, the alderman, not to take up his crutch to accompany her, for he was now "of a certain age." But with these, and a few other exceptions, we have heard this significant expression applied solely to ladies.

As to the meaning of the words, we confess that we are so completely at fault that we do not thoroughly understand whether they imply censure or commendation. The air of sarcasm and contempt with which they are commonly delivered leave us to conclude that the former is intended to be conveyed; yet we cannot but think that the words themselves signify the latter, if they have any signification at all. For, conscious as we are of the uncertainty of female fancies, the doubts they entertain on the most minute point, the hesitation which they display alike, in the refusal of an equipage or a thimble, an earring or a husband, we certainly consider it no small praise in a woman if she is found to be "certain" in anything. Nevertheless, so attached are we all to our folly and our self-conceit, that we are unwilling even to be commended for the exercise of those good qualities which we call mean and contemptible. Hence it is that our fair friends, who cruelly exult in the ambiguity of uncertain wills, uncertain wishes, and uncertain smiles, reject with disdain the honour (which we must allow would be inconsistent) of possessing—"a certain age."

The discovery of the time at which this epoch is fixed baffles our utmost diligence. We are rather disposed to place it at no particular number of years in the life of man, but to allow it to vary its period according to the disposition and manner of life of each individual. We would make it a sort of interregnum between manhood and age, between declin: and imbecility. According to our idea, the certain age of the officer would last from the first to the final breaking up of his constitution; the certain age of the drunkard would extend from the first fit of the gout to the last shake of the head of his physician; the judge would find himself in a certain age, from the time when he quits the bench to the time when he is unable to quit the sofa; and the coquette must submit to the provoking definition of a certain age, from the day on which rouge and enamel first become necessary, to the silent melancholy day on which rouge and enamel will be unavailing.

According to this arrangement, a certain age would be that restless uneasy space which elapses between our first warning to prepare for another world and our final summons to enter it. That period is to some of long, to others of shorter duration; but we believe there are few to whom this brief, this insufficient space for preparation is not conceded; there are few who are not warned by some previous sign or visitation that their sand is almost run out, that a new state of existence awaits them, that their days upon this earth are numbered. The phrase which we hear so frequently, and disregard, seen in this light will indeed inspire sombre and salutary ideas; for ourselves, we look upon a certain age as if it were the last veil which conceals from us the visions we dread to see; the last barrier which shuts us from that unexplored country on which we fear to tread; the last pause between experience and doubt,—the last dark silent curtain which separates Time from Eternity.

NOT AT HOME.

"An Englishman's house is his castle."

"Not at home," said her ladyship's footman, with the usual air of nonchalance, which says, "You know I am lying, but—*n'importe !*"

"Not at home," I repeated to myself, as I sauntered from the door in a careless fit of abstractedness. "Not at

Home !"—how universally practised is this falsehood ! Of what various, and what powerful import? Is there any one who has not been preserved from annoyance by its adoption? Is there any one who has not rejoiced, or grieved, or smiled, or sighed at the sound of "Not at Home?" No! everybody (that is everybody who has any pretensions to the title of somebody) acknowledges the utility and advantages of these three little words. To them the lady of *ton* is indebted for the undisturbed enjoyment of her vapours, the philosopher for the preservation of solitude and study, the spendthrift for the repulse of the importunate dun.

It is true that the constant use of this sentence savours somewhat of a false French taste, which I hope never to see engrafted upon our true English feeling. But in this particular who will not excuse this imitation of our refined neighbours? Who will so far give up the enviable privilege of making his house his castle, as to throw open the gates upon the first summons of inquisitive impertinence or fashionable intrusion? The "morning calls" of the dun and the dandy, the belle and the bailiff, the poet and the petitioner, appear to us a species of open hostility carried on against our comfort and tranquillity ; and, as all stratagems are fair in war, we find no fault with the ingenious device which fortifies us against these insidious attacks.

While I was engaged in this mental soliloquy, a carriage drove up to Lady Mortimer's door, and a footman in a most appallingly splendid livery roused me from a reverie by a thundering knock. "Not at Home !" was the result of the application. Half a dozen cards were thrust from the window ; and, after due inquiries after her ladyship's cold, and her ladyship's husband's cold, and her ladyship's lapdog's cold, the carriage resumed its course, and so did my cogitations. "What," said I to myself, "would have been the visitor's perplexity, if this brief formula were not in use?" She must have got out of her carriage ; an exertion which would ill accord with the *vis inertiæ* * (excuse Latin in a schoolboy) of a lady, or she must have given up her

---

* Every one knows the gradations of vis, visit, and visitation ; *vis inertiæ*, therefore, signifies an idle visit.

intention of leaving her card at a dozen houses to which she is now hastening, or she must have gone to dinner even later than fashionable punctuality requires! Equally annoying would the visit have proved to the lady of the house. She might have been obliged to throw "The Abbot" into the drawer, or to call the children from the nursery. Is she taciturn? She might have been compelled to converse. Is she talkative? She might have been compelled to hold her tongue : or, in all probability, she sees her friends to-night, and it would be hard indeed if she were not allowed to be "Not at Home" till ten at night, when from that time she must be "At Home" till three in the morning.

A knock again recalled me from my abstraction. Upon looking up, I perceived an interesting youth listening with evident mortification to the "Not at Home" of the porter. "Not at Home!" he muttered to himself, as he retired. "What am I to think? She has denied herself these three days!" and, with a most loverlike sigh, he passed on his way. Here again what an invaluable talisman was found in "Not at Home!" The idol of his affections was perhaps at that moment receiving the incense of adoration from another, possibly a more favoured votary : perhaps she was balancing, in the solitude of her boudoir, between the Vicar's band and the Captain's epaulettes ; or weighing the merits of Gout with a plum, on the one side, against those of Love with a shilling, on the other. Or, possibly, she was sitting unprepared for conquest, unadorned by cosmetic aid, rapt up in dreams of to-night's assembly, where her face will owe the evening's unexpected triumph to the assistance of the morning's "Not at Home."

Another knock! Another "Not at Home!" A fat tradesman, with all the terrors of authorized impertinence written legibly on his forehead, was combating with pertinacious resolution the denial of a valet. "The Captain's not at home," said the servant. "I saw him at the window," cried the other. "I can't help that," resumed the laced Cerberus, "he's not at home."

The foe was not easily repulsed, and seemed disposed to storm. I was in no little fear for the security of "the castle," but the siege was finally raised. The enemy retreated, sending forth from his half-closed teeth many threats, intermingled with frequent mention of a powerful ally in the person of Lawyer Shark. "Here," said I, resuming my meditations, "here is another instance of the utility of my theme. Without it, the noble spirit of this disciple of Mars would have been torn away from reflections on twenty-pounders by a demand for twenty pounds; from his pride in the King's Commission, by his dread of the King's Bench. Perhaps he is at this moment entranced in dreams of charges of horse and foot! He might have been roused by a charge for boots and shoes. In fancy he is at the head of serried columns of warriors! His eyes might have been opened upon columns of shillings and pence. In fancy he is disposing of crowns! Horrible thought! he might have been awakened to the recollection that he has not half-a-crown in the world!"

I had now reached the door of a friend, whom, to say the truth, I designed to dun for an article. Coming in the capacity of a dun, I ought not to have been surprised that I experienced a dun's reception. Nevertheless, I was a little nettled at the "Not at Home" of my old friend. "What," said I, recurring to my former ideas, "what can be Harry's occupation that he is thus inaccessible? Is he making love, or making verses? Studying Euclid or the *Sporting Magazine?* Meditating on the trial of the Queen last October, or the trial for King's next July?" For surely no light cause should induce one Etonian to be "Not at Home" to another.

As is usual with persons in my situation, who are accustomed to speculate upon trifles, from which no fixed principle can be deduced, I negatived the theory of one moment by the practice of the next. For, having returned from my perambulations, I seated myself in my study, with pen, ink, and a sheet of foolscap before me; and, finding myself once more "at Home," enjoined the servant to remember that I was "Not at Home" for the rest of the day.

MUSÆ O'CONNORIANÆ.

LETTER FROM PATRICK O'CONNOR, ESQ.

Enclosing Metrical Versions in the Greek and Latin Tongues.

DEAR MR. COURTENAY,—It is both a shame and a sin that no attempt is made to perpetuate the memory of those excellent ballads with which the languages of Ireland, England, and Scotland abound. For whereas the said languages are allowed by all men of real taste to be Gothic and semi-barbarous, it is incumbent upon us to endeavour to preserve whatever good they do contain by putting it into another dress. You know Mr. O'Doherty has preceded me in this praiseworthy attempt by his admirable version of Chevy Chace, "Persæus ex Northumbriâ," &c., which I have compared with the English ballad so often that I can hardly tell which is the original. When about to exercise my talents in this line, I held much question with myself whether I should assimilate my metre to that of my original, as is the case in the above-mentioned admirable work, or embody the ideas of my author in the rhythm of the ancient Greeks. For of the former design I do not consider myself altogether incapable; in proof of which I enclose a brief specimen of my abilities in this line—viz., a song from a MS. collection of poems in the possession of John Jackson, Esq., rendered by Patrick O'Connor, with all the original rhymes miraculously preserved.

I weep, girl, before ye,	Premore dolore,
I kneel to adore ye,	Uror amore,
My bosom is torn asunder,	Anima fit furibunda ;
Maiden divine, O,	Madeo vino,
In generous wine, O,	Et tibi propino
I pledge thee, Rosamunda !	Salutem, Rosamunda.
To a pipe of tobacco,	Victa tabaco,
And plenty of sack, O,	Victaque Baccho,
Passions and flames knock under;	Flamma mi fit moribunda ;
I'm hasty and heady,	Ebrius dedi
With lots of the deady ; —	Venerem et te Di-
Hang thyself, Rosamunda !	abolo, Rosamunda.

I trust this sample will be sufficient to convince you that when I turn my talents to the monkish style which the author above alluded to has chosen I shall come very little behind my prototype. For the present, however, I have judged that the metres of antiquity are more classical, and consequently more worthy of a place in the *Etonian*.

With regard to the poem itself, it is not, I believe, generally understood that Looney, the hero of it, is the descendant of the celebrated Phelim MacTwolter, who, in the year 1750 A.D., fought that celebrated pugilistic encounter with Patrick MacNevis, which is the subject of admiration and encomium in the sporting circles of Carrickfergus. It is gratifying to me to be able to notice this genuine son of Hibernia, because the Boxiana of modern criticism, dwelling with delight upon the minor glories of a Corcoran, a Randall, or a Donnelly, have by some strange neglect omitted all mention of the surpassing brilliancy of the merits of Phelim MacTwolter. This is the more remarkable as the above-mentioned fight was made the subject of a stanzaic heroic poem, remarkable for the animation and geniality which is preserved throughout. MacNevis, who it seems was little better than a braggadocio, gave the challenge. This is described with great force and simplicity. The landlord's daughter of the Shamrock public-house, who is said to have had a penchant for little Phelim, had been boasting of her lover's pugilistic fame.

MacNevis leaped up from his seat,
  And made his bow and told her,
" Kathleen, I'll fight for your dear
    sake
Along with fierce MacTwolter."

Surgebat MacNevisius,
  Et mox jactabat ultro,
" Pugnabo tui gratiâ
  Cum fero MacTuoltro."

Does not this remind us strongly of Homer's Paris?

Ἀυτὰρ ἔμ' ἐν μέσσῳ καὶ ἀρηΐφιλον Μενέλαον
Συμβάλετ', ἀμφ' Ἑλένῃ καὶ κτήμασι πᾶσι μάχεσθαι.

The address of MacNevis to his antagonist upon meeting him in the ring is conceived in the same style of ferocious grandeur. He sees him applying himself to the bottle, and exclaims—

While you can see blue ruin, joy !	Frater, dum tibi manet lux,
Pull deeper yet and deeper ;	Bibe ruinæ poculum :
By George ! you shall return from	Redibis hinc, per Georgium !
hence,	Utrumque cassus oculum.
Without an open peeper.	

Observe that the expression "blue ruin" is very poetical, but my version of it is also prophetical—a charm unknown to the original. Phelim's reply is beautiful—

Don't tip me now, my lad of wax,	Ne sis, O cerâ mollior,
Your blarney and locution,	Grandiloquus et vanus ;
Och ! sure you ar'n't a giant yet,	Heus bone ! non es gigas tu,
Nor I a Lilliputian.	Et non sum ego nanus.

Here again the author, of course, had Homer in his eye—

Μήτι μευ, ἠύτε παιδὸς ἀφαυροῦ, πειρήτιζε.

And again—

Πηλείδη, μὴ δή μ' ἐπέεσσί γε, νηπύτιον ὣς,
Ἔλπεο δειδίξεσθαι.

The contest, which, it is possible, I may by-and-by transmit to you at length, is described with a minuteness which far exceeds Virgil's Dares and Entellus, or even the pugilism of the *Sporting Magazine.* The modest MacTwolter is, as he deserves to be, the victor. The poem concludes in a high strain of triumph—

So Victory to Phelim gave	Victoria dedit Phelimo
A wife of fair renown ;	Uxorem valde bonam ;
And with that wife she gave besides	Et dedit cum uxore hâc
To him a silver crown.	Argenteam coronam.

I must now cease to comment upon this fascinating character, and proceed, without further delay, to the celebration of the amour of his descendant. Looney Mac-Twolter is well known to you, as you have frequently heard the identical ballad from the lips of Frederick Golightly. I shall therefore give you my promised translation of it, without note or preface. Give it a classical name —"an Eclogue," or "an Idyll," or "an Elegy," or what you will.

I.

Oh, whack! Cupid's a mannikin,
   Smack on my heart he hit me a polter;
Good lack, Judy O'Flannikin!
   Dearly she loves nate Looney MacTwolter.
Judy's my darling, my kisses she suffers;
     She's an heiress, that's clear,
     Fot her father sells beer;
He keeps the sign of the Cow and the Snuffers;
     She's so smart,
     From my heart
     I cannot bolt her.
Oh, whack, Judy O'Flannikin!
She is the girl for Looney MacTwolter.

II.

Oh, hone! good news I need a bit!
   We'd correspond, but larning would choke her.
Mavrone!—I cannot read a bit;
   Judy can't tell a pen from a poker.
Judy's so constant, I'll never forsake her;
     She's true as the moon—
     Only one afternoon
I caught her asleep with a humpbacked shoemaker.
     She's so smart, &c.

ά.

'Αλαλη· τι μικρον ἐστι
βρεφος οὐλιον Κυθηρης,
ἐμε δ' ἐγκρατει βελεμνῳ
προς καρδιαν ἐνυξεν.
ἀλαλη· τι φημ'; Ιουδιθ
ἀπο Φλαννικιν φιλεῖ με,
τον Λουνιαν φιλεῖ με,
τοκον εὐπρεπη Τυολτρου.
μελι και το νεκταρ ἀμον
ἀπαλη πεφυκ' Ιουδιθ·
το δ' ἐμον, χαριεσσα θυμῳ,
γλυκερον φιλημα πασχει.
ἐφανη δ' ἀρ', οὐκ ἀδηλως,
μεγαλου λαχουσα κληρου.

ὁ πατηρ γαρ, εὐ τοδ' οἰδα,
πομα κριθινον πιπρασκει,
ὑπο σημα δ' ἡ καθηται
βοος ἡδε και πυραγρας.

Χαριεσσα δ' ἡ πεφηνε·
τοσον, ὡς νιν οὐ δύναιμην
ἀπο καρδιας ἀπωσαι·
ἀλαλη· μαλιστ' Ιουδιθ
ἀπο Φλαννικιν με τερπει,
τον Λουνιαν με τερπει,
τοκὸν εὐπρεπη Τυολτρου.

β'.

'Οτοτοι· τι γραμμ' ἀπ' αὐτης
καλος ἀγγελος γενοιτ' ἀν·
ἀποροισι δ' ἀν πλοκαισιν
σοφια νιν ἀγχονωη.
'Οτοτοι· τα γραμματ' οὐδεις
ἐδιδαξε μ', ἡ δ' Ιουδιθ

γραφιδ' οὐτι και σιδηρον
πυρεσειστικον διεγνω·
μελι και το νεκταρ ἀμον
ἀπαλη πεφυκ' Ιευδιθ·
οὐδ' εὐφρονως ἐγωγε
καταλειψομαι ποτ' αὐτην·

ἐφάνη γὰρ, ὡς σελήνη,   ὑποδέμνιας ξυνευνου
παναληθινη νεανις·   σκολιῷ γε βυρσοδεψῃ·
ἀλλ', ἑσπερας πεσουσης,
ἐληψαμην ποτ' αὑτης   χαριεσσα δ' ἡ πεφηνε, κ. τ. λ.

PATRICK O'CONNOR.

Port St. Dermid, near Ballinocrasy,
December 28, 1820.

[NOTE.—The Greek Version, to which this paper was written as a preface, was the composition of the late John Louis Petit, subsequently Vicar of Uplands, Shifnal, Salop.]

THE KNIGHT AND THE KNAVE.

AN OLD ENGLISH TALE.

"REGINALD!" said the old Baron. It is striking, and fashionable, and classical, to hurry my reader thus *in medias res;* else it had been my duty to have informed him that the *dramatis personæ* whom he finds upon the scene are the son and grandson of the redoubted Hugh d'Arennes, who did good service by the Conqueror's side at the field of Hastings. In common with the distinguished chiefs of William's army, he had received large grants of land, which his enterprising spirit, and his interest with the monarch and his successor, had tended to augment. His heir, however, the present head of the illustrious family, had rather studied the security than the aggrandizement of his possessions, and had grown to a green old age in retirement and seclusion, as far as was compatible with his high rank and exalted situation. The younger speaker of the colloquy was of a character, the description of which may be dismissed as easily. Not having been obliged, like the other young men of his time, to take an active part in the divisions which agitated the period of the reign of the second Henry, Reginald had not acquired the firm and energetic tone of

mind by which the sons of the nobility were distinguished.
He had been accustomed to shape his conduct, in the most
trifling concerns, according to the advice and judgment of
his father; and consequently, when deprived for a short
period of his monitor, seemed utterly incapable of thinking
seriously, or rather seemed to have made a religious vow
against thinking at all. This hopeful descendant of the
noble Sir Hugh had arrived at the age of twenty, was
possessed of a listless, yet handsome, set of features; a
careless, yet commanding figure; a true English head at
the cup, and a true English hand at the quarrel. And now,
having gone through the interruption, which ought to have
been the introduction, let us proceed.

"Reginald!" said the old Baron, with a slight inclination
of the head, which he was in the habit of using when he
wished to throw dignity into his admonitions.

"Ears hear thee," said the son, without stirring from the
huge oaken table upon which, after the fatigues of the chase,
he was reclining.

"I have ordered that we should be alone, my son," said
the old man, "because I have to discourse to thee a matter
which deeply and nearly concerns thy welfare. Pour for
thy father, Reginald."

Reginald obeyed; and, after performing for himself the
same office, resumed his attitude, with an aspect which was
ludicrously divided between the resolution to attend and
the propensity to inattention.

"Twenty years have gone by, Reginald, since thou didst
become the hope of the house of which thou wilt shortly be
the head. Ere thou hast other twenty years to look back
upon, thou wilt have lost the guidance of thy father, and I
shall sleep by the side of mine."

"Sir Hugh sleeps in the abbey," said Reginald.

"He doth," resumed his adviser. "He was a knight of
name and fame, and wielded a good sword at Hastings."

"As touching the sword," said Reginald, totally unconscious of any metaphorical meaning implied in his father's
words, "it hangs above him in the abbey. Marry, it is
somewhat rusty, but nevertheless a good sword."

"But, Reginald, to come to the point——"

"Thou dost remind me how that it was broken against

the fifth rib of Egwulph, surnamed the Impetuous, a good knight and a true—although a Saxon."

The look of the young man had in it something of animation as he expressed his hereditary contempt of the Saxon race. To his father, however, this demonstration of feeling did not seem altogether so welcome as it might have been upon another occasion. He contracted his huge shaggy eyebrows, turned his eyes from his son to the wine-cup, and from the wine-cup to his son, stroked his chin, folded his arms, and, in short, assumed an attitude of thought, which was little less ridiculous than the thoughtlessness of his companion. After a pause of some minutes, he began to speak, sending out his words with all the caution and circumspection of a Fabius.

"Of a truth, Reginald, the Saxon thanes are in breeding and courtesy rough, and in no way able to compete with the bearing of our Norman knights; but they are not, as thy speech would signify, altogether to be contemned. There is among them much might of arm, and courage of heart; and Sir Hugh was wont to say there were few cravens at Hastings."

Reginald made no reply: he was deep in mental researches after the probable cause of the Baron's unaccustomed eulogium upon a race so universally vilified. Finding himself unable to solve the mystery, he waited in silence for some further clue. The old man looked as if to see whether his words had made any impression upon the prejudices of his hearer; and, not being able to ascertain the fact, proceeded: "There is Leofwyn of Kennet Hold," said he, "his better never drew bow : his grandfather stood before Harold when De Rocroi had him down. He hath riches and retainers, such as never had King of England. Ill befall the man that thinks scorn of Leofwyn of Kennet Hold."

"He is our near neighbour," said Reginald. "I have heard that he hath a braver horse than is my black steed Launcelot, and hounds whose equals the world cannot show. He hath a daughter, too, if fame speak rightly, a lady of a most noble presence ; and he hath a falcon——"
Here he was interrupted by the old Baron, who, as if weary of the circumlocution by which he had been endeavouring

to bring about his object, observed dryly: "It is to that lady, Reginald, I would see thee wedded."

Reginald fixed himself upright upon the table on which he had been extended, and, opening wide his large languid eyes, gazed upon his father with a mute expression of astonishment. The latter, though a little daunted by the silence with which his proposition had been received, proceeded to explain the causes and consequences of his design. It is needless to accompany him through his detail, which, to say truth, was somewhat prolix. It is sufficient to state that the lands of the Saxon looked tempting in the eyes of the Norman lord; and that, in times of such danger and difficulty, it seemed prudent to conciliate the friendship of those who were powerful in their immediate vicinity, and especially those who were attached to the Saxon succession.

Now the Baron, while he detailed his hopes, and his fears, and his designs, fancied that he had made in this scheme a notable hit of policy, and from time to time looked up to the listener's face for the approbation to which he thought himself entitled. Reginald, however, perceived that his castle-building would meet with obstacles which the architect had never contemplated; and began to be of opinion that a friendly alliance between Norman and Saxon sounded very like an amicable treaty between hound and hare, or a peaceable union between fire and water. To these thoughts he was unwilling to give utterance: a dispute, and upon such a subject, was a thing to which he had an insuperable reluctance: he therefore quietly acquiesced in his father's reasoning, and, after stipulating that in this matter no trouble should fall upon himself, composed himself in a quiet slumber, while the Baron was recounting the particulars of his ten years' courtship of Marie, the beautiful heiress of Roger de Vesnoy, the last lord of Battiswold.

The old man, contented with this calm compliance on the part of his son, proceeded forthwith to put his favourite scheme in execution. For many weeks was his brain disturbed by the anxiety which he felt for the result of his negotiations: there were messages, and letters, and heralds, and stipulations, and breakings off, and reconciliations, more than sufficient to perplex the thoughts of a far more able diplomatist. Meantime the person who was to bear the principal part in the play which was now in rehearsal, ate, drank, and slept, talked of his horses and hounds, and his escutcheon, and thought of nothing less than of his fair unseen intended, Elfrida of Kennet Hold. Finally, the treaty was completed more successfully than the violent temper of Leofwyn gave reason to expect; and Reginald received orders to prepare for an immediate journey to receive the bride he had never courted. The first impression upon his mind was that it was passing strange that the pride of a Saxon thane, nay, the pride of a Saxon heiress, could be with such facility subdued.' Reflection, however, was not his province; and, banishing as quickly as possible the intrusive idea, he prepared himself to obey his father.

On the morrow he set out. The manuscript from which I draw my information describes, with much prolixity, the accoutrements of himself and his steed; from whence it makes a considerable digression to the changes in the fashions of dress, and the peculiar merits of various breeds of horses. It then makes honourable mention of his attendants, and dwells upon certain scandalous anecdotes connected with their family concerns. The last-mentioned points I deem it right to omit altogether; and upon the others I must be more concise than is the chronicler whom I follow, the erudite Henricus Wykeleius.

It appears that Reginald, although a bigot to the manners and prejudices which his Norman ancestry had entailed upon him, had, upon this occasion, in compliance with the request of his father, assumed the costume of the Saxons. So much had the natural ease and gracefulness of his frame been improved by constant exercise and knightly sports, that the unaccustomed dress seemed to be no restraint or inconvenience to him; and his limbs were as free in the long Saxon robe as they had been wont to be in the short Norman tunic. He reined his horse with a skill which at once excited and curbed his impetuosity, while it set off to the best advantage the forms of both the animal and his rider. Of this, however, neither of them stood in need. Launcelot was one of the noblest steeds that ever bore armed knight to the lists; and Reginald, in spite of the want of animation which was so evident in his features, was really a handsome and well-proportioned youth. Had his education been suited to his talents, or the qualifications of his mind kept pace with those of his body, few warriors might have won lady's love so lightly as Reginald d'Arennes.

Of his followers, which were six in number, four were merely retainers of little note or name. Of the remaining two some notice must be taken. The first was Roger Naylis, an old and approved dependent, who was his companion upon this journey for the purpose of obviating by his prudence and experience those dangers into which the hot heart or light head of his young master might hurry him. The other was a personage of a description not quite so common. This was Robin Garnet, who had long been in Reginald's service, in triple capacity of page, associate, and fool. His was a character, of which, in the compass of this tale, it will be impossible to give the reader any idea. In it was to be found the most extraordinary mixture of cunning and folly, blindness and foresight, thoughtlessness and thought. His actions were generally those which no one but a madman would commit ; yet the means by which he extricated himself from their consequences were those which none but a man of great acuteness would hit upon. He was the son of poor parents, but had rendered himself, by his talents for frolic and buffoonery, so necessary to the young lord, that he was looked upon almost in the light of his foster-brother. He rode a small piebald nag, which formed a whimsical contrast with the large black courser of his master. His dress was that of an ordinary page ; his form, though small, was not inelegant ; and his features, though not handsome, had an arch expression about them, which looked very ludicrous, when compared with the lifelessness of Reginald's.

Nothing more need be said of him save that the extremes of cunning and idiotcy which his conduct perpetually exhibited had conferred upon him two denominations, which were alternately applied as they became by turns appropriate. When the former predominated, he was termed "Robin the Wily;" and when the latter resumed its influence, his appellation was "Robin the Witless."

Upon the present occasion Reginald was not a little annoyed that he was compelled to converse with his father's old counsellor, to the exclusion of the humorous partner of his follies. From this inconvenience, however, he was soon relieved. Before he had gone many miles he was met by a messenger from Leofwyn, who, after various excuses and apologies, informed him that his lord had vowed a vow that two men of Norman blood should never cross his threshold together; and that he therefore requested his future son-in-law to dismiss such of his train as fell under this interdict. The young lord certainly was not greatly displeased, when, upon examination, it was found that Robin was the only one of his followers who was not excluded by Norman lineage from the hall of the Saxon thane. Nevertheless, when his aged attendant whispered his suspicions of meditated treason, and intimated the propriety of returning, he gazed on the adviser, and then on the page, and then on the messenger; and expressed, by look and word, his usual sentiment in all such dilemmas—"I doubt!"

"The hall of Leofwyn is open," said the messenger; "shall I say that the guest dallieth? The Lady Elfrida is in her bridal robe; shall I say that the bridegroom delayeth his purpose?" "I will go with thee," said Reginald.

"For my part, I say nought," observed Naylis, "but life may be preserved, and life may be thrown away; and one against a hundred is fearful odds. Fathers will weep when children die; it matters not whether by the naked sword or the poisoned cup." "I will return with thee!" said Reginald.

"Of a surety," said Robin, "there is a venture both ways. If we advance, life is perilled; and if we retreat, the lady is lost." "I know not whether to go or to return?" said Reginald.

"I will return to my master," said the messenger; "peradventure he will send to thee that shall remove thine apprehensions. Hasten not on the way. Marry! it is well that the Lady Elfrida should wait the leisure of Reginald d'Arennes;" and, turning his horse's head, he was preparing to depart, when Naylis seized his reins, exclaiming : "Not so, Sir Discourteous ! By our Lady thou departest not so lightly. Sir Reginald wendeth to Kennet Hold, and if a hair of his head be injured thou diest, an thou wert Leofwyn's first-born ! "

"Norman hound !" cried the messenger, with an exclamation of surprise, "hast thou divined——but no ! thy thoughts were no parties to thy lips, and I war not for a random word. I will go with ye—rather than your master should lose his bride. By the soul of Hengist, it were pity !" As he spoke he removed his hand, which he had laid upon the hilt of his dagger, and bent upon Reginald a look in which there was much and deep signification, although the standers-by were unable to read its import. Naylis led his young lord apart, and spoke a few words in an earnest whisper. Reginald still seemed irresolute ; he began to reply hastily in a tone between soliloquy and expostulation.

"Thou sayest right well, Roger, and with discretion ; yet, by my spurs, a younger head had given warmer counsel ! How think you, my masters, were it not a pleasant tale to tell that Reginald d'Arennes fled from the bright eyes of his bride? Yet, as thou sayest, Roger, there is danger in this adventure ! Not that I heed shaft or spear, bill or battle-axe, in the hand of a Saxon ; thou knowest I am no craven, Roger ! But then, as thou sayest, Roger—my father, I do believe my death-wound would be his ! I will return to him—yet would he be shamed by my return ! I will go on—or rather, I will not ; thou shalt hasten back to him, Roger, and tell him—hum ! I doubt !"

How long the contest might have lasted it is impossible to determine ; the remaining attendants were beginning to hazard surmises respecting the eligibility of a night lodging *sub dio*, when Robin the Wily sprung with a kind of harlequin step before his patron, and, throwing himself into the attitude of a despairing maiden, sang, in a ludicrously plaintive voice, some stanzas of a popular air, which may be thus modernized :—

> Oh ! I am drest in my bridal vest,
>   The feast is on the board !
> And whither fleeth my father's guest ?
>   Whither Elfrida's lord ?

I look to the east, and I look to the west,
  The evening moon is toward ;
But I see not yet my father's guest,
  I see not Elfrida's lord !

Why am I dight in my kirtle of white,
  My silken snood withal ?
For not to-night that craven knight
  Will cross my father's hall.

She hath torn outright her kirtle of white,
  Her silken snood withal ;
And not to-night that craven knight
  Will cross her father's hall !

"I will go on to Kennet Hold," said Reginald. There was something in the look of the page, more than in the words he uttered, which had so deeply inspired his master with that strongest of all incentives, the dread of ridicule, that his determination was now inflexible. Well was it said by the learned monk, Bedo Camerarius, "the resolution of a strong mind giveth way to argument, but the obstinacy of a weak one never !" Naylis was of the same opinion : he held another conference with his master in whispers; the result of which was that Reginald exchanged his loose robe for the rich suit of armour which was borne after him by his attendants.

They were preparing to separate upon their respective journeys, when they discovered the first fruits of Reginald's hesitation in the departure of their purposed hostage. No orders had been given for his forcible detention; and he had accordingly taken advantage of the consultation which had engaged the attention of the party to effect his retreat. "The hawk without a collar hath but brief thraldom," said Robin. "Thou art right, knave," said Naylis; "had thy counsel been earlier, yon slave should have made experiment of the weight of a Norman gyve. But it matters not. Though the Saxon have the temper of his own Zernbock, and the Furies to boot, he dare not—surely he dare not ! Well I wot our master would work so deep a requital that the heads of twenty such miscreants should appear cheap ransom !"

"Fare thee well, good Naylis," said Reginald; "bid my

father be of good cheer, and do honour to his son's bridal! Ha! ha! Thou hast still thy misdoubtings and thine apprehensions—I know thy mind!" "Would thou didst know thine own but half as well!" muttered the old man, as he turned slowly round, followed by the Norman attendants. The steeds, as if rejoicing to be again in motion, arched their proud necks, and flung back their thick manes in the wind: the clattering of their hoofs arose, and sank, and died into silence.

Reginald and the knave, Robin, journeyed some miles without converse. The latter seemed to be thinking of nothing but his new doublet, and the former seemed to be thinking of nothing at all. After a considerable pause, the Knight began the conversation. "I am doubting, Robin——"

"It is a wise man that solveth his own doubts!" returned his attendant.

"I am doubting, Robin," continued Reginald, "whether thou or I be the greater fool!"

"A gibe! a gibe!" cried the jester; "thy reasons, most convincing disputant? thy proofs, most inventive master? thine arguments, most incontrovertible Knight? Marry, an thou make me the greater fool, it will ill become the servant to be greater than his master."

"Imprimis, thou art a fool by thy name, which is Witless!"

"I will have license to make reply," said the jester; "thou art a fool to call a wise man by a fool's name."

"Secondly," resumed Reginald, "thou art a fool by thy face!"

"Who is to choose," said his antagonist, "between the folly that is seen on the face and the folly which is spoken from the tongue?"

"Thirdly, thou art foolish in thy designs."

"By Saint Swithin," cried the respondent, "thou hast the better of me there, for designs formest thou none."

"Fourthly, thou art a fool by thine occupation!"

"There thou hast spoken well," said the page; "I am serving-man to Sir Reginald d'Arennes."

"Finally, Robin," said Reginald, relapsing into taciturnity, "thou knowest that thou art a fool positive!"

"Thou hast the better of me again, Reginald," said the complaisant lackey, "for thou art greatly a fool, and surpassingly a fool—but never a positive one."

Reginald did not hear the import of his follower's reply; or at least made no answer to it. They proceeded for some minutes in silence, at a brisk pace, when Reginald suddenly stopped, and exclaimed, "We have wandered from our track!"

"Not a whit, not a whit," replied his companion, "do not I know the turnings and the windings of the way? Is it not the fourth time that I have journeyed with thee on this path? Firstly, when thou didst do penance at the Abbey of Brixhelm; secondly, when thou didst pillage the fat friar of Torney Low; thirdly, when thou wert, at thine own pleasure, a suitor to the miller's daughter of Nesselray; fourthly, when thou art, at thy father's pleasure, a suitor to the thane's daughter of Kennet Hold. Truly the fool's counsel is nought; but I hold the pillage more profitable than the penance, and the miller a cheaper bargain than the thane. Trust me, if there be in the hall of the Saxon another giant such as he that escaped from us even now, there will be stronger trust in the speed of black Launcelot than in the plating of thy Milan corselet."

"He was, indeed," said Reginald, "firm of sinew and large of bone; he was, withal, free in his deportment, and ruled that sorrel courser full knightly; and, as thou sayest, Robin, he bore in his hand a battle-axe, against which ribs of steel were but weak protection."

They had now proceeded far on their journey, and were winding round a thick forest; the extremities of which were skirted by brushwood to a very considerable extent. Reginald continued to discuss the personal appearance of the herald of his father-in-law in a manner which showed he was by no means deficient in natural observation. "He had the tone of one not unused to command, and an eye right noble and piercing; nevertheless, he is but a Saxon; and ill betide the day when Reginald d'Arennes shall fear to cope with twenty Saxons."

"Especially," said Robin, with an expression of countenance more than usually arch, "when Reginald d'Arennes hath by his side so true an esquire. Well thou knowest I am a shrewd knave, and a wily!"

At this moment a shrill whistle rung in their ears, and five or six stout yeomen rushed from the thicket, seized Launcelot's rein, and dragged his rider from the saddle ere he could raise his war-cry, or draw his sword from its sheath. Robin was treated with no more ceremony than his master, and both were hurried through the coppice. Reginald seemed lost in astonishment; he made no resistance, and uttered no word. Robin was not so quiet in his sufferings; his alarm broke out in various unconnected exclamations: "Saints be merciful to me! The limbs of a Roland or an Oliver could not stand this harrying! And the fair tunic that was given me but yester-even is rent like a withered leaf! Truly, my masters, these bushes are over-sharp for a delicate frame. Well I wot my sides are torn as it were with the barbed points of twenty arrows; and Sir Reginald heeds no more the brambles than if they were damosels' arms! See now! Some are born to a corselet of steel, and some to a tunic of cloth! Saint Christopher befriend me! I confessed myself but yesterday! Bethink ye, my masters, why compass ye the death of an innocent man! The bough hath reft me of my cap! Hold, for the love of mercy! I am a poor knave and a witless!'

To such lamentations no answer was returned, save an occasional peal of laughter. Knight and knave were borne rapidly onward, through paths which not only seemed impervious to the tread, but were hardly penetrable to the sight. At length, a sudden winding in their track brought them into a large open space, which appeared to have been cleared out in the middle of the forest. Here an extraordinary scene burst upon them, which not a little heightened the astonishment of the young lord, and even checked for a space the wailings of his attendant.

In a spacious area, surrounded by lofty trees, which seemed admirably calculated for the concealment of parties met for the prosecution of illicit designs, various groups of men were widely scattered. They appeared to be principally composed of the lower sort of peasantry, who, having no dependence on any one but those to whom they had been born subject, were liable to be called, at a moment's warning, to engage in the quarrels of their feudal lord.

D

And such seemed to be the purpose which had collected together the force I am endeavouring to describe. Some few were clad in the complete defensive armour of that period, and might be supposed to be those retainers who were more immediately attached to the person of their chief. There were others who were prepared for less regular warfare by the boar-spear or the Norman cross-bow; and others, again, who made little military display beyond the knife which was stuck in their girdle or the rude mace that lay beside them.

A short distance apart from these groups two figures were engaged in conversation, one of whom appeared to be the leader of the party. He was a tall, powerful man, apparently little more than thirty years of age; he seemed to have been inured to toil and danger; and his manner, at once graceful and dignified, gave the idea of one who had been bred up alternately in the camp and the court from his earliest years. His countenance was handsome, but nevertheless unpleasing; for its features indicated a knowledge of the world which partook strongly of dissimulation, and a valour which would not scruple to exert itself in a bad cause. His dress was a mailed shirt, unadorned by any extraneous decoration; but the richly wrought hilt of the dagger which he wore by his side proved that he was a person of no ordinary rank. His attendant was an esquire, who appeared to receive with much deference the communications of his superior.

Reginald and his attendant were immediately conducted into the presence of this chieftain. He had been conversing with his companion in a manner and tone of much hauteur; but when, upon turning round, he beheld the heroes of my story, every appearance of this kind immediately vanished; his brow was in a moment perfectly calm, and his look wore all the pliability and condescension which an able diplomatist knows so well how to assume.

"Sir Knight," he began, "I am, it is true, a stranger to thee, but I have confidence that those features, and that bearing, bespeak one of the house of d'Arennes." Reginald bowed, in token of acquiescence; and his new acquaintance (who, by-the-by, had received pretty certain intelligence beforehand of the rank of the person he was addressing) proceeded : " The disturbed state of our realm, Sir Knight, must be my excuse for a measure which courtesy would else have shrunk from. It must also excuse the interrogation which it constrains me to put. With what purpose hast thou journeyed hither?"

Reginald seemed not sufficiently recovered from his surprise to make reply. Robin answered for him, "Marry, with the purpose of journeying back again."

"Thou wouldest do well to keep thy counsel, friend," said the querist; "thy flippant tongue might elsewhere procure thee a cap and bells; but here, trust me, it will exalt thee to little else than the bough that waves over my head. I would pray of thee," he continued to Reginald, " brief answer and speedy."

Reginald seemed somewhat roused from his torpidity by the overweening tone in which he was addressed : " Hither I came," he said, "with the purpose of a bridal, and in bridal garment; mantle and cap have I already exchanged for hauberk and helm ; and, by thy goodwill, wedding and wassail will briefly be transmuted to quarrel and fray."

"Art thou so warm for a fray?" said the stranger. "It is the better; thou hast gentle blood within thee, although thy first address did belie it wofully. What if I were to lead thee to a fray, where an estate shall be had for the buckling on of thy harness, and an earldom shall be the requital of every blow? How sayest thou, Reginald d'Arennes? Is not prince's favour more worth the winning than lady's love? and is not the possession that is the guerdon of service in field more honourable than the dower that is sued for on bended knee?"

Reginald seemed again frozen into inanimation. Alike ignorant of the person who spoke to him, and of the purport of what he spoke, he had recourse to his never-failing response, "I doubt." Robin again stepped forward with his ballad admonition, which I shall again endeavour to modernize, "albeit unused to the rhyming mood."

> 'Tis merry, 'tis merry, in fair greenwood,
>   When birds are blithely singing ;
> 'Tis merry, 'tis merry, in foughten field,
>   When blows are bravely ringing.

"On to the fight !" saith King Arthure,
  "Accurst be he that flies !
Riches and fame to him·that lives !
  And bliss to him that dies !

Why lingerest thou, Childe Celadon ?"
  Out spoke that cunning knave,
"The brightest gift thy crown can give,
  What boots it in the grave !"

The very prudent and natural suggestion of "Childe Celadon" seemed to have a marvellous effect upon Reginald, and would probably have influenced his reply, had not the attention of his interrogator been called off by another circumstance. To this we must also attribute the safety of the songster's neck, which, had not this seasonable interruption taken place, would have been ill worth a minute's purchase.

A messenger had suddenly arrived, and been conducted into the presence of their unknown captor. He appeared to have come from a long distance; and the disordered state of his dress, together with the fatigue which was apparent on his pale countenance, sufficiently proved that he had not spared whip or spur on the journey. He delivered to the chief the letters of which he was the bearer, and retired in silence. The chief broke open the packet; anxiety was strongly marked on his countenance; yet his features changed not, as he read his advices : it was difficult to form a conjecture whether he was rejoiced or displeased by their contents. He called to him his esquire. They held a brief conference apart.

"Cold news, Eustace ! The Flemings have been beaten ! The slaves fled as the first weapon leaped from its sheath. De Lucy's powers are drawn together, and Bohun hath Leicester prisoner."

"Then it were well to seek shelter while the tempest is yet coming on. It will blow a fierce wind ere long !"

"Let it blow," said the chief, drawing himself up to the full height of his figure; "there are those that shall weather the gale. What, Eustace ! Thinkest thou that in caves, or in castles, or in fastnesses, there is safety for those whom Henry calls traitors? Our refuge is in battle-field, our trust in ready sword. I have advanced my foot in this quarrel, and yon oak is not fixed more firmly."

"I am ready to serve thee in good and in ill: I am ready to live and to die with thee; but it were sheer madness, with thy single force, to——"

The chief interrupted him by unfolding his letters and pointing to several names which were mentioned in them, speaking hastily as he went on. "Archetil is up in arms—Ferrars is with us—Roger de Moubray hath good bowmen—Hamo de Mascie will not flinch—Hugh Bigod will not be idle in a rising—Clare and Gloucester may be won; and, let but Williams hear the news of our arming, the North shall see a hundred thousand Scottish spears ere a hundred men are afoot against us. It is no time for dallying; and this place, though for forty-eight hours it hath concealed our ill-assorted levy, is no safe abode for men engaged in this warfare. We must endeavour to join my brother at the setting of to-morrow's sun." Eustace bowed, and was preparing to withdraw, but was recalled. A few sentences were exchanged, in which the name of Reginald was frequently mentioned, and he was then summoned before his captor.

"Reginald d'Arennes," said the Knight, in a low tone of voice, "thou seest before thee Richard de Mallory. For himself he hath little claim to expect that his name should have been breathed in thine ear, but thou wilt know him better as the brother of the renowned Archetil de Mallory, who with many brave companions, which at a more fitting time shall be enumerated to thee, is now in arms against usurpation and tyranny. What sayest thou? Wilt thou continue to disgrace, by thine inactivity, the name of thine ancestor? or wilt thou join thy name to the list of these valiant nobles, buckle thy fortune to thy sword, and win an earldom by my side?"

Now Reginald was by no means deficient in natural penetration, although he had not the firmness of character which was requisite to act upon its suggestions; he saw, therefore, that the attempt of these "valiant nobles," like the many other conspiracies by which the reign of Henry II. was perpetually threatened, would probably have for its conclusion confiscation and death. He was not very ready to embark in an undertaking of this nature, until he had conferred with the Baron upon its expediency, and had calculated the chances for and against success. Upon the present occasion, therefore, he succeeded with much difficulty in pleading his approaching bridal as an excuse for declining the offer of his new acquaintance.

Richard de Mallory, however, appeared by no means satisfied with the apology; the less so, when upon inquiry he heard that the lady whose unseen charms detained the young lord from the field was of Saxon descent. That the scion of so illustrious a stock should intermarry with that contemned race was an idea which startled the prejudices of the proud Norman; insomuch that he evidently entertained serious doubts of the truth of the narration. "Elfrida of Kennet Hold!" he muttered to himself; "named not the Saxon whom our spies brought hither this morning the name of Kennet Hold?"

"He did," replied Eustace.

"Lead him hither," said De Mallory; and instantly, from one of the avenues which led into the forest, some armed men brought forth a captive Saxon, in whom Reginald immediately recognized the messenger who had escaped from his baffled followers in the morning. The Saxon also bestowed a glance of recognition upon his fellow-captive. "Saxon," said De Mallory scornfully, "what saidst thou was thy name? for in truth the appellations of thy race dwell not long in Norman remembrance."

"I am called," said the prisoner, looking on Reginald as he spoke, "Lothaire, the first-born of Leofwyn of Kennet Hold. Thy name, Richard de Mallory, is not unknown to me: thou art one of those who have raised up the subjects against the king, and the sons against the father. But the work needed not thine agency. It shall be long ere a Norman shall know peace on the throne of Harold; long ere the gods of the Saxons shall cease to revenge upon the head of his descendants the usurpation of the first William."

"I asked not for thy forebodings; nor knew I that I had a prophet in my camp. One more question shall I ask thee. Shall Reginald d'Arennes wed thy father's daughter?"

Lothaire seemed much embarrassed by the question: he hesitated for some time; until at last, smiling, as if he had found the means of releasing himself from some difficulty, he looked at Reginald with an unintelligible expression of countenance, and replied, " He rideth with that purpose."

" It is enough," exclaimed the chief. "The Norman knight that can stoop to wed with the daughter of a Saxon franklin is no fellow in arms for Richard de Mallory. Let them wend on their way together. Where is the fool? It were a pity to deny him such fit company."

And with this sarcasm the three captives were suffered to depart, being first obliged to swear a binding oath not to divulge what they had seen and heard in their confinement. Reginald suffered himself to be reconducted to the place where he had been seized, without betraying any unusual emotion either of joy or resentment; but Lothaire cast back upon the Norman leader frequent glances expressive of the most determined hate, and a disposition to make a speedy and an ample return for his discourteous hospitality. Their horses were brought to them, and they again set forward upon their errand with no injury but what was occasioned by the long delay they had experienced. It was near sunset, and there seemed little possibility of their reaching Kennet Hold before nightfall. They pushed on, however, at a brisk pace. It may be doubted whether Reginald was altogether pleased with the new companion he had met with in the person of Lothaire, who accompanied him unasked, and threw upon him at whiles a look which spoke anything rather than brotherly love. Robin kept a respectful distance, for he seemed to have for the Saxon youth no stronger predilection than his master.

Meantime the mind of the rebel chief was little disturbed by the disastrous intelligence which he had received. The leader, upon whom his party had placed the greatest reliance, was taken; and the easy defeat of the Flemings had taught him a lesson which every one that embarks in a great undertaking should learn betimes—that it is a perilous thing to put trust in foreign auxiliaries. Yet so accustomed was he to this irregular mode of warfare, and so inured to all the vicissitudes to which the fickle temper of

Dame Fortune might subject him, that his mind was at this moment perfectly calm, and hardly rested a thought upon the perilous situation in which he found himself placed. He seated himself at the rude banquet, which his followers were now preparing, with perfect indifference, although the possibility of his enjoying another tranquil meal was at least a matter of doubt. After some time spent in noisy revelling—for when their assistance was required in an affair of so much danger, the chief thought it no scorn to join in the merriment and court the goodwill of his vassals —Richard began to reflect upon his interview with his two captives; and, with a contemptuous smile, he asked who was the Saxon divinity to whom they must attribute the loss of so able a coadjutor in the person of Reginald d'Arennes.

A dozen sturdy voices were lifted up at once, in commendation of the Lady Elfrida. Her tall and commanding stature—her long flaxen hair—her dignified countenance— her cheeks, whose bright complexion invited the flattery which they blushed to hear—and her light blue eye, whose glance beamed so mildly on the meek, and met so proudly the gazes of the proud—were alternately the themes of admiration. At last the chieftain, impatient of these rapturous effusions, which he began to think were endless, poured out his last cup "To the health of the Rose of Kennet Hold," and deserted the board. He busied himself for a time in giving the necessary orders for their departure early in the ensuing morning; and then, calling Eustace aside, exclaimed: "We will ourselves look upon this Saxon beauty: by our Lady, if she deserve but one half of the praises of these boors, she may haply be the companion of our onward march." And with these words, attended by his esquire, De Mallory strode from the enclosure.

While this scene was going on, Reginald and his companion had made considerable progress on their journey, and were within a·few miles of its termination; yet not a word had been exchanged between them. They looked from time to time towards each other, apparently with a mutual feeling of dislike, if not of apprehension. At last Lothaire led the way to conversation, in a tone which betrayed a strong disposition to offer an insult, although the disposition appeared to be checked or subdued for a time by the counter-agency of some equally powerful motive.

"Sir Reginald," said he, "knowest thou the qualities which are required in him who would sue for the hand of my sister Elfrida?"

"I have doubts touching this matter," replied Reginald.

"Methinks," rejoined his companion, "it were worth the while to instruct thyself further, ere thou settest foot on my father's threshold; for, of a truth, Elfrida hath a right Saxon spirit and a right Saxon speech: she hath proud eyes, that smile on whom they list and frown on whom they will; and proud thoughts, that respect not so much the glittering of the corselet as the valour of the knight that wears it."

This was somewhat like a thunderclap to poor Reginald. He had anticipated no difficulties of this nature: the timidity of his nature would have shrunk back with horror from the mention of a protracted courtship. In short, he had expected a path strewn with roses, and he found it beset with briars; he came to wed an obedient and passive bride, and he began to suspect she was little better than an intractable virago. After having spent some moments in reflections of this nature, he gave utterance to his secret musings in a brief soliloquy:

"I am doubting whether or no I shall proceed.

He was answered by a loud laugh from his intended brother-in-law, who proceeded forthwith to dispel the apprehensions which he had himself excited.

"Cheer thee, noble Knight; be not afraid for a woman. Thou hast, princely Reginald, many valorous and knightly qualities, the least of which might win a richer bride than the daughter of Leofwyn and the sister of Lothaire. Surely thou dost obtain honour at those splendid jousts, from which thou knowest our Saxon habits do utterly revolt; and, doubtless, thou hast skill in foreign music, which thou knowest our Saxon ears do utterly detest; and thou art also ski led in that foreign language which thou knowest a Saxon doth so loath, that he would have his tongue torn from his throat rather than give utterance to its accents."

"Brother," said Reginald, who began to perceive the necessity of conciliating Lothaire, "I have meddled but little with courts, and, in my ignorance of these accomplishments, I am a perfect Saxon. But I prithee tell me, in love and fellowship, by what means or endeavours it is possible for me to win the goodwill of thy sister."

"I will show thee," said Lothaire. "First, thou must learn to speak, not tardily through thy teeth, as is thy present method, but boldly, openly, and fearlessly, as one man should do to another."

"Whether this be possible, I doubt," observed Reginald.

"Secondly," said his instructor, "at my father's board thou must not be too ready to relinquish the goblet."

"I will do thee reason—I will do thee reason, Sir Lothaire," returned Reginald. "Marry, I shall need but little instruction upon that head." And he strained his eye as he spoke in the direction of Kennet Hold, as if he would measure the space which lay between his lip and the flagon.

"Thirdly," resumed Lothaire, "thou must hate a Norman as thou wouldest hate the foul fiend."

"I do," cried Reginald; "I do hate a Norman: the Norman we parted from e'en now, Richard de Mallory. A blight upon him! He hath bound me, scoffed at me, worried my body and my mind, until I can scarcely keep my saddle on my journey or recollect whither the journey tendeth. A murrain on the proud knight! Doth he fancy that I care aught whether the father or the son hath the better? whether the Henry I serve be called the second or the third?"

"If I may risk prophecy," muttered the Saxon, "thou wilt never see the third Henry wearing his father's crown. We have worn the yoke of your tyrants long enough; and it is time that the throne of Alfred should be again filled by one of his descendants. Despised and oppressed as we are, there are still true Saxons enow to drive ye headlong from the land ye have spoiled."

The two young men continued to ride as far apart as courtesy and their roads would permit, and the line of conversation into which they had fallen did not seem likely to promote kinder feelings between them. Reginald's national prejudices began to rise high within him, and to overpower the want of energy which was his failing. " Sir Lothaire," he replied doggedly, "methinks thou hast forgotten Hastings."

"Sir Knight," said his companion, in a melancholy voice, "it is not possible for thee or for me to forget Hastings. Thine ancestor did obtain there power, and title, and riches ; mine did win nothing but honour and his grave. The chance may be ours in another field. If valour and desert in arms had had their meed the bastard of Normandy had never set foot upon the corpse of Harold."

"Thou errest, thou errest, good brother," said Reginald unthinkingly; "the single arm of King William was sufficient to beat down Harold and his brothers to boot. Thine ancestor himself, Sir Lothaire, was light in the balance when weighed with the least of our Norman chivalry ! "

"Norman liar !" exclaimed Lothaire, and immediately giving his horse the spur, and causing him to make a demi-volte, which brought him close to his companion's side, he raised his ponderous arm, and dealt with his mailed hand so terrible a blow between the corselet and headpiece of his future brother-in-law, that Launcelot reeled upon his haunches, and his rider fell to the ground without sense or motion. Lothaire gazed for a moment upon the fallen Knight ; and then, after beckoning to Robin to come up, put his horse into a hand gallop, and continued his route.

Robin, when the formidable Saxon was out of sight, ventured to approach the scene of the fracas. Piteous was the sight which presented itself. Launcelot was standing beneath a neighbouring tree, still trembling with the shock he had received. Reginald lay motionless in the dust : his bright armour was soiled with earth and blood, which gushed out plentifully from his mouth and nostrils. Robin took off his helmet, and endeavoured, by throwing water over his features, to restore animation. After having spent a long time in the vain endeavour, he looked upon his fallen patron with an expression of utter despair, and muttered to himself, "My master is certainly dead ; and there will be no wedding, nor revel, nor wassailing." He continued for some minutes in deep contemplation, and then exclaimed, "An my project hold good, I will be revenged on the Saxon churl." And with these words he began to disarm his master.

While these incidents were taking place among those personages to whom our attention has been hitherto confined, the state of the inhabitants of Kennet Hold was such as calls for our notice. The MS., indeed, from which I draw this narrative, goes through all the minute particulars of Reginald's journey, until it sets him down at the gate of his father-in-law; but, to avoid greater prolixity than is necessary, I will reserve this explanation for my *dénouement*, and for the present leaving my hero on his bed of earth, I will introduce my reader, without further delay, to the hall at Kennet Hold.

Everything seemed to be in a state of unusual confusion at the residence of the Saxon. This was, no doubt, partly to be attributed to the extraordinary preparations made by the cooks, and to the wish of the domestics to appear in the sprucest attire before the eyes of the Norman guest. But there was something more than this in the bustle which pervaded Kennet Hold. There seemed to be in every countenance, from the swineherd to the thane, the consciousness of some concealment, some unspeakable secret lingering on the lips, and awaiting a fit opportunity for disclosure. Many of the menials were staring at each other in silence, although they had abundant occupation before them; and many were looking inordinately busy, although it was their chance to have nothing to do. The expression of their faces was various. In some you could perceive little more than a repressed desire to laugh; but on the features of the higher sort of vassals you might read pride, contempt, resentment, together with a visible exultation, which plainly told that all these vindictive feelings were on the eve of gratification.

Leofwyn himself was seated on the chair of his hall, beneath a scarlet canopy, in all the rude state which his Saxon prejudices permitted. He was of short stature, with a round good-humoured face, which spoke, as plainly as face could speak, that its owner was willing to be upon friendly terms with the rest of the world, if the rest of the

world would give him leave. In fact, Leofwyn was of a
disposition to prefer the beginning of a banquet to the
conclusion of a broil; and if he had been at liberty to
consult his own inclination, there would have been much
wine, and but very little blood, poured out annually by the
retainers of Kennet Hold. Many causes, however, conspired
to make these pacific qualities of no effect. In the first
place, the chief had an hereditary feud to support against
the invaders of the land; and, although he himself saw
nothing in these foreigners which should deserve his male-
diction, he deemed it his·duty to hate them most religiously,
because his father had done so before him; secondly, his
son Lothaire was of a terribly violent temper, and was always
seeking an opportunity for embroiling his father with some
Norman landholder; and thirdly, this opportunity was frequently afforded by the predatory attacks of the surrounding
nobles.

In the retaliation which Leofwyn exercised for these
outrages he frequently put in practice some cunning and
jocose device, which accorded ill with the professions of
hate and enmity which he was perpetually making. For
instance, it appears that when the vassals of Sir Robert de
Vallice had made considerable depredations upon the
Saxon's swine, he carried off the only son of the offender,
and, after confining him in company with the porkers for a
night and a day, sent him back to Sir Robert, with a
message that "he had sent him his swineherd also." Such
freaks as these had among his dependents secured to him
the reputation·of having a right sharp wit: among his
powerful neighbours he was considered little better than a
madman, in consequence of which, amidst the oppressions
to which his race was daily subject, he had been allowed to
pass his days in despised security.

Upon the present occasion it seemed that he had some
unusually clever design in view. He was perpetually giving
some instructions to the domestics, in a tone of voice
mysteriously low, and again relapsing into deep and silent
meditation. In short, in the anxiety which he evinced for
the approaching nuptials, he showed all the assiduity and
precaution of a modern match-maker. Reginald did not
come at the appointed time; the old man began to grow

impatient; he asked for his son. "Lothaire," replied one of
the attendants, "bore forth thy message in the morning,
being desirous of looking on the Norman guest. He hath
not yet returned." "It is the better," said Leofwyn to
himself. "His hastiness might defeat what my prudence
hath devised. Nevertheless, I cannot but marvel at his
stay. Is the bride apparelled?" "She is: the maidens
have been busied about her head-gear since noonday.
Marry they have no light task; for the hair they decorate
hath been but little used to the operation." "Peace!"
said Leofwyn.

Hours passed away in rapid succession, evening came
gradually on; and still there were no traces or tidings of
Reginald d'Arennes. The Saxon's choler began to rise
in earnest. "Surely," he muttered inwardly, "surely, that
hot-brained fellow Lothaire hath not overturned the structure my counsel hath been so long a-building; mischief
light upon him if he hath dared to make or to meddle!
The forward boy is ever at bullying and drawing of swords.
Boys' play, boys' play; but it were a brave thing to put
this slight upon the Norman. Marry, hang him if he hath
despoiled my daughter of her husband."

Suddenly his soliloquy was interrupted by the blast of
horn announcing the arrival of strangers. Leofwyn leaped
from his seat in an ecstasy; but immediately resumed it,
with a studied look of gravity, that restrained the inclination
of merriment which was predominant among his dependents.
Every one, therefore, was silent, as the folding-doors were
slowly unclosed, and the major-domo introduced to the
presence of his lord—Sir Reginald d'Arennes.

He was greeted by his future father-in-law with cold and
distant courtesy, which he returned in a manner of still
greater reserve. "Sir Knight," said Leofwyn, "it is my
will that thy nuptials be solemnized ere thou sittest down
to the banquet. My son Lothaire is choleric (his guest
gave an involuntary motion of assent); and if he should
return before the wedding, I know not whether thy head
might not lie in the castle-moat sooner than on the bridal
pillow." The bridegroom shuddered.

"Is the Lady Elfrida attired?" continued Leofwyn, in a
tone of mock gravity, which was exceedingly ludicrous.

The attendants caught the infection, and many unrepressed jests circulated among them, as they departed to bear their lord's summons to his daughter.

Presently Elfrida made her appearance. The bridegroom started as she entered the hall : perhaps the exterior qualifications of the Saxon beauty might not altogether correspond with the exaggerated reports which his ears had greedily drunk. Her figure might be called elegant, but was certainly too short to deserve the appellation of dignified ; her face might be deemed pretty, but the pertness which was its prevalent characteristic disqualified it for the epithet of beautiful. Instead of the soft yellow hair which her adorer had expected, he beheld a profusion of dark brown ringlets ; and in lieu of the languishing blue eye, which he deemed would have dissolved him into rapture, he met the glance of a sparkling black one, in which there lurked a very strong inclination to laugh in his face. To his disappointment, however, if he felt any, Reginald gave no vent ; he seemed to have a great reluctance to unclose, in the presence of Saxons, either his visor or his lips. Both parties betrayed a wish to have the ceremony performed as speedily as possible ; and the nuptials of Sir Reginald d'Arennes with Elfrida, the daughter of Leofwyn of Kennet Hold, were accordingly celebrated in the chapel which was attached to the residence of the Saxon. The Lady Elfrida was splendidly attired ; but, in other respects, the nuptial rites were graced with little pomp save the attendance of a large body of Leofwyn's retainers, who, bearing in their hands each a flaming torch, cast an air of rude magnificence over the scene.

A sumptuous banquet awaited them upon their return to the hall. The merriment of the vassals was loud and unremitting. The bridegroom, however, did not seem to enjoy the situation in which he found himself placed. He fidgeted upon his seat, and turned his eyes alternately to the ceiling and to the wall, as if he suspected that more than half the joviality of the party was at his expense. His embarrassment was increased by the malicious endeavours of his bride, who rallied him upon his gravity and look of despondency, in a style to which he had evidently no spirits to reply.

It must be confessed that the young man's suspicions were not altogether without foundation. The occupants of the lower part of the board, who, of course, were the most obstreperous in their mirth, were, from time to time, indulging themselves in very acute criticisms upon the figure and features of their master's son-in-law. These did not altogether answer their expectations. Much as they contemned the Normans, they had pictured to themselves, in the person of Reginald d'Arennes, a countenance noble even to sternness, and a bearing at once courteous and martial. They knew he was a Norman, but they also knew he was a handsome and a friendly Norman; in consequence of which they had made up their minds to hate him, and, at the same time, to find nothing in him worthy of hate. They were much surprised, therefore, when they found the young Knight so perfectly different from the image report had drawn. His face seemed perfectly void of all expression of majesty or valour. At present its predominant expression was embarrassment, mingled with a strong tincture of fear; but there was a slight curve upon the lips, and a sly twinkle under the eye, which betrayed a strong disposition to cunning and risibility. His figure appeared slender and diminutive, and a gorgeous steel harness hung dangling about it, as if the bark of the forest oak had been stripped off to give an appearance of strength to the willow. This was all very strange: the attendants looked, and laughed, and wondered; and Leofwyn showed no disposition to check their humour. Indeed he seemed to participate cordially in their malicious propensities.

"Sir Knight," said he, "methinks there is in thy demeanour a greater degree of bashfulness than thy noble presence and thy lofty lineage do warrant."

"It is a feeling," replied the guest, "which I have inherited from my mother Bridget—I mean, from my mother the Lady Marie," he added, turning very pale.

"Ha, ha!" exclaimed his entertainer; "now, by my verity, I dreamed not thy father had been so gay in his young days. What! play the Lady Marie false! Come, come, it was ill done, ill done; she was a lady of most excellent carriage; it was ill done. But be not cast down,

The sin was not thine. Pledge me, noble Reginald. Thou standest in need of refreshment; for, in truth, thy look is weariness itself, and thou art as silent as the oaken board on which thou leanest. Come, come, the pigment is worth the tasting."

Reginald blushed, and seemed doubting whether it were not well to make a precipitate retreat. The Lady Elfrida turned away her head, and let down her veil, with a gesture of affected horror at the indelicate sallies of her father. Nothing daunted, the old man continued his pertinacious system of annoyance, while the domestics applauded, by ill-repressed acclamations, the surprising jocularity of their lord.

" Thou art sparing of thy food, Sir Knight ; but doubtless thou art used to other diet than this : the board of a Saxon thane hath but little to tempt the palate of the son of a Norman noble."

"Thou wrongest thine own hospitality, noble thane," replied the other, collecting his spirits, and making an effort to be polite. "Womanly indeed should I be, if I were not used to harder fare than this! My father, the forester— that is, I mean, my father, the baron." And again Reginald looked confused, and paused, and was silent.

"Cheer thee, noble Reginald," said his host; "thou art wearied with thy journey, and thy wits wander." "Perchance," said the fair Elfrida, "Sir Reginald hath lost them on the way !" The menials echoed applause, and Reginald looked yet more foolish than before. " Thou dost belie thy character strangely," continued the old man; "fame hath told us that in the whole shire there is not a jollier boon companion nor a truer lover of the cup." " It is true that Sir Reginald d'Arennes hath had that reputation," replied the Norman, "and his best friends have judged that he would do well to put it away." " By the holy Confessor," cried Leofwyn, "not upon his wedding-day ! Out upon the idea ! What, ho ! Osric, fill up for Sir Reginald. Pledge me, gallant Knight. The health of thy bride—of Elfrida !"

" I will do thee reason," said Reginald, raising the cup to his lips; but, at the mention of the name of Elfrida, some of the vassals burst into such a clamorous fit of laughter that he set it down in astonishment.

Leofwyn remarked his surprise, and endeavoured to dispel it. "Thou seest, good son, that there is a kind of pageant toward, at which these boors are marvellously pleased; but be not the less inclined to join in our banquet. We wait but for the arrival of my son Lothaire, and all disguise shall be stripped off." "Disguise!" cried the guest, dropping the cup, and starting from his seat, "a murrain on the tell-tale! How didst thou learn——" "Nay, my son," said the Saxon, as if endeavouring to retract an unguarded expression, "we are all somewhat disguised—in liquor."

Reginald resumed his seat, and, in a short time, began to drink most valorously, as if striving to drown in the rich pigment some unpleasant suspicions. By degrees, his head, which was evidently weaker than the one fame had attributed to Reginald d'Arennes, began to be overpowered by the frequent potations which were forced upon him by his host; and while Leofwyn and his retainers, and even the modest Elfrida, were immensely amused by his awkward situation, the hapless bridegroom showed the effects of Saxon hospitality in rhapsodical and unintelligable exclamations.

"Of a truth, good thane, thy drink is marvellous good! marvellous good is thy drink! Better have not I tasted since we rifled old Ambrose, the hermit of Torney Low! Very rich was the old rogue: he had store of gold and of silver, and an admirable cellar withal. Right merry we were and jovial; and, for the hoary man, we made him sit by the board, and chaunt a merry stave. That did I; for truly my fellow thief had some quirks of conscience. Health to the old man! May his bags and his cellar be replenished before next Whitsuntide! What care I for abbot and friar, mitre and cowl! I roam through glade and greenwood, over hill, and rock, and stream, free as the hawk, free as the passing wind. Marry, I had forgot how I have linked myself to a wife! Kiss me, fair Elfrida! I love thee very much, Elfrida; but thou knowest, when war calleth us away, we soldiers leave ye like a whistle. How dost thou, old father-in-law, how dost thou? Of a verity, thy face is as black as a November cloud, and that spear by thy side is wondrous sharp: it is well I have a Milan

corselet. Mark ye my Milan corselet, father and bride?
The zecchins that were paid for it! It hath not borne
blow yet. Certainly I like not blows; but the lace of my
helmet is snapped in twain. Thy son, most noble Leofwyn,
could explain unto thee the manner of it. Surely it was a
mighty blow, and a perilous, given with a strong arm and
a right goodwill. Launcelot shook like an aspen leaf.
Howbeit, noble Saxon, thy drink is marvellous good; it
maketh a man valorous, and doth as it were put to flight
the whimsies, and the visions, and the phantasies of the
brain. Fill up, valiant Leofwyn! Plague on them that
flinch! Mine harness is much soiled for a wedding garment, but I shall wear a new doublet to-morrow. A blight
upon the brambles in the coppice! How now, good
father-in-law, why dost thou not speak? Thy face is as
round as the bowl, and as silent as the roasted crab that
is floating within it. Fill up! Off with care! Shall I not be
merry, when steel, and nobility, and a wife are put upon
my shoulders?"

"My lord groweth complimentary," said Elfrida, hardly
able to speak for laughter. "I do feel afraid that the air of
Kennet Hold, and the drink it affords, have somewhat
unsettled his brains!"

"Beautiful Elfrida," said the bridegroom, "true it is that
the brains of Sir Reginald had a terrible knock this day,
and thy brother knows whence it came; but we will forget
these quarrelsome topics, and give up the evening to
merriment. My brains are as firm as thine own. Marry,
the wine is marvellous good!" He was sinking gradually
into intoxication.

"I marvel wherefore Lothaire delayeth his coming," said
Leofwyn.

"Truly," replied Elfrida, "it were well to conclude the
farce without him. I am weary of this mummery."

"Mar-vel-lous good!" repeated the Norman, and closed
his eyes.

"Girl," said Leofwyn, "thou speakest foolishly; until my
son's return we will keep up the disguise."

"Disguise!" cried Reginald, recovering some little sense
of what was going forward. "Who talked of disguise? Was
it thou, most rustic Leofwyn, or thou, most black-browed

Elfrida? Who talked of disguise? I care not. If I am
not——"

A loud and piercing shriek interrupted the speaker. You
might have thought all the maidens of the shire had conspired to deafen the ears of the Saxon proprietor. A door
was suddenly flung open, and a warder, with terror and
consternation pictured on every limb and feature, rushed up
to the daïs, and bending his head as if to receive the chas-
tisement which his negligence would call down, exclaimed,
"The Lady Elfrida hath been taken away from the castle!"

It were difficult to describe minutely the astonishment
which pervaded the hall. Vassals and menials of every
degree snatched their arms and fled from the apartment.
Nothing was heard but inquiries, and weeping, and
imprecations. Nothing was known but that the lady had
been within the last few minutes carried off by a strange
knight mounted on a swift bay horse, and attended by one
follower. It was supposed that he must have entered and
departed by swimming the moat, which, as it was now
midnight, was an attempt by no means impracticable. He
had been seen by a peasant who was returning from an
adjacent forest; his lovely prize was thrown across a led
palfrey, and appeared to be in a swoon.

All was confusion. The retainers of Leofwyn ran to and
fro in all directions but the right one. Armour resounded
with a dismal clang, as it was hastily thrown over the
shoulders of the domestics; torches were flinging their
red glare in every direction; the voices of the pursuers were
repeated by frequent echoes, as they shouted and called to
one another through the darkness. In the meantime the
chief personages in the hall were in a situation partaking
strongly of the ludicrous. The black-eyed damsel, who
had figured throughout the banquet as the daughter of
Leofwyn, had cried out, as the warder had delivered his
news, "My dear mistress, my poor mistress!" and fainted
upon her throne. The bridegroom had been in some
measure roused from his intoxication, but was still unable
to collect his ideas, so as to form any idea of the origin or
meaning of the tumult. Leofwyn appeared to be in a state
of mental stupefaction. In spite of the foibles of the old
man's character, he was doatingly fond of his daughter;

and the news of her loss, coming in the midst of revelry, seemed to have withered him like a thunderbolt. He sat still, looking on the confusion with a vacant gaze, and inquiring from time to time, "Is my daughter well? How fares it with the Lady Elfrida? Does she not come to her old father?" These three personages, therefore, remained quietly upon their seats, while every one around them was in commotion; like the bronzed images in modern halls, that hold their candelabras so calmly, while the guests are all in the bustle of departure.

Things remained in this disagreeable position for some minutes, when the blowing of a horn, and a loud talking and shouting without, announced that something had taken place. Presently, accompanied by a crowd of peasants half accoutred for the pursuit, Lothaire entered the hall. Leofwyn raised his head, and being in some measure recalled to his recollection by the sight of his scn, repeated his inquiry, "Is my daughter well?"

"She is well!" said Lothaire, "and I am well! No thanks to my new friend, the doughty Sir Richard de Mallory, from whom, to say truth, mine headpiece hath received a most mischievous contusion. Thanks to thee, good steel," he continued, taking off his helmet, and surveying the deep indenture which appeared on its summit; "had not thy temper been true, thy master's head had lain on the couch from which no man lifteth himself up." He was interrupted by a thousand interrogatories, a great proportion of which proceeded from Leofwyn, who had by this time recovered from the effects of his sudden shock, and began to feel great curiosity to know the particulars of the story.

"I know but little of the matter," said Lothaire; "ye see I have been overthrown in no light fashion"—(they perceived for the first time that his apparel bore marks of a recent fall)—"and in truth had it not been for the intervention of my good friend in the ragged doublet, I had hardly lived to tell ye the tale."

"Of whom dost thou speak?" said Leofwyn.

"That is more than I can tell," replied the young Saxon. "Not many paces hence did I encounter the valorous Sir Richard, who is now, peace be with him, no longer a man of this world. I had a heavy stroke, as ye may witness; nevertheless, it was my horse's fault, or I had not been so foiled. I believe another minute would have caught the last breath of Lothaire, but for the help of the aforesaid knight of the ragged doublet. By the sword of Harold! he overthrew that proud Norman as if he were wrestling with a child. I saw not his features, but by his apparel he seemed to be the esquire of thine hopeful son-in-law, Reginald d'Arennes. But ye will see him presently."

Lothaire was supported from the hall, and put under the care of the leech; for his wound, although he made so light of it in his story, wore a dangerous appearance.

As he retired, another loud acclamation announced the arrival of Elfrida's deliverer. A tall, well-made figure advanced towards the daïs, clad, as Lothaire had intimated, in a short ragged doublet, with a small cap which was quite insufficient to confine the long dark tresses that floated luxuriantly down his neck. His arm supported the real Elfrida, whose personal charms amply deserved the encomium which had been lavished upon them in the forest. Animation seemed hardly restored to that beautiful form. Her eyes were half closed and her cheek very pale.

"Providence be thanked," cried Leofwyn, "that my child is restored to me!"

Now it has been already hinted that Elfrida was possessed of a disposition somewhat untractable; in fact, loth as I am to speak aught ill of the fair sex, I must confess that the Lady Elfrida partook, in no trifling degree, both of the fantastic whims of her father Leofwyn and the violent obstinacy of her brother Lothaire: The reader, therefore, will not be surprised when he hears that the Saxon beauty, bowing respectfully to her father, thus addressed him:

"Not to thee, my father, not to thee is thy daughter restored; in good and in evil, in life and in death, she shall abide with her preserver—with him who hath delivered her from the grasp of the spoiler."

"Thou art mad, my child!" said the old man in astonishment; "the knight that sued for thee thou didst contemn and reject, and wilt thou now wed with his serving-man?"

Elfrida appeared to recollect the circumstances which had preceded her capture, the suitor who had solicited her hand, and the deceit which she had conspired to put upon him: she looked up to the daïs, and beheld Bertha, her waiting-woman, seated by the side of the Norman guest; she glanced round and met the eye of her preserver turned upon her with an expression of the deepest adoration. She looked no further, but immediately, addressing her father, said:

. "Why should it not be so, my father? To-day thou hast married thine handmaid to the Knight; to-morrow thou shalt marry thy daughter to the Knave."

Her unknown deliverer at these words began to stare about him; he gazed upon his dress, upon his attendants, upon Elfrida; and then, with all the embarrassment of a performer who comes forward to play in a pageant without the smallest acquaintance with his part, observed: "This morning was I a knight, mounted on a goodly steed, and clad in goodly apparel; but whether I am now Norman or Saxon, knight or knave, by my grandfather's sword—I doubt."

Leofwyn stared; his large eyes were dilated into a truly comic expression of astonishment. "Who art thou?" he cried at last to the bridegroom; "art thou Reginald d'Arennes, or must we hang thee for a rogue?"

"Peace, good father-in-law," said the sham Reginald, shaking off his drunkenness, and leering around him with an arch look of self-satisfaction; "I am not Reginald d'Arennes, but yet as good a man! I am Robin, the son of Egwulph; truly a cunning knave, and a wily."

"I do begin to perceive," said the waiting-woman, Bertha, looking on the sham Reginald with a disappointed air, "that our plot hath altogether failed."

"Mine hath fared no better!" said the knave, returning a glance of equal disappointment upon the mock Elfrida. "In this I have been but a silly knave, and a witless!"

Dost thou comprehend, gentle reader, the circumstances which led to these mistakes? or is it necessary for me to inform thee that the knave Robin proceeded to Kennet Hold in Reginald's apparel, with the purpose of revenging, by his wedding with the heiress, the death of his master,

which he fancied had been occasioned by the heir; that at
Kennet Hold the said knave met with the counterplot which
had been prepared by the jocose Saxon, and became the
husband of the maid instead of the mistress; that Reginald,
recovering from his swoon after the departure of his attendant, advanced towards Kennet Hold, and encountered, in
his way, his new acquaintance, Richard de Mallory, from
whom he had the good fortune to rescue the life of Lothaire
and the honour of Elfrida?

There is yet one point unexplained. The reader must
be aware that a considerable interval took place between
the memorable blow given by Lothaire and his rencontre
with De Mallory. Upon this point the MS. makes mention
of Winifred, a certain arch-damsel, who——but Decorum
puts her forefinger on her mouth—I have done.

Rather than desert a long established custom, I proceed
to state that the personages of my tale lived and loved to
a green old age. Robin died before it was thoroughly
decided whether he was more properly termed "the Wily"
or "the Witless." Reginald, it appears, never got rid of his
old trick of hesitation, for it is upon record that, when he
told the story of his adventures to Cœur de Lion, at the
siege of Acre, and was asked by the humorous monarch
whether the knight or the knave were the more fortunate
bridegroom, he scratched his chin for a few minutes, played
with his sword for a few more, and replied slowly, "I have
doubts as touching this matter."

MAD—QUITE MAD!

"Great wits are sure to madness near allied."—DRYDEN.

IT has frequently been observed that Genius and Madness
are nearly allied; that very great talents are seldom found
unaccompanied by a touch of insanity, and that there are
few bedlamites who will not, upon a close examination,

display symptoms of a powerful, though ruined, intellect. According to this hypothesis, the flowers of Parnassus must be blended with the drugs of Anticyra; and the man who feels himself to be in possession of very brilliant wits may conclude that he is within an ace of running out of them. Whether this be true or false, we are not at present disposed to contradict the assertion. What we wish to notice is the pains which many young men take to qualify themselves for Bedlam, by hiding a good, sober, gentleman-like understanding beneath an assumption of thoughtlessness and whim. It is the received opinion among many that a man's talents and abilities are to be rated by the quantity of nonsense he utters per diem, and the number of follies he runs into per annum. Against this idea we must enter our protest; if we concede that every real genius is more or less a madman, we must not be supposed to allow that every sham madman is more or less a genius.

In the days of our ancestors, the hot-blooded youth who threw away his fortune at twenty-one, his character at twenty-two, and his life at twenty-three, was termed "a good fellow," "an honest fellow," "nobody's enemy but his own." In our time the name is altered; and the fashionable who squanders his father's estate, or murders his best friend—who breaks his wife's heart at the gaming-table, and his own neck at a steeple-chase—escapes the sentence which morality would pass upon him, by the plea of lunacy. "He was a rascal," says Common Sense. "True," says the World, "but he was mad, you know—quite mad."

We were lately in company with a knot of young men who were discussing the character and fortunes of one of their own body, who was, it seems, distinguished for his proficiency in the art of madness. "Harry," said a young sprig of nobility, "have you heard that Charles is in the King's Bench?" "I heard it this morning," drawled the Exquisite; "how distressing! I have not been so hurt since poor Angelica (his bay mare) broke down. Poor Charles has been too flighty." "His wings will be clipped for the furture!" observed young Caustic. "He has been very imprudent," said young Candour.

I inquired of whom they were speaking. "Don't you

know Charles Gally?" said the Exquisite, endeavouring to turn in his collar. "Not know Charles Gally?" he repeated, with an expression of pity. "He is the best fellow breathing; only lives to laugh and make others laugh; drinks his two bottles with any man, and rides the finest mare I ever saw—next to my Angelica. Not know Charles Gally? Why everybody knows him! He is so amusing! Ha! ha! And tells such admirable stories! Ha! ha! Often have they kept me awake"—a yawn—"when nothing else could." "Poor fellow!" said his lordship; "I understand he's done for ten thousand!" "I never believe more than half what the world says," observed Candour. "He that has not a farthing," said Caustic, "cares little whether he owes ten thousand or five." "Thank Heaven!" said Candour, "that will never be the case with Charles: he has a fine estate in Leicestershire." "Mortgaged for half its value," said his lordship. "A large personal property!" "All gone in annuity bills," said the Exquisite. "A rich uncle upwards of fourscore!" "He'll cut him off with a shilling," said Caustic.

"Let us hope he may reform," sighed the Hypocrite; "and sell the pack," added the Nobleman; "and marry," continued the Dandy. "Pshaw!" cried the Satirist, "he will never get rid of his habits, his hounds, or his horns." "But he has an excellent heart," said Candour. "Excellent," repeated his lordship, unthinkingly. "Excellent," lisped the Fop, effeminately. "Excellent," exclaimed the Wit, ironically. We took this opportunity to ask by what means so excellent a heart and so bright a genius had contrived to plunge him into these disasters. "He was my friend," replied his lordship, "and a man of large property; but he was mad—quite mad. I remember his leaping a lame pony over a stone wall, simply because Sir Marmaduke bet him a dozen that he broke his neck in the attempt; and sending a bullet through a poor pedlar's pack because Bob Darrell said the piece wouldn't carry so far." "Upon another occasion," began the Exquisite in his turn, "he jumped into a horse-pond after dinner in order to prove it was not six feet deep; and overturned a bottle of eau-de-cologne in Lady Emilia's face, to convince me that she was not painted. Poor fellow! The first experiment cost him a dress, and the second an heiress." "I have heard," resumed the Nobleman, "that he lost his election for —— by lampooning the mayor; and was dismissed from his place in the Treasury for challenging Lord C——." "The last accounts I heard of him," said Caustic, "told me that Lady Tarrel had forbid him her house for driving a sucking-pig into her drawing-room; and that young Hawthorn had run him through for boasting of favours from his sister!" "These gentlemen are really too severe," remarked young Candour to us. "Not a jot," we said to ourselves.

"This will be a terrible blow for his sister," said a young man who had been listening in silence. "A fine girl,—a very fine girl," said the Exquisite. "And a fine fortune," said the Nobleman; "the mines of Peru are nothing to her." "Nothing at all," observed the Sneerer; "she has no property there. But I would not have you caught, Harry; her income was good, but is dipped, horribly dipped. Guineas melt very fast when the cards are put by them." "I was not aware Maria was a gambler," said the young man, much alarmed. "Her brother is, Sir," replied his informant. The querist looked sorry, but yet relieved. We could see that he was not quite disinterested in his inquiries. "However," resumed the young Cynic, "his profusion has at least obtained him many noble and wealthy friends." He glanced at his hearers, and went on: "No one that knew him will hear of his distresses without being forward to relieve them. He will find interest for his money in the hearts of his friends." Nobility took snuff; Foppery played with his watch-chain; Hypocrisy looked grave. There was long silence. We ventured to regret the misuse of natural talents, which, if properly directed, might have rendered their possessor useful to the interests of society and celebrated in the records of his country. Every one stared, as if we were talking Hebrew. "Very true," said his lordship, "he enjoys great talents. No man is a nicer judge of horseflesh. He beats me at billiards, and Harry at picquet; he's a dead shot at a button, and can drive his curricle-wheels over a brace of sovereigns. "Radicalism," says Caustic, looking round for a laugh. "He is a great amateur of pictures," observed the Exquisite, "and is allowed to be quite a connoisseur in beauty; but there," simpering,' "every one must claim the privilege of judging for themselves." "Upon my word," said Candour, "you allow poor Charles too little. I have no doubt he has great courage—though, to be sure, there was a whisper that young Hawthorn found him rather shy; and I am convinced he is very generous, though I must confess that I have it from good authority that his younger brother was refused the loan of a hundred when Charles had pigeoned that fool of a nabob but the evening before. I would stake my existence that he is a man of unshaken honour—though, when he eased Lieutenant Hardy of his pay, there certainly was an awkward story about the transaction, which was never properly cleared up. I hope that when matters are properly investigated he will be liberated from all his embarrassments; though I am sorry to be compelled to believe that he has been spending double the amount of his income annually. But I trust that all will be adjusted. I have no doubt upon the subject." "Nor I," said Caustic. "We shall miss him prodigiously at the Club," said the Dandy, with a slight shake of the head. "What a bore!" replied the Nobleman, with a long yawn. We could hardly venture to express compassion for a character so despicable. Our auditors, however, entertained very different opinions of right and wrong! "Poor fellow! he was much to be pitied: had done some very foolish things—to say the truth was a sad scoundrel—but then he was always so mad." And having come unanimously to this decision, the conclave dispersed.

Charles gave an additional proof of his madness within a week after this discussion by swallowing laudanum. The verdict of the coroner's inquest confirmed the judgment of his four friends. For our own parts we must pause before we give in to so dangerous a doctrine. Here is a man who has outraged the laws of honour, the ties of relationship, and the duties of religion; he appears before us in the triple character of a libertine, a swindler, and a suicide. Yet his follies, his vices, his crimes, are all palliated or even applauded by this specious *façon de parler*—"He was mad—quite mad!"

THE BOGLE OF ANNESLIE;

OR, THE THREE-CORNERED HAT.

A TALE.

"An' ye winna believe i' the bogle?" said a pretty young lassie to her sweetheart, as they sat in the door of her father's cottage one fine autumn evening. "Do you hear that, mither? Andrew 'll no believe i' the bogle."

"Gude be wi' us, Effie!" exclaimed Andrew, a slender and delicate youth of about two-and-twenty, "a bonny time I wad hae o't, gin I were to heed every auld wife's clatter."

The words "auld wife" had a manifest effect on Effie, and she bit her lips in silence. Her mother immediately opened a battery upon the young man's prejudices, narrating how that on Anneslie Heath, at ten o'clock at night, a certain apparition was wont to appear, in the form of a maiden above the usual size, with a wide three-cornered hat. Sundry other particulars were mentioned, but Andrew was still incredulous. "He'll rue that, dearly will he rue't!" said Effie, as he departed.

Many days, however, passed away, and Effie was evidently much disappointed to find that the scepticism of her lover gathered strength. Nay, he had the audacity to insult, by gibes and jests, the true believers, and to call upon them for the reasons of their faith. Effie was in a terrible passion.

At last, however, her prophecy was fulfilled. Andrew was passing over the moor, while the clock struck ten; for it was his usual practice to walk at that hour, in order to mock the fears of his future bride. He was just winding round the thicket which opened to him a view of the cottage where Effie dwelt, when he heard a light step behind him, and, in an instant, his feet were tripped up, and he was laid prostrate on the turf. Upon looking up he beheld a tall muscular man standing over him, who, in no courteous manner, desired to see the contents of his pocket. "De'il be on ye!" exclaimed the young forester, "I hae but ae coin i' the warld." "That coin maun I hae," said his assailant. "Faith! I'se show ye play for't then," said Andrew, and sprang upon his feet.

Andrew was esteemed the best cudgel-player for twenty miles round, so that in brief space he cooled the ardour of his antagonist, and dealt such visitations upon his skull as might have made a much firmer head ache for a fortnight. The man stepped back, and, pausing in his assault, raised his hand to his forehead, and buried it among his dark locks. It returned covered with blood. "Thou hast cracked my crown," he said, "but yet ye sha' na gang scatheless;" and, flinging down his cudgel, he flew on his young foe, and, grasping his body before he was aware of the attack, whirled him to the earth with an appalling impetus. "The Lord hae mercy on me!" said Andrew, "I'm a dead man."

He was not far from it, for his rude foe was preparing to put the finishing stroke to his victory. Suddenly something stirred in the bushes, and the conqueror, turning away from his victim, cried out, "The bogle! the bogle!" and fled precipitately. Andrew ventured to look up. He saw the figure which had been described to him approaching; it came nearer and nearer; its face was very pale, and its step was not heard on the grass. At last it stood by his side, and looked down upon him. Andrew buried his face in his cloak: presently the apparition spoke —indistinctly indeed, for its teeth seemed to chatter with cold:

"This is a cauld an' an eerie night to be sae late on Anneslie Muir!" and immediately it glided away. Andrew lay a few minutes in a trance; and then, arising from his cold bed, ran hastily towards the cottage of his mistress. His hair stood on end, and the vapours of the night sunk chill upon his brow as he lifted up the latch and flung himself upon an oaken seat.

"Preserve us!" cried the old woman. "Why, ye are mair than aneugh to frighten a body out o' her wits! To come in wi' sic a flaunt and a fling, bare-sconced, and the red bluid spatter'd a' o'er your new leather jerkin! Shame on you,

Andrew! in what mishanter hast thou broken that fule's head o' thine?"

"Peace, mither!" said the young man, taking breath, "I hae seen the bogle!"

The old lady had a long line of reproaches, drawn up in order of march, between her lips; but the mention of the bogle was the signal for disbanding them. A thousand questions poured in, in rapid succession. "How old was she? How was she dressed? Who was she like? What did she say?"

"She was a tall thin woman, about seven feet high!"

"Oh Andrew!" cried Effie.

"As ugly as sin!"

"Other people tell a different story," said Effie.

"True, on my Bible oath! And then her beard——"

"A beard, Andrew!" shrieked Effie; "a woman with a beard! For shame, Andrew!"

"Nay, I'll swear it upon my soul's salvation! She had seen saxty winters and mair, afore e'er she died to trouble us!"

"I'll wager my best new goun," said the maiden, "that saxteen would be nearer the mark."

"But wha was she like, Andrew?" said the old woman. "Was she like- auld Janet that was drowned in the burn forenaint? or that auld witch that your maister hanged for stealing his pet lamb? or was she like——"

"Are you sure she was na like *me*, Andrew?" said Effie, looking archly in his face.

"You—pshaw! Faith, guid mither, she was like to naebody that I ken, unless it be auld Elspeth, the cobbler's wife, that was blamed for a' the mischief or misfortunes o' the kintra roun', and was drowned at last for having 'sense aboon the lave.'"

"And how was she dressed, Andrew?"

"In that horrible three-cornered hat, which may I be blinded if ever I seek to look upon again!—an' in a lang blue apron——"

"Green, Andrew!" cried Effie, twirling her own green apron round her thumb.

"How you like to tease ane!" said the lover. Poor Andrew did not at all enter into his mistress's pleasantry, for he laboured under a great depression of spirits, and never lifted his eyes from the ground.

"But ye hae na tauld us what she said, lad!" said the old woman, assuming ·an air of deeper mystery as each question was put and answered in its turn.

"Lord! what signifies it whether she said this or that! Haud your tongue, and get me some comfort; for, to speak truth, I'm vera cauld."

"Weel mayest thou be sae," said Effie, "for indeed," she continued, in· a feigned voice, "*it was a cauld an' an eerie night to be sae late on Anneslie Muir.*"

Andrew started, and a doubt seemed to pass over his mind. He looked up at the damsel, and perceived, for the first time, that her large blue eyes were laughing at him from under the shade of a huge three-cornered hat. The next moment he hung over her in an ecstasy of gratitude, and smothered with his kisses the ridicule which she forced upon him as the penalty of his preservation.

"Seven feet high, Andrew?"

"My dear Effie!"

"As ugly as sin?"

"My darling lassie!"

"And a beard?"

"Na! na! now you carry the jest o'er far!"

"And saxty winters?"

"Saxteen springs, Effie! Dear, delightfu', smiling springs!"

"And Elspeth, the cobbler's wife! Oh, Andrew, Andrew! I never can forgie you for the cobbler's wife! And what say you now, Andrew—is there nae bogle on the muir?"

"My dear Effie, for your sake I'll believe in a' the bogles · in Christendie!"

"That is," said Effie, at the conclusion of a long and vehement fit of risibility, "that is, in a' that wear 'three-cornered hats.'"

ON THE PROPOSED ESTABLISHMENT OF
A PUBLIC LIBRARY AT ETON.

WE are very glad to be able to announce that, after the Easter holidays, a public library for the use of the school will be established by subscription, at Mr. Williams's. We are very glad of it, not for our own sake, for before it shall rise to any degree of importance we shall be inhabitants of this spot no longer; our very names will be forgotten among its more recent inmates. But we hail with joy this institution, for the sake of the school we love and reverence, to which we hope it will prove, at some future period, a valuable addition.

The plan admits of one hundred subscribers—viz., the one hundred senior members of the school. If any of these decline to become members, the option will descend to the next in gradation. The subscription for the first year will be 10s. 6d. after the Easter, Election, and Christmas holidays; in future 10s. 6d. will be paid after the two latter vacations only. The library will consist of the classics, history, &c.; and subscribers will be allowed, under certain regulations, to take books from the room. Of course a thing of this kind has not been set on foot without the concurrence of the higher powers; and the head-master has assisted the promoters of it by his approbation, as well as by liberality of another description. We trust that Eton will not long continue to experience the want of an advantage which many other public schools enjoy.

We had intended to send the foregoing loose remarks to press, in order to request as many of our schoolfellows in the upper division as are willing to become subscribers to leave their names with Mr. Williams, at whose house the library will be established. But as we were preparing to send off the manuscript, an old gentleman, for whom we have a great respect, called in, and looked over our shoulder. He then took a chair, and observed to us : " This will never

E

do !" He took off his spectacles, wiped them, put them on again, and repeated : "This will never do !

"I, sir, was an Etonian in the year 17—, and, being a bit of a speculator in those days, had a mind to do what you are now dreaming of doing. I addressed myself forthwith to various friends, all of them distinguished for rank, or talent, or influence, among their companions. I began with Sir Roger Gandy, expatiated on the sad want of books which many experienced, and asked whether he did not think a public library would be a very fine thing? 'A circulating one,' he said ; 'oh yes, very !'—and he yawned. There was taste !

"The next to whom I made application was Tom Luny, the fat son of a fat merchant on Ludgate Hill. Poor Tom ! He died last week, by-the-by, of a surfeit. Well, sir, I harangued him for some time upon the advantages of my scheme, to which he gave his cordial assent. Finally I observed that, of course, it would not be very expensive. 'Expensive !' he said ; 'oh yes, very !'—and he walked off. There was liberality !

"Next I besieged Will Wingham. I made my approaches as before, with great caution, and at last summoned the garrison to surrender. 'Books !' he exclaimed, 'I haven't one but a Greek Grammar, with all syntax out.' 'And do you think,' I resumed, 'that an Etonian can do well without them?' 'Do well !' he said ; 'oh yes, very !'—and he laughed. There was a wish for improvement !

"Now, my good Peregrine," continued the old gentleman, putting his feet up upon the hobs of my fire, and looking very argumentative, "what do you say to all this ?"

The old gentleman is

> Laudator temporis acti
> Se puero.

He left the room piqued, when we hurt his prejudices by replying, "Nothing, sir, but that the Etonians of 1821 are not, we will hope, the Etonians of 17—."

———

THE MISTAKE;

OR, SIXES AND SEVENS.

" Be particular to observe that the name on the door is ——."
Morning Chronicle, April 1821.

IT is a point which has often been advanced and contested
by the learned, that the world grows worse as it grows
older; arguments have been advanced, and treatises written,
in support of Horace's opinion—

Ætas parentum pejor avis tulit
Nos nequiores, mox daturos
Progeniem vitiosiorem.

The supporters of this idea rest their sentence upon
various grounds: they mention the frequency of crim. con.
cases, the increase of the poor-rate, the licentiousness of the
press, the celebrity of *rouge et noir*.

There is, however, one circumstance corroborative of
their judgment, to which we think the public opinion has
not yet been sufficiently called. We mean the indisputable
fact that persons of all descriptions are growing ashamed of
their own names. We remember that when we were dragged
in our childhood to walk with our nurse, we were accustomed
to beguile our sense of weariness and disgust by studying
the names, which, in their neat brass plates, decorated the
doors by which we passed. Now the case is altered. We
have observed elsewhere that the tradesmen have removed
their signs; it is equally true that the gentlemen have
removed their names. The simple numerical distinction,
which is now alone emblazoned upon the doors of our dwell-
ings, but ill replaces that more gratifying custom, which, in a
literal sense, held up great names for our emulation, and
made the streets of the metropolis a muster-roll of examples
for our conduct.

But a very serious inconvenience is also occasioned by
this departure from ancient observances. How is the
visitor from the country to discover the patron of his
fortunes, the friend of his bosom, or the mistress of his

heart, if, in lieu of the above-mentioned edifying brass plates, his eye glances upon the unsatisfactory information contained in 1, 2, or 3 ?   In some cases even this assistance is denied to him, and he wanders upon his dark and comfortless voyage, like an ancient mariner deprived of the assistance of the stars.

Our poor friend, Mr. Nichol Loaming, has treated us with a long and eloquent dissertation upon this symptom of degeneracy; and certainly, if the advice *experto crede* be of any weight, Mr. Nichol's testimony ought to induce all persons to hang out upon the exterior of their residences some more convincing enunciation of their name and calling than it is at present the fashion to produce.

Nichol came up to town with letters of introduction to several friends of his family, whom it was his first duty and wish to discover.   But his first adventure so dispirited him, that, after having spent two mornings at an hotel, he set out upon his homeward voyage, and left the metropolis an unexplored region.

He purposed to make his first visit to Sir William Knowell, and, having with some difficulty discovered the street to which he had been directed, he proceeded to investigate the doors, in order to find out the object of his search.   The doors presented nothing but a blank !   He made inquiries, was directed to a house, heard that Sir William was at home, was shown into an empty room, and waited for some time with patience.

The furniture of the house rather surprised him.   It was handsomer than he had expected to find it; and on the table were the *Morning Chronicle* and the *Edinburgh Review*, although Sir William was a violent Tory.   At length the door opened, and a gentleman made his appearance. Nichol asked, in a studied speech, whether he had the honour to address Sir William Knowell?   The gentleman replied that he believed there had been a little mistake, but that he was an intimate friend of Sir W. Knowell's, and expected him in the course of a few minutes.   Nichol resumed his seat, although he did not quite perceive what mistake had taken place.   He was unfortunately urged by his evil genius to attempt conversation.

He observed that Sir W. Knowell had a delightful house, and inquired whether the neighbourhood was pleasant.

"His next neighbour," said the stranger, with a most incomprehensible smile, "is Sir William Morley." Nichol shook his head; was surprised to hear Sir William kept such company—had heard strange stories of Sir W. Morley —hoped there was no foundation—indeed had received no good report of the family! The mother rather weak in the head—to say the truth under confinement; the sister a professed coquette—went off to Gretna last week with a Scotch officer; Sir William himself a gambler by habit, a drunkard by inclination—at present in the King's Bench, without the possibility of an adjustment——"

Here he was stopped by the entrance of an elderly lady leaning on the arm of an interesting girl of sixteen or seventeen. Upon looking up, Nichol perceived the gentleman he had been addressing rather embarrassed; and "hoped that he had not said anything which could give offence." "Not in the least," replied the stranger; "I am more amused by an account of the foibles of Sir W. Morley than any one else can be; and of this I will immediately convince you. Sir William Knowell resides at No. Six— you have stepped by mistake into No. Seven. Before you leave it, allow me to introduce you to Lady Morley—who is rather weak in the head, and, to say the truth, under confinement; to Miss Ellen Morley, a professed coquette, who went off to Gretna last week with a half-pay officer; finally "—(with a very low bow)—" to Sir William Morley himself, a gambler by habit, and a drunkard by inclination —who is at present in the King's Bench, without the possibility of an adjustment!"

SENSE AND SENSIBILITY.

"Hâc in re scilicet unâ
Multum dissimiles." HOR.

IN a visit which we paid some time ago to our worthy contributor, Morris Gowan, we became acquainted with two characters; upon whom, as they afford a perfect counterpart to Messrs. "Rhyme and Reason," recorded in a former paper, we have bestowed the names of Sense and Sensibility.

. The Misses Lowrie, of whom we are about to give our readers an account, are both young, both handsome, both amiable: Nature made the outline of their characters the same, but Education has varied the colouring. Their mother died almost before they were able to profit by her example or instruction. Emily, the eldest of the sisters, was brought up under the immediate care of her father. He was a man of strong and temperate judgment, obliging to his neighbours, and affectionate to his children; but certainly rather calculated to educate a son than a daughter. Emily profited abundantly by his assistance, as far as moral duties or literary accomplishments were concerned; but for all the lesser *agrémens* of society, she had nothing to depend upon but the suggestions of a kind heart and a quiet temper. Matilda, on the contrary, spent her childhood in England, at the house of a relation, who, having imbibed her notions of propriety at a fashionable boarding-school, and made a love-match very early in life, was but ill-prepared to regulate a warm disposition and check a natural tendency to romance. The consequence has been such as might have been expected. Matilda pities the distressed, and Emily relieves them; Matilda has more of the love of the neighbourhood, although Emily is more entitled to its gratitude; Matilda is very agreeable, while Emily is very useful; and two or three old ladies, who talk scandal over their tea, and murder grammar and reputations together, consider Matilda a practised heroine, and laugh at Emily as an inveterate Blue.

The incident which first introduced us to them afforded us a tolerable specimen of their different qualities. While on a long pedestrian excursion with Morris, we met the two ladies returning from their walk; and, as our companion had already the privileges of an intimate acquaintance, we became their companions. An accurate observer of human manners knows well how decisively character is marked by trifles, and how wide is the distinction which is frequently made by circumstances apparently the most insignificant.

In spite, therefore, of the similarity of age and person which existed between the two sisters, the first glance at their dress and manner, the first tones of their voice, were sufficient to distinguish the one from the other. It was whimsical enough to observe how every object which attracted our attention exhibited their respective peculiarities in a new and entertaining light. Sense entered into a learned discussion on the nature of a plant, while Sensibility talked enchantingly of the fading of its flower. From Matilda we had a rapturous eulogium upon the surrounding scenery; from Emily we derived much information relative to the state of its cultivation. When we listened to the one, we seemed to be reading a novel, but a clever and an interesting novel; when we turned to the other, we found only real life, but real life in its most pleasant and engaging form.

Suddenly one of those rapid storms, which so frequently disturb for a time the tranquillity of the finest weather, appeared to be gathering over our heads. Dark clouds were driven impetuously over the clear sky, and the refreshing coolness of the atmosphere was changed to a close and overpowering heat. Matilda looked up in admiration—Emily in alarm; Sensibility was thinking of a landscape—Sense of a wet pelisse. "This would make a fine sketch," said the first. "We had better make haste," said the second. The tempest continued to grow gloomier above us: we passed a ruined hut, which had been long deserted by its inhabitants. "Suppose we take refuge here for the evening," said Morris. "It would be very romantic," said Sensibility. "It would be very disagreeable," said Sense. "How it would astonish my father!" said the heroine. "How it would alarm him!" said her sister.

As yet we had only observed distant prognostics of the tumult of the elements which was about to take place. Now, however, the collected fury of the storm burst at once upon us. A long and bright flash of lightning, together with a continued roll of thunder, accompanied one of the heaviest rains that we have ever experienced. "We shall have an adventure!" cried Matilda. "We shall be very late," observed Emily. "I wish we were a hundred miles off," said the one hyperbolically. "I wish we were at home," replied the other soberly. "Alas! we shall never get home to-night," sighed Sensibility pathetically. " Possibly," returned Sense dryly. The fact was that the eldest of the sisters was quite calm, although she was aware of all the inconveniences of their situation ; and the youngest was terribly frightened, although she began quoting poetry. There was another and a brighter flash, another and a louder peal : Sense quickened her steps—Sensibility fainted.

With some difficulty, and not without the aid of a con-veyance from a neighbouring farmer, we brought our companions in safety to their father's door. We were of course received with an invitation to remain under shelter till the weather should clear up ; and of course we felt no reluctance to accept the offer. The house was very neatly furnished, principally by the care of the two young ladies ; but here again the diversity of their manners showed itself very plainly. The useful was produced by the labour of Emily ; the ornamental was the fruit of the leisure hours of Matilda. The skill of the former was visible in the sofa-covers and the curtains, but the latter had decorated the card-racks and painted the roses on the hand-screens. The neat little bookcases, too, which contained their respective libraries, suggested a similar remark. In that of the eldest we observed our native English worthies—Milton, Shakespeare, Dryden, and Pope ; on the shelves of her sister reclined the more effeminate Italians—Tasso, Ariosto, Metastasio, and Petrarch. It was a delightful thing to see two amiable beings with tastes so widely different, yet with hearts so closely united.

It is not to be wondered at that we paid a longer visit than we had originally intended. The conversation turned, at one time, upon the late revolutions. Matilda was a terrible Radical, and spoke most enthusiastically of tyranny and patriotism, the righteous cause, and the Holy Alliance : Emily, however, declined to join in commiseration or invective, and pleaded ignorance in excuse for her indiffer-ence. We fancy she was apprehensive of blundering against a stranger's political prejudices. However that may be, Matilda sighed and talked, and Emily smiled and held her tongue. We believe the silence was the most judicious; but we are sure the loquacity was the most interesting.

We took up the newspaper. There was an account of a young man who had gone out alone to the rescue of a vessel in distress. The design had been utterly hopeless, and he had lost his life in the attempt. His fate struck our fair friends in very different lights. "He ought to have had a better fortune," murmured Matilda. "Or more prudence," added Emily. "He must have been a hero," said the first. "Or a madman," rejoined the second.

The storm now died away in the distance, and a tranquil evening approached. We set out on our return. The old gentleman, with his daughters, accompanied us a small part of the way. The scene around us was beautiful; the birds and the cattle seemed to be rejoicing in the return of the sunshine, and every herb and leaf had derived a 'brighter tint from the rain-drops with which it was spangled. As we lingered for a few moments by the side of a beautiful piece of water, the mellowed sound of a flute was conveyed to us over its clear surface. The instrument was delightfully played: at such an hour, on such a spot, and with such companions, we could have listened to it for ever. "That is George Mervyn," said Morris to us. "How very clever he is!" exclaimed. Matilda. "How very imprudent," replied Emily. "He will catch all the hearts in the place!" said Sensibility, with a sigh. "He will catch nothing but a cold!" said Sense, with a shiver. We were reminded that our companions were running the same risk, and we parted from them reluctantly.

After this introduction we had many opportunities of seeing them; we became every day more pleased with the acquaintance, and looked forward with regret to the day on which we were finally to leave so enchanting a neighbourhood. The preceding night it was discovered that the cottage of Mr. Lowrie was on fire. The destructive element was soon checked, and the alarm quieted; but it produced a circumstance which illustrated, in a very affecting manner, the observations we have been making. As the family were greatly beloved by all who knew them, every one used the most affectionate exertions in their behalf. When the father had been brought safely from the house, several hastened to the relief of the daughters. They were dressed, and were descending the stairs. The eldest, who had behaved with great presence of mind, was supporting her sister, who trembled with agitation. "Take care of this box," said Emily: it contained her father's title-deeds. "For Heaven's sake preserve this locket!" sobbed Matilda; it was a miniature of her mother!

We have left, but not forgotten you, beautiful creatures! Often, when we are sitting in solitude, with a pen behind our ear and a proof before our eyes, you come, hand in hand, to our imagination! Some, indeed, enjoin us to prefer esteem to fascination—to write sonnets to Sensibility, and to look for a wife in Sense. These are the suggestions of age; perhaps of prudence. We are young, and may be allowed to shake our heads as we listen!

MR. LOZELL'S

ESSAY ON WEATHERCOCKS.

"Round he spun."—BYRON.

WE have a great respect for a Weathercock! There is something about it so springy, so sprightly, and, at the same time, so complying and so accommodating, that we are not ashamed to confess that we have long taken it for our model. It changes sides perpetually, yet always preserves one unvaried elevation; it is always in motion, yet always remains the same. We could look at a Weathercock for hours!

To us, however, it has another charm, independent of its intrinsic good qualities. Its name, not less than its character, recalls to our recollection a family which is entitled, in the highest degree, to our esteem; of which we should never cease to think, even if our memory were not daily sharpened by the little remembrancer, which is at once their namesake, their crest, and their model.

The family of the Weathercocks is one of considerable

antiquity. The first of the name, whom we find distinguishing himself in any extraordinary degree, is Sir Anthony Weathercock of Fetherly, Staffordshire; who changed his party seven times during the unfortunate dissensions between the houses of York and Lancaster. And this he contrived to do with so much tact, that he was a considerable gainer by his six first defections. By his seventh he certainly sustained a trifling loss—he lost his head!

It is a well-known observation, that the descendants of surpassingly great men are often either blockheads or idiots. The present instance certainly affords us an exemplification of the truth of the remark. The successor of this genuine Weathercock was a poor weak fellow, who had no more idea of turning to the rightabout, without compulsion, than he had of breakfasting without beef. Upon his refusing to deliver up the castle of Nounhame to the celebrated Warwick, he was besieged, compelled to surrender, and immediately hung up upon the gates of the fort, to learn to behave like his forefathers.

The religious prosecutions which followed the union of the White and Red Roses afforded fresh opportunity for the manifestation of the merits of the Weathercocks. Theirs was almost the only family of any note in England which did not lose one or other of its members from the indiscriminate fury of superstition. The head of the house appears to have embraced as many religions, and more wives, than Henry himself; and a younger branch is said to have been, within a week, a serving-man in the train of Gardiner and a clerk in the household of Cranmer. But we are forgetting that we and our friends live in 1821, and that we shall weary the patience of our reader by tracing those dry historical facts *ab ovo*.

The Weathercock family, or rather that branch of it with which we are at present concerned, resides on a large and productive estate in Leicestershire. We have spent much time with them, and have had several opportunities of studying their peculiar merits. Their mansion affords a perfect college for mutability; everything is kept in readiness to be destroyed or refitted, removed or replaced, at a minute's warning. It is quite delightful to see how new fashions of furniture come in and go out; how the faces of the servants are continually altered; how the hour of meals, the regulation of the parterres—in short, the whole system of domestic economy is always subjected to some new ephemeral arrangement, which must soon give way to another equally new and equally ephemeral. To us, we say, this is delightful. But one seldom finds two tastes alike. Many pronounce the Weathercocks to be quite crazed; and many decide that "they are mighty good kind of people, but have very odd whimsies!"

The disposition for change, which is inherent in the family, has produced very strange effects upon their place of residence. The house was originally a good stout old-fashioned house, remarkable for nothing but the antiquity of its pictures and the size of its dining-hall. But its name and character have shifted considerably since it came into the possession of my worthy friends. It has been alternately a Hall, an Abbey, a Castle, and a Lodge; nay, during the life of the late Sir Adonis Weathercock, it became, for a few months, a Cottage. The proprietor, however, in this instance, gave up his design before it had affected anything beyond the windows. The mansion bears more permanent marks of its other metamorphoses. On one side it has the square turrets and battlements of the feudal system; on another, the flowery-pointed arch of a Gothic cathedral. One of the owners of the place thought proper to sink a moat round his habitation; but he afterwards filled it up, and converted it into a circular gravel walk. Another had a fancy for erecting some solid Doric pillars; he, doubtless, much improved their appearance, by placing upon them a beautiful Chinese veranda. Similar observations are suggested by an inspection of the interior of the building. You may almost read a history of two or three centuries in the reliques of their manners which are scattered in every apartment. War has been carried on with tolerably equal success between Lely's portraits, Gainsborough's landscapes, and Bunbury's caricatures. A cast of a Hercules looks somewhat angrily upon a mandarin, who is his next neighbour; and a timorous Venus maintains her post with great obstinacy, although her divine presence is invaded by the scaly folds of an enormous dragon. There are bronzes and Cupids, oaken tables and mahogany tables, drab papering and crimson papering, high mantelpieces and low mantelpieces, Dresden china and French china; everything is superb, everything incongruous, everything unfinished.

The old park has been reduced to the same state. A scrupulous homage has been paid to every new mode of cultivation; a thousand emendations, and additions, and improvements have been successively introduced. But it is easier to plant new customs than to eradicate the old. Lycaon was turned into a beast, but he retained his old habits of atrocity. Arachne was transformed into a spider, but she did not forget her spinning. The park of the Weathercocks has, in like manner, assumed various novel shapes, without losing the traces of its old ones. At one time it was dressed out in all the stiff regularity of alleys and arcades; at another, it was dubbed a "wilderness," and was immediately laid waste by a terrible inroad of shrubs and weeds without number. In one part your eye rests upon the muddy vestiges of an artificial cascade; in another, your foot stumbles over a heap of rubbish, which has been produced by the demolition of an artificial ruin. Some people object to these things; for my part, I own I am delighted with them. They show a proper distrust of one's own opinion, a decorous compliance with the unstable will of the world, an eager spirit of enterprise; in short, they prove that the Weathercocks have not an ounce of obstinacy in their composition

Sir Wilfrid Weathercock, the present head of the family, is a cheerful and hale man, between forty and fifty years of age. He is about the middle stature, although, upon some occasions, by the affectation of a fashionable stoop, he appears somewhat dwarfish; while, upon others, by the assumption of a military gait and a pair of high heels, he bids fair to be accounted a giant. With a self-denial worthy of a Cincinnatus, he has avoided all offers of place or pension, all invitations to embark in public life; he has confined his manifold talents and his extraordinary versatility to the limits of his own estate. Perhaps, indeed, his determination, in this respect, may have been a prudent one; for, although any ministry would have been benefited by the unusual facility with which Sir Wilfrid would have flown from

patriotic speeches to taxation and gagging bills, from
prayers for peace to declarations of war, from professions
of economy to measures of profusion; yet it must be
confessed that his reluctance to remain a minute stationary
would have driven him from one side of the House to the
other oftener than is seemly in a public man. Let it be
understood that we speak with all due deference and respect
for the numerous precedents which are to be found in our
English history. Leaving great statesmen to settle this point,
we can only express our opinion that our friend has certainly acted best for his own comfort, by choosing a quiet
privacy, where he may "change every hour," undisturbed
by the malevolence of envy or the violence of faction.

His education was, in his youth, sadly neglected. Indeed,
his father fluctuated so long, first between Eton and Westminster, and afterwards between Cambridge and Oxford,
that it is marvellous to me how little Wilfrid picked up
any education at all. He has, however, obtained just so
much learning as enables him to cry up the Greeks and the
Latins alternately, and to flirt with all the nine Muses in
succession. He escaped the fatigue of deliberation in the
choice of a profession, by the death of his father; who left
him, in very early life, the heir to all his fortune, all his
friendships, and all his follies. He spent his first two years
upon the estate, occupied in reflections of no very serious
import: such as, whether his coat should be red or green,
whether his hunter should be bay or brown, whether his
equipage should be a barouche or a curricle. So far all was
sunshine; but some tempestuous days were approaching.
It was suggested to him that the ancient family of the
Weathercocks ought to have an heir to its honours and
possessions. No evasion would serve; Sir Wilfrid must
take a wife. He was now in a novel and a disagreeable
dilemma. In any trifling part of his domestic economy, in
the livery of his servants, in the arrangement of his dinner-
table, in the fashion of his plate, he would have bowed
without a murmur to the decision of his friends; but to
inflict upon himself a wife was a thing so utterly unlooked
for and unprepared for, that Sir Wilfrid paused. He hesitated and decided, and hesitated again, through three years;
at the termination of which he broke his leg in a fox-chase,
grew quiet in consequence, sold his hounds, and looked out

for a wife. Then another perplexity occurred. Who was to be the happy woman? He could never resolve to make so invidious a distinction.

"It is very true," said poor Sir Wilfrid, "that Miss Dormer has a very fine face, but then I never much admired her nose. I certainly have always preferred her cousin, although that unfortunate cast of the eye—well, well, I am a young man, and, as my aunt says, 'there is no hurry!' Miss Rayner is very beautiful, and has such charming dark hair—I always liked dark hair; yet I don't know if light is not as pretty—prettier sometimes, as for instance Miss Chevier's—only she is so insipid; I think Lady Mary is more fascinating, but then she is so terribly satirical. Perhaps her sister would make a better wife—if she was not such a fool!"

He consulted in this manner with himself for a long time : half the belles of the county were ready to pull caps for him, but he "prattled with fifty fair maids, and changed them as oft." At last, in a fit of courage, he flung himself at the feet of his chosen one, talked some rhapsodies, sighed some sighs, and awaited his sentence. The lady was sorry, very sorry—and she was flattered, highly flattered—and she was sure, quite sure—it would only be attributed to her own want of discernment, that she declined the favour, the honour, the distinction, the—— He heard no more ; he hesitated ! Should he leave the room? Yes!—no! —yes! And he escaped as well as he could.

He has continued to this day a bachelor. In spite of all intrigue, all solicitation, all persecution, he has remained, in this one instance, obstinate. In all others he is a real Weathercock. He builds cottages, apparently with no object but pulling them down ; and pulls them down, apparently with no object but that of building them up : he is a Tory one hour and a Whig the next, and takes in the *Chronicle* and *Courier* alternately ; he seldom reads more than half a number of a periodical work, and never wears the same coat above a month. In his conversation he pursues the same plan—or rather want of plan—

Modo reges atque tetrarchas,
Omnia magna, loquens ; modo "sit mihi mensa tripes, et
Concha salis puri, et toga, quæ defendere frigus,
Quamvis crassa, queat ——."

In short—in manner, in language, in business, and in
pleasure, he sets an admirable example of mutability, which
we shall always make it our study to imitate—especially
when we take up our pens.

Of Sir Wilfrid's nephew and heir we shall here say
nothing, as his character has been elsewhere noticed by
another hand, under the name of Arthur Clavering. We
pass on, therefore, to the Baronet's maiden sister, Lady
Rachel Weathercock, who is nowise deficient in the
peculiarities for which her family is remarkable. Lady
Rachel has now attained her fiftieth year; the caprices and
follies of her youth have gradually subsided; and, in many
points, she has become more stationary than a Weathercock
ought to be. Her character, however, is just saved by one
little ingredient, by which a person who is unacquainted
with her habits may be not a little puzzled. Lady Rachel
is an inveterate reader, an inveterate talker, and an inveterate arguer. You might therefore suppose that few subjects
could be started upon which the lady would not ground a
dispute; but it is no such thing. Her ladyship possesses
such a delightful pliability of opinion, that it is hardly
possible to differ from her upon any topic. We have heard
her advocate and abuse every school of painting or poetry
in almost immediate succession. She combats to-day the
very opinions she maintained yesterday; yet, upon the first
semblance of a contradiction, she veers round forthwith, and
proves herself a more accommodating antagonist, if possible,
than the Neapolitans. Mr. Oakley was three hours in conversation with her; and though the burden of his song was
No, No, No, he was unable to pick a quarrel. Like Sir
Robert Bramble and Job, "they couldn't disagree—and so
they parted."

The only remaining member of the family is Sir Wilfrid's
niece. How delightful is your mutability, charming
Leonora! You are like a chess-board which is chec-
quered with black and white squares alternately; or a
melodrama, in which the tears of Tragedy are relieved by
the follies of Farce; or a day in April which blends rain
with sunshine, summer with winter; or the *Etonian*, in
which the serious is united with the absurd, and pathos is
intermingled with puns. What a wardrobe must be yours!
To-day you assume the costume of the victim Mary—

to-morrow that of the executioner Elizabeth ; you put off
the diamonds of the queen for the garland of the peasant,
the curls of the coquette for the veil of the nun.   Your
voice has a thousand tones; your lips have a thousand
smiles—all of them distinct, yet all of them engaging !   You
are always the same, yet always varying ; consistent only in
your inconsistency !   Be always so !   We will build a fane in
the most beautiful region of Fancy, where no two flowers
shall wear the same hue, no two days be of the same length
or temperature : light gales shall breathe from all points of
the compass by turns, and clear streams shall vary their
course every hour; stability shall be sacrilege—and Leonora
shall be the Goddess of the Temple.

GOLIGHTLY'S ESSAY ON BLUES.

A FRAGMENT.

LADY DABBLE is a True Blue.   She is a meddler in
literature of every sort and description.   Poetry and prose,
pamphlets and plays, sermons and satires, overtures and
odes—all are her hobbies, all are the objects of her
patronage, all are subjects of her harangues.   At her
house is the synod held : where criticism and tea are
poured out together, where sweet sugar and sweeter
sonnets melt in delicious unison.   It is delightful to spend
a few hours at Lady Dabble's *conversazione.*   All inferior
wits and witlings flit around her like twinkling stars ; while
her ladyship, with her full-moon face—but it strikes us that
this is a very old simile.

Of all Blues we think the Light Blue is our favourite.
Mark the surprising difference which exists between Emilia,
the Light Blue, and her sister Sophia, the Dark Blue.
Sophia is a fine vessel, properly supplied with everything
requisite for a long voyage ; but a villanous slow sailer.
Emilia is the same vessel, but certainly it has thrown out a
vast quantity of ballast.   To speak in plainer language,
Sophia talks learnedly, and puzzles you ; Emilia talks

learnedly, and amuses you; the latter sets you a laughing, and the former sends you to sleep. A good painter will select for his picture only the most agreeable parts of the landscape which lies before him; a good talker will notice the more pleasing points of his subject, while he will throw aside the tedious. But, alas! Emilia will describe a statue, while Sophia is treating of a finger; and the Light Blue will analyse the "Iliad," while the Dark Blue is discussing the Digamma.

Fannia is a fair one, who endeavours to unite the extreme of fashionable dress with the extreme of unfashionable Blue-ism. Mr. Hodgson made a vile pun (as usual) when he denominated her a Blue *Belle.*

The only remaining Blue of whom we shall here make mention is Eva, the Sky-Blue. The habit of talking sentiment, in which the Sky-Blue commonly indulges, is in general sufficiently annoying; but in the person of Eva, far be it from us to apply to it such an epithet. Eva is always in heroics: she never speaks a sentence which is not fit to go into a German romance. All this sits very well upon youth and beauty, but in age and ugliness it is insufferable. Eva has a pretty pair of blue eyes, a finely polished neck, an enchanting white arm, and a voice withal, which is never heard but in a whisper, an aria, or a sigh. She has, in short, such a talent at turning our brains, that our Secretary has not inappositely styled her "Blue Ruin."

OLD BOOTS.

> "Whose conceit
> Lies in his hamstring, and doth think it rich
> To hear the wooden dialogue and sound
> 'Twixt his stretched footing and the scaffoldage."
>
> SHAKESPEARE.

I HAVE got a pair of old boots.

I bought them at Exeter last summer, and they withstood all the malice of Devonshire paviours in a most inconceivable style. The leather was of a most editorial consistency, and the sole resembled a quarto. It was in them that I revisited the desolate habitation of my infancy; it was their heavy clanging sound which echoed through those deserted apartments. It was in them, too, that I tottered upon the perilous summit of the Ness; and it was in them that I got wet to the knees in the disagreeable tempest which waited upon the Dawlish regatta. How many pleasant moments, how many dear friends, do they recall to my recollection! It was with their ponderous solidity that I astonished the weak nerves of one, and trod upon the weak toes of another. Every inch of them, old and *emeriti* as they are, is pregnant with some delightful, some amiable sensation. It was in them that I excogitated the first number of the *Etonian*— they shall live to look upon the last! I cannot say they were ever very elegant in shape or texture. Like the genius of my friend Swinburne, they possessed more intrinsic strength than outward polish. They served me well, however, and travelled with me to town.

I happened to put them on one wet morning in April. Whatever form or fashion they formerly boasted was altogether extinct; they were as shapeless as an unlicked cub, and as dusky as a cloud on a November morning. I beheld their fallen appearance with some dismay. "I shall be stared at," I said; "I had better take them off!" But I thought of their former services, and resolved to keep them on.

They had brought their plated heels from the country, and they made a confounded noise upon the pavement as I walked along. Ding, dong, they went at every step, as if I carried a belfry swung at my toes. "This is a disagreeable sort of accompaniment," I said. "I had better dismiss the musicians." Just at that moment a young baronet passed me, attended by a fine dog. The dog was in high spirits, and made rather too much noise for the contemplative mood of his master. "Silence, Cæsar! Be quiet, Cæsar!" No, it was all in vain, and Cæsar was kicked into the gutter. "That was cruel!" I said, "to dismiss an old servant, because he was a note too loud! I think I will keep my boots!"

I walked in the Park with Golightly. By the side of my stable footcase his neat and dapper instep cut a peculiarly smart figure; it was a Molossus *tête-à-tête* with a Pyrrhic; an Etonian's skiff moored alongside of a coal-barge. Golightly's meditations seemed to be of the same cast; he once or twice turned his eyes to the ground, as I thought with no very complacent aspect. "My friends grow ashamed of me," I said to myself; "I must part with my boots!" As I made up my mind to the sacrifice, Lady Eglantine met us, with her husband. She was constantly looking another way, nodding familiarly to the young men she met, and endeavouring to convince the world how thoroughly she despised the lump of earth which she was obliged to drag after her. "There is a woman," said Frederick, "who married Sir John for his money, and has not the sense to appear contented with the bargain she has made. What can be more silly than to look down thus upon a man of sterling worth, because he happened to be born a hundred miles from the metropolis?" "What can be more silly?" I repeated inwardly; "I will never look down on my boots again!"

. We continued our walk, and Golightly began his usual course of strictures upon the place and the company. Hurried away by the constant flow of jest and wildness with which he embellishes his sketches, I soon forgot both the boots, which had been the theme of my reflections, and the moral lessons which the subject had produced. There was an awkward stone in the way! Oh my unfortunate heels! I broke down terribly, and was very near bringing my companion after me. I rose, and went on in great dudgeon. "This will never do," I muttered; "this will never do! I must positively cashier my boots!" I looked up: an interesting girl was passing, leaning on the arm of a young man, whose face I thought I recognized. She looked pale and feeble; and, when my friend bowed to her with unusual attention, she seemed embarrassed by the civility. "That is Anna Leith," said Golightly; "she made an imprudent match with that young man about a year ago, and her father has refused to see her ever since. Poor girl! She is in a rapid decline, and the remedies of her physicians have no effect upon a broken spirit. I would never cast off a beloved object for a single false step!"

"I will keep my boots," I exclaimed; "though they make a thousand!"

ON THE DIVINITIES OF THE ANCIENTS.

To a person inquiring into the manners and customs of ancient nations, the religion which they professed and the gods which they worshipped will always appear objects of the greatest curiosity. And this will not be wondered at when we remember how intimately the religion of a State must necessarily be connected with its civil policy. In former times, when ignorance and superstition flourished side by side, the aid of a divinity was required for the carrying into effect of the most frivolous designs. No poem could succeed until the Muses were called upon in a well-rounded hexameter, no war could prosper until Mars was propitiated by a sufficiency of roast beef. The ancients appear to have had some faint idea of the ubiquity of the Deity ; but, not comprehending how such a faculty had been vested in a single divinity, they formed to themselves a set of superior powers, calculated to attend upon every emergency, from Jupiter, the god of thunder, to Tussis, the god of coughing. It is therefore evident that the consideration of the religious ideas of the ancients must be inseparably united with the study of the other parts of their history.

In the remarks which I am about to make upon this subject, I must request that one or two preliminaries may be kept in mind. First, that the characters of the constant supporters of the *Etonian* may not be implicated in the blunders of an occasional correspondent; and, secondly, that I may not be understood as endeavouring to compose a regular essay or treatise upon the topic which is before me. I have no more the inclination than I have the ability to attempt such a task. The observations which I shall have occasion to make will be merely the unripe fruit of an hour of leisure; merely a few unconnected hints, thrown out at random for your amusement, Mr. Editor, and that of my fellow-citizens. If they are pleased with them, they will thank me, and I am sufficiently repaid : if not—*n'importe*—they will at least give me credit for good intentions.

The first point which I shall notice is the opinion which the ancients entertained of the power and authority of their heavenly rulers. And as the study of fallen religions is principally useful as it shows to us the superiority of that religion which can never fall, let us first see upon what footing Christianity stands in this respect. In my eyes, and in the eyes of every one upon whom the light of revelation has dawned, the mention of a God presupposes an idea of infinite, irresistible, indisputable power. One cannot form the most remote conception of a deity whose powers or existence should be in any way limited. One of the distinguishing attributes of Christianity is that with its God nothing is impossible. He is omniscient, omnipresent, omnipotent. Can we say the same of the gods of the heathen —"the gods of wood and stone, the work of men's hands?"

Alas! alas! They raised ghosts, and they raised tempests; they scolded, and they thundered; they drank nectar, and drove doves: but when anything serious was to be done— when a battle was to be decided, or an empire overthrown, they were frequently as powerless to slay or to save as the sceptre which they wielded or the cloud which they bestrode. Let us call before us some of the most formidable, and examine into their pretensions to Olympus.

Come down, then, Jupiter, from the little pedestal on which I have placed your plaster effigy! Come down, father of men and gods, counsel-giving, wide-thundering, cloud-compelling! Come down, thou who overthrowest the Titans and abusest thy wife; thou who art so fond of the voice of prayer and the smoke of hecatombs; thou who hast so many epithets and so many sons; thou who governest Olympus and meritest Bridewell! Where are thy frowns and thy nods? thy muscles and thy sinews? thy darts and thy decrees? Where are the looks which appal—the blows which destroy? Where is the unbroken chain—the insatiable vulture? Where are the Cyclopes who forge the lightning, and the poets who forge the Cyclopes? Alas! Jupiter, amidst all thy terrors, in heaven or on Ida, in feasting or in wrath, in poetry or in prose, thou wert a quack, Jupiter, a most contemptible quack; so utterly destitute of everything that could ensure respect; so miserably deficient in everything that could inspire fear; such a pitiful compound of ignorance and knowledge, of strength and imbecility, of vanity and vice—that if the days of thy sovereignty could return again —if thou couldst again be fed upon sacrifice and flattery, I swear by thine own beard I would as soon be an Irus as a Jupiter.

The truth is that the religion of the ancients, as far as it can be collected from their writings, partook in no small degree of predestination. Yet it is enveloped in so much obscurity, that it is very difficult for us—nay, it might have been very difficult for them—to define where the supremacy of fate should stop and the authority of the gods commence. We find some unfortunate divinity perpetually endeavouring to overthrow some State which is destined to stand, or to destroy some hero who is destined to live; although the said divinity has an innate perception that his struggles in either instance must eventually be fruitless. I know that these ideas may be said to be founded solely on the marvellous fictions of the poets; but, let me ask, would Diomedes have ever inflicted a wound upon Mars, if Homer had seen in Mars a formidable being? or would Juno have ever strutted and stormed through the Æneid, if Virgil had cared a sixpence for her displeasure? When I see these liberties taken with the gods in writing, I feel convinced that equal liberties will be taken with them in life; when I find an immortal and an invincible being knocked on the head or run through the belly at the mercy of a terrestrial wit, I naturally conclude that in the country where such a phenomenon takes place few persons will boggle at a perjury from the apprehension of a thunderbolt. But this is not all. There seems to have existed an idea that a time was approaching when the great offspring of Saturn would be hurled down from the seat he occupied, and subjected to an ignominious destiny, if not to utter annihilation. This is one of the most singular and unaccountable points in their system of faith. Without going into discussions, to which I am unequal, upon the origin and import of this notion, I must express my surprise at the blindness of those who dressed up a figure loaded with all these debilities as their supreme power, and installed him in the seat of universal dominion.

As I have been making allusions to the introduction of

the gods in the battles of the Epics, I shall proceed to say
a few words upon the subject. The worthy gentry of
Olympus, resembling men in their vices, their passions,
their liability to pain, and their delight in carnage, made a
very tolerable figure in a fair stand-up fight. Their
characters could suffer very little from their making use of
brazen arms, riding in wooden chariots, and wrestling with
antagonists of mere flesh and blood. Mars, to be sure,
would have done better if he had refrained from howling;
and Juno would not have lost in dignity if she had been a
little more cautious in boxing the ears of Diana. But, upon
the whole, these people are very good matter for the poet;
and I would as lief meet them in an hexameter as in a
temple.

But it is a very different thing when the person of the
only true God is to be introduced in a poem. A pigmy in
poetry may trifle with the thunders of Jupiter; but a
Hercules should beware how he handles the terrors of
Jehovah. A rhymer may talk what nonsense he pleases of
a mythology which consists of fiction and tinsel; but he
should be afraid to touch upon a theme in which there is
truth, and eternity, and power. It is for this reason that I
can never read without disgust those passages of Tasso in
which the divine agency is degraded to the level of the
machinery of the poem.

When, however, the description falls into the hands of
one who is able to do justice to it, see how the glories of
the heathen mythology sink before the effulgence of the
living God. Search the most celebrated descriptions of
heathen writers; and where, in the brightest moments of
inspiration, will you find a passage that can for a moment
be compared with that of the Psalmist?

"The earth trembled and quaked; the very foundations
of the hills shook, and were removed, because He was
wrath. There went a smoke out in His presence, and a
consuming fire out of His mouth, so that coals were kindled
at it. He bowed the heavens also and came down, and it
was dark under His feet. He rode upon the cherubims and
did fly: He came flying upon the wings of the wind. He
made darkness his secret place; His pavilion round about
Him with dark water, and thick clouds to cover Him. At

the brightness of his presence His clouds removed; hailstones and coals of fire. The Lord also thundered out of heaven, and the Highest gave His thunder; hailstones and coals of fire. He sent out His arrows and scattered them; He cast forth lightnings and destroyed them. The springs of waters were seen, and the foundations of the round world were discovered, at Thy chiding, O Lord, at the blasting of the breath of Thy displeasure."

When I look at the famous nod of Jupiter—

'Η, καὶ κυανέῃσιν ἐπ' ὀφρύσι νεῦσε Κρονίων,
'Αμβρόσιαι δ' ἄρα χαῖται ἐπερρώσαντο ἄνακτος
Κρατὸς ἀπ' ἀθανάτοιο· μέγαν δ' ἐλέλιξεν Ὄλυμπον—

I have before me a distinct image of a handsome terrible-looking man, sitting on a throne, and shaking his head; but when I read the passage which I have quoted above, I find no clear image represented; I feel only a dark and undefinable sensation of awe—a consciousness of the presence of the Deity, visible, yet clothed with darkness as with a veil.

Look now at the terrible magnificence with which Ezekiel has overshadowed the Almighty. After a gorgeous description of the attendant ministers, he says—

"And there was a voice from the firmament that was over their heads, when they stood and had let down their wings. And above the firmament that was over their heads, was the likeness of a throne, as the appearance of a sapphire stone, and upon the likeness of the throne was the likeness as the appearance of a man upon it. And I saw as the colour of amber, as the appearance of fire round about within it, from the appearance of his loins even upward, and from the appearance of his loins even downward, I saw as it were the appearance of fire, and it had brightness round about. As the appearance of the bow that is in the cloud in the day of rain, so was the appearance of the brightness round about. This was the appearance of the likeness of the glory of the Lord. And when I saw it, I fell upon my face, and I heard a voice of one that spake."

My quotations are running to a great length; nevertheless I cannot refrain from transcribing the splendid description

of the Messiah, in which our own Milton has united the
above two passages :—

> Forth rushed with whirlwind sound
> The chariot of Paternal Deity,
> Flashing thick flames, wheel within wheel withdraw
> Itself instinct with spirit, but convoyed
> By four cherubick shapes ; four faces each
> Had wondrous ; as with stars their bodies all
> And wings were set with eyes, with eyes the wheels
> Of beryl, and careering fires between ;
> Over their heads a crystal firmament,
> Whereon a sapphire throne inlaid with pure
> Amber, and colours of the showery arch.
> He in celestial panoply all armed
> Of radiant Urim, work divinely wrought,
> Ascended ; at his right hand Victory
> Sate eagle-winged ; beside him hung his bow
> And quiver, with three-bolted thunder stored ;
> And from about him fierce effusion rolled
> Of smoke and bickering flame, and sparkles dire.
> Attended with ten thousand thousand saints
> He onward came ; far off his coming shone ;
> And twenty thousand (I their number heard)
> Chariots of God, half on each hand were seen.
> He on the wings of cherub rode sublime,
> On the crystalline sky in sapphire throned.

After having transcribed three such passages as these,
I am in no mind to return at present to the dirt and
filth of Pagan superstition, and I shall hasten to a conclusion.

I have been digressing from my original proposition,
until at last I have left the Divinities of the Ancients, and
set to work at proving that Homer and Virgil are far
inferior to David, Ezekiel, and Milton, which after all is a
very easy task, and not very new. I intended to have
made this a very learned paper, to have talked much of
Egypt, a little of M. Belzoni, and several other matters
which I have not time to enumerate. Here, however, is
the fruit of my labours ; I am too lazy, or too busy, to alter,
or add, or erase ; in thus rambling through five or six pages,
instead of labouring through fifty, my time has been expended, I am sure, more pleasantly to myself, and I hope
as agreeably to my readers.

REMINISCENCES OF MY YOUTH.

"Admonitu locorum."—CICERO.

IT is the seventh day of my revisiting! The burst of almost painful affection which came over me as I first trod upon the scene of brighter hours, and the glow of heart and brow, which seemed like a resuscitation of feelings and passions that have long lain dormant in forgetfulness— these have gradually died away ; but there has succeeded, dearest spot, a mellowed fondness for you, which, were I to live an eternity with you, would remain through that eternity imperishable. I now am delighted to muse upon the sweetness of those recollections, whose overpowering throb I at first could hardly endure ; and love to call up before me those imaginings, which at first rushed upon me with the overwhelming force of a cataract. I look around me! A spirit seems to be sitting on every house-top, lingering in every grove ; incidents in themselves the most humble, objects in themselves the most mean—like insects preserved in amber—derive nobility and beauty from the colours which memory has thrown around them!

There are associations in the names and the aspects of places which it is impossible for us to restrain or subdue. Who shall gaze upon the Capitol, and not think upon the Cæsars? Who shall roam round Stonehenge, and not shudder at the knife of the Druids? Who shall be a sojourner in Eastcheap, and not enjoy sweet visions of Shakespeare? My native village! Less celebrated are the worthies whose images you recall to my imagination, but they are recalled in colours as constant and as vivid. How can I look upon your sports, without thinking of those who were my companions when I joined in them? How can I listen to the voice of your merriment, without thinking of those from whom in other days it sprung?

Before me is the tavern! The lapse of years has hardly bored an additional excavation in its dusky window-curtain, or borrowed a single shade from the boards of its faded sign

But its inmates have vanished ; their laughter is no longer heard in their place ; and the red-brick wall of the Ship stands before me like the cemetery of their mirth, their wit, and their good-humour.   In my youth I was wild—blame me you that have never been so—and I loved to mingle in this scene of rustic joviality, to listen to the remarks of untutored simplicity, to envy those who had grown grey untainted by the corruptions of "this great Babel," and to feel how truly it was said,

> Where ignorance is bliss,
> 'Tis folly to be wise.

Many years ago I looked upon these boyish pursuits with an eye very different from that which is now cast back towards them.   Many years ago, I thought nothing disgraceful which was not incompatible with innocence in myself and charity towards my fellow-creatures.   What would you have?   I have grown more prudent, and I am not so happy.

The great room of this humble building was the curia of the village.   In it the patriarchs of the place held their nightly sittings, and discussed ale and politics with unremitting assiduity.   There was no inebriety, no tumult, no ill-mannered brutality in their sessions ; everything was conducted with the greatest order and tranquillity ; the old men assembled with all the gravity, with all the earnestness, perhaps with much of the wisdom, of great statesmen. Alas ! ye profane ones, ye smile.   Ye look with contempt upon my rustic curia and my weather-beaten statesmen. And what are the great ones of this earth ?   Shall not the beings of a more exalted sphere contemplate with equal scorn the wranglings of more honoured senates ?   You turn with disgust from the eloquence of a Huggins or a Muggins !   Look ye then to the oratory of a Cicero, to the patriotism of a Brutus, or, if you will, to the commanding energies of a Pitt and a Fox !   Years roll on, and—what are they ?

However, call it a curia, or a club, or what ye will, custom had established in this mansion a meeting of all the wise heads and all the choice spirits of the hamlet.   At first the members of it were very independent of all party considerations, and each was too conscious of his own individual merits to become a hanger-on of any more important potentate. Whatever subject was tabled, whether it were the Holy Alliance or the Holy Church—the taste of the new tap or the conduct of the new member—every one said what he thought, and had no idea of bowing to the opinion of his neighbour. In process of time, however, this laudable spirit of liberty and equality began, as in other places, to decline. Some of the members became idle and complaisant, others waxed mighty and overbearing; until at last the Parliament of —— became subservient to the will and wishes of a single ruler, and Jeremiah Snaggs took his place in my memorandum-book as the first Dictator.

He had lived many years in the place, so that he was well known to most of its inhabitants—to some too well. He had long enjoyed the office of collector of the taxes in —— and its neighbourhood, and had contrived to grow rich, as some whispered not by the most creditable methods. However that might be, he was rich, and, as the patriarchal simplicity of the spot declined, many began to look with ill-concealed covetings upon the possessions of Jeremiah Snaggs. He had built to himself a mansion by the roadside, with a small garden in front; and there was a very extraordinary appendage to it, which excited much speculation among his unsophisticated contemporaries, and which he denominated a veranda. For some time he remained shut up in his citadel, and seemed to contemn the courtesies and repel the approaches of the inferior beings who moved around him. Afterwards, however, he found the solitude of his home (for he was a bachelor) insupportable; and he emerged gradually from his retirement, and condescended to join in the social assemblies of his neighbours. He joined them not as a fellow-citizen, but as a sovereign; he came among them, not to brighten their festivity, but to chill their good-humour; his presence was not an assistance, but a restraint. Nevertheless, he was the great man of the place, and in a short time his word was law among its inhabitants. Whether the ascendency was owing rather to the talents which he occasionally displayed, or to the dinners which he occasionally gave, I cannot say. Thomas the boatbuilder, who till now had the credit of being a staunch Whig, and the boldness to avow it, drew in his horns; his patriotism, his oratory, his zeal shrank into nothing before the fiat of the Tory bashaw. He made indeed a violent opposition when Jeremiah proposed the introduction of port wine in lieu of the malt which had hitherto been the inspiration of their counsels, and he was somewhat refractory when the dictator insisted upon turning out the seats of the last generation and introducing modern chairs. But upon both points the boatbuilder was outvoted; and in obedience to Mr. Snaggs the senators dozed upon nauseous port, and fidgeted upon cane bottoms, for the space of six years. Look now! You smile at the disputes of a Thomas and a Snaggs! Yet why? What is there of greater moment in those of a Londonderry and a Brougham?

A period, however, was soon put to this terrible system of misrule: an old favourite of the hundred returned from fighting his country's battles, in which occupation he had been perseveringly engaged for the last fourteen years. Sergeant Kerrick was disgusted with the innovations of the day, and set vigorously to work to drive them before him, as he expressed himself, at the point of the bayonet. The sergeant was always a fine man, but he was now a cripple into the bargain; he had always majestic black eyes, but he had now the additional advantage of having a cut over both; he had always the two legs of Hercules, but now— glorious destiny!—he had only one to stand upon. He was irresistible! The veranda, the roast mutton, the will —all, all was forgotten. In a short time Snaggs was beat by unheard-of majorities; a week—and the tide of Whitbread's best was turned into its proper channel; another—and the cane-bottoms were kicked ignominiously from the Parliament. Thomas the boatbuilder, who had seceded in disappointment, was brought back in triumph; the dictator in vain attempted to check the progress of the revolution! baffled, defeated, insulted on all sides, he retired from the field in dismay, and died within a week afterwards from the falling of his veranda. His death produced no sensation; for it was evident that the man of war had been already installed in his place.

The Sergeant bore his faculties right meekly, and

promoted the restoration of *l'ancien régime* to the utmost of his abilities. During his administration people began to talk with some little degree of freedom, although at first they were much awed by the laurels and the scars of their president. They had a wondrous idea of the wisdom he had attained upon his travels. How could they talk of politics in his presence? Why, gracious! he had held the Emperor o' Russia's stirrup at Petersburg, and taken off his hat to the Pope o' Rome—ay! and caught a glimpse o' Boney to boot. Then, as to religious matters! why the Vicar was nothing to him : he had seen some nations that pray cross-legged, and some that pray in the open air, and some that don't pray at all; and he had been to St. Peter's, and a place they call the Pantheon, and all among the convents and nunneries, where they shut up young folk to make clergymen of them. It is not surprising that all this condensation of knowledge produced much veneration in the neighbourhood; it wore off, however, rapidly, and his companions began to enjoy the tales of. his hardships, his privations, his battles, and his triumphs, without any feeling of distance or dissatisfaction. Enchanted by the stories he told, enchanted still more by the enthusiasm with which he told them, the *Patres Conscripti* began to despise their hitherto pacific habits ; they carried their sticks on their shoulders, instead of trailing them on the ground ; they longed

> To follow to the field some warlike lord ;

all of them began to look big, and one or two made some proficiency in swearing. By the edict of the dictator, the Biblical prints which were ranged round the chamber made room for coloured representations of Cressy and Agincourt ; and the table was moved into such a situation as to give sufficient room for the manual exercise. The women of the village began to be frightened ; Matthew Lock, a fine young man of eighteen, ran away to be listed ; Mark Fender, a fine old man of eighty, lost an eye in learning parry tierce ; two able-bodied artisans caught an ague by counter-marching in a shower ; apprehensions of a military government began to be pretty general—when suddenly the dictator was taken off by an apoplexy. *Ibi omnis effusus*

labor! He died when the organization of the corps was
just completed; he was carried to his final quarters in great
state, and three pistols and a blunderbuss were fired over
his grave. Why should we contemn his lowly sepulchre?
He died—and so did Alexander.

The warlike Tullus was succeeded by the pacific Numa.
Kerrick, the sergeant, was succeeded by Nicholas, the
clerk. The six months during which the progeny of Mars
had held the reins of government, had unsettled everything; the six weeks which saw Nicholas in his stead set
everything in its place again. In the course of a few days
it was discovered that drab was a better colour than red,
and that an oyster-knife was a prettier weapon than a
bayonet. In this short reign the magnates of the place
imbibed a strong taste for literature and the arts. The
blunderbuss was exchanged for the "Pilgrim's Progress,"
and one of the pistols for the "Whole Duty of Man."
Nicholas himself was a man of considerable acquirements;
he was the best reader in the place next to the Vicar, and
by dint of much scraping and perseverance he had
managed to fill two shelves with a heterogeneous confusion
of ancient and modern lore. There was an odd volume of
the "History of England," sundry ditto of sermons, an
account of "Anson's Voyage Round the World," and "The
righte Pathe toe Welle-Doinge," by Geoffry Mixon. There
was also a sage treatise on Ghosts, Spectres, Apparitions,
&c., which instigated me to various acts of atrocity, to which
I shall presently allude.

Nicholas had presided over the conclave for four months
in uninterrupted tranquillity, when an incident occurred
which put the firmness of his character to the test. The
Parliament had just finished their second jug one evening,
and were beginning to think of an adjournment, when a low
rumbling noise, like the echo of distant thunder, was heard,
and in a moment afterwards the door, as it were spon-
taneously, flew open, and a spectre flew in. It is needless
for me to describe the spectre: it was, *selon règle*, above the
common height, with pale cheeks, hollow voice, and staring
eyes. It advanced to the dictator's chair, and moaned, in
an audible murmur, "I am thine evil genius, Nicholas!
Thou shalt see me at church on Sunday." And then it

immediately vanished, nobody knew how or where. Well indeed it might, for few of the company were qualified to play the spy on its motions. The clerk, however, is said to have kept his seat with great firmness; and all avowed that they had followed his example. Howbeit, unless my memory fails me, there was a whisper that the saddler contrived to be looking under the table for a sixpence, and the exciseman's sooty appearance told dirty tales of the chimney. The clerk was much importuned not to hazard himself in the church upon the fated Sabbath; but upon this point he was obstinate: it was finally agreed to conceal the matter, and in the event of the apparition's reappearance to set the minister at him.

On the Sunday (for I suppose the reader is aware that I was intimately acquainted with the causes of the alarm) it was very amusing to watch the different faces of terror or expectation which appeared at public worship, to mark the quivering hue on the sallow cheek of the exciseman, and listen to the querulous intonation of the clerk's Amen. When at last the sermon was concluded, Nicholas gave his final twang in such a manner that to my ears it resembled an *Io pæan.* He rose from his knees with a countenance of such unmingled, unrepressed triumph, that I could no longer restrain myself! I laughed. Alas! dearly did I rue, unhappy wight, that freak of sacrilegious jocularity.

"And is this all!" See now; you laugh at this deception because a foolish boy was its instrument, and an honest clerk its victim. Have you not often pored, with romantic interest, upon tales of impostures equally gross? Have you not read with horror the celebrated warning of Dion? Have you not shuddered at, "I am thine evil spirit, Brutus; thou shalt see me again at Philippi?" and yet

What's in a name?
"Nicholas" will raise a sp'rit as well as "Brutus."

The dictator's seat was soon after vacated. Ellen, the Vicar's daughter, had died some years before; and her father, finding himself unable to reconcile himself to the residence which she had so long endeared to him, prepared to quit the village. It was supposed that poor Nicholas was overpowered by the misfortune of his patron: certain it is that he

F

died very quietly one fine summer's evening, quite prepared for his end, and in the fullest possession of his faculties. He was followed to his grave by as sincere a crowd of mourners as ever wept at a poor man's obsequies. There is no urn, no column, no monumental splendour where he sleeps! But what of this? Nicholas is dust—and so is Cheops.

One more name lives in my recollection. The old clerk bequeathed his library and his authority to his favourite, Arthur. Arthur!—he had no other name. That of his father was unknown to him, and he was taken from life before his merits had earned one. He was a foundling. He had been left at the old clerk's door some years before I was born; and Nicholas had relieved the parish of the expense, and had educated him with all the attention of a father. I will not relate the whisper which went about at the time, nor the whispers which succeeded afterwards. Arthur grew in health and beauty, and was quite the pet of the neighbourhood; he had talents too, which seemed designed for brighter days ; and patience, which made even his bitter lot endurable. He used to write verses which were the admiration of the synod; and sang his hearers to sleep occasionally with all the good-nature imaginable. At last a critic of distinguished note, who was spending a few months near the hamlet, happened to get a sight of the boy's poetry, and took a fancy to him. He taught him to read and recite with feeling; pointed out to him the beauties and the errors of the models which he put into his hands; and, on his departure, gave him the works of several of our modern worthies, and promised that he would not forget him. However he did forget him, or gave no symptoms of his remembrance.

The old clerk died, and Arthur felt alone in the world. Still he had many friends ; and when the first burst of his regret was over, comfortable prospects again began to dawn upon him. He again mingled in the society of the village; and the dictator's chair in the chimney-corner, which had been vacated during this short interregnum, was given up to him cheerfully. He was beloved, esteemed, looked up to, by every one. Another circumstance, too, seemed likely to add to his happiness: he fixed his affections on a young woman, the daughter of an inhabitant of the place; his passion was returned with interest, and the latter opposed no obstacle to its gratification.

On a sudden his whole appearance and behaviour was altered. He seemed as if awaking from a delightful dream; nothing which he had loved or pursued appeared to have charms for him any longer. When he was questioned as to the cause of his depression, he hinted obscurely that "it was no matter; the infamy which his parents had heaped upon him he would bear alone; he would entangle no one else in the misery which was and must be his own portion." This was all the explanation he gave; but it was enough to show that he had given himself up to the dominion of a morbid sensibility, which must finally be his destruction.

He ceased to lead, as he formerly was wont to do, the opinions and pursuits of his neighbours. They had always bowed to his criticisms, his logic, his lectures; but criticism, logic, and lectures were now silent. He would sit in the chair of dignity hour after hour, and utter no word: sometimes, however, he would appear to shake off, with a painful struggle, the feelings which oppressed him, and would break out suddenly into flashes of a broad but irresistible humour, which Burns, in his brightest moments, could not have surpassed; and then he would relapse again into gloom and taciturnity. But his mind, thus kept in a state of continual agitation and excitement, was sinking fast beneath it. The girl, too, whom he loved, was wretched through his refinement of passion. She believed herself slighted, and her coldness aggravated his torments. This could not last! It did not.

One day he did not make his appearance in the village. One of his friends, going to his cottage, found the door fastened; and, upon calling, received no answer. The neighbourhood became alarmed; and several of his acquaintance searched in vain for him. He was not by the stream, where he often sat in solitude till the noxious dew fell round him; nor in the grove, where he used to listen to the nightingales till fancy filled up the pauses in their songs; nor by the window, where he would stand and gaze unconsciously till the sight of that dear face drove him from the scene of enchantment. At last they forced open his door; I entered with them. The poor youth was sitting at his writing-table, in his old patron's armchair; the pen seemed to have just fallen from his hand; the ink on its nib was hardly dry; but he was quite still, quite silent, quite cold.

His last thoughts seemed to have been spent upon the stanzas which were on the table before him. I will transcribe them, rather as an illustration of his story than as a specimen of his talents. Some of the lines gave rise to a conjecture that he had been the author of his own death, but nothing appeared to warrant the suspicion.

I have a devil in my brain!—
 He haunts me when I sleep,
And points his finger at my pain,
 And will not let me weep:
And ever, as he hears me groan,
He says the cause is all my own.

I shall be calm anon!—I had
 A pleasant dream of bliss;
And now they tell me I am mad—
 Why should I mourn for this?
My good, kind parents! Answer ye,
For what I am, and am to be.

Alas! I have forgotten, dear,
 The pledging and the vow;
There is a falsehood in my tear,
 I do not love thee now:
Or how could I endure to go,
And look, and laugh, and leave thee so?

Thou shalt not come to my caress,
 Thou shalt not bear my name;
Nor sorrow in my wretchedness,
 Nor wither in my shame;
Mine is the misery and the moan,
And I will die—but die alone!

Him too I saw carried to his narrow dwelling-place. In his latter days he had been regarded by his companions with a kind of superstitious awe; and, as his coffin fell with its solemn, reverberating sound, into its allotted space, the bearers looked upon each other with an expression of conscious mystery, and many shook their heads in silence. I lingered round the spot when they departed, and planted a rose upon his humble mound.

I was to leave the village the next day in order to fix my abode among the haunts of busy men. In the evening, feeling a melancholy which I could not shake off, I took up my hat and wandered towards the churchyard. From a distance I perceived a bright and delicate figure hastily retiring from my approach. I leaned over the remains of the kind, the enthusiastic, the affectionate! The rose which I had planted there glistened beneath the moon. It was not the dew: it was something more clear, more precious—it was one beautiful tear! I had rather have such a tear on my grave than a pyramid of marble.

ON TRUE FRIENDSHIP.

"Infido scurræ distabit amicus."—HORACE.

How very seldom do we find any one who has a relish for real friendship—who can set a due value upon its approbation, and pay a due regard to its censures! Adulation lives, and pleases; truth dies, and is forgotten. The flattery of the fool is always pungent and delicious; the rebuke of the wise is ever irksome and hateful. Wherefore, then, do we accuse the Fates when they withhold from us the blessings of friendship, if we ourselves have not the capacity for enjoying them?

Schah Sultan Hossein, says an old Persian fable, had two favourites. Mahamood was very designing and smooth-tongued; Selim was very open and plain-spoken. After a space, the intrigues of Mahamood had the upper hand, and Selim was banished from the court. Then Zobeide, the mother of the Sultan's mother, a wise woman, and one learned in all the learning of the Persians, stood before the throne, and spoke thus :—

"When I was young I was said to be beautiful. Upon one occasion a great *fête* was to be given. The handmaids dressed my hair in an inner apartment. 'Look,' said one, 'how bright are her eyes!' 'What a complexion,' said another, 'is upon her cheeks!' 'What sweetness,' cried a third, 'in her voice!' I grew sick of all this adulation. I sent my woman from me, and complained to myself bitterly. 'Why have I not,' I cried, 'some friend on whom I can rely; who will tell me with sincerity when the roses on my cheeks begin to fade and the darkness of my eyebrows to want colouring? But alas! this is impossible.'

"As I spoke, a beneficent Genius rose from the ground before me. 'I have brought thee,' he said, 'what thou didst require: thou shalt no longer have occasion to reproach the Prophet for denying thee that which, if granted, thou wouldst thyself destroy.' So saying, he held forth to me a small locket, and disappeared.

"I opened it impatiently. It contained a small plate, in shape like a horseman's shield, but so bright that the brightness of twenty shields would be dim before it: I looked, and beheld every charm upon which I valued myself reflected upon its surface. 'Delightful monitor!' I exclaimed, 'thou shalt ever be my companion; in thee I may safely confide; thou art not mercenary, nor changeable; thou wilt always speak to me the truth—as thou dost now!' and I kissed its polish exultingly, and hastened to the *fête*.

"Something happened to ruffle my temper, and I returned to the palace out of humour with myself and the world. I took up my treasure. Heavens! what a change was there! My eyes were red with weeping—my lips distorted with vexation; my beauty was changed into deformity—my dimples were converted into frowns. 'Liar!' I cried, in a frenzy of passion, 'what meanest thou by this insolence? Art thou not in my power, and dost thou provoke me to wrath?' I dashed my monitor to the earth, and went in search of the consolation of my flatterers!"

Zobeide here ceased. I know not whether the reader will comprehend the application of her narrative. The Sultan did—and Selim was recalled.

THE COUNTRY CURATE.

"Tenui censu, sine crimine notum,
Et properare loco, et cessare, et quærere, et uti."—HOR.

IT was with feelings of the most unmixed delight that on
my way to the north I contemplated spending one evening
with my old friend Charles Torrens. I call him my friend,
although he is six or seven years my senior; because his
manners and his habits have always nearly resembled those
of a boy, and have seemed more suitable to my age than
to his. Some years ago, partly in consequence of his
own imprudence, the poor fellow was in very low circumstances; but he has now, by one of those sudden freaks of
fortune which nobody knows how to account for, become
sleek and fat, and well-to-do in the world; with a noble
patron, a pretty wife, and the next presentation to a living
of a thousand a year.

I arrived at the village of —— about sunset, and inquired for the house of Mr. Torrens. Of the children to
whom I applied no one seemed to understand me at
all; at last one of them, a 'cuter lad than his companions, scratched his head for half a minute, and exclaimed,
"Oh! why, sure, you mean Master Charles, our curate!
Gracious! to think of calling him Mr. Torrens!" I afterwards learned that this hopeful disciple had the office of
looking to the curate's night-lines. However, he led me to
the house, giggling all the way at the formality of "Mr.
Torrens." I was prepared by this to find my old acquaintance as warm, and as wild, and as childish as ever.

His residence was a red brick dwelling-house, which you
would call a house by right and a cottage by courtesy: it
seemed to possess, like the owner, all requisites for hospitality and kindness, and to want, like him, all pretensions to
decoration and show. "This is as it should be," I said
to myself; "I shall sleep soundly beneath such a roof as
this;" and so I threw up the latch of the garden-gate, and
went in. Charles was in the kitchen garden behind the

house, looking at his strawberry beds. I walked round to meet him. I will not describe the pleasure with which we shook hands : my readers well know what it is to meet a dear and cherished friend after a long absence. I know not which was the happier of the two.

"Well," he said, "here I am, you see, settled in a snug competency, with a dry roof over my head, and a little bit of turf around me. I have had some knowledge of Fortune's slippery ways, and I thank my stars that I have pretty well got out of her reach. Charles Torrens can never be miserable while there's good fishing every hour in the day in his lordship's ponds, and good venison every Sunday in the year in his lordship's dining-room. Here you see me settled, as it were, in my *otium cum dignitate*, without a wish beyond the welfare of my wife and the ripening of my melons ; and what gives my enjoyments their greatest zest, Peregrine, is, that though the road to them was rather a hilly one, I kept out of the gutters as well as I could. What is it Horace says, Peregrine ?

> Neque majorem feci ratione malâ rem,
> Nec sum facturus vitio culpâve minorem ;—

that is, I did not grow rich like a rascal, and I sha'n't grow poor like a fool ; though (thanks to my uncle, the Nabob) I can afford to give a young friend a bed and a breakfast, without pinching myself and my servants the next week ! But, bless me ! how I am letting my tongue run on. I haven't introduced you to Margaret yet ;" and so saying, he took my arm, and hurried me into his drawing-room. His bride was a very pleasing woman—a lover might well call her a beautiful one ; she seemed about one-and-twenty, and possessed every requisite to confer happiness upon a husband of my friend's wandering habits. She had sufficient good-nature to let him wander abroad, but she had, at the same time, sufficient attractions to keep him at home ; her forbearance never scolded him for his stay at another's hearth, but her good sense always took care to make his own agreeable to him. A clever wife would have piqued him, a silly wife would have bored him : Margaret was the *aurea mediocritas*, and I could see that he was sincerely attached to her.

The next morning I walked into his library, and was not a little amused by the heterogeneous treasures which it presented. Paley seemed somewhat surprised to find himself on the same shelf with "The Complete Angler," and Blair, in his decent vestment of calf-skin, was looking with consummate contempt upon the morocco coat of his next neighbour, Colonel Thornton. A fowling-piece, fishing-rod, and powder-horn were the principal decorations of the room.

On the table was a portfolio containing a variety of manuscripts, unfinished sermons, stanzas, complete in all but the rhymes; bills, receipts, and recipes for the diseases of horses. Among them I found a little memorandum-book for 1818 : it contained a sketch of his way of life previous to his accession of fortune. I transcribed four days of it, and hope he will thank me for putting them in print.

" Monday, 10 o'clock.—Breakfast. *Mem.* My clerk tells me admirable coffee may be made with burnt crusts of bread—an ingenious plan and a frugal! Am engaged to eat my mutton with the Vicar of the next parish, so that I have leisure to speculate for to-morrow. 12 o'clock.—Rode over to my Aunt Picquet's. N.B. A plaguy old woman, but has excellent cherry-brandy, and all the fruits of Alcinous in her garden. Managed to oblige her by conveying home some fine pines in a basket. 5 o'clock.—Dinner. Old Decker, his wife, and young Decker of Brasenose. *Mem.* Young Decker a great fool, but takes good care of the cellar. On my return sent my pines to the Hall (know Sir Harry's have failed this year), and received, per bearer, an invitation to join in the eating to-morrow.

" Tuesday.—After breakfast a water-excursion with the Hon. F. Goree. The poor little fellow very ingeniously fell out of the boat. I contrived to catch him by the collar in time to prevent him from spoiling his curls; but he was quite outrageous because I ruined his neckcloth. *Eh bien !* I lose nothing, for I never compassed a dinner with the Countess yet. 7 o'clock.—Dinner at the Hall. A large party. Began my manœuvres very badly, by correcting a mistake of the old gentleman's about ' Hannibal, the Roman general ;' recovered my ground, unconsciously, by a lucky dispute I had with his opponent in politics. A good dinner. Hinted how much I preferred a saddle of mutton cold. Praised the wine and drank it with equal avidity. In the evening played the flute, joined in a catch, and took a beating at chess from her ladyship with all imaginable complacency. Have certainly made great progress at the Hall. Must dance with the Baronet's daughter at the ball on Thursday.

" Wednesday.—Wet morning. Nothing to be done. Cold saddle, with compliments, sent over from the Hall. Pocketed the affront and dined on the mutton.

" Thursday.—My mare has sprained her shoulder. How am I to get to the rooms to-night? 1 o'clock.—Walked out. Met young Lawson. Hinted Rosinante's calamity, and secured a seat in the curricle. 10 o'clock.—The curricle called. L. nearly lodged me in a ditch. *Au reste*, a pleasant drive. *Mem*. To dine with him at six to-morrow, and he is to take me in the evening to a quadrille at the Landrishes'. The rooms very full. Certainly intended to dance with the Baronet's beauty. Made a villanous mistake, and stood up with Caroline Berry. My Roxana avoided me all the rest of the evening. How stupid! Have certainly ruined myself at the Hall!"

This sort of life must have been very annoying to such a man as Charles Torrens; however, he has now freed himself from it. "Good-by," he said, as we shook hands, and parted; "you'll come to us again, Perry. I was a harum-scarum dog when you knew me last; but if the river of life is rough, there is nothing like an affectionate wife to steady the boat!"

ESSAY ON THE POEMS OF HOMER, AND THE MANNERS ˙OF THE AGE IN WHICH HE LIVED.

"Philo-Musus" has sent us an essay, of considerable length, upon the merits and beauties of the Art of Poetry. We are persuaded, however, that of such merits and beauties none of our readers need to be informed; and therefore "Philo-Musus" lies at our publisher's till called for.

We are going, however, to make some observations upon one advantage to be derived from poetry, which our good friend has altogether omitted. We mean the power which it possesses of handing down to posterity an exact picture of the customs and manners of a very distant age. By its aid we can trace through successive years the variations which gradually take place in warfare and in letters, in habits and in costume; we can gaze with reverence upon the superstitions which have become extinct, and smile upon comparing the nascent follies of the age of demigods with the full-blown follies of the age of men. Homer, as he stands pre-eminent among the ancient bards in all other requisites, is equally so in this. Notwithstanding the force of his numbers, the fertility of his invention, the grandeur of his story, and the excellency of the moral precepts which are interspersed throughout it, we are inclined to value him less upon these considerations than upon the faithful representation which he has given us of the manners of his heroes. For these reasons we have put his name at the top of this paper, although in the course of it we shall probably indulge ourselves in more frequent digressions than ever the old gentleman himself made use of. To those who had rather have from us a well-digested essay than a series of straggling remarks, we must say what we have often said before:—"We are boys, and we have not the presumption to suppose ourselves capable of criticising the studies, or regulating the taste, of our schoolfellows.

Our aim has not been, and is not, to instruct, but to amuse."
With this preface, we put our Homer before us, mend our
pen, and begin.

The "Odyssey," which describes the travels and sufferings
of an individual, has, of course, more numerous sketches of
private life than the "Iliad," the actors in which seem, as it
were, to be upon a public stage, and to stalk in the tragic
buskin from one end of the poem to the other. But we
cannot help wondering at the manner in which the poet
has so frequently interwoven in his most gorgeous descriptions some allusion to the commerce or the arts of his
countrymen; his similes, in particular, are perpetually
borrowed from the works of the farmer or the mechanic.
Some have found fault with Homer upon this head, arguing
that the images which he introduces are, in some instances,
too mean for the dignity of the epic style. He has been
defended from the charge by abler pens than ours; and therefore we shall only observe, at present, that allowing these
passages to be blemishes, they are blemishes more valuable
to us than the greatest beauties could have been : if his
descriptions of rustic manners are faults, Homer, like his
own Achilles, would be less interesting were he less faulty.

The first observation which occurs to us (for we intend to
write, like sentimental ladies, quite at random) is that the
besiegers of Ilium were ignorant of one of the fiercest pests
of modern times, coined money.

> Ἔνθεν ἄρ' οἰνίζοντο καρηκομόωντες Ἀχαιοί,
> Ἄλλοι μὲν χαλκῷ, ἄλλοι δ' αἴθωνι σιδήρῳ,
> Ἄλλοι δὲ ῥινοῖς, ἄλλοι δ' αὐτοῖσι βόεσσιν,
> Ἄλλοι δ' ἀνδραπόδεσσι·

> Each, in exchange, proportioned treasures gave;
> Some brass, or iron ; some an ox, or slave.

Not a word in the bargain of pounds, shillings, and pence.
If these noxious ideas had then existed, we should have had
the sellers of the wine exclaiming, in the style of one of our
old ballad writers :

> Noe pence, nor halfpence, by my faye,
> But a noble in gold so round !

And we should have had the buyers replying, in all the lengthy insolence of Homeric compounds :

> I have gold to discharge all that I call !
> If it be forty pence, I will pay all.

Again, when Agamemnon endeavours to appease the anger of Achilles by the offer of sumptuous presents, he presents him with a magnificent list of the cities in his gift ; and, in order to describe the value of them, is obliged to have recourse to the vague epithets of " εὖ ναιομένα "— " ποιήεσσαν "—" βαθύλειμον "—" ἀμπελόεσσαν." Now, if Homer's heroes had understood anything of coinage, the poet would have avoided all this circumlocution, and presented us at once with a clear statement of the yearly revenues, in the style of the above-quoted songster :

> For Plumpton Park I will give thee,
> With tenements fair beside ;
> 'Tis worth three hundred markes by the yeare,
> To maintain thy good cow-hide.

This, however, is mere jesting. The next consideration we shall offer will be a more serious one. How happy were the men of that age ! They had no such crime as forgery, no discussions about stocks, no apprehensions of a paper currency. There was no liability to imposition ; no necessity for pamphlets. At the present crisis, when the increase of forgery and the dread of national bankruptcy occupy so large a portion of public attention, we, in common with other more practised quacks, come humbly forward with our nostrum. Is it not "a consummation devoutly to be wished" that Britain would consent to forego the use of these horrible mischief-workers, these bits of silver, or of silver paper, and return contentedly to the original method of traffic, making her payments in oxen or in sheep ? The veriest bungler may forge a shilling, but the veriest adept would find it plaguy difficult to forge an ox.

If it be true that the ancient Greeks were thus ignorant of stamped money (for we are only repeating what has been observed upon the subject before us), it cannot but surprise us that they had made so great a proficiency in other arts, without the use of what appears in modern times absolutely indispensable to social intercourse.   From the descriptions of Homer they should seem to have been, in a great measure, in possession of our arts, our ideas of policy, our customs, our superstitions.   Although living at so remote a period they enjoyed many of our luxuries ; although corrupted and debased by the grossest of religious codes, they entertained many of our notions of morality : the most skilful artisan, and the most enlightened sage, may, even in our days, find in the poems of Homer always an incitement to curiosity, and frequently a source of instruction.

Many a lady of *ton* (if ladies of *ton* were in the habit of studying Homer) would be astonished at learning that her last new lustres would sink into insignificance by the side of the candelabras of Alcinous :

> Χρύσειοι δ' ἄρα κοῦροι ἐϋδμήτων ἐπὶ βωμῶν,
> Ἕστασαν, αἰθομένας δαΐδας μετὰ χερσὶν ἔχοντες,
> Φαίνοντες νύκτας κατὰ δώματα δαιτυμόνεσσιν.

> Refulgent pedestals the walls surround,
> Which boys of gold with flaming torches crowned ;
> The polished ore, reflecting every ray,
> Blazed on the banquets with a double day.

Nor would she be less amazed, upon turning from these inanimate attendants, and learning the number and duties of the housemaids :

> Πεντήκοντα δέ οἱ δμωαὶ κατὰ δῶμα γυναῖκες, κ. τ. λ.

> Full fifty handmaids form the household train ;
> Some turn the mill, or sift the golden grain ;
> Some ply the loom ; their busy fingers move
> Like poplar-trees when Zephyr fans the grove.

Indeed, throughout his whole description of the palace and gardens of Alcinous, the poet seems to have expended all his ideas of luxury and magnificence.   The colouring of the picture must of course be supposed to be much heightened by the graces of fiction and ornament ; but nevertheless the objects of it must certainly have been sketched from the manners and usages which were before the eyes of the designer.   Upon the first of these passages it is to be observed that the Greeks of those days were ignorant of any contrivance in the way of lamps: they banqueted or deliberated by the light of fires or the blaze of torches—rude even in their refinements and barbarous in their most surpassing splendour. As to the fifty housemaids, we must recollect that it was necessary to retain a great number of female attendants, where the women had the charge of almost every menial employment, and the males seemed to live for little else but pleasure and war.

One example we may derive from the rude manners of that age, which it would be well if the more polished society of this would remember and imitate: we allude to the constant reliance which was placed upon religion in affairs of every kind. No voyage was commenced—no war undertaken—no treaty concluded—without a recurrence of sacrifice and ceremony. Hence the extraordinary sanctity which was always attached to the persons of their priests; hence also the veneration which was paid to their poets; for as the themes of their earliest songs were generally the praise or the actions of some member of their multifarious mythology, the celebrators partook of the honours which were paid to those whom they celebrated; and the verse which flowed in the name of any of their divinities was supposed to proceed from their immediate inspiration. Princes therefore generally retained in their household a bard or sage (for the terms were nearly synonymous), though we are not so wicked as to suppose that the office of fool, among the ancient Saxons, bore any analogy to that of bard among the ancient Greeks. There is an example of this custom in the opening of the "Odyssey" which has always pleased us very much. The poet has been describing the debauchery and insolence of the suitors of Penelope—

> A brutal crowd,
> With insolence, and wine, elate and loud.

And when his readers are disgusted by the extravagance and luxury which revels in the property of another, he introduces, by way of relief to the glaring colouring of the rest of the picture, the person of an old man, who still retains the post which he had held under Ulysses, and is compelled reluctantly to sweep the strings of his lyre by the mandate of the dissolute usurpers:

Κῆρυξ δ' ἐν χερσὶν κίθαριν περικαλλέα θῆκε
Φημίῳ, ὅς ῥ' ἤειδε παρὰ μνηστῆρσιν ἀνάγκη·
Ἦτοι ὃ φορμίζων ἀνεβάλλετο καλὸν ἀείδειν·

To Phemius was consigned the chorded lyre,
Whose hand reluctant touched the warbling wire ;
Phemius, whose voice divine could sweetest sing
High strains, responsive to the vocal string.

This, however, is a custom by no means peculiar to the
Greeks. We know that each of the Highland clans
retained a bard expressly for the purpose of celebrating the
clan and its chief. We imagine we have seen something
of the same kind mentioned relative to the American and
Indian tribes.

The subject of the " Iliad " of course calls forth long and
spirited descriptions of the mode of warfare in use among
the ancient Greeks. This appears to us to exhibit plainer
marks of barbarism than any other part of their character.
They had all the untutored ferocity, the dependence on
personal strength or courage, which is characteristic of the
earliest ages, without the studied manœuvres and the
laboured machines which malicious invention afterwards
introduced. The greatest quality inherent in a commander
was not skill of head, but strength of limb ; few seemed to
lay claim to any nobler distinctions than those which were
to be found in the space between their shoulders. We
know not whether the rude struggling of these uncultivated
warriors is not a more interesting spectacle than the cold-
blooded massacres of modern days. In the hand-to-hand
conflict of two princes there is passion, and fury, and
enthusiasm, for which we look in vain to the cold and
calculating tactics of *l'art militaire.*

The war, indeed, of those times was naturally deficient in
everything technical or scientific. It abounded in instances
of individual devotion and of desperate enterprise, but had
no means of supplying by art the defect of numbers, or of
overcoming an obstinate enemy by a regular siege. It
rather resembled the foray of a few pillaging tribes, than the
contest between two powerful nations.

We shall see nothing to wonder at in this their undis-
ciplined warfare, when we remember that piracy, which it so

nearly resembled, was a mode of life to which they were greatly addicted. They saw in it nothing dishonourable; but on the contrary esteemed it a brave and worthy employment: their greatest heroes exercised it without the smallest scruple. They rather gloried in their robberies, and recounted with a feeling of pride their achievements and their plunder. Here again there is a manifest similarity between their ideas and those of the Highland clans. We do not know indeed if a very close parallel might not be drawn between the greaved Greek and the plaided mountaineer. We shall throw out a hint or two upon the subject, and recommend the plan to Mr. Golightly, if he wishes to be witty in our next Number.

In the first place, the love of rapine which we have just mentioned is inherent in both: the towns which fall beneath the ravages of the Greek are probably little superior in importance to the villages which excite the cupidity of the Scot. Both nations possess the same romantic notions of individual bravery: both value their booty rather from its being the prize of battle, than from the weight of the gold, or the number of the cattle, of which it consists. And to say the truth, when we behold, on the one side, Achilles retiring from his conquests, with his captives, and his treasures, and his beeves; and when we see, on the other, the chieftain of some kilted cian returning to his native fastnesses, and driving the fat of the land before him, we hardly know which of the two cuts the more respectable figure. Why do we attach such splendid ideas to the terror of Troy ? His rival is a more picturesque object for the design of the painter, he is as muscular a model for the chisel of the sculptor ; but the piracies of the Mountaineer will never be celebrated like the piracies of the Myrmidon ; for, alas ! Gaelic will never sound so classical as Greek !

Many of the superstitions of the one nation bear a striking resemblance to those of the cther. Both of them believe that their sages have the faculty of foreseeing and predicting future events ; both of them place great reliance on signs and auguries ; both imagine that the soul exists after death, and that it continues to take an interest in the pursuits and the friends whom it left upon earth. Much as

we are attached to the fooleries of our old friends before Troy
—to the victims, and the priests, and the oracles, we must
confess that, to our taste, the plaided seer, rapt up in his
vacant trance of second-sight, is a more interesting and a
more poetical object than all the mummeries of Delphos
or Dodona. But there is one point in this legendary
species of religion, in which the similarity appears to
us rather remarkable. We allude to that extraordinary
union of the opposite doctrines of free-will and predestination, which so forcibly obtrudes itself upon our notice
in examining the traditions of both countries. To discuss
this point at any length would require a greater portion
of time than we can devote to it; and we shall therefore content ourselves with observing that the fabulous
self-devotion of Achilles, who is said to have remained at
Troy, although conscious that he was destined to die there,
appears to us to have taken its rise from those notions of an
unavoidable fate which Homer so frequently expresses.
But this trait, which, as has been often observed, adds such
an exalted merit to the character of the hero, has many
parallels in the conduct of the Scottish clansmen, whose
chieftains we frequently find going with alacrity to battle,
although feeling a consciousness that they are seeking their
death. But look you there again!—the self-devotion of the
Mountaineer will never be celebrated like the self-devotion
of the Myrmidon; for, alas! Gaelic will never sound so
classical as Greek!

Another conspicuous ingredient in the character of both
is the pride which both take in ancestry. The Greek and
the Highlander take an equal delight in tracing the river
of their blood through distant generations, although we
fancy that the latter pays rather the most attention to
the purity of the stream. When he looks over the tree of
his genealogy, and exults in the glorious names which he
finds among its foliage, his feelings are not the less honest,
nor his happiness the less fervent, because he sees no
Jupiter in the root and no Venus perched among the
branches. And truly we do not see why the descent of the
Greek is of greater moment than the descent of the Scot,
except that patronymics in _ides_, and _ion_, and _iades_ have
certainly a nobler sound than plain, simple, unsophisticated

Mac. But look you there again!—the ancestry of the Mountaineer will never be celebrated like the ancestry of the Myrmidon; for, alas! Gaelic will never sound so classical as Greek!

When any important quarrel calls for a union of the forces under their numerous petty princes, the gathering of the Greek nations is precisely the gathering of the Highland clans. In both the commander-in-chief is chosen by the vote of the assembled leaders; in both, his authority is cramped and frustrated by the exclusive allegiance which is owed by each separate clan to its respective chieftain. In both, as may be supposed from the ill-concocted materials of which both armies are composed, quarrels and dissensions are perpetually taking place. And why are not the disputes of the tartans as worthy of song as the disputes of the spears and the helmets? They often arise from the same passions; they often spring from equally insignificant causes; they often lead to equally tragical results. But look you there. again!—the quarrels of the Mountaineer will never be celebrated like the quarrels of the Myrmidon; for, alas! Gaelic will never sound so classical as Greek!

We might go on to trace the simile, in the same strain, through many other qualities and customs. We might instance their mutual fondness for athletic exercises—the absolute authority exercised by the chiefs over the persons of their followers—the belief prevalent among both nations of the efficacy of music and charms in the cure of wounds —the custom of being constantly attended by large dogs— the union of heart and hand, which in both cases exists between the chief and his foster-brother. But this is idle— the *tout-ensemble* of the Mountaineer will never be celebrated like the *tout-ensemble* of the Myrmidon; for, alas! Gaelic will never sound so classical as Greek!

And now that we come to the end of what ought to have been ended a page ago, we recollect that we have been wandering through a great tract of paper; and we hear Mr. Golightly bellowing in our ears a reproof, in which we fear our readers will join him: " Mr. Swinburne, Mr. Swinburne, *Quid ad rem?*"

THE WEDDING:

A ROMAN TALE.

"Oh! snatched away in beauty's bloom,
  On thee shall press no ponderous tomb!"
                                        BYRON.

By the side of the Latin Way, amidst many other mementoes
of fallen greatness or faded beauty, there arose a small
pillar of white marble, bearing neither emblem nor inscription. The singular simplicity of its appearance frequently
excited the attention and inquiries of the passers-by, but
no one gratified their curiosity. She whom that marble
commemorated was known to few ; and those who remembered her told not of her virtues, for they shrank from the
pain they felt in the recital.

Julia was the daughter of distinguished and wealthy
parents, in the reign of Tiberius. She was an only child,
and had been educated with the fondest attention. When
she attained her eighteenth year she was very beautiful :
she was taller than most women ; her nose was aquiline,
her hair dark and glossy ; the smile that played on her lips
was provokingly arch, and in her large blue eyes dignity
was inexpressibly combined with tenderness. The qualities
of her heart were not inferior to those of her person ; so
that it is not to be wondered at that the hand of Julia was
solicited in marriage by the heirs of many of the first
families in Rome.

But she had early given away her affections to the son of
her father's brother. Young Cœlius was younger than his
cousin, and fortune had given him a lower station in life
and a humbler property. He was very handsome, however,
very accomplished, and perfectly amiable ; so that the
parents of Julia made no difficulty of acceding to the match.
The preliminary ceremonies had been gone through : the
hallowed straw * had been broken between the young

* *Stipula.*   Hence the term stipulation.

couple; the dower had been settled; the augurs had been consulted, and had returned a favourable answer. Finally, Cœlius had presented to his future bride the sacred ring which was to be the pledge of their eternal affection. It was a plain circle of gold, with the inscription "*in æternum!*" It was customary to put these rings upon the fourth finger of the left hand, because it was imagined that a vein ran immediately from that finger to the heart. It was a foolish superstition, but Cœlius was observed to shudder when Julia placed her ring upon the wrong finger.

One of the rejected suitors of Julia was a favourite with the Emperor. When our tale is of a creature so pure and so unhappy as Julia, we cannot waste our time in describing the characters of the wretches by whom her death was effected. It is enough for our purpose to say that Marcius made use of the influence he possessed in such a manner that the father of Julia trembled for his fortune and his life; he began to retract the engagements by which he was bound to his nephew, and to devise plans for the marriage of his daughter with the court favourite.

Cœlius was an orphan. He had been educated under the same roof with Julia; and his guardians had hitherto been amply repaid for the expense of his maintenance by the reflection that they were instructing the husband of their child. Now, however, they began to be vexed by having him always before their eyes; they saw that the accomplishment of their scheme was impossible while he remained with their daughter, and they prepared to remove him. The union of those affectionate hearts was procrastinated for a long time upon various pretences; at last the young man was sent, in order to complete his education, upon a tour, with permission to return in a year and claim his betrothed bride.

The year passed sadly away. He was forbidden to keep up any correspondence with his cousin until its expiration. At last the happy June arrived which allowed him to return—which permitted him to meet the gaze of those bright eyes, in whose sight only he seemed to live. He flew to Rome on the wings of expectancy!

As he approached the dwelling-place of his hopes, his

thoughts, his happiness, circumstances occurred which filled him with the gloomiest forebodings. Several of his young acquaintance; when they met him, shook their heads, and endeavoured to avoid his address. As he passed by the mansion of his once-contemned rival, he observed a slave clad in unusual finery; and "What!" he said, "is Marcius to feast the Emperor to-day?" "Marcius," said the slave, "will feast a fairer guest—he will bring home his bride to-night!" Cœlius started as if a viper had crossed his path; but he recovered himself immediately. "It was but a suspicion!" he said, "and I will have done with it!" He said no more, but ran on with desperate impetuosity to the well-known door. He heeded not the malicious rumours, and the compassionate whispers, which were circulated around him: with a fluttering heart and faltering step he hurried to the chamber which had been the scene of their last parting. As he put his hand upon the door, a thousand visions flocked upon his brain. "Then she was good, and affectionate, and beautiful, and true; and she looked upon me so tenderly, and spoke to me so kindly;—and now, will her look be as tender, and her voice as kind? I will be in suspense no longer!" He thrust open the door and stood in her presence.

She was sitting at the window, half-shaded from his view by some beautiful orange-trees. She did not seem to have observed his entrance; for she did not rise from her seat, nor move her head from the delicate white hand which was supporting it. "Julia!" he cried, in a voice of the wildest passion; but she did not stir. "Julia," he said, coming nearer, and speaking in a calmer tone; still she was motionless. "Julia," he whispered gently, bending his head over the orange-blossoms. Their lips almost met; she started from him as if from profanation. "Cœlius!" she exclaimed, "this must not be! I have broken the holy cake* with another! To-night I shall be the wife of Marcius."

He lifted his hands to Heaven; a curse rose to his lips. "May the vows you have falsified—may the hopes you have blighted—may the heart you have broken—— But no, Julia," he continued, as he gazed upon her rayless eye, and

* The ceremony was rarely, if ever, used in the reign of Tiberius.

her colourless cheek; "you have suffered much—and I cannot—I cannot reproach you!" He hid his tears with his hands, and rushed into the street.

She had indeed suffered much! Her face had become pale and emaciated, her step melancholy and slow: she no longer took her wonted care in arranging her dress, or setting in order her luxuriant hair; but this was not the alteration which had shocked her unfortunate lover—it was the languor which had succeeded to her natural liveliness, the despondency in her every accent, the absence of soul in her every look!

The evening came, and the ceremony was near at hand. Julia suffered her attendants to adorn her, reckless herself of the pains they took and the decorations they bestowed. They put upon her a long white robe, quite plain; it would have well set off the bloom of her loveliness, but upon the paleness of her sorrow it seemed to sit like a shroud. They made large masses of her hair to flow dishevelled down her neck, and mingled with it locks of wool, to signify that, in her new station, she was to imitate the purity of the vestals, whose peculiar emblem it was. The extremities of her long ringlets were curled and arranged with the steel of a lance; and among her attendants there were many pretty flutterings and drawings-back as they handled so terrible a comb. Then they suffered her to wait in quiet the approach of the bridegroom. He was not long in his coming. They drew over her head the crown of vervain, and concealed her deathlike features beneath the flame-coloured veil. They put on, too, the yellow slippers, which it was the fashion for brides to wear: they were so contrived as to add considerably to the height, but Julia's was so much diminished by sadness and disease, that even with this assistance she did not seem near her usual stature

It was night; and she was borne to the house of her husband by the light of flambeaux. Three young persons, whose parents were still living, were her conductors. Two supported her, and Julia indeed stood in need of support; the third walked before her, bearing a torch of pine. A distaff and spindle, a child's coral, and other emblems of her future duties, were carried behind her. Her friends and relations also followed, each bearing in his arms some present to the new married couple. Cœlius was among them, but he concealed his face in the folds of his gown, and his smothered sighs attracted no observation.

At last they came to the threshold of the bridegroom : it was tastefully adorned with wreaths of flowers ; and woollen fillets, smeared with oil, were hung round to keep out enchantments. The master of the house stood at the door, and the crowd gathered round it to witness the conclusion of the ceremony.

They asked her, according to custom, under what title she came ? She had opened her lips to answer, when Cœlius ran forward and threw himself between Marcius and his beloved. "Oh ! no, no ! " he cried ; " I cannot hear it ! —do not, do not kill me quite ! " "Back, back ! " she said, shuddering. "Shall I not obey my father ? " The youth heard not—saw not ; he was led away, senseless and unresisting ; and the ceremony proceeded. Again she was asked under what title she came ; and she answered, as was prescribed for her, in a low but distinct tone, " Ubi tu Caius, ego Caia ! " * They lifted her from the ground, for it was reckoned an evil omen to touch the threshold in her entrance. They lifted her from the ground, and she spoke no word, and made no struggle. But ere they had set down her foot upon her husband's floor, she trembled with a convulsive quivering, and her head fell back upon the youth who supported her left shoulder. Again they put down their burden, but it was quite motionless ! They tore the veil from her head—her look was fixed and quiet— her eye open and dull ! She was quite dead !

* This was the customary response, signifying, "Where you are the master I shall be mistress."

PRIVATE CORRESPONDENCE OF PEREGRINE COURTENAY.

I.

PEREGRINE OF CLUBS TO GEORGE OF ENGLAND.

MAY IT PLEASE YOUR MAJESTY,

I AM your loyal subject, and an editor. I am induced to address you in print by three considerations. First, I am like yourself, a King ; although my c'aim to the title is not quite so legitimate as your Majesty's. Secondly, I am an author, and it is much the fashion with authors of the present day to indite letters to the Crown. Thirdly, I am enthusiastically fond of novelty in every shape ; and I flatter myself I am going to strike one—·a letter to the King, without an ounce of politics in its composition.

I am not going to offer my congratulations upon "glorious accession," " recent successes," or " the flourishing state of our manufactures ; " neither am I going to present you with memorials relating to " excessive taxation," " starving weavers," or " Ilchester Gaol." I am myself too tired of flattery and abuse to offer such insipid dishes to the palate of a brother monarch. No, Sire ! I am about to offer you some observations upon that part of your Majesty's dominions which falls more immediately under the notice of the King of Clubs—the Royal Foundation of Eton.

May it please your Majesty, I have been long a member of it, and I am sure that (*exceptis excipiendis*) you have not in any part of your sovereignty five hundred better disposed subjects than are to be met with in its "antique towers." I shall not therefore be repulsed with harshness if I lay before you a few of the grievances, or the fancied grievances, under which we labour.

I think it was in the year 1814 that I first saw your

Majesty at Frogmore. The Emperor of Russia was there, and the King of Prussia, and Blucher, and Platoff, and sundry other worthies, whom were I to attempt to enumerate the line would reach out "to the crack of doom." One single individual of that illustrious body could have drawn all London to the Monument, if he had promised to exhibit himself in the gallery; and we, favoured alumni, had the privilege of staring by wholesale. I never shall forget the reception of those illustrious potentates. All voices were loud in hurras, all hats were waving in the air; and there was such a squeezing, and pushing, and shouting, and shaking of hands, and treading on toes, that I have often wondered how I escaped in safety from the perils into which my enthusiasm threw me.

Never shall I forget the soul-enlivening moment when your Majesty, stepping into the midst of our obstreperous group, proclaimed aloud, "A whole holiday for the Emperor of Russia." (Cheering.) "A whole holiday for the King of Prussia." (Renewed cheering.) "Now, my boys," you said, with a good-humoured laugh that set Whiggism and awe at defiance, "I must add my mite"—and there was long, loud, reiterated, unanimous, heartfelt cheering. In that look of yours there were years of intimacy. The distinction which rank had placed between us seemed at once overturned; you raised us up to your own level, or rather you deigned to come down for a moment to ours. One could almost have imagined that you had been yourself an Etonian, that you had shared in our amusements, that you had tasted of our feelings !

It was a proud evening for Eton, but a troublesome one for those who made it so. The warmth of an English welcome is enough to overpower any one but an Englishman. Platoff swore he was more pestered by the Etonians than he had ever been by the French; and the kind old Blucher had his hand so cordially wrung that he was unable to lift his bottle for a week afterwards. To your Majesty the recollection of that evening must have been one of unmingled gratification. You had enjoyed that truly royal pleasure, which springs from the act of bestowing pleasure upon others; you had been applauded by Etonians, as the patron of Etonians ought to be ; you purchased more than three hundred whole hearts at the price of only three whole holidays.

It would be needless, as it would be endless, to enumerate all the instances of Royal favour which since that time have been extended towards our Foundation ; I have not room to give an extended narration of the cricketing at Frogmore, nor to describe your Majesty's visit to our Triennial Montem. One subject, however, there is, the omission of which would be both irksome to myself and ungrateful to your Majesty. I mean the gracious liberality which gave to the school your lamented father had so constantly esteemed the permission to attend at his obsequies, and follow their patron to his grave. That unsolicited attention, and the delicate manner in which the notice of it was conveyed to us, live still in our hearts. They proved to us that you were aware of the loss we had sustained; they proved to us that by your munificence that loss would be alleviated or repaired.

Having thus performed what I conceived to be my duty, by expressing the sense we entertain of your Majesty's bounty, let me call your attention to the situation in which we are now placed.

Eton is a soil which has been used to the sun of Royal patronage, and, if that invigorating heat is withheld, what can be expected but that the earth should be unproductive, and that its plants should fade? This is a most comfortable doctrine, inasmuch as it enables us to set down to your Majesty's account all the degeneracy which modern Eton is said to exhibit. The remedy is as obvious as the evil. Pay us a visit! Are our cricketers weak in the arm? Your patronage shall add vigour to their sinews! Are our poets weak in the head? Your encouragement shall give new life to their hippocrene! Are our alumni diminishing in numbers? Beneath your influence recruits shall tumble in like locusts! Are they diminishing in stature? They shall grow like mustard beneath a Royal smile.

This, however, is all theory and speculation. There are many who will attribute our degeneracy to other causes, and many who will deny that there is any degeneracy in the case at all. I am now going to mention a specific grievance, the

existence of which no one can deny, and to which your
Majesty alone can apply a remedy.   During the life of your
father we enjoyed three annual holidays, under the de-
nomination of " King's visits ;" and the enjoyment of them
had become so much a thing of course, that few were aware
upon how short a tenure we held our blessings.   They are
gone !   We have no " King's visits," because your Majesty
has never visited Eton.

It seems to be pretty well determined that your Majesty,
sooner or later, will visit some place or other.   Some
recommend a visit to Hanover, some recommend a visit to
Ireland—I recommend a visit to Eton.   It will be less
troublesome, less expensive, and less formal, than either of
its rival proposals.   It will be soonest begun, and it will be
the soonest over.   It would be without a hundred inconveniences which would wait upon your two other
journeys.   At Eton, you would not be bothered by counts
and courtiers ; you would not be stifled with Phelims and
·Patricks ; you would not he pestered with German addresses,
as at Hanover; and you would not have to dine with the
Mayor and Corporation, as at Dublin.

The time of your visit I will not presume to point out.   If
you happen to come on the fourth of this month, you will
find certain illicit proceedings going on, which I cannot in
this place describe.   I can tell you, however, that we shall
have a splendid show, and a band that shall play "God
save the King," *ad infinitum*.   If you prefer being present
at our public speeches, as your Majesty's father occasionally
was, you will hear much embryo oratory and see much
sawing of the air.

To be serious—may it please your Majesty, I think you
ought to come to Eton.   Let us have due notice of the
honour intended us, and you shall be received in a style
worthy both of us and of you.   Come, and by your coming
disperse over the face of Etona her wonted smile : paste
another bright leaf into her annals : give a new excitement
to her talents, her studies, and her amusements.   You need
not come in state : you must not depart in a hurry : bring
to us as many smiles, and as few lords, as you please : above
all, drive away for an hour the formality of dress and

manner which public life enjoins ; come to us provided with an English heart, and dressed in the Windsor uniform.

On Windsor Bridge you shall be met by the Fellows with "God save the King," and, as you step into College, you shall be saluted by my friend the Captain with a Latin address. This shall not detain you longer than three minutes and a half; and Sir Benjamin Bloomfield shall hold the watch. You will then be conducted to all the lions of the College, amongst which you will feel particularly interested in the new library established last month, and you will probably put a small donation into the hands of Mr. Hawkins, the Treasurer. After your peregrinations you will have the option of taking a cold collation with the Provost, or a hot beefsteak with the King of Clubs. If you prefer the former, my duty for the day is over ; but if, as I prognosticate, your choice falls upon the latter, the talents of Mr. Rowley shall be forthwith put in requisition. We will give your Majesty a real English dinner, and a hearty welcome. I will not present my book unless your Majesty desires it, and your Majesty shall not be required to knight any of the Club, unless you would condescend to confirm the title of my worthy friend Sir Thomas. We will be very merry, may it please your Majesty, and we will have your Majesty's favourite punch, if your Majesty will give us the recipe. Mr. Oakley shall be driven from the Club-room, and we will make our furious Whig, Sir Francis, sing loyal staves in honour of the occasion. If this does not bring you to Eton, I don't know what will— that's all.

In the evening your Majesty shall return to—bless my soul, I had forgotten the holidays. But your own good-nature will prompt you. I have finished my epistle, and— may it please your Majesty.

(Signed)   PEREGRINE.

II.

PEREGRINE COURTENAY TO MR. BENJ. BOOKWORM.

[Mr. Courtenay is both surprised and grieved to hear that the unwarrantable curiosity of the public has cast a sacrilegious eye upon
his private correspondence; and that his private letter to a
brother monarch has been made the subject of animadversions
totally unjustifiable. To prevent mistakes, he thinks it necessary to
inform the public that his private correspondence is—*not to
be read.*]

MY DEAR BENJAMIN,

ALLOW me to congratulate you upon the happy termination
of your literary labours. Allow me to congratulate you,
not hypocritically, or sarcastically, or triumphantly, but
sincerely, and as a friend. We have been long opposed to
each other, as writers; and although the sword of attack
was sheathed by me almost as soon as it was drawn, on
your side its point has been constantly protruded in a very
threatening attitude. I mean not to complain of this; I
will say nothing but what is civil and conciliatory; it would
be unmanly in me to do otherwise, now that my adversary
is *hors du combat.* Well then, you have said your say, and
we will, if you please,

> Leave this keen encounter of our wits,
> And fall to something of a slower method.

I have heard it remarked, my good Benjamin, that your
last number is somewhat dear. I must confess, and I
believe you must confess, that the matter contained therein
is somewhat scanty; but nevertheless, as it is the last time
I shall have an opportunity of patronizing you, I have not
grudged you my shilling. You have taken leave very
decently, or, in the words of the old housewives, "You
have made a good end!" I must say I rather envy you.
But there is one passage in your last scene which rather
surprised me:

"If the *Etonian* has behaved in a manner unworthy of its
conductors towards the *Salt-Bearer*, there is no reason that
I should retaliate a single word upon them!

My magnanimous rival! Let us go over the grounds of our squabble temperately.

I was originally, as you know, the conductor of a small miscellany in manuscript; I was requested to establish a periodical publication in its place. I declined it, on the ground that the talent of Eton was not adequate to such an undertaking. Soon after the *Salt-Bearer* was advertised. I felt a curiosity to know something of its authors, because, had the work been conducted by any person upon whose discretion or authority I could rely, I should have been glad to have supported him to the best of my abilities. I made inquiries, without effect, among such of my school-fellows as were most distinguished for genius or industry : it was suggested to me that the *Salt-Bearer* was not actually set on foot by an Etonian, or at least not by one at that time belonging to the school. I made inquiries upon this point at your bookseller's, and could get no answer. Was it not natural enough for me to believe that my suspicions were correct? I did believe so, and I made no secret of my belief. Was I obliged by any motive of justice to withhold my ideas respecting one who voluntarily thrust himself in a mask before the public? Who has any scruple in expressing his opinions relative to Junius?—or the Scotch novelist—or *John Bull?*

Well! the work appeared, and if I thought that it was not calculated to advance the credit of Enton, my judgment may have been erroneous; but it was t' Bjudgment of many persons, wiser far than either Persgrine Courtenay or Benjamin Bookworm. I expressed that judgment, and my reasons for it, very openly; and again I must ask, by what principle should I have been withheld from doing so? There were one or two cuts at myself in your *début*, but they were so insignificant that I cannot even censure you for making use of them.

The work proceeded, and some friends, who took more interest in my little manuscript miscellany than it deserved, wished me to publish some extracts from it, in order to do away the stain which the reputation of Eton had suffered from the writings of the *Salt-Bearer*. It is needless for me to explain why the project of the *Selection* was given up, and that of the *Etonian* substituted in its place. Suffice it to say that the hearty promises of support which I immediately received convinced me that those of my schoolfellows whose good opinion I wished to enjoy were not displeased at the steps I had taken.

When the first number of the *Etonian* was in a state of forwardness, I received from a friend, whom no one can know without esteem, some very witty remarks upon the *Salt-Bearer*, intended for insertion in the King of Clubs; it had been my intention to refrain from any mention of your publication, but the remarks in question amused me so much that I felt very loth to withhold them from my readers. While I was thus wavering, your fourth number appeared, in which I was alluded to in a most extraordinary manner. I have not room to quote the whole of your attack. I was accused of "rancour," "malice," "pride," "hatred" —and a variety of ill-natured offences.

Alas! the infirmities of human nature! I confess it, Mr. Bookworm, I flew into a most devouring passion. I lost my temper, Mr. Bookworm, and I shouted, "To arms!" And, truth to say, a youth like me, who had all his life preserved a good, respectable, quiet, silly sort of character; who had always had a great propensity to sitting indoors, and a great horror of duelling; who had borne no reputation more disgraceful than that of "Sap," no nickname more opprobrious than that of "Toup"—I say, Mr. Bookworm, such a youth as this is apt to fly off at a tangent, when he was fulminated at by so horrible an assailant. I repeat it—I lost my temper; I hurried to the printing-office; and I not only discharged the light javelin* which had been put into my hands by my friend, but took from my own armoury a less keen, but more ponderous weapon, which you may look for in the "Second Meeting of the Club." I confess it; I was very abusive. But my abuse lighted upon literary, not moral character. I believe I accused you of dulness, stupidity, presumption; I am not sure if I did not call you a blockhead! But if I had said one word of "malice," "rancour," or "hatred," I should have felt it my duty to apologize for it long ago!

Well! No. I., with all its severity, went forth to the

---

* The greater part of the satire here alluded to was retrenched in our Second Edition.

world; I grew cool, and I was sorry that I had been so violent. I said to myself, "If the author of this work receives my attack in silence, and honours me with not one word in reply, he will take a high ground, and obtain a superiority over me which I shall never be able to recover." This made me very uneasy.

By-and-by your next number appeared! I was happier than you can conceive! Every sarcasm I had uttered was answered by one twice as furious; if Peregrine was angry, Benjamin was mad. I hugged the dear invectives with delight: as you waxed more wrathful I waxed more pleased; and at last, when, as the climax of my happiness, I found that you had been carping at the "Lines to ——," those lines which would have done honour to any living poet; those lines which, had they appeared in your columns, would have made the *Salt-Bearer* worthy of immortality— then I flung down the book in transport, and exclaimed, " Our enemies are the best friends we have!"

From that time to the present the *Etonian* has never renewed the contest. The answers, however, which you have published to the strictures of a correspondent upon Wordsworth and Coleridge have shown that the *Salt-Bearer* was somewhat reluctant to lay down the cudgels. There was also an occasional sly hit at Peregrine—especially one on the score of plagiarism, which the author did not think fit to support by any examples. You remember the lines "To a Young Lady on her Fourteenth Birthday," inserted in your fourth number? You have accused me of plagiarism, but I did not retaliate. Neither was I severe upon your literary connection with a certain Mr. H., because I believe that connection was at least commenced when you were ignorant of the man's notorious character.

And now, after the furious reply in your fifth number, and the occasional hits in its successors, you come forward and say, "There is no reason that I should retaliate a single word." The palpable absurdity of this generosity must be so evident both to yourself and your readers that I need say no more upon the subject.

At all events our warfare is now over. I know not what your feelings may be towards me, but I assure you that in mine not a particle of hostility exists: if I may use the

G

expression, I have shaken hands with you, not *re verâ*, but by a poetical license. I feel no reluctance in allowing that the prose composition of your latter numbers has exhibited many signs of improvement; and that if the support you have received has been no greater than I believe it to have been, the editor of the *Salt-Bearer* has gone through his work respectably.

You and I, Mr. Bookworm, have made much noise in our day, and have excited, among our fellow-Etonians, a greater sensation than two such insignificant beings ever excited before. There has been much talk about us, which has now, I believe, ceased; and there has been much hot blood between us, which has now, I trust, grown cool. For my part, I can look back to our early disputes as if they were the events of a former age; and detect our respective blunders and mistakes as calmly as if I were making the same examination into the conduct of our great-grand-fathers.

When I throw a glance over the journey which our Etonian writers have travelled, I fancy that I see three different routes leading towards the same point. In the centre, Messrs. Griffin and Gildrig are riding a couple of clever nags, at a good round trot: on one side, Mr. Bookworm is bestriding what is commonly termed "a safe cob for an infirm gentleman," which scrambles over his ground in such a manner that the spectators imagine he will come to a dead stop every instant; on the other side is Mr. Courtenay, whip and spur, whip and spur, the whole way—up hill and down hill, bush and briar, furze and fence, it is the same thing. Mr. C., they say, never uses a curb; and the animal occasionally waxes so formidably obstinate that he has infinite difficulty in keeping his seat.

The meaning of all this is, that it would have been well for you to have had a little less discretion, and for me to have had a little more; it would have been well for you to have drunk a little more punch, and for me to have drunk a little less. But what could I do? The *Salt-Bearer* appeared, and was voted milk and water! It was necessary for me to prepare a more potent beverage. I will venture to assert, that if the *Microcosm* itself had appeared immediately after the *Salt-Bearer*, its success would have been precarious. Eton wanted something more pungent ! The *Etonian* substituted the punch-bowl for the tea-pot ; and people ran away from Mr. Bookworm's best Bohea to see Mr. Golightly squeezing the lemons.

I, Peregrine Courtenay, as is well known, am a very sober long-faced sort of editor, somewhat of a friend to a quiet pint of ale or a social glass of old port, but a most abominable enemy (I hope Sir Thomas will not be angry) to everything that bears the name of downright jollification. I was therefore not less surprised than my friends at finding myself a member—nay, the president of a club—so formidably jovial. Many times during the first week of my reign did I turn round in an absent fit and exclaim, " How in the name of sobriety did I come here ? " However, finding that there were no spirits in our punch-bowl saving the spirit of good-humour, and no danger of intoxication saving the intoxication of success, I gradually became reconciled to my situation, and can now get drunk, in print, with very tolerable success. With you, however, my dear sir, I am quite sober. I would not have ventured to obtrude myself upon your retirement in a condition of which you could have disapproved. I do assure you, upon the word of an editor, that I have drunk nothing this morning but some " Meanders of Sensibility," by " Juvenis,' very weak and corky indeed ; and some " Tricklings from Tweed," by "Allen-a-Dale," the first bottle of which has poisoned half the Club.

I have been remarking upon the birth of you and me. Let me now look back to your decease, and forward (alas !) to my own.

You have taken leave of your readers, I must say, pretty decently. I regret, however, that you have not thought fit to disclose to the world the names of your several correspondents, and the papers for which you are indebted to them. I regret it not, believe me, from any silly curiosity, but merely from a regard for your own character. I wish you had shown (I know you could have shown) that it was not your hand which put " rancour " and "malice" and "hatred" into your fourth number ; that it was

G 2

not your ingenuity which coined that unlucky null*æ* in your fifth. But, however—you have delivered your farewell address, and I am getting ready mine. On the 28th of July—I weep as I think of it—the Club will be dissolved, and the *Etonian* will be no more.

In the concealment of your correspondents' names, I think I shall not imitate you. It is at present my intention to adopt a contrary line of conduct. I am actuated in this by two very opposite motives—by a feeling of modesty and a feeling of pride. Modesty induces me to take care that I may not be commended, as I have been, for writings which are another's ; and that others may not be abused, as they have been, for writings which are mine. Pride, on the other hand, compels me to wish that my name may appear in print, coupled with names which are, and long will be, a part of our most triumphant recollections. When I reflect exultingly on the powerful minds upon which Peregrine Courtenay has leaned for support, I would fain hope that in after years he may continue to share in their praises—to partake of their immortality !

I shall be very sorry, Mr. Bookworm, to give up my editorship ; and yet, upon second thoughts, I think I shall be very glad. To say the truth—the plain, honest, un-varnished, unsophisticated truth—editorship is a desperate bore. *Eh bien!* I did not encounter it voluntarily ! As Shakespeare says, "Some are born great, some achieve greatness, and some have greatness thrust upon them !"

What a bore it is to have an idle contributor ! "My dear Mr. Montgomery ! your pen has been dry a long time, and we can ill do without you." "I will go to work immediately, Mr. Courtenay ; what shall it be ?—another essay !" "Excellent !" "But then I'm so idle ! or another Somnium ?" "Admirable !" "But then I'm so idle ! or another poem in the *Ottava Rima ?*" "Inimitable !" "But then I'm so in-com-pre-hen-si-bly idle !"

What a bore it is to be criticized by a blockhead ! "Mr. Editor, the public opinion of your merits is higher than it should be." "I beg your pardon, sir, but I think you are singular in your opinion." "Mr. Editor, your levities are disgusting !" "I beg your pardon, sir, but I think you are mistaken !" "Mr. Editor, your impertinence is insufferable !" "I beg your pardon, sir, but I think you are——"

What a bore it is to have a troublesome contributor. "Mr. Moonshine, it's absolutely impossible for me to insert your ode." "My ode! oh! dock it, and dress it, and alter it; I leave it quite to your judgment; you'll oblige me—really now!" "I have made a few corrections here, Mr. Moonshine. I hope you approve." "Approve! why zounds! Courtenay, I won't swear, but you've cut out the sting, the point, the attraction of the whole. Look here, man, what have you done! Bless me! what have you done with Urien's beard?" "Urien's beard, sir! Oh! Urien's beard was too long, a great deal too long, sir; flowed through three stanzas and a half. I have used the razor, shaved him pretty close, indeed!" "Ignorance! May you never have a beard of your own to shave, or a razor to shave with! And, murder! sir, what have you done with Ætna—my 'ejaculated flames,' my 'vomit of sulphur,' and my 'artillery of Tellus?'" "Why, really, sir, without a joke, your Ætna was too loud—too loud, a great deal, sir; and you have put too much fire in it—oh! by far too much fire; more fire than Ætna ever vomited since she swallowed her first emetic!" "Fire, Mr. Courtenay! You have left my verses cold as the love of a blockhead, or Sir Thomas Nesbit before his morning's draught! However, sir, I depend on my picture of Melpomene in my last strophe! Don't you think it must strike, Mr. Editor?" "Strike, sir! I have struck it out!" "Struck it out! struck out Melpomene! What! the 'pale blue eye,' and the 'gaze of wonderment,' and the 'long dishevelled hair,' and the dagger, and the bowl!" "It went to my heart, sir, to strike out a bowl of any sort, but it was the most insipid bowl I ever tasted!" "Go to the devil, Mr. Courtenay!" "I am going there this minute, Mr. Moonshine; but, upon my honour, the ode can't go with me!"

What a bore it is to be pointed at! What a bore it is to be laughed at! What a bore it is to correct manuscripts! What a bore it is to correct proofs! What a bore it is to scribble all day! What a bore it is to scribble all night! What a bore it is to—— But I will stop before I work myself into a fever!

Helas! My trammels are indeed heavy upon me; but you have got rid of yours. Whether you have retired to your Sabine farm, or to the sacred recesses of Granta; whether you are chopping logic, or chopping cabbages; whether you are invocating Mathesis or the Muse; whether you are dreaming of problems or of proof-sheets—of the Senate House or of second editions;—assure yourself, Mr. Bookworm, that the best wishes of Peregrine Courtenay are with you; and allow him to conclude, as he began, by congratulating you most sincerely.

Yours editorially,

Peregrine Courtenay.

III.

PEREGRINE COURTENAY TO THE PUBLIC.

My dear Public,

How rejoiced I feel in being able to rid myself of all weighty affairs for a few minutes, and sit down to a little private conversation with you. I am going, as usual, to be very silly, and very talkative, and I have so much to say that I hardly know where to begin.

Allow me to congratulate you upon the flourishing state of your affairs. There has been a Coronation, and you have had lighting of lamps, and drinking of ale, and breaking of heads, to you heart's content; and there are two new novels coming from Sir Walter, and the King is going to Ireland, and Mr. Kean is come from America, and—here is No. X. of the *Etonian!* How happy you must be!

But you will have to pay an extra shilling for it. I hope you will not be angry. The fact is, that the approaching conclusion of our work has put into our contributors such a spirit of goodwill and exertion, that we found it quite impossible to comprise their benefactions within our usual limits, although I myself gave up to them many of my own pages, and burned several first-rate articles, especially one

"On the Digamma," which would have had a surprising effect. For, to parody the poet,

Those write now, who never wrote before,
And those who always wrote, now write the more.

And you will be satisfied, I think, with the augmentation of bulk and of price, when you consider what you would have lost if such a step had not been adopted. Perhaps you might not have had "The Bride of the Cave ;" perhaps you might not have had "The Hall of my Fathers ;" perhaps you might not have had—oh, yes ! you certainly should have had "Maimoune," though it had filled our whole number. But you would not have had my "Private Correspondence," which I should have regretted extremely, although my modesty hints to me that you would not have cared a rush about the matter.

I used to promise, you will remember, that in all and in each of our numbers, twenty pages only should be devoted to our foreign correspondents. This resolution was, I believe, rigidly adhered to during the existence of the *Salt-Bearer ;* but since his exit I have grown more idle and less scrupulous. In our present number you will find a much greater proportion of matter from the Universities. I tell you so fearlessly, because you are, in no small degree, a gainer by the fraud.

When I look back on my life, my dear public, I cannot help thinking what a life of impudence, what a life of hoaxing, what a life of singularity, I have led. If all the brass I have shown in my writings could be transferred to my monument, my memory would be immortal. I have told, in print, more lies than ever Munchausen did ; and, in the sphere of my existence, have been guilty of as much deceit as the Fortunate Youth. As for the "Letter to the King," however, I can't, for the life of me, see a grain of impertinence in its composition ; all I wonder at is that it did not procure a holiday for Eton, nor knighthood for Sir Thomas, nor a thousand a year for myself. Nevertheless, in spite of the mortifying silence with which my communication was received, I am happy to observe that our Etonians continue very loyal. On the night of the Coronation, when the mob said "Queen !" the boys said "King !" and many, forthwith, risked their own crowns in behalf of his Majesty's. But whether this proceeded from the love of loyalty, or the love of blows, must remain a question.

Howbeit, I am not naturally addicted to impudence, or hoaxing, or singularity. To convince you of this, I had at one time an intention of drawing up a memoir of my own life, containing an accurate detail of my thoughts and words and actions during the whole period which my memory comprehends. I found it very difficult to settle the title of my book. Should it be the stately "Life of Peregrine Courtenay, Esq., of the College of Eton, foolscap octavo"? or should it be the quaint "Notice of a Gentleman who has left Long Chamber?" or should it be the concise and attractive "Peregriniana"? It was a weighty affair; and I abandoned the design before I could settle the point. For I at last began to believe, my public, that this is all of which you ought to be informed—that I have lived long at Eton, and that have I edited the *Etonian;* that I am now bidding farewell to the first, and writing the epilogue of the other.

I leave Eton at a peculiarly auspicious time. Her cricket is very good this year (I wish we could have had a meeting with Harrow, but *Diis aliter visum est*), and her boats are unusually well manned, and there are in her ranks more youths of five-feet-ten than I have seen for a long time. She has also just effected the establishment of a public library, which has been so spiritedly supported by our *alumni* themselves, and by the friends of the school, that it is already rising into importance. And, thanks to the exertions of many who have been our friends, and a few of our correspondents, she maintains a high ground at the Universities. I am bound for Cambridge myself; but this is nothing at all to concern you, inasmuch as I do not mean to edit a *Cantab.*

I resign my office too at a propitious moment, before time has quelled the enthusiasm with which it was entered upon—before warmth and impetuosity have yielded to weariness and disgust. My spirits are still unabated, my friends are still untired, and you, my public, are still kind! I might have waited to experience the sinking of the first, the anger of the second, and alas! the fickleness of the third. It is well that I stop in time.

I have two drawers of my bureau filled, almost to bursting, with divers manuscripts; I am afraid to open either of them, lest somebody passionate, or somebody stupid, or somebody wearisome should stare me in the face. Of these compositions, my pages witness against me that I have promised insertion to many, and my conscience witnesses against me that I ought to have given insertion to many more. I don't know what to do with them. I have some thoughts of sending them to my publisher's in a lump, or bequeathing them as a legacy to my successors. I believe, however, my better plan may be to put them up to auction. Amongst the numerous authors, great and small, good and bad, who are at the present day wasting their pen, ink, paper, and time, in "doing honour to Eton," I cannot but think that some of my literary treasures would fetch a pretty good price. There are all the articles, of which we have at various times given notice; some of which I know our readers are dying to see. But these form but a trifling part of the heap; I will subjoin a few specimens of my wares, but catalogues shall, of course, be printed previous to the sale.

Several "Reminiscences"—very useful for writers who wish to recollect what never occurred.

A few "Visions," "Musings," "Odes," &c.—a great bargain to any young person who wants to be interesting, or unintelligible.

"Edmund Ironside, an Old English Tale," in the style of "The Knight and the Knave," very valuable—in consequence of the *Quarterly's* hint about "Ivanhoe."

"Thoughts on the Coronation," to be had for a trifle, as the article is a common one, and will not keep.

A great many "Classical Tales," strongly recommended to those authors who are not learned, and wish to be thought so.

A large bundle of "Notices to Correspondents," admirably adapted to the use of those who have none.

A portfolio of cursory hints, remarks, puns, introductory observations, windings-up, &c., capable of serving any purpose to which the purchaser likes to put them.

With such a repository, it will be evident that, if the Fates were willing that I should proceed in my undertaking, I should be in no want of support. This, however, is not the decree of the Destinies; I must go, and like him who

Oft fitted the halter, oft traversed the cart,
And often took leave, but seemed loth to depart,

I continue to say to you, I am " going, going, going," while you methinks are waiting with the uplifted hammer, impatient to pronounce me "gone!"

Everybody, who wishes to do anything worthy of record, is anxious to know what will be said of him after his decease. I am thinking what will be said of me, after my literary death.

I fancy to myself a knot of ladies, busy with their Loo and scandal. The tenth, the last number of the *Etonian*, is brought upon the carpet, and every one flies at Peregrine in the flirting of a fan. "So he's gone, is he! Well, it's time he should; he was getting sadly tiresome;"—"and so satirical;"—"and so learned;"—"as for all his Greek, I'm sure it must be very bad, for Lord St. Luke can't construe me a word of it, and he was three years at Oxford;"—"and that abominable ' Certain Age!'"—"and that odious ' Windsor Ball'"—"Oh! positively we can never forgive the ' Windsor Ball!' I have not bought a copy since!" Pray be quiet, ladies; I never meant one of you—never, on the word of an editor! Howbeit, if the cap fits——you know what I would say, though politeness shall leave it unsaid.

Then I picture to my mind a set of sober critics taking my reputation to pieces, as easily as you would crack a walnut. "Peregrine. Courtenay?—ay! he was a silly, laughing fellow. He had some spirit; yes—and a tolerable rhyme now and then; but he had no sense, no solidity; he was all froth, all evaporation. He was like the wine we are drinking—he had no body! 'Where did you get this wine, Mr. Matthew?'" And so I am dismissed

Then I begin to think of what is much more interesting to me. What will be the talk of my schoolfellows? I fancy that I hear their censures, and their praises not sparingly bestowed. I fancy that I am already taken up with kindness, or laid down with a shrug! "The *Etonian!* oh! the last number is out, is it? How does it sell?

Some of it was good, but I wish they had less of their
balaam, as they call it ! And then all the punch was low—
horribly low ; and all that slang about the Club !—and that
foolish picture on the cover !—and then the puffing and the
puns ! For my part, I never saw a grain of wit in it—and
the sense was in a still less proportion ! In short, it was
bad, oh ! very bad ! but, I don't know how, it certainly did
amuse one, too !"

Such are the sounds which haunt my imagination in my
leave-taking. And ever and anon, I put my prayer to the
Goddess with the brazen trumpet, who proclaims the titles
and the exploits of great men : "Fame, Fame, when I am
removed from the scene of my exertions, let me not be
quite forgotten ! let me be talked of with praise, or let me
be talked of with censure; but let me, at all events, be
talked of ! Whether I be remembered with pardon or with
condemnation, I care little—so that I be only remembered."

I wish all manner of success and prosperity to the
members of the Club, my affectionate coadjutors. Mr.
Sterling, I have no doubt, will make an exemplary Vicar,
and Mr. Lozell will do excellent well to say his "Amen."
Mr. Musgrave will be a capital whip, unless he breaks his
neck in the training; and Sir Francis Wentworth will
probably rise to great honours and emoluments—when
the Whigs come in. Golightly will die with a jest in his
mouth, and a glass in his hand. Bellamy will live with
elegance in his manners, and · love in his eye. Oakley will
be a spiteful critic ; and Swinburne an erudite commentator.
As for Gerard, he will go forward on his own path to
eminence, destined to shine in a nobler arena than that of
a schoolboy's periodical, and to enjoy more worthy ap-
plauses than those of Peregrine Courtenay.   ·

And I, my dear public, shall walk up the hill of life as
steadily as I can, and as prosperously as I may. For the
present I have wiped my pen, and given a holiday to the
devils; but if, at any future period, I should, in my bounty,
give to your inspection a political pamphlet, or a treatise on
law, a farce or a tragedy, a speech or a sermon, I trust that
you will have a respect for the name of Peregrine Courtenay,
and be as ready with your pounds, shillings, and pence, as
I have always hitherto found you.

One word more. I have been much solicited to have my own effigies stuck in the front of my work, done in an editorial attitude, with a writing-desk before me, and a pen behind my ear; and I am aware that this is the custom of many gentlemen whom I might be proud to imitate. Mr. Canning figures in front of the *Microcosm*, and Dr. Peter Morris presents his goodly physiognomy in the vanguard of "Peter's Letters." And I know, what has often before been remarked, that when the public sit down to the perusal of a work, it imports them much to be convinced whether the writer thereof be plump or spare, fair or dark, of an open or a meditative countenance. Would any one feel an interest in the fate of Tom Thumb, who did not see a representation of the hero courting inspection, and claiming, as it were, *in propriâ personâ*, the applause to which his exploits entitle him? Would any one shudder with horror at the perilous adventures of Munchausen, who could not count the scars with which they are engraven on the Baron's physiognomy? In opposition to these weighty considerations, I have two motives which forcibly impel me to adopt a contrary line of conduct. In the first place, I am, as is known to all my acquaintance, most outrageously modest. I have been so from my cradle. Before I ever entered upon a public capacity, a few copies of a caricature came down to our Eton bookseller, one of which contained a figure of a starved poet. One of my friends carelessly discovered a resemblance between the said starved poet and your humble servant, the consequence of which was that your humble servant bought up, at no inconsiderable expense, all the copies of the said print, and committed them to the flames. And now, if I were to see my own features prefixed to my own writings; if I were to imagine to myself your curiosity, my public, criticizing expression of countenance as well as expression of thought, and lines of face as well as lines of metre, I could not endure it—I should faint! Yes, I should positively faint.

I have another reason; another very momentous one. I once heard a lady criticizing the "Lines to ——." How beautiful were the criticisms; and how beautiful was the critic! I would have given the riches of Mexico for such a review, and such a reviewer. But to proceed with my story —thus were the remarks wound up:—"Now do, Mr.

Courtenay, tell me who is the author? What an interesting looking man he must be!"

From that moment I have been enwrapt in most delightful day-dreams. I have constantly said to myself, " Peregrine, perhaps at this moment bright eyes are looking on your effusion; and sweet voices are saying, 'What a pretty young man Mr. Courtenay must be!'" And shall I publish my picture, and give them the lie? Oh, no! I will preserve to them the charity of their conjectures, and to myself the comfort of their opinion.

And now what rests for me but to express my gratitude to all who have assisted me by their advice or their support, and to beg, that if, in discharging my part to the best of my abilities, it has been my misfortune to give offence to any one of them, he will believe that I sinned not intentionally, and forgive me as well as he can.

I have also to return thanks to many gentlemen who have honoured me by marks of individual kindness. It would be painful for me to leave this spot without assuring them, that in all places, and under all circumstances, I shall have a lively recollection of the attention they have shown me, and the interest they have expressed in my success.

But most of all, I have to speak my feelings to him who, at my earnest solicitations, undertook to bear an equal portion of my fatigues and my responsibility—to him who has performed so diligently the labours which he entered upon so reluctantly—to him who has been the constant companion of my hopes and fears, my good and ill fortune—to him who, by the assiduity of his own attention, and the genius of the contributors whose good offices he secured, has ensured the success of the *Etonian.*

I began this letter in a light and jesting vein, but I find that I cannot keep it up. My departure from Eton and the *Etonian* is really too serious a business for a jest or a gibe. I have felt my spirits sinking by little and little, until I have become downright melancholy. I shall make haste, therefore, to come to a conclusion. I have done, and I subscribe myself (for the last time),

My dear Public,

Your obliged and devoted servant,

PEREGRINE COURTENAY.

ABDICATION OF THE KING OF CLUBS.

WE, PEREGRINE, by Our own choice, and the public favour, King of Clubs, and editor of the *Etonian*, in the ninth month of Our reign, being this day in possession of Our full and unimpaired faculties both of mind and body, do, by these presents, address Ourselves to all Our loving subjects, whether holding place and profit under Us, or not.

Inasmuch as We are sensible that We must shortly be removed from this state of trial, and translated to another life, leaving behind Us all the trappings of royalty, all the duties of government, all the concerns of this condition of being, it does seem good to Us, before We are withdrawn from the eyes of Our dearly beloved friends and subjects, to abdicate and divest Ourselves of all the ensigns of power and authority which We have hitherto borne; and We do hereby willingly abdicate and divest Ourselves of the same.

And be it, by all whom it may concern, remembered, that the cares and labours of Peregrine, sometime King of Clubs, are henceforth directed to another world; and that if any one shall assume the sceptre and the style of Peregrine, the first King of Clubs, such person is a liar and usurper.

Howbeit, If it shall please Our trusty subjects and counsellors to set upon Our Throne a rightful and legitimate successor, We will that the allegiance of Our people be transferred to him; and that he be accounted supreme over serious and comic, verse and prose; and that the treasury of Our Kingdom, with all that it shall at such time contain, song, and sonnet, and epigram, and epic, and descriptions, and nondescripts, shall be made over forthwith to his charge and keeping.

And for all acts, and writings, made and done during the period of Our reign, to wit, from the twentieth day of October, anno Domini eighteen hundred and twenty, to the twenty-eighth day of July, eighteen hundred and twenty-one, inclusive, we commit them to the memory of men, for the entertainment of our friends and the instruction of posterity.

Further, If any one shall take upon himself the office of commenting upon any of the deeds and transactions which have taken place under Our administration, whether such comment shall go forth in plain drab or in gaudier saffron and blue, We recommend to such person charity and forbearance, and in their spirit let him say forth his say.

And be it hereby known, that for all that has been said or done against Us, during the above-mentioned period, whether by open hostility or secret dislike, We do this day publish a general and hearty Amnesty : And We will that all such offences be from henceforth committed to oblivion, and that no person shall presume to recall to Our recollection such sins and treasons.

And We also entreat that if, in the course of a long and arduous administration, it has been Our lot to inflict wounds in self-defence, or to wound, unknowingly, those who were unconnected with Us, the forgiveness which We extend to others will be extended by others to Us.

And We do, from this day, release from all bond, duty, and obligation those who have assisted Us by their counsel and support ; leaving it to all such persons to transfer their services to any other master, as seemeth to them best.

We decree that Our punchbowl be henceforth consecrated to Our lonely hours and our pleasant recollections; that no one do henceforth apply his lips to its margin ; and that all future potentates in this state of Eton do submit to assemble their privy council around a coffee-pot or an urn.

And We most earnestly recommend to those dear friends, whom We must perforce leave behind Us, that in all places and conditions they continue to perform their duties in a worshipful manner, always endeavouring to be a credit to the Prince whom they have so long honoured by their service.

And now, as Our predecessor, Charles of Germany, in the meridian of his glory, laid down the reins of empire, exchanging the court for the cloister, and the crown for the cowl—even so do We, Peregrine of Clubs, lay down the pen and the paper, exchanging celebrity for obscurity, punch

for algebra, the printing-office for Trinity College. And
We entreat all those who have Our welfare at heart to
remember Us sometimes in their orisons. And so We
depart.

PEREGRINE.

Given in our Club-room, this twenty-eighth
day of July, A.D. 1821.

THE UNION CLUB.

A.D. 1823.

> The Union Club, of rhetorical fame,
>   Was held at the Red Lion Inn,*
> And there never was Lion so perfectly tame,
>   Or who made such a musical din.
> 'Tis pleasant to snore, at a quarter before,
>   When the Chairman does nothing in state,
> But 'tis heaven, 'tis heaven, to waken at seven,
>   And pray for a noisy debate!

"WHAT'S the question?"—"Reform." "What! the old
story!"—"Yes, the old story; the common good against
the Commons' House; speechifying *versus* starvation!"
"Oh, but you're a red-hot Radical?"—"Yes, that's my
key; every man is red-hot who is deep read!" "Reform
in Parliament?"—"Yes, the only thing men are agreed
upon; for the Outs can't carry it, and the Ins can't bear it."
"Infamous! split me!"—"Order, order! Gentlemen
will be so good as to take their seats. The question for
this evening's debate is: 'Would Reform in Parliament have
been conducive to the welfare of the country at any period
previous to the year 1800?' To be opened by Mr. Pattison
of St. John's."

And the honourable opener immediately mounts his
hobby, and proceeds at a rapid rate over a level road,
panting and blowing like a courier. Off he goes! Mounts

* In Petty Cury, Cambridge.

at Magna Charta, breakfasts with the Long Parliament, dines with William and Anne, and finds himself comfortably at home in the state of the nation.

* " We have heard of a time, Mr. President, when England was the envy and the terror of the whole world; we have heard of a time when commerce flourished, and the quartern loaf was sold for a penny-halfpenny; but these things are now altered; bread has risen, as stocks have fallen; we lose time in debates, and we lose men in battle; and are not all these things owing to Mr. Pitt? Unfortunate man ! he had it in his power to make his country happy, and he has left it miserable ; all of it encumbered with penury and taxation, and half of it fettered by a damnable religious restriction. Yes, Mr. President, from the fear of rebellion and revolution, the Protestants are wretched and spied upon ; and from the dread of the Holy Alliance, the Pope, the Pretender, the Arch-Fiend Napoleon, and the Devil, the Catholics are oppressed and persecuted."

Here the honourable member is jerked from his hobby by an orthodox hiss from the corner, and he sits down among the comments of the crowd. " What do you think of the opener? "—" Why, I think he's all

> Public debts,
> Epithets,
> Foul and filthy, good and great,
> Glorious wars,
> British iars,
> Beat and bruise
> Parlez-vous,
> Frenzy, frown,
> Commons, Crown,
> Ass and pannier,
> Rule Britannia !—
> How I love a loud debate ! "

> Then the Church shakes her rattle, and sends forth to battle
> The terror of Papist and sinner,
> Who loves to be seen as the modern Mæcenas,
> And asks all the poets to dinner.

† " Mr. President,—I rise to express my dissent from the honourable opener with regard to the Catholics. With

---

* Pattison.   † Bulwer—afterwards Lord Lytton.

respect to the question of debate, my sentiments are entirely those of the late Charles James Fox. He was a man adorned by every manly virtue that can adorn and dignify a man—*Propria quæ maribus tribuuntur, mascula dicas.* But with regard to the Catholics, when I remember the times of the Bloody Queen Mary, when I call to mind the horrible massacres she perpetrated—the helpless old women that were depopulated—I cannot sufficiently restrain my feelings to hear the Catholics commended without expressing my dissent."

> Then the gentleman Attic, with tales Asiatic
> And body that bends with a grace,
> The maker of jeers that led us for years,
> The prime Staple-Ton of the place.

* " Mr. President,—From the look of virtuous indignation with which the honourable gentleman arose from his seat, I expected to have heard something worthy of a Blair or a Benson, a Confucius or a Nebuchadnezzar; but lo ! when my hopes were wrought up to the highest pitch, the honourable gentleman has suddenly reseated himself, and I do not even understand the purport of his sudden ebullition. Once upon a time a sudden darkness over-spread the town of Ching-Chong-Foo; the sun and the moon and the stars were hidden, all business was suspended, all hearts were astounded. The mathematician Sing-Su said it was an eclipse ; the Bishop Chit-Quong said it was the Devil ; and the Chancellor Hum-lum said that he doubted : when suddenly there flew down from the skies, extending his wings over all the city, a stupendous cock ; he soared majestically down—sullenly—slowly ; and when they expected from him the voice of Azrael the Destroyer, or the Mandate of Mahomet the Prophet, he said—nothing, Mr. President, but Cock-a-doodle-doo !"

" Why the devil do you laugh ? "—" Laugh ! why because it's all

> Indian Stories,
> Damn the Tories,
> None but he can rule the State,
> Wise magicians,
> Politicians,

* Stapleton.

> Foreign lands,
> Kings and wands,
> Fiends and fairies,
> Dromedaries,
> Laugh at Boodle's,
> Cock-a-doodles—
> How I love a loud debate !"

Then up gets a youth with a visage of truth,
　An omen of good to our islands,
Who promises health and abundance of wealth
　To our Oatlands, and Wheatlands, and Ryelands.

* " Mr. President,—I had not intended to address you
on the present question ; but some observations which
have been made on the character of George the Third
prevent me from remaining silent. If I use any strong
expressions, I trust they will be attributed to the violence
of my feelings." (Refers to a paper.) " When I remember,
Sir, that in the reign of George the Third the purest
blessings of Heaven were shed upon us, and that Mr. Pitt
was Prime Minister ; that the powers of darkness were
scattered before us, and that the combined fleets of France
and Spain were defeated—above all, when I reflect that
all the nine Muses migrated from Pindus to England, and
that Mr. Southey was the Poet Laureate—I cannot help
saying that George the Third, who reigned so gloriously,
and lived to an advanced period of life, was very wise, very
prudent, and very triumphant. In short, Sir, I do not fear
to affirm that he was very good."

And the honourable gentleman halts as systematically as
a posthorse knocked up or a timepiece run down. " Very
perfect in his lesson ! "—" Oh, very ! but it's all

> Sigh and simper,
> Whine and whimper,
> Kings and princes, Church and State ;
> Cut and dried,
> Ill applied,
> Nightly taper,
> Pen and paper,
> Audience dozing,
> How composing !
> Would 'twere shorter !
> Milk and water !—
> How I love a loud debate !"

---

* Ryland of St. John's.

> But the favourite comes, with his trumpets and drums,
>   And his arms and his metaphors crossed ;
> And the audience—O dear !—vociferate "Hear !"
>   Till they're half of them deaf as a post.

And the honourable gentleman, after making the grand tour in a hand canter, touching cursorily upon Rome, Constantinople, Amsterdam, Philadelphia, and the Red Sea ; with two quotations, two or three hundred similes, and two or three hundred thousand metaphors, proceeds to the tune of

*" We, Mr. President, have indeed awful examples to direct us or deter. Have we not seen the arms of the mighty overpowered, and the counsels of the wise confounded ? Have not the swords of licentious conquest, and the fasces of perverted law, covered Europe with blood, and tears, and mourning ? Have not priests and princes and nobles been driven in beggary and exile to implore the protection of rival thrones and hostile altars ? Where is the sacred magnificence of Rome ? Where the wealth and independence of Holland ? Where the proud titles of the German Cæsars ? Where the mighty dynasty of Bourbon ? But is there yet one nation which has retained unimpaired its moral and political strength ? One nation, whose shores have ever been accessible to a suppliant, and never to an enemy ? One nation which, while the banners of her foes have been carried in triumph to half the capitals of the world, has seen them only suspended over her shrines as trophies ? One nation, which, while so many cities have been a prey to hostile fires, has never seen her streets lighted up but with the blaze of victorious illumination ? History and posterity will reply, 'That country was England.' Let them not talk to us of their philosophy and their philanthropy, their reason and their rights ! We know too well the oratory of their Smithfield meetings, and the orgies of their midnight clubs ! We have seen the weapons which arm, and the spirit which nerves them. We have heard the hyæna howl, till the raving which excited dismay provokes nothing but disgust. Amid the railings of disappointed ambition, and the curses of

* Macaulay.

factious hate ; amid the machinations of the foully wicked,
and the sophistries of the would-be wise, we will cling to
our fathers' banner—we will rally round our native rock.
Mr. President, that banner is the Charta of our rights—that
Rock is the British Constitution !"

"Bravo !" "Can't say I quite caught the line of
argument." "Argument! Fiddlestick! Quite gone out
except for opponencies ; and then for the language,
and the feeling, and the style, and all that sort of thing—
oh ! nobody can deny that it was all

> Oratoric,
> Metaphoric,
> Similes of wondrous length ;
> Illustration,
> Conflagration,
> Ancient Romans,
> House of Commons,
> Clever Uriel
> And Ithuriel,
> Good old king,
> Everything !—
> How I love a loud debate !"

> With his sayings and saws, his hems and his haws,
> Another comes up to the scratch ;
> While Deacon and Law unite in a yaw !   [*Yawning.*
> And the President looks at his watch.

And the honourable gentleman, after making a long
journey and plunging up to his knees in dirt, bog, and
quagmire ; after taking up many strong positions and much
valuable time, after bruising the Bishops and the table,
and twisting his argument and his sleeve in twenty different
ways, proceeds to wake the members with a joke.

* "Mr. President,—I am out of all patience when I
hear the poor abused because they wish to reform the
Constitution. Why, when you have taken from them all
they have got, and all they hope to get, what can they do ?
Why, they complain, to be sure ; and as soon as they
complain, like the poor fellow who was tried for stealing a
pair of leather breeches, and found guilty of manslaughter,

* Ord.

the unfortunate rabble—though why they are called rabble the Attorney-General only knows, I'm sure I don't—but, as I said before, the unfortunate rabble are prosecuted upon *ex officio* informations, or persecuted by a Bridge Street gang, which I look upon as a combination of fiends against our Constitution—that is, what we've got left of it, which to be sure is but little, whatever the honourable gentlemen opposite may think, who seem to be very much amused at the idea—but as I said before, the unfortunate rabble, like the poor fellow who was tried for stealing a pair of leather breeches and found guilty of manslaughter, is tried for high treason and found guilty of being ragged, and so is hung, fined, imprisoned, or sent to Botany Bay, or Australasia as the Vice-Chancellor calls it, according to the will and pleasure of His Majesty's Attorney and Solicitor-General. But the honourable gentleman would let the poor starve, while the rich take coffee and snuff, talk religion, and buy into the stocks; provided my Lord this and my Lord that may keep their mistresses and their boroughs, all the scum, all the *canaille* may be cut down by the dozen. The honourable gentleman cares no more for the poor than the country gentleman did—a good, honest, well-meaning man—who lost so many turnips that he wanted to make turnip-stealing a capital offence. The country gentleman and the honourable gentleman argue on the same ground—they are on the same bench—there they are ! "

" Bravo ! " " Bravo ! " " Pray, Sir, how long has that young gentleman been on his legs ? "—" Really I can't tell, I was so much amused at his

Admirable,
Bang the table,
' Sir, although its getting late,'
Opposition,
Repetition,
Endless speeches,
Leather breeches,
Taxes, hops,
Turnip-tops,
Leather 'em, lather 'em,
Omnium-gatherum—
How I love a loud debate ! "

> Mr. Punnett, whose vows are put up for the House
>   As if he was born to the trade,
> Would chafe if we close with the ayes and the noes,
>   And break up before we have—prayed !

And accordingly, after the honourable gentleman has abused, *ad libitum*, all persons not freeholders who wish to have votes, and told us, "as for such people, now we have got 'em down, keep 'em down ;" he is succeeded by the laureate jester of the society. The honourable gentleman plunges into a sea of puns, passes a few modest strictures on the freedom of the press, likens Frederick the Great to a thief, and Mr. Bartholomew to the devil ; and at last betakes himself, like all poets, to abusing his friends.

* "Not being disposed, Mr. President, to pun it in a decidedly personal manner through any more of the honourable gentleman's speech, I proceed to say a few words in reply to my honourable friend who preceded him. But I conceive, Mr. President, when I see how much the table of the House has suffered from the fist of the honourable gentleman, I may be somewhat afraid of the knock-down arguments of my honourable friend. Let him not commit violence on our persons or our property ; let him not frighten the freshman or annihilate the Soph. He is already the Ord of this House, let him not make himself the Lord of it ; we give him an inch, let him not take an ' L.' But I conceive, Sir, that my honourable friend will attend to no suggestion of mine. He is a Republican, a Radical, a Revolutionist, a Fury, a Firebrand ; but, however hot may be the doctrines he now advocates, I would whisper in his ear : ' You were once something far more reasonable ; yes, though you may now be a rioter or a regicide, yet, as the poet says, You were a Whig, and thereby hangs a tale !' I have detained the House too long, and will make haste to conclude. I have been censured for mixing too much of the ludicrous with the debates of the House. It has been said of me that the thread of my argument is drawn from the tassel of my cap, that the point of my jokes is drawn from the belles of Barnwell. Mr. President, I

---

* Praed.

plead guilty to the charges, and the House must be well aware that the insignia of my profession were never anything but the cap and bells ! "

> Quite divine
> Peregrine,
> Never shall we see his mate ;
> Fun and flams,
> Epigrams,
> Leering, lying,
> Versifying,
> Nodding, noting,
> Quibbling, quoting,
> ' Thief ! ' and ' Bore ! '
> ' Lie ! ' no more —
> How I love a loud debate ! "

Then up gets the glory of us and our story,
  Who does all by logic and rule,
Who can tell the true diff'rence 'twixt twopence and threepence,
  And prove Adam Smith quite a fool.

* " Mr. President,—I had intended to have addressed the meeting at considerable length, but as the ground I meant to occupy has been entirely and successfully anticipated by my honourable friends, I shall not dwell upon the crying and terrible demand there is for Parliamentary Reform, but shall confine my observations to the existing aggression of France upon Spain.   For it is not so much the question whether France or Spain shall be victorious ; it is not so much the question whether that 'alter Achilles,' the Duke d'Angoulême, with his miserable and half-starved myrmidons, or General Mina and his patriots, shall be vanquished ; the question is, whether the nefarious and accursed principles of foreign aggression and tyranny, the principles of despotism and usurpation, shall triumph eternally over the principles of freedom; whether worse than Scythian ignorance and barbarism shall crush the progress of science and enlightened understanding ; whether that holy knot of confederated despots (who I trust in heaven will ere long meet their well-earned reward of the halter)—whether they are to dictate laws and constitutions to the rest of mankind; whether that hellish power which has crushed the

* Charles Austin.

freedom and trampled on the genius of Italy shall crush the freedom and trample on the genius of the rest of the world ; whether we, who boast ourselves freeborn Englishmen, shall tamely look on and see the rights of nations and the rights of man assaulted and violated ; whether we are to listen with submission and humility to the insolent decrees of the Autocrat of the Russias ; whether we are to cringe and subscribe to the proclamation of a semi-barbarian who dares to issue his mandate to the world—a mandate which is nothing but an ignorant tissue of Syrio-Calmuc jargon and cacophony."

> But Lord ! Sir, you ask a more difficult task
> That aught in the son-shop of Burchill,
> If you ask me to dish up, like many a Bishop,
> The eminent words of the Church-ill !

* " Mr. President,—The honourable opener of this debate called Mr. Pitt an unfortunate man ; now I think him a very fortunate man. He went about, like Jeremy Diddler, borrowing sixpence from every one who was fool enough to lend him, and died before he was called on to refund. We have heard the prosperous state of the country referred to. Now, Sir, everybody that can pay for his passage is going to the Cape ; for though a man likes his bed, he leaves it when he finds it full of fleas. The distresses of England have also been alluded to. Now, Sir, with regard to Lord George Gordon's riots, they were like Tom Thumb's giants —the Minister made the riots first, and then he quelled them."

" Does any other honourable gentleman wish to address the House ? I shall proceed to put the question. It is carried that Parliamentary Reform would not be beneficial, by a majority of 77 to 13. (Hear ! hear ! hear !) There is a motion on the boards, ' That an adequate supply of chairs for the reading-room be provided— proposed by Mr. Moore, of Caius.' "

† " Mr. President,—It is not often that I rise to address this society ; nor should I on the present occasion, but that I see so strong a necessity for interference, that I

---

* Churchill.   † Moore.

should deem it a dereliction of my duty were I to remain silent. In those things which regard our intellectual and moral improvement, this society should be more especially attentive to its interests; but I have observed with regret and concern that there is by no means an adequate supply of chairs in our reading-room, and I therefore move that a fit supply be immediately procured."

* " Mr. President,—I have observed with great satisfaction the interest which the honourable gentleman takes in the welfare of this society; but as in an inn, where there are nine beds, and ten travellers to sleep in them, one bed must carry double or one traveller must go without; so, in the present case, if upon any occasion the honourable gentleman should find ten chairs in the reading-room occupied by ten individuals, I should recommend him to make them determine by lot which of them shall hold him on his knees!"

" Well, Sir, what do you think of the Union ? "—" Why, Sir, I think it's all

Bow, wow,
What a row,
Money lost, and laurels earned ;
Constitution,
Elocution,
Whig and Tory,
Oratory,
Hauling, bawling,
' Order ' calling,
Headache, dizziness,
No more business—
Sirs, the meeting is adjourned."

---

* Prosser.

MY FIRST FOLLY.

"L'imagination grossit souvent les plus petits objets par une estimation fantastique jusqu'à remplir notre âme."—PENSÉES DE PASCAL.

> "I have spent all my golden time,
> In writing many a loving rime :
> I have consumed all my youth
> In vowing of my faith and trueth ;
> O willow, willow, willow tree,
> Yet can I not beleeved bee."—OLD BALLAD.

"Do you take trifle?" said Lady Olivia to my poor friend
Halloran.

"No, Ma'am, I am reading philosophy," said Halloran;
waking from a fit of abstraction, with about as much consciousness and perception as exists in a petrified oyster, or
an alderman dying of a surfeit. Halloran is a fool.

A trifle is the one good thing, the sole and surpassing enjoyment. He only is happy who can fix his thoughts, and
his hopes, and his feelings, and his affections, upon those
fickle and fading pleasures, which are tenderly cherished
and easily forgotten, alike acute in their excitement and
brief in their regret. Trifles constitute my *summum bonum*.
Sages may crush them with the heavy train of argument
and syllogism ; schoolboys may assail them with the light
artillery of essay and of theme ; Members of Parliament may
loathe, doctors of divinity may contemn—bag wigs and big
wigs, blue devils and blue stockings, sophistry and sermons,
reasonings and wrinkles, Solon, Thales, Newton's "Principia,"
Mr. Walker's "Eidouranion," the King's Bench, the bench of
Bishops—all these are serious antagonists ; very serious !
But I care not ; I defy them ; I dote upon trifles ; my
name is Vyvyan Joyeuse, and my motto is "Vive la
Bagatelle!"

There are many persons who, while they have a tolerable
taste for the frivolous, yet profess remorse and penitence for
their indulgence of it ; and continually court and embrace

new day-dreams, while they shrink from the retrospect of those which have already faded. Peace be to their ever-lasting laments and their ever-broken resolutions! Your true trifler, meaning your humble servant, is a being of a very different order. The luxury which I renew in the recollection of the past is equal to that which I feel in the enjoyment of the present, or create in the anticipation of the future. I love to count and recount every treasure I have flung away, every bubble I have broken; I love to dream again the dreams of my boyhood, and to see the visions of departed pleasures flitting, like Ossian's ghosts, around me, "with stars dim twinkling through their forms." I look back with delight to a youth which has been idled away, to tastes which have been perverted, to talents which have been misemployed; and while in imagination I wander back through the haunts of my old idlesse, for all the learning of a Greek professor, for all the morality of Sir John Sewell, I would not lose one single point of that which has been ridiculous and grotesque, nor one single tint of that which has been beautiful and beloved.

Moralists and misanthropists, maidens with starched morals and matrons with starched frills, ancient adorers of Bohea and scandal, venerable votaries of whispering and of whist, learned professors of the compassionate sneer and the innocent innuendo, eternal pillars of gravity and good order, of stupidity and decorum—come not near me with your spare and spectacled features, your candid and considerate criticism. In you I have no hope, in me you have no interest. I am to speak of stories you will not believe, of beings you cannot love; of foibles for which you have no compassion, of feelings in which you have no share.

Fortunate and unfortunate couples, belles in silks and beaux in sentimentals, ye who have wept and sighed, ye who have been wept for and sighed for, victims of vapours and coiners of vows, makers and marrers of intrigue, readers and writers of songs—come to me with your attention and your salts, your sympathy and your cambric; your griefs, your raptures, your anxieties, all have been mine; I know your blushing and your paleness, your self-deceiving and your self-tormenting.

so com'è inconstanta e vaga
Timida, ardita vita degli amanti,
Ch'un poco dolce molto amaro appoggia ;
E so i costumi, e i lor sospiri, e i canti
E'l parlar rotto, e'l subito silenzio,
E'l brevissimo riso, e i lunghi pianti ;
E qual è 'l mel temprato con l'assenzio.

All these things are so beautiful in Italian ! But I need not
have borrowed a syllable from Petrarch, for shapes of
shadowy beauty, smiles of cherished loveliness, glances of
reviving lustre, are coming in the mist of memory around
me ! I am writing "an ower true tale ! "

I never fell seriously in love till I was seventeen. Long
before that period I had learned to talk nonsense and tell
lies, and had established the important points that a delicate
figure is equivalent to a thousand pounds, a pretty mouth
better than the Bank of England, and a pair of bright eyes
worth all Mexico. But at seventeen a more intricate
branch of study awaited me.

I was lounging away my June at a pretty village in Kent,
with little occupation beyond my own meditations, and no
company but my horse and dogs. My sisters were both in
the South of France ; and my uncle, at whose seat I had
pitched my camp, was attending to the interests of his constituents and the wishes of his patron in Parliament. I
began after the lapse of a week to be immensely bored ; I
felt a considerable dislike of an agricultural life, and an
incipient inclination for laudanum. I took to playing
backgammon with the rector. He was more than a match
for me, and used to grow most unclerically hot when the
dice, as was their duty, befriended the weaker side. At
last, at the conclusion of a very long hit, which had kept
Mrs. Penn's tea waiting full an hour, my worthy and wigged
friend flung deuce-ace three times in succession, put the
board in the fire, overturned Mrs. Penn's best china, and
hurried to his study to compose a sermon on patience.

Then I took up reading. My uncle had a delightful
library, where a reasonable man might have lived and died.
But I confess I never could endure a long hour of lonely
reading. It is a very pretty thing to take down a volume
of Tasso or Racine, and study accent and cadence for the

benefit of half a dozen listening belles, all dividing their attention between the work and the work-basket, their feelings and their flounces, their tears and their trimmings, with becoming and laudable perseverance. It is a far prettier thing to read Petrarch or Rousseau with a single companion, in some sheltered spot so full of passion and of beauty that you may sit whole days in its fragrance and dream of Laura and Julie. If these are out of the way, it is endurable to be tied down to the moth-eaten marvels of antiquity, poring to-day that you may pore again to-morrow, and labouring for the nine days' wonder of some temporary distinction, with an ambition which is almost frenzy, and an emulation which speaks the language of animosity. But to sit down to a novel or a philosopher, with no companion to participate in the enjoyment and no object to reward the toil, this indeed—oh! I never could endure a long hour of lonely reading; and so I deserted Sir Roger's library, and left his Marmontel and his Aristotle to the slumbers from which I had unthinkingly awakened them.

At last I was roused from a state of most Persian torpor by a note from an old lady, whose hall, for so an indifferent country-house was by courtesy denominated, stood at the distance of a few miles. She was about to give a ball. Such a thing had not been seen for ten years within ten miles of us. From the sensation produced by the intimation you might have deemed the world at an end. Prayers and entreaties were offered up to all the guardians and all the milliners; and the old gentlemen rose in a passion, and the old lace rose in price. Everything was everywhere in a flurry; kitchen, and parlour, and boudoir and garret— Babel all! *Ackermann's Fashionable Repository*, the *Ladies' Magazine,* the *New Pocket-book*—all these, and all other publications whose frontispieces presented the "fashions for 1817," personified in a thin lady with kid gloves and a formidable obliquity of vision, were in earnest and im- mediate requisition. Needles and pins were flying right and left; dinner was ill-dressed that dancers might be well-dressed; mutton was marred that misses might be married. There was not a schoolboy who did not cut Homer and capers; nor a boarding-school beauty who did not try on a score of dancing shoes, and talk for a fortnight of Angiolini. Every occupation was laid down, every carpet was taken up; every combination of hands-across and down the middle was committed most laudably to memory; and nothing was talked, nothing was meditated, nothing was dreamed, but love and romance, fiddles and flirtation, warm negus and handsome partners, dyed feathers and chalked floors.

In all the pride and condescension of an inmate of Grosvenor Square, I looked upon Lady Motley's "At Home." "Yes," I said, flinging away the card with a tragedy twist of the fingers, "yes: I will be there. For one evening I will encounter the tedium and the taste of a village ball. For one evening I will doom myself to figures that are out of date, and fiddles that are out of tune; dowagers who make embroidery by wholesale, and demoiselles who make conquests by profession: for one evening I will endure the inquiries about Almack's and St. Paul's, the tales of the weddings that have been and the weddings that are to be, the round of courtesies in the ball-room and the round of beef at the supper-table: for one evening I will not complain of the everlasting hostess and the everlasting Boulanger, of the double duty and the double bass, of the great heiress and the great plum-pudding:

> Come one, come all,
> Come dance in Sir Roger's great hall."

And thus, by dint of civility, indolence, quotation, and antithesis, I bent up each corporal agent to the terrible feat, and " would have the honour of waiting upon her ladyship," —in due form.

I went: turned my uncle's one-horse chaise into the long old avenue about an hour after the time specified, and perceived by the lights flashing from all the windows, and the crash of chairs and carriages returning from the door, that the room was most punctually full, and the performers most pastorally impatient. The first face I encountered on my entrance was that of my old friend Villars; I was delighted to meet him, and expressed my astonishment at finding

him in a situation for which his inclination, one would have
supposed, was so little adapted.

"By Mercury," he exclaimed, "I am metamorphosed—
fairly metamorphosed, my good Vyvyan; I have been
detained here three months by a fall from Sir Peter, and
have amused myself most indefatigably by humming tunes
and reading newspapers, winding silk and guessing conun-
drums. I have made myself the admiration, the adoration,
the very worship of all the coteries in the place; am
reckoned very clever at cross purposes, and very apt at
'What's my thought like?' The squires have discovered I
can carve, and the matrons hold me indispensable at loo.
Come! I am of little service to-night, but my popularity
may be of use to you. You don't know a soul! I thought
so—read it in your face the moment you came in. Never
saw such a——— There, Vyvyan, look there! I will introduce
you." And so saying my companion half limped, half
danced with me up to Miss Amelia Mesnil, and presented
me in due form.

When I look back to any particular scene of my
existence, I can never keep the stage clear of second-rate
characters. I never think of Mr. Kean's Othello without
an intrusive reflection upon the subject of Mr. Cooper's
Cassio; I never call to mind a gorgeous scattering forth of
roses from Mr. Canning, without a painful idea of some
contemporary effusion of poppies from Mr. Hume. And
thus, beautiful Margaret, it is in vain that I endeavour to
separate your fascination from the group which was
collected around you. Perhaps that dominion, which at
this moment I feel almost revived, recurs more vividly to
my imagination, when the forms and figures of all by whom
it was contested are associated in its renewal.

First comes Amelia the magnificent, the acknowledged
belle of the county, very stiff and very dumb in her
unheeded and uncontested supremacy; and next, the most
black-browed of fox-hunters, Augusta, enumerating the
names of her father's stud, and dancing as if she imitated
them; and then the most accomplished Jane, vowing that
for the last month she had endured immense *ennui*, that
she thinks Lady Olivia prodigiously *fade*, that her cousin

Sophy is quite *brillante* to-night, and that Mr. Peters plays the violin *à merveille*.

"I am bored, my dear Villars—positively bored! The light is bad and the music abominable; there is no spring in the boards and less in the conversation; it is a lovely moonlight night, and there is nothing worth looking at in the room."

I shook hands with my friend, bowed to three or four people, and was moving off. As I passed to the door I met two ladies in conversation. "Don't you dance any more, Margaret?" said one. "Oh no," replied the other, "I am bored, my dear Louisa—positively bored! The light is bad and the music abominable; there is no spring in the boards and less in the conversation; it is a lovely moonlight night, and there is nothing worth looking at in the room."

I never was distanced in a jest. I put on the look of a ten years' acquaintance and commenced parley. "Surely you are not going away yet! You have not danced with me, Margaret: it is impossible you can be so cruel!" The lady behaved with wonderful intrepidity. "She would allow me the honour—but I was very late; really I had not deserved it." And so we stood up together.

"Are you not very impertinent?"

"Very; but you are very handsome. Nay, you are not to be angry; it was a fair challenge and fairly received."

"And you will not even ask my pardon?"

"No! it is out of my way! I never do those things; it would embarrass me beyond measure. Pray let us accomplish an introduction: not altogether a usual one, but that matters little. Vyvyan Joyeuse—rather impertinent, and very fortunate—at your service."

"Margaret Orleans—very handsome, and rather foolish —at your service!"

Margaret danced like an angel. I knew she would. I could not conceive by what blindness I had passed four hours without being struck. We talked of all things that are, and a few beside. She was something of a botanist, so

H

we began with flowers; a digression upon China roses
carried us to China—the Mandarins with little brains, and
the ladies with little feet—the Emperor—the Orphan of China
—Voltaire—Zayre—criticism—Dr. Johnson—the Great
Bear—the system of Copernicus—stars—ribbons—garters—
the Order of the Bath—sea-bathing—Dawlish—Sidmouth—
Lord Sidmouth—Cicero—Rome—Italy—Alfieri—Metastasio—fountains—groves—gardens; and so, as the dancing
concluded, we contrived to end as we began, with Margaret
Orleans and botany.

Margaret talked well on all subjects and wittily on
many. I had expected to find nothing but a romping
girl, somewhat amusing, and very vain. But I was out
of my latitude in the first five minutes, and out of my
senses in the next. She left the room very early, and
I drove home, more astonished than I had been for many
years.

Several weeks passed away, and I was about to leave
England to join my sisters on the Continent. I determined
to look once more on that enslaving smile, whose recollection had haunted me more than once. I had ascertained
that she resided with an old lady who took two pupils, and
taught French and Italian, and music and manners, at an
establishment called Vine House. Two days before I left
the country, I had been till a late hour shooting at a mark
with a duelling pistol, an entertainment, of which, perhaps
from a lurking presentiment, I was very fond. I was returning alone when I perceived, by the light of an enormous
lamp, a board by the wayside bearing the welcome inscription, "Vine House." "Enough," I exclaimed, "enough!
One more scene before the curtain drops. Romeo and
Juliet by lamplight!" I roamed about the dwelling-place
of all I held dear, till I saw a figure at one of the windows
in the back of the house, which it was quite impossible to
doubt I leaned against a tree in a sentimental position,
and began to chant my own rhymes thus :—

> Pretty coquette, the ceaseless play
>   Of mine unstudied wit,
> And thy dark eye's remembered ray
>   By buoyant fancy lit,

And thy young forehead's clear expanse,
Where the locks slept, as through the dance,
   Dreamlike, I saw thee flit,
Are far too warm, and far too fair,
To mix with aught of earthly care ;
But the vision shall come when my day is done,
A frail and a fair and a fleeting one !

And if the many boldly gaze
   On that bright brow of thine,
And if thine eye's undying rays
   On countless coxcombs shine
And if thy wit flings out its mirth,
Which echoes more of air than earth,
   For other ears than mine,
I heed not this ; ye are fickle things,
And I like your very wanderings ;
I gaze, and if thousands share the bliss,
Pretty capricious ! I heed not this.

In sooth I am a wayward youth,
   As fickle as the sea,
And very apt to speak the truth,
   Unpleasing though it be ;
I am no lover ; yet, as long
As I have heart for jest or song,
   An image, sweet, of thee,
Locked in my heart's remotest treasures,
Shall ever be one of its hoarded pleasures ;
This from the scoffer thou hast won,
And more than this he gives to none.

"Are they your own verses?" said my idol at the window.

"They are yours, Margaret! I was only the versifier; you were the muse herself."

"The muse herself is obliged to you. And now what is your errand? For it grows late, and you must be sensible— no, that you never will be—but you must be aware that this is very indecorous."

"I am come to see you, dear Margaret—which I cannot without candles—to see you, and to tell you that it is impossible I can forget——"

"Bless me! what a memory you have. But you must take another opportunity for your tale; for——"

"Alas! I leave England immediately."

"A pleasant voyage to you! There, not a word more; I must run down to coffee."

"Now may I never laugh more," I said, "if I am baffled thus." So I strolled back to the front of the house and proceeded to reconnoitre. A bay-window was half open, and in a small neat drawing-room I perceived a group assembled : an old lady, with a high muslin cap and red ribbons, was pouring out the coffee; her nephew, a tall awkward young gentleman, sitting on one chair and resting his legs on another, was occupied in the study of Sir Charles Grandison ; and my fair Margaret was leaning on a sofa, and laughing immoderately. "Indeed, miss," said the matron, "you should learn to govern your mirth; people will think you came out of Bedlam."

I lifted the window gently, and stepped into the room. "Bedlam, madam!" quoth I, "I bring intelligence from Bedlam ; I arrived last week."

The tall awkward young gentleman stared ; and the aunt half said, half shrieked, "What in the name of wonder are you?"

"Mad, madam! very particularly mad! Mad as a hare in March or a Cheapside blood on Sunday morning. Look at me! do I not foam? Listen to me! do I not rave? Coffee, my dear madam, coffee ; there is no animal so thirsty as your madman in the dog-days."

"Eh, really!" said the tall awkward young gentleman.

"My good sir," I began. But my original insanity began to fail me, and I drew forthwith upon Ossian's. "Fly! receive the wind and fly ; the blasts are in the hollow of my hand, the course of the storm is mine!"

"Eh, really!" said the tall awkward young gentleman.

"I look on the nations and they vanish; my nostrils pour the blast of death ; I come abroad on the winds ; the tempest is before my face ; but my dwelling is calm, above the clouds ; the fields of my rest are pleasant."

"Do you mean to insult us?" said the old lady.

"Ay! do you mean to insult my aunt?—really!" said the tall awkward young gentleman.

" I shall call in my servants," said the old lady.

" I am the humblest of them," said I, bowing.

" I shall teach you a different tune," said the tall awkward young gentleman, "really!"

"Very well, my dear sir; my instrument is the barrel-organ;" and I cocked my sweet little pocket companion in his face, "Vanish, little Kastril; for by Hannibal, Heliogabalus, and Holophernes, time is valuable, madness is precipitate, and hair-triggers are the word! Vanish!"

" Eh, really!" said the tall awkward young gentleman, and performed an *entrechat* which carried him to the door: the old lady had disappeared at the first note of the barrel-organ. I locked the door, and found Margaret in a paroxysm of laughter. "I wish you had shot him," she said, when she recovered; " I wish you had shot him: he is a sad fool."

" Do not talk of him; I am speaking to you, beautiful Margaret, possibly for the last time! Will you ever think of me? Perhaps you will. But let me receive from you some token that I may dote upon in other years; something that may be a hope to me in my happiness, and a consolation in calamity; something—nay! I never could talk romance; but give me one lock of your hair, and I will leave England with resignation."

" You have earned it like a true knight," said Margaret; and she severed from her head a long glossy ringlet. "Look!" she continued, "you must to horse, the country has risen for your apprehension." I turned towards the window. The country had indeed risen. Nothing was to be seen but gossoons in the van and gossips in the rear, red faces and white jackets, gallants in smock-frecks and gay damsels in grogram. Bludgeons were waving, and torches were flashing, as far as the gaze could reach. All the chivalry of the place was arming and chafing, and loading for a volley of pebbles and oaths together.

I kneeled down and kissed her hand. It was the happiest moment of my life! "Now," said I, " *au revoir*, my sweet Margaret!" and in a moment I was in the lane.

"Gentlemen, be pleased to fall back! Farther yet—a few paces farther! Stalwart kern in buckskin, be pleased to lay down your cat-o'-nine-tails! Old knight of the plush jerkin, ground your poker! So, fair damisel with the pitch-fork, you are too pretty for so rude an encounter! Most miraculous Magog with the sledge-hammer, flit! Sooty Cupid with the link, light me from Paphos. Ha! tall friend of the barrel-organ, have you turned staff officer? Etna and Vesuvius! Wild fire and wit! Blunderbusses and steam! Fly! Ha! have I not Burgundy in my brain, murder in my plot, and a whole train of artillery in my coat-pocket?" Right and left the ranks opened for my egress, and in a few minutes I was alone on the road, and whistling "Lillibullero."

This was my first folly. I looked at the lock of hair often, but I never saw Margaret again. She has become the wife of a young clergyman, and resides with him on a small living in Staffordshire. I believe she is very happy, and I have forgotten the colour of her eyes.

POINTS.

"Peregrine," said Lady Mary, "write."
"I will make a point of it, may it please you ladyship."

"O mes enfans! quelles âmes que celles qui ne sont inquiètes que des mouvemens de l'écliptique, ou que des mœurs et des arts des Chinois!"   MARMONTEL

How far our happiness may be advanced or endangered by the indulgence of a lively interest in all things and persons that chance throws in our way, is a point on which I never could make up my mind. I have seen the man of feeling rapt up in the fervour of his affection or the enthusiasm of his benevolence, and I have believed him perfectly happy; but I have seen him again when he has discovered that his affection had been wasted on a fool, and his benevolence lavished on a scoundrel, and I have believed him the most wretched of men. Again, I have looked on the man of the world in an hour of trouble or embarrassment, and I have envied his philosophy and his self-command; but I have marked him too in the day of revel and exultation, and I have shrunk from the immobility of his features and the torpor of his smile.

I could never settle it to my satisfaction. Acute pleasure seems to be always the forerunner of intense pain, and weariness the inseparable demon which dogs the steps of gratification. I have examined all ranks and all faces; I have looked into eyes and I have looked into folios; I have lost patience and I have lost time; I have made inquiries of many and enemies of not a few; and drawn confessions and conclusions from demoiselles who never had feelings, and from dowagers who have survived them, from bards who have nourished them in solitude, and from barristers who have crushed them in Westminster Hall. The choice spirit who is loudest at his club to-night will be dullest in his chambers to-morrow, and the girl who is merriest at the dance will infallibly be palest at the breakfast-table. How shall I decide? The equability which lives, or the excitement which dies? The beef without the mustard, or the mustard without the beef?

Chance, or my kind stars, for I am very often inclined to believe in their agency, especially on fine moonlight nights, has flung me into a circle of acquaintance, where the pleasures and the pains attendant upon these different tempers of mind are continually forced upon my notice, and hold me delightfully balanced, like Mahomet's coffin, between earth and ether. Davenant Cecil is a being as thoroughly made up of sympathies and affections as ever was a puppet of springs or a commentator of absurdities. He never experienced, he never could endure five minutes of calm weather; he is always carried up into the heaven and down again into the deep; every hope, every exertion, every circumstance, be it of light or of grave import, is to him equally productive of its exaltation or its depression ; like the Proserpina of fable he is in Olympus half the year, and in Tartarus the other. Marmaduke Villars has about as much notion of raptures and enthusiasm as a Mohawk chief entertains of turtle soup, or a French milliner of the differential calculus. Except that he prefers claret to port, and Drury Lane to Covent Garden, and eau de Montpellier to eau de Cologne, I doubt whether he is conscious of any predilection for one thing or any aversion to another. Marmaduke is like Ladurlad in everything except "the fire in his heart, and the fire in his brain ;" and Davenant is the Sorcerer Benshee, who rode on a fast horse, and talked with many, and jested with many, and laughed loudly, and wept wildly for the things he saw ; yet was he bound by his compact to the fiend to sit at no table, and to lie on no couch, and to speed forward by night and by day, sleeping never, and resting never, even till his appointed hour.

A short time ago Davenant and myself received an invitation to spend a few days with Villars. His favourite hunter, Sir Peter, had thrown him or fallen with him, I forget which, and after being a little put to rights, as he expressed it, at the little country place where the accident happened, he had been removed to the Hall, and ordered to keep himself quiet. There seemed to be some chance of his compliance with this admonition, as the rest of his family were all absent, and there was not a house within five miles; but in order to counteract these favourable symptoms as much as possible, he summoned us to his sofa. Cecil and Villars are the antipodes of one another ; and, as is commonly the case, are the fondest friends upon all occasions, because they never can agree upon one.

We went accordingly, and were rejoiced to find our friend, pale to be sure, and very intimate with crutches, but still apparently free from pain, and enjoying that medicinal level of spirits which is a better preservative against fever than you will easily find from the lancet or the draught. He congratulated himself upon the safety of his nose, which Mr. Perrott the apothecary had pronounced broken, and only lamented the loss of his boot, which it had been necessary to cut from his leg. In a short time we quite forgot that he was in the slightest degree damaged, and conversed on divers topics without any intrusive compassion for his flannel and his slipper.

And first, as in duty bound, we began to discuss the *Quarterly Magazine*, and its past success, and its future hopes, and its patrons, and its contributors. Davenant was wonderfully angry because some " fathomless blockheads " found obscurities in his lyrical poem. " If there were any descendings into the deep fountains of thought, any abstruse researches ' into the mind of man'—in short, to speak plainly, if there were anything in the poem which a man might be very proud to risk his reputation upon, then one might be prepared for darkness and coldness in this improving and understanding age ; but a mere fancy piece like this, as simple in design as it is in execution—you know, Marmaduke, that incapacity to comprehend must be either gross stupidity or supreme affectation."

" I think much may be said for the ' blockheads,'" observed Marmaduke, shaking his head.

" You think no such thing," said Davenant, " and you feel that you think no such thing : I shall detest you, Villars, if you ' write yourself down an ass,' merely for the sake of telling me I am one."

" You know, my dear Davenant," said Villars, " you know you never detested any body in your life, except, perhaps, a few of the commentators upon Shakespeare, and the critic who considered Campbell the first poet of the day and Wordsworth the second. But seriously, I cannot conceive why you are ruffled about your verses ; you know they are admired, as Mr. Rigge says of his soap, by all the best judges ; not to go out of our own circle, you know Lady Mary, and Tristram, and Gerard, who are worth all the world, think them about the best things going ; nay, I am not clear that our good friend Joyeuse has not some suspicion of the kind, only he never speaks a word of truth upon any subject. And, loaded as you are with all these accumulated commendations, you want to add the weight of my valueless voice to your burthen, and to——"

"There never was a man more mistaken; what should I care for your opinion? It is not worth a straw, it is not worth 'Gertrude of Wyoming' to me. But I am in a passion when I see a tolerably clever man making a fool of himself wilfully. I read the poem to your sister, and she understood it perfectly."

"Then you persuaded her first that she was a clever girl, and she thought her comprehension would confirm the idea. I will wager a beauty against a bottle, or a haunch of venison against a page of rhyme, or 'The Pleasures of Hope' against 'The Excursion,' or any other boundless odds which you like to suggest, that with the same object in view she shall admire the Iliad or dote upon the Koran."

"There is no answer to such an argument. All I know is, that Amelia found nothing difficult in the poem."

"What! she told you so, I suppose."

"No; her eyes did."

"Then her eyes lied confoundedly. Never, my dear Davenant—never, while you live, believe in the language of the eyes. I would rather believe in the miracles of Apollonius, or the infallibility of the Pope of Rome, or the invincibility of the French army. I believed a pretty piercing pair once, which told me the wearer was very fond of a particular person, and I cultivated my whiskers accordingly, and did double duty at my glass. By Paphos and its patroness, she went off in a month with a tall captain of fusiliers, and left me to despondency and the new novel."

" And you longed to be so deceived again," said Davenant.

"No; it was very fatiguing. Never, while you live, believe in the language of the eyes. But you will, because you were born to be a fool, and you must fulfil your destiny. As Rousseau says—he is somewhere about the room——"

"I have him in my hand," said Davenant; "what a delightful little book! I dote upon the size, and the binding, and the type, and the——"

"Yes; he was of great service to me a fortnight ago, when my hurt was rather annoying at night. My people prescribed opium, and I used to take Jean Jacques instead. But this way is my treasure-house of reading : *eh ! le voici !*" And he led us up to a bookcase where was conspicuously placed an immense edition of Voltaire, and began taking down the volumes and expressing the dotage of his delight with wonderful rapidity. "Ah ! Alzire ! charming—and Merope; you are going to talk about Shakespeare, Davenant. Hold your tongue !—a noisy, gross, fatiguing— no, no : the French stage for me.!—*Eh ! ma belle Zaïre !*— the French stage for me !—*tout dort, tout est tranquille, et*— and Candide ! oh ! I could laugh for a century. *Et puis— la Pucelle ! oh, pour le coup——*"

And *le coup* came with a vengeance; for Davenant, who hates a French play worse than poison, had just found something overpoweringly ridiculous in the woes of " L'Or- phelin de la Chine," and bursting into an ungovernable shriek of laughter, dropped some six or seven quarto volumes upon the wounded foot of our unfortunate stoic. He fell on the floor, in agony, and almost in a passion.

"Damnation !—*n'importe !* My sweet Davenant, how could you—— Peregrine, my good fellow, do pull the bell ! Horrible ! Why, Cecil, how out of your wits you look ! *Ave Maria ! Vive la bagatelle !* Why you look like a *diable !*—like a physician called in too late—*mort de ma vie !*—or like a—*monstre !*—like a wood demon at the English Opera House. Ring again, Courtenay ! Ha, ha !— I play.d one myself once—*Oh ! que c'est affreux !*—for a wager, ha, ha !—Oh !—with a long torch, ha, ha !—fire and brimstone !—with long black hair—*peste !*—but it would never stand on end like yours ! *oh que non !* Ring again, Courtenay !—*Eh ! Perpignan !* here has been a fall ! a fall, —as they say upon 'Change. *Cher Perpignan :* take me to bed, Perpignan ; take it easy—*doucement !* Ah ! the wood demon, Davenant ! I shall never get over it !—ha, ha !— Oh !——"

And thus was Marmaduke carried off, laughing, and screaming, and jesting, and swearing, by turns. His medical attendant was summoned, and we saw him no more that night; he sent us word that he was as well as could be expected, but that he should never get over the wood demon, in spite of which consolatory intelligence Davenant wore a Tyburn countenance the whole evening.

We met, however, the next morning, and proceeded most laudably to remember nothing of the accident but its absurdity. "I never found Voltaire heavy before," said Villars, shaking Davenant by the hand; "but you poets of the Lake are so horribly in the habit of taking liberties with your own feet that you have no compassion at all for those of your friends. Mercy upon my five toes! they will not meet in a boot for a twelvemonth; and now, *àpropos de bottes*, we must have some breakfast."

Rain confined us to the house, the newspapers were full of advertisements, and the billiard-table was undergoing repair. Davenant endeavoured to define intensity, and I endeavoured to sleep; Marmaduke struck his sister's tambourine, and the great clock struck one. We began to feel as uncomfortably idle as a gaol-bird who has just been put in, or a Minister who has just been turned out. At last some notice was taken of two miniatures of our friend and his sister, which had been done many years ago, and now hung on opposite sides of the mantelpiece, gazing tenderly at one another in all the holiday magnificence which was conferred by laced cap and pink ribbons upon the one, and by sky-blue jacket and sugar-loaf buttons upon the other. Hence we began to talk of painting, and of "Raphael, Correggio, and stuff," until it was determined that we should proceed to make a pilgrimage through a long gallery of family portraits, which Marmaduke assured us had been covered with commendations and cobwebs ever since he left his cradle. He hobbled before us on his crutches, and made a very sufficient cicerone. Marmaduke has no wit; but he has a certain off-hand manner which often passes for it, and is sometimes as good a thing.

"'That old gentleman," he began, pointing to a magnificent fellow in rich chain armour, whose effigies occupied one end of the gallery, "that old gentleman is the founder of the family. Blessings on his beard! I almost fancy it has grown longer since I saw it last. He fought inordinately at Harfleur and Agincourt, was eminently admired and bruised, won a whole grove of laurels, and lost three fingers and a thumb. See, over his head is the crest which was his guerdon; a little finger rampant, and the motto blazoned gorgeously round, '*Mon doyt est mon droit!*'"

"A splendid servant of the sword," said Davenant; "what a glorious scope of forehead, and what a lowering decision in the upper lip. A real soldier! He would have cleft down a dozen of your modern male *figurantes!*"

"Perhaps so," replied Villars; "but you see he made a bad hand of it, notwithstanding. His nephew, there, is something more soberly habited, but he was not a jot less mad. Who would dream of such a frenzy in sackcloth and sad countenance? He was a follower of Wyckliffe before it was the fashion, and——"

"An excellent piece of workmanship too! I like to see some fury in a man's faith. Who can endure a minister of the gospel mounting his pulpit at Marylebone, with his well-ordered bands, and his clean manuscript, and his matter-of-fact disquisition, and his matter-of-course tone! That bald apostle has lips I could have listened to: he might have been an enthusiast, or a bigot, or a madman, or e'en what you will; but he has a show of zeal, and an assumption of authority; there is fire about the old man!"

"There was once," said Marmaduke, "for he was burned in Smithfield. Come hither, here is a young fellow you will admire—Everard the Beautiful (by the way, they say he is like me), who fell in love with the pretty Baroness de Pomeroy. He used to sing under her balcony at midnight, out of pure gallantry, and out of all tune; catching sighs from the high window, and colds from the high wind. He was full three years wailing and whispering, and dreaming and dying, and smarting in the left breast, and sonneting in the left turret. At last came the fifth act of the drama, death and happiness blended together with strict poetic propriety; the fates threw him into her arms one night, and the baron threw him into the moat one morning."

"I loathe and detest that eternal sneer of yours. You believe and feel, Marmaduke, although you are too weak to confess it, that the life you have described, a turbid unresting sea of passion and anxiety, and hope and fear, and brief calm and long madness, is worth—oh! twenty times over—the sleepy river of a pedant's philosophy, or the dirty ditchwater of your own clumsy indifference."

"Why, my dear Davenant," said Marmaduke, quietly, "you know love has its ditch-water occasionally; my poor ancestor found it so. But pass on. Here is a courtier of Queen Elizabeth's day, lying on the green sward in despondency and an attitude, with a myriad of cares and a bunch of daffy-down-dillies in his bosom. There is your true cavalier; a health to short wit and long spurs, blue eyes and white satin! The race has been quite extinct since rapiers went out and political economists came in."

"I wish," muttered Cecil, "I wish I had lived with those men. To have had Spenser for my idol, or Sydney for my friend—to have held Leicester's mantle at court, or Raleigh's back-hand at tennis—to have stormed a town with Drake, or a bottle with Shakespeare—by Elizabeth's ruff, it would have been worth an eternity! That was your age for choice spirits!"

"You will find very choice spirits at the Hummums," said Marmaduke; "but we are getting into the Great Rebellion. It abounded in good subjects—for the pencil, I mean, not for the prince. Never was the land so sorely plagued with dire confusion and daubed canvas. There is silly Sir Lacy who lost his head, and was none the poorer; and sillier Sir Maurice, who lost his lands, and was many acres the poorer: and there is honest Sir Paul, who came in with the Restoration, and wrote my favourite song. Ha, Davenant!

> " ' For prince or for prig.
> Long locks or flowery wig,
> I don't care a fig !— .
>   Fill the glasses.
> So I may hold my land,
> And my bottle in my hand,
> And moisten life's sand
>   While it passes.' "

There was a curious portrait a little farther on—a beautiful and interesting woman, as far as neck and bosom could give us any information ; but in place of her countenance was painted a thick black veil. I asked for her history. "Oh," said Villars, "that damosel was called Priscilla the Penniless. She was wonderfully killing, but of course that is not the reason she is veiled. Her uncle, the existing head of the family, struck her face out of the picture, and her name out of his will, because she married a young Roundhead, who had no merit but his insolence and no fortune but his sword."

"What a detestable fool !" said Davenant, meaning the uncle.

"I think she was," said Marmaduke, meaning the niece. "*Mais allons ;* let me show you one more set of features, and we will adjourn. Here is my earliest and most complete idea of feminine beauty. Down on your knees, Davenant, and worship. The fairy-like symmetry of the shape, and the pretty threatening of the right arm, and the admirable nonchalance of the left, and the studied tranquillity of the black hair, and the eloquent malignity of the dark eyes, and the exquisite caprice of the nose, and the laughing scorn of her little lips ! By Venus' dimple, Davenant, I have stood here, and talked rhapsodies to her for hours."

"Pray give us one now," said Cecil, laughing.

"I will. Fairest of Nature's works ! perfection in duodecimo ! I speak to you, and you do not hear ; I question you, and you do not answer : but I read your taste in your dress, and your character in your countenance. You are the brightest of all earthly beauties. You would call me a blockhead if I called you a goddess ; you are fashioned for a drawing-room, and not for Olympus—for champagne, and not for nectar ; you are born for conquest and for mirth, to busy your delicate brain with the slaves of to-day, and to snap your delicate fingers at the slaves of yesterday ; epigrams only are indited to your charms, witticisms only are uttered in your presence ; you think laughter the elixir vitæ, and a folio of theology poison ; you look with contempt on the Damon who has died for your sake, and with kindness on the fool who bows to the ground and vows he is 'yours entire,' head and hand, pen and pistol, from infancy to age, and from shining ringlet to shoe-ribbon!"

"Admirable!" cried Cecil, "and after all the woman is nothing extraordinary."

"*Chacun a son goût,*" said Villars.

"She has no poetry about her," said the first.

"I never write poetry about anybody," said the second.

"She is not guilty of intellect," said the reviler.

"She is guilty of coquetry," said the admirer.

"She would never understand Milton," said the poet.

"She would dance divinely," said the fashionable.

"You are over head and ears in love," said Davenant, laughing immensely.

"She died anno Domini seventeen hundred!" said Marmaduke, with inestimable gravity; and so we left the gallery.

We parted from our friend the next morning. If perfect indifference and composure in all trials and temptations can constitute happiness, Villars will be a happy man; but there is something repulsive in his very happiness. Which shall I prefer? Marmaduke, with his unsunned and unclouded weather, or Davenant, with his eternal alternation of bright glow and fleeting shower?

I could never settle the point.

LEONORA.

POOR Alonzo! He was the best friend that ever drank Xeres: he picked me out of the Guadalquivir, when I deemed I had said my last prayer.

It was a very conciliating introduction. I never in my life made a friend of a man to whom I was introduced in a formal kind of way, with bows from both parties, and cordiality from neither. I love something more stirring, more animated; the river of life is at best but a quiet stupid stream, and I want an occasional pebble to ruffle its surface withal. The most agreeable introductions that ever fell to my lot were these—my introduction to Pendragon, who was overturned with me in the York Mail; my introduction to Eliza, who contrived to faint in my arms on board the *Albion* packet; and my introduction to Alonzo, who picked me out of the Guadalquivir.

I was strolling beside it on a fine moonlight night, after a brilliant and fatiguing party, at which the Lady Isidora had made ten conquests, and Don Pedro had told twenty stories: I was tired to death of dancing and iced waters, glaring lights and lemonade; and as I looked on the sleepy wave, and the dark trees, and the cloudless sky, I felt that I could wander there for ever, and dream of poetry, and— two or three friends.

The sound of a guitar and a sweet voice waked me; I do not know why I always associate the ideas of pleasant tones and bright eyes together; but I cannot help it, and of course I was very anxious to see the musician of the Guadalquivir. I clambered, by the aid of cracked stones, and bushes which hung to them, to the summit of a low wall; and looking down perceived a cavalier sitting with a lady under a grove of sycamores. The cavalier seemed to have seen hardly seventeen winters; he was slender and tall, with a ruddy complexion, black hair, and a quick merry eye. The lady appeared full five years older; her eyes were as quick, and her ringlets as black, and her complexion as warm, but more delicate: they were evidently brother and sister; but that was a matter of indifference to me.

I heard a Spanish song upon the fall of the Abencerrage. and another upon the exploits of the Cid: then the lady began an Italian ditty, but she had not accomplished the first stanza when a decayed stone gave way, and carried me through all the intricacies of bush and bramble into the cold bed of the river. I could not swim a stroke.

I remember nothing more until the minute when I

opened my eyes, and found myself in a pretty summer-house, very wet and very cold, with Alonzo and his sister leaning over me. "For the love of heaven" were the first words I heard, "run, Alonzo, to call the servants."

"I wait," said Alonzo, "to hear him speak. If he be a Frenchman he goes to the bottom again."

The Fates be thanked that I was born in Derbyshire, and called Sir Harry my father; if I had bathed in the Seine instead of the Derwent, I had rued my parentage bitterly. Alonzo detested the French.

From that time we were always together. They were orphans, and had scarcely a relation in the world except an aunt who had gone to the cloister, and an uncle who had crossed the sea, and a rich cousin who had betaken himself St. Jerome knew whither; but Alonzo, who had a much nearer concern in the matter, seemed to know little enough about it. They had travelled much, and Leonora was mistress apparently of the literature of all Europe; yet they went rarely into company, for they doted upon one another with a love so perfect and so engrossing, that you might have fancied them, as they fancied themselves, alone in the world, with no toil and no pleasure, but solitary walks, and songs of tenderness, and gazings upon one another's eyes. If ever perfection existed in woman, it existed here. I do not know why I did not fall in love with Leonora; but to be sure I was in love with five or six at a time.

A few months flew delightfully away. Leonora taught me Spanish, and Alonzo taught me to swim. Every morning was occupied with romantic excursions by water or by land, and every evening was beguiled with literary conversation or music from the loveliest voice and the most eloquent strings that ever I had the fortune to listen to. And when we parted, we parted with warm hearts, and pleasant anticipations, and affectionate tears. In two brief years those hearts were separated, and those anticipations were blighted for ever, and those tears were exchanged for tears of bitterness and of mourning.

The troubles of Spain commenced; and my poor Alonzo joined the Patriots, and fell in his first campaign. Leonora had been—not a heroine, for I hate heroines—but a noble woman. She herself had decorated the young victim whom she sacrificed to her country's good; she had embroidered the lace on his uniform with her own hand; she had given him the scarf which was found turned round his arm on the field; and she had smiled mournfully as she bade him wear it till some one more beautiful or more beloved had chosen him for her knight. And when he had girded on his father's sword, and lingered with his hand upon his courser's mane, she had said "farewell" in a firm voice, and wept while she said it.

It was on a journey to Scotland that I passed through the small village in which the Spanish lady had shrouded her fading beauty and her breaking heart. I sent up my name to her, and was admitted into her little drawing-room immediately. Oh! how altered she seemed that day. All the colour had disappeared from her cheek, and all the freshness from her lip; she had still the white hand and arm, which I had seen running so lightly over the strings of her theorbo, but they were wasted terribly away; and though her long dark locks were braided as carefully as they had been in happier days, they did not communicate the idea of brightness and brilliancy which they had been wont to scatter over her countenance. She endeavoured to rise from the sofa as I entered; but the effort was too great for her, and she sat down without speaking. She was evidently dying; and the contrast between the parting and the meeting, and the vague vision of the past and the melancholy reality of the present, struck me so forcibly and so sadly, that I stayed with my hand on the door and burst into tears.

"We are not to weep thus," she said; "he fell like a true Spaniard, and I only regret that I was not born a man, that I might have put my rifle to my shoulder and died with my hand in his. Pray sit down; it is a long time since I have seen any friend who can talk to me of the old days."

I suggested that she ought to endeavour to think less of the losses she had endured, and to dwell more cheerfully on the tranquillity which might yet be in store for her. "I

should despise you now," she answered, " if I could think
this advice came from your heart.   What! you would have
me forget him, whose life was my dearest pleasure, and
whose death is my greatest pride.   Look at this ring," and
she took off a small gold one, and made me remark its
motto—*fiel a la muerte ;* " he would not have bade me wear
this in remembrance of him, if he had not known that he
was doomed to perish, if he had not known too that I
should be happy afterwards in thinking and dreaming of
him."   Then she began to recall minutely every scene and
circumstance of our intimacy ; inquiring about every study
or amusement we had meditated or enjoyed together,
whether I had bettered my flute-playing, whether I had
studied landscape, whether I had finished Calderon.   She
wearied herself with talking ; and then, leaning her head on
the cushions, desired me to take up a book from the table
and read to her, that she might hear whether my pronun-
ciation was improved.

I took up the first that presented itself; it was only a
manuscript book, containing many scraps and fragments
from different authors in her brother's writing.   I laid it
down again, and took up the next : it was a Dante which
I had given her : I opened it at random and began to read
the story of Francesca.   When I came to the celebrated
lines —

> Nessun maggior dolore
> Che ricordarsi del tempo felice
> Nella miseria——

" I do not believe a word of it" she said.   " I would not
lose my recollection for all Mexico."

I took leave of her soon : for I saw that my presence
agitated and wearied her.   When I had parted from her
before, she had given me a miniature of herself, which she
had painted in all the glow of health and spirits, and ardent
affections, which then so well became her.   Now she gave
me another which had been her task or pleasure in sickness
and solitude.   I do not know why I turn from the first with
its fine hues and sparkling lustre, to gaze upon the paleness
and languor of the other, with a deeper feeling of melancholy delight.

When I returned from Scotland after the lapse of two months, Leonora was dead. I found the sexton of the village, and desired him to point out to me the spot where she rested. There was a small marble slab over her remains, with the brief inscription, " Leonora.—Addio ! " I stood for a few minutes there, and began to moralize and murmur. " It seems only yesterday," I said, " that she was moving and breathing before me, with all the buoyancy and beauty of her blameless form and her stainless spirit ; and now she lies in her purity and her loveliness."

" She lies in a pretty grave," said the old sexton, looking with apparent satisfaction on his handiwork.

" She does, indeed, good Nicholas ; and her loveliness is but little to the purpose ! "

DAMASIPPUS.

DAMASIPPUS.	GETA.
SYRINX.	MARSYAS.
CYANE.	A MESSENGER.

Scene—ROME. *A Cook's Shop.* *Time*—NIGHT.

DAM. [*entering.*] Hilloa ! black dweller in darkness ! Hilloa ! monarch of perfumes and placentæ ! How long am I to kick my royal feet before thy damnable dwelling-place, like a half-buried ghost before Charon, or a half-witted Grecian before Troy ? Shrivelled imp of Hades, answer me ! Was it for me—for me, reptile, the lord of all misrule, the bosom friend of every felon and flagon in Rome, the deepest drinker that ever kissed Chian—saving always the Emperor, whom the Fates and the Furies preserve !—was it for me to stand for an hour, roaring " Syrinx, Syrinx," louder than ever poet cried Evoe ! over his sour verses and sour vinegar, with not a hand of those who live by me to take the bolt from the door and the seal from the bottle? Now, by Pollux——

SYR. Prince of patrons——

DAM. I tell thee, foul fiend, all Rome has been at my heels, hooting and hallooing, sweating and swearing, making a very chaos of greasy caps and grievous imprecations, red flambeaux and faces almost as red, cooks and cobblers, slaves and centurions, money borrowers and money lenders. By Pollux, again I say, Themison is not more weary when he has prescribed for his twentieth patient, nor Palemon, when the last disputant of his hundred has murthered grammar and great Julius together.

SYR. Merciful lord——

DAM. Hecate! We are come to a pretty pass, when a man of my blood may not walk in the dark, and swear in a mask, and kiss a girl in the Capitol, and cudgel a usurer in the Suburra—but fathers, and brothers, and cousins—ay, by the gods of the hearthstone! and mothers and aunts to boot—must start up, like the Argonaut's harvest, scouring and screaming in all the streets of Rome and all the dialects of its provinces. Marry, hang them! Is there no respect or reverence for my this year's chariot, or my last year's fasces? Nay, then, honour may hide in a cloaca, and fashion walk a-foot; patricians shall patronize the tunic, and consulships be sold for an as.

SYR. Most munificent of revellers——

DAM. And for thee, scum of Ethiopia, for thee to keep thy supporter and thy sovereign lingering thus long before thy threshold, and listening to the cries, and the curses, and the distant murmurs of a mob. May I never fling Venus again, may I never lip Mela's Falernian, may the black plague poison my pickles, may the green jacket fail in the circus, if ever I danced the client so long—no, not before the Emperor's gate—no, not under Triphenion's window, though she be witty, and wicked, and gay, and golden-haired, the fairest and the fondest of the daughters of Corinth! Epona! belike thou hast forgotten me; there is nothing to be remembered in my forehead and my features! Look at me, villain, slave—who am I?

SYR. My most admirable and excellent master, I lick thy

foot. Thou art the supreme of sin and song, the chief choice of charioteers, the love of all thy slaves, the envy of all the Senate, priest of pledgings and king of cups, the Mars of midnight, the Cupid of costume, the Jupiter of all joviality!

DAM. Excellent well! I had not deemed thy recollection so good; marry, thou mayest perhaps recollect the far-back landing, and the lorn look, and the chalked sole, and the bored ear; and thou mayest perhaps have some slight vision of thrushes fried to dust, and boars burned to powder, and the inflicted scourge, and the threatened crucifixion. I thought that withered skin of thine had undergone metempsychosis, or that thou hadst found the two springs of Lethe in Vindicta and Vertigo.

SYR. Prince of men, it is not so lightly that I forget my native dust, or the hand that raised me from it. All I have is thine own; take of it to eat or to drink, or to wear or to waste; set thy slipper on my head, and crush my brains beneath thee; give me thy dagger, and let me pledge a health to thee in my best heart's blood.

DAM. Honest Syrinx, I forgive thee! let there be new peace and old wine between us. Ha! little Cyane, where hast thou hidden thy mirth and mitra? Come hither, little Cyane! What! I warrant me thou wert afraid of me, because my frown was somewhat grim, and my posture somewhat gladiatorial. But mine anger is vanished; I am as cold as the snows of Hæmus, or the pleadings of Pedo. Sit by me, Cyane; we will have music anon.

CYA. Now, by Venus, I had not dreamed we should see you again, Damasippus! Have you been grieving with the jaundice or grappling with the Gauls? Have you hunted Parnassus and the columns, or cultivated philosophy and a beard? Ah! now I bethink me; there were two tormentors who kept your sweet looks from us; soldier and sophist they were, uncle and father. Tisiphone whip them for it! And what hast thou done with them, dear Damasippus: him of the civic crown, with his sword and buckler, his sour look and sagum; who prated to you of cohorts and conquests, warfare and wounds, Syria and Armenia, Ister and Rhine? and him of the Stoic school, with his good morals and grave face, his short breath and long speeches, who only lived for profitless dispute, and endless enthymeme, and meaningless maxim, and senseless syllogism. Mercury! but they were a valuable pair to all the lovers of laughter.

DAM. They were, Cyane, they were; but they were loathsome poisoners of enjoyment, and detestable marrers of mettle. Here is to the quiet of their encampment. Mine uncle—the gods be thanked for that—is with the Prætor in Spain; and my father—the gods be thanked for that too—is with his ancestors in the Flaminian; and I am here, sweet Cyane—the gods be thanked for that, above all—sufficiently merry and reasonably drunk. I thought I should have died before supper. A hundred plagues have haunted me since daybreak. My head was out of order, and my physician out of town; and my mistress broke an appointment, and my curricle broke down; and the theatres were empty, and the courts were full; and merry Marcus was swearing in the sullens, and solemn Saleius was reciting in the baths. Phœbus blight him for it! A decree of the Senate would never stop that eternal babbler; it would be easier to silence the Danube. Does he think that man, whose life is fourscore years, has nothing to study and care for here but warrior and amazon, epic and ode, maidens shrieking in sapphics and heroes howling in hexameters?

CYA. Nay now, sweetest soul of mine, you are very rude to the poets. May I never see a solidus again, if I do not love a poet as I love my own soul! They are all so humble, and so obedient, and so starving. Poor Saleius never fingers a denarius, but it comes straight to us at the Jews' gate. And then he is so happy and so agreeable, and so fond of his liquor and his laurels; and after his second cup, "Cyane," says he. "did you never hear my Orestes? Never, I'll be sworn! Woe for thy education, Cyane; thou wert born among savage barbarians, and suckled by tigresses, and cradled in rocks and stones. But it shall be amended. 'Learning,' as Ovid sung before me,

"'Learning and love are good lustrations,
And purify all rude sensations,'"

And then he throws himself into an attitude thus, takes off his cup with a tragic smack of the lips, and "Cyane," quoth he, "thou shalt hear sounds which Hercules might have earned by the repetition of his old labours, which Cleopatra might have bought with the brightest jewel in her crown. Their melody might make a client pause when he throws his first glance on the sportula, or a lawyer when the last drop of his clepsydra is putting him into a passion and a gallop. They might wake a Stoic from his mutterings, or a spendthrift from his debauch, or a lover from his dream, or a Christian from his cloud-worship. Listen; I am to recite them at Carus's to-morrow, and would fain have thy judgment, Cyane, on my voice and manner. By Phœbus, there is some fascination in both, and I could tell thee of some bright-haired ladies who have thought so. Ha!" Upon which I compose my features into a greedy gaze of admiration, and bid Syrinx hold the bottle, and Marsyas hold his tongue; and so my man of loud verses and cheap drink prologuises.

DAM. Let me bathe my lips in the Chian but once more, and so begin, Cyane: thou art an incomparable mimic; Bathyllus is but dirt by thy side.

CYA. What will you have then, sweet Damasippus? Œdipus, the expounder of riddles, or Ajax, the slaughterer of sheep? Medea, with her brats and dragons, or Orestes, with his rags and snakes? for he has stored me with specimens of all.

DAM. The last, I pray thee, the last; let me hear what Orestes says to his tormentors, that I may know how to answer mine. Marry, the fiends in the fish market are becoming so tumultuous now, that a nobleman knows not wherewithal to reply, unless he ransacks the poets for complimentary language.

CYA. Thus then: "It is necessary that thou shouldst understand, Cyane, how that Orestes is the murderer of his mother—a wicked thing, by Themis, a wicked thing; but justifiable in particular cases. Æmilius argued it so the other day, and saved his client—Publius it was, who had succeeded somewhat too suddenly to an inheritance. Alas, avarice never walks abroad, but she carries aconite fastened to her girdle. But as I said, Orestes has murdered his mother, and he rushes upon the stage with long hair, and short breath, and torn garments, and wandering eyes; and fifty furies are in readiness without, with snaky ringlets and blazing torches, which thou knowest, little Cyane, are the adornments which the furies most conceit. When Serranus played his Megæra, the torches went out; but those things shall be better cared for when I——but I lose time; listen! Orestes begins thus, faltering a little from fear, as is natural:

> " ' Dark goddesses, swift-footed, serpent-haired,
> Red-eyed, black-lipped, hell's offspring, earth's annoy,
> Avaunt, I spit upon ye ! King Apollo,
> Lord of the beaming bow and echoing string,
> Fair-browed, far-darting, Prince of Poetry,
> Art thou a juggler ? are thine oracles
> Mere webs for witching flies? Behold ! they come !
> Railing and roasting, scampering and scaring,
> All hot from hissing Tartarus ! O God,
> Pæan, Lycean,
> God of music, god of day,
> Delian, Patarean,
> Help, help ! and let me see an
> End of these calamities as soon as I may.' "

DAM. Ha! ha! May Æsculapius put life into my father's ashes, if I do not love thee entirely. The poet is under infinite obligations to thee; if thou wouldst only study this trade, the dirty Quirites would run from their bread—by Pollux! I think they would run from their games, to hear thee. And now the answer, pretty Saleius, the response of the Avengers !

CYA. Let me unfasten my mitra, and perform it in costume. There! "Now, Cyane," he says, "thou must suppose, what doubtless thou hast already suspected, that the goddesses rush in with their shrivelled arms and terrible eyebrows, dancing, in groups of three or four, a dance dreadful to look upon, such a dance as Pomponia's slave performs when he is whipped, or Paulus's mistress when she is intoxicated; thus, Cyane, a rapid agitation of the right foot, then a corresponding movement of the left, with vibrations of·the arms and contortions of the neck in

unison. Presently the chief of them chants these terrible
verses in a low and dismal scream :

> "' Ye raven-headed goddesses,
>> Who, in your cloudy bodices,
> Hover with me around this ball of earth,
>> And ever love to mix
>> Dark drops from your own Styx
> With every rivulet of living mirth,
>> Fit followers of mortality,
>> Fine teachers of morality,
> Eternal servants of the Olympian thunder,—
>> Dwellers in mirky mists,
>> By whose unyielding wrists
> Strong frames are racked, fine heart-strings rent asunder,—
>> Come hither, solemn sisters,
>> Rain, rain your boils and blisters,
> Heart-thrilling ache, swift stripe, and searing cinder,
>> Come hither, oh ! come hither,
>> And let him waste and wither,
> Roaring like twenty bulls, and rotting into tinder ! '"

DAM. Ho ! ho ! ho ! Stop, dear girl, or thou wilt murder
me indeed ; thou art very Saleius from head to foot. Investigate the flagon and proceed : I would bring thee to the
Emperor's hearing, Cyane, had I not some scruples of
jealousy in my composition. But thou must be chary of
thy parlous wit, for those singing birds are marvellously
inflammable ; I have known them in their wrath more rude
than a Briton and more robust than a rhinoceros. Codrus
broke my skull in the first week of my consulship, because
I asked him how often he had dined upon his Theseid ;
and Serranus has written five-and-twenty lampoons upon
me, because I told him that Podalirius recommends cold
water for a December cup. And I need not tell thee that
these male sempstresses of absurdities have at their beck
and bidding sword and dagger, plague and pestilence,
balista and bowl—ay, by my head, and lightning-flash
and thunder-bolt to boot, and the whole armoury of
the skies. But go on, sweetest of all the Furies ; maledic-
tions from such lips as thine are worth blessings from any
others.

CYA. I have done ! Never was Sibyl more weary after

an hour's raving. But Damasippus hath noticed none other of his friends. Geta is here, and Parmeno, and little Amphitryon, and tall Antigonus. Come, do throw away a word upon them; it is long since they have looked upon their master.

DAM. Geta, worthy Geta, sovereign reducer of ringlets and princely mower of beards, how fares the world with thee! Well, as I can divine by thy red nose and round external. What! do the gallants still linger to babble truth and falsehood in the shade of thy dominion? Come, let us know what scandal is toward.

GET. I prate scandal! Now Mercury forbid! It is true that idle persons do consort to me often; and as my worshipful master knows, much talk will arise of princes and patricians, and matters with which the like of Geta are little concerned. But do I ever report a syllable? Now Mercury forbid! 'Twas but yesterday that young Nasica was telling of the quarrel between Aurelius and his wife; did you hear? She must go on the arena forsooth; nothing would serve her but helm and sword, glory and fencing. "Why not," quoth the lady; "was not Julia in training with Capella, and had not Lucia foiled her master after three week's learning?" Marry, Aurelius was but little moved by authority or precept. He stilled her arguments by oaths, and sold her paraphernalia by auction; carried her into the country on a lean mule, and confined her in what he calls his Tusculan, where he collects together gems he cannot name, and books he cannot read, busts with broken noses and bailiffs who talk philosophy.

DAM. Bravo! and has the lady laid her propensities on the shelf?

GET. No; she has put her baggage on board; she has gone off to sea with that long armed destroyer of tigers, Cleobulus. The amphitheatre never saw a firmer hand or a quicker eye. But do I ever mention the story? Now Mercury forbid! Then there was merry Tiberius—ha, ha! a clever young fellow, and one who stands well with the court; and he was telling how Sulpicia tore the old Prætor's hair to shreds, because he had never read Homer, and whipped a slave to death because he brought her some perfumes wrapt up in a page of old Horace. A strong woman, and terrible when moved! But do I circulate these tales? Now Mercury forbid!

DAM. Thou art the most silent of babblers, the most veracious of liars, the most honest of knaves! I would trust in thy keeping, dear Geta, all secrets that men strive most to conceal; I would breathe in thine ear my successful amours and my anonymous writings, my own merits and the failings of my friends.

GET. Ah! Damasippus was always witty with his slaves. But I suppose you have not heard of the tumult at Glycerion's last night. I have heard mention of nought else to-day. Valla has said nothing of the Gauls, and Varus has been silent upon his lawsuit.

DAM. Prithee, now what was the manner of it?

GET. You know Glycerion—the little light-eyed Lesbian. And you know Titus too; and you used to cling as constantly to his side as the lictors to the consul or the duns to Flaminius. Well; he was shivering before her door last night in a thin cloak and sullen mood, with a lute in his hand, and a garland on his head, and perfumes enough on his apparel to convert Tartarus into Ida, and make Atinia herself endurable. A rival comes up; a young fellow in a long robe, masqued, and walking on tiptoes. Swords are drawn—crossed—thrusts given and returned; and Titus discovers that the sober votary of pleasure, the quiet Clodius, the dissipated Hippolytus, is no other than—— Guess now! You may study until a second Virgil rises, until the sun sets at daybreak, until I talk Greek, until my wife talks reason, and you shall never come near the mark. No other, by Jupiter and his transformations, than his studious and stern brother Caius.

DAM. Now, by Pollux, I am glad of it! Caius is a handsome young fellow, and deserves not spoiling by learning and sobriety.

GET. But the beauty of the jest remains behind. They explain—coalesce—beat the door from its hinges, and find in the citadel Caius's long-winded and long-bearded tutor, wrinkled Terentius, solacing his tired brain with stewed vegetables, golden smiles, and a goblet of damaged Falernian.

DAM. I will sacrifice a hecatomb. Thus it should ever be.

GET. But do I tell these stories? Do I repeat what may hurt reputation?—Now Mercury forbid! They told me, and it is indeed true, but do I repeat it?—now Mercury forbid!—that Aurunculeia was seen in the Suburra three nights ago in a mantle and hood, hastening to meet Lentulus, the——

DAM. Aurunculeia! Now, by Olympus and all its sojourners, I will drive the foul falsehood down thy black and calumnious throat. Withered imp of iniquity, cunning scatterer of poison, lie there; I put my sword's point to thy throat, and recommend to thee silence and thy last testament.

SYR. Noble Damasippus!

MARS. Sweet prince, have mercy!

DAM. Mercy is not for him! He shall never smooth a chin or fabricate a lie again. Come hither, Cyane: take off thy scarlet slipper, girl, and beat him till he confesses.

CYA. Good Damasippus, do not be thus moved by a slave!

GET. Slave, quotha? I beg no mercy, I! Mercury forbid! I will speak out, and be gagged for no man. What now, master of the whip and wheel, do you dream that you are in the company of your cattle, where lash and blow are law? I do most cordially hate thee; and I tell thee, moreover, that if thou comest, braving it and bullying it with loud tongue and long rapier, I have here a stout flagon of Saguntum, which has made flaws in heads of stouter manufacture, and——

DAM. Why, thou foul-mouthed blasphemer of greatness!

GET. Thou impotent imitator of buffoons!

DAM. Thou idol of cobblers!

GET. Thou scorn of nobility!

MAR. SYR. CYA. In the name of the gods, Damasippus! Jove! there will be a goodly tumult!

MESSENGER [*without.*] What, Syrinx—Syrinx, I say!

SYR. See now, if the Prætor be not here with a force!

Mess. Syrinx, I say—is Damasippus here to-night?
Dam. Well, fellow, who sends for Damasippus?
Mess. Truly, one that must send and find. The Emperor.
Dam. The Emperor! Hang ye, pestilent curs, give me my sandals. Quick!—and my cloak. So! am I steady, Syrinx? Thy venomous wine hath somewhat—— Adieu, Cyane; I will visit ye again ere long. A pest upon the Emperor!

MY FIRST FLAME.

Alderman Greenfat lives, from three to seven p.m., in joyous anticipation of the delights that hour will bring upon its wing. He tastes in fancy the never-cloying richness of the turtle, which if Jupiter had reigned now would have made Jupiter a candidate for civic honours; the invigorating flavour of the punch, which at once heightens the zest of the last and prepares the palate for the following dainty; the turbot, the venison, the champagne, the Burgundy—all are present to his imagination. Delicious! But seven o'clock arrives. What is the consummation? The meat is cold, or the wine is hot; the servants are awkward, or the next neighbour is a bore; repletion—indigestion—satiety—gout —the devil!

Lady Bauble waits patiently from March to May for the new Waverley novel, indulging perhaps in an occasional flirtation with Granby or a brief and hurried visit to Brambletye House, but turning eagerly from both to the prospect which the unnamed name of the Great Unknown opens before her imagination. Her visions are full of strange and appalling ideas. Some new· Meg Merrilies appears to start into terrible existence; some second Balfour lifts up the sword of the Lord and of Gideon;

Amy Robsart is regenerate, Front de Bœuf blasphemes again. But the three volumes come out, and present her with a commonplace bully or an everyday coquette— a lady who chatters at an evening party, a lord who figures in the *Morning Post.* "This really is too bad," says Lady Bauble, yawning; "I must absolutely give up Sir Walter!"

Captain Eustace is ordered to Rangoon. Delightful dreams are his—dreams of success and of reputation, of promotion and of pay, of armies discomfited, of stockades stormed, of midnight glimpses of the King of Ava's harem, of curry prepared in the King of Ava's kitchen! A few short weeks, and the fairy vision fades with a vengeance : he finds an empty camp, and a crowded hospital ; a weary surgeon, and a burning sun ; a rifleman in every bramble-bush, and a rheumatism in every bone.

O that our hopes could last for ever! That we and the objects of our desire could run on, like the fore and hind wheels of a chariot, always close but never united. That we could be contented to let our enjoyments go on like the lamp of the Rosicrucians, burning and dazzling eternally ; without advancing towards them the profane step which, by the essence and law of their nature, must destroy and crush them in a moment!

It is now about ten years since I left the residence of my respectable uncle and guardian in order to pay a visit of a few weeks to some friends at a neighbouring watering-place. My guardian, Sir Abraham, was in his day something of a character—and by-and-by I may sketch his portrait. For the present I shall only quote, as faithfully as I can, the old gentleman's parting admonition, for so constantly and unremittingly had he laboured at my education, up to the age of sixteen, that he considered six weeks of absence a long period, and six miles an infinite distance.

"Hark ye, Frederic!" he began; "all young men are fools—very well! Some are more fools than others ; there are degrees of comparison, but all are fools—very well! You I hold to be particularly and peculiarly a fool ; no fault of mine—very well! Now you have been for the last two

years pestering me with ravings and reveries about every
pretty face that fell in your way; verses you have written,
and they are my abomination—very well! I have found
stanzas to Chloe in my shaving-pot, and sonnets to
Araminta in the blank leaves of the Annual Registers—
very well! You are going to-day to my cousin Sir Andrew's;
nobody to fall in love with there—too sensible a man; insists
on a crooked nose in his laundress, and prefers a humpback
to a ten years' character in his choice of a dairymaid—very
well! But hark you, sir! you may meet, at some of those
hotbeds of frivolity and fevers, which are called card-parties,
routs, balls, and I know not what beside—I say, sir, you may
meet a girl called Adèle Lepicq—a fantastical name forsooth,
but ladies are as fine now in their appellations as they are in
their costume—very well! What's in a name? I tell you,
Frederic, if ever you mean to play the fool to any purpose,
fall in love with that girl. Why, sir, she is rich enough to
buy up the Bank of England—to keep even a ballad-monger
from starving! Talk of beauty—sentiment—affection! What
are these to a rent-roll like hers? I tell you, a shape is as
well set off by Mechlin lace as by brown holland; and a
white neck is mere moonshine, till it has a diamond necklace about it. Bah!—very well!"

So spoke my revered relation, and the impression produced on my mind was that which similar speeches have
produced on similar minds ever since old men were
arbitrary and young men wilful. I sell myself for gold!
I barter the first flush of the young heart's emotion for
what in poetry was always trash! I bend my knees to
awkwardness or ugliness! I bow in adoration to malice
and insipidity!

I set off, however, and found the stage which was to be
my conveyance occupied by a fox-hunter and a brace of
Militia officers, who were discussing the case of a poor man,
named, for his sins, John Smith. He had been severely
wounded in a duel. I listened with great interest to the
usual interesting details—the chaises ordered at five in the
morning; the vain attempt at a reconciliation; the ground
measured; the surgeon in attendance; the firing, the dropping; the deep regret of the antagonist; the absconding;

I

the apprehension of danger. All this was very well; but when, after going through the action, they proceeded to investigate the cause, what was my astonishment at finding that all this, which was to engross conversation for a week and fill the newspapers for a month, was occasioned by the fascinations of Adèle Lepicq!

"I never would risk my life for deformity," said I, in a fit of enthusiasm. "Deformity!" quoth the foe of foxes, opening his eyes very wide; "why she is a divinity! Venus was a wax doll to her—Diana a dowdy! One glance of her might charm a statue from its pedestal, or inspire the Bench of Bishops with wit!" And then all three joined in a sort of chorus of eulogy, which conveyed to me no definite idea of form or feature, but expressed simply the conviction of the speakers that every perfection of both had been collected by the munificence of a bountiful destiny in the person of Adèle Lepicq.

I arrived at my journey's end pretty considerably puzzled, and not a little annoyed. I fortified myself, however, in my preconceived dislike of my guardian's angel, by remembering that wealth and want of ideas, loveliness and imbecility, were perfectly compatible qualities. "Some silly uneducated heiress—all heiresses are silly and uneducated —who knows nothing but what she has learnt from her glass, and likes no one who does not corroborate daily its assertions; who votes literature *mauvais ton*, and would rather look into a coffin than a quarto." So thought I with myself as I lounged into Sir Andrew's library, in the pride of my mathematical studies, to take down Laplace from the neglect in which I flattered myself he had slumbered for years. Laplace was gone; and the card, which according to the custom of the place accounted for the vacancy on the shelf, informed me that the appropriator of the treasure was Adèle Lepicq.

I was petrified. But distrust is slow to depart, when it has once been admitted. "A Blue, then—who studies Aristotle, I warrant, and criticizes Plato! who keeps a journal in Hebrew, and scribbles notes in the arrow-headed writing! She has, I doubt not, an album—full of doggerel compliments and pen-and-ink drawings, a cabinet of shells and fossils, a museum of butterflies and beetles! After all, the days were blest when women attempted nothing beyond embroidery and the making of puddings!" And with these charitable reflections I sat down to dinner. There was at table a detestable story-teller; I have met him often since, and have heard his fifty-nine stories fifty-nine times over; but on this occasion it was as much as he could do to get through one of them. It was about an *omelette soufflée:* how he was very partial to an *omelette soufflée;* how he ate an *omelette soufflée* seven times a week in Paris; how he never tasted a good *omelette soufflée* out of France except once; how a very romantic incident belonged to that *omelette soufflée;* how it was composed by a beauty—an heiress of sixteen; how she had studied the whole theory of an *omelette soufflée* for her father's gratification, because the old man could not live without an *omelette soufflée.* This tale, interrupted of course by the usual accidents which disturb at a dinner-table the most experienced narrator, concluded by a rhapsody concerning filial duty, and her who was the gastronomical example of its excellence— Adèle Lepicq.

I began to be infinitely plagued by this continual recurrence of Monsieur Tonson in the shape of a reigning toast, But I was haunted for more than a week by unceasing and unpitying rumours. The shops were full of Adèle bonnets and Lepicq shawls; the musicians dedicated their quadrilles to Miss Lepicq; the Poet's Corner in the newspaper had always its stanzas to A—— L——. By her the harp I admired at Schneider's had been bespoken; the Arabian I noticed at the riding-house was breaking for her. By degrees my imagination became more and more engrossed by the thought which was thus eternally forced upon its notice. I began to delight in forming conjectures about the extraordinary being who did all things, and all things well. First, I painted her reserved, retiring, shrinking from her own praises, and winning, in consequence, many more than she deserved. Then I drew her wild, piquante, with a little dash of the masculine, and spirits enough to provoke the advances which her pride checked in a moment. Sometimes she was alone by the side of a river stream, reading Shake-

I 2

speare, and weeping unconsciously as she read; presently afterwards she was galloping along the hard sands of the sea-shore, her horse starting in vain from the echoing waters, and her hair floating long and dark upon the ocean breeze. She was my thought by day, my vision by night. I became like the lunatic who beholds, whithersoever he turns his eyes, an unvarying attendant figure, distinct in shape and hue to his own sight, but impalpable and unperceived to the gaze of others.

But I had never seen her, and I left the place in all the tortures of unsatisfied curiosity. If I was to meet her at a ball, she had a plaguy cold, and was confined to her room; if I looked for her on the public walk, she was the only person between the ages of seven and seventy who was not there; if I went to the theatre, she patronized the concert; if I rode on the downs, she rambled in the forest.

It was nearly a twelvemonth afterwards that I was one of three hundred who crowded, almost to bursting, two small drawing-rooms, not a hundred miles from Cavendish Square. I had picked up a lost fan, while the hurry and bustle of departure was going on, and was examining it in a fit of vacant abstraction, when I heard some charitable old lady annoying her friends with officious inquiries: "Where is Miss Lepicq's fan?" "Who has seen Miss Lepicq's fan?" "Where can Miss Lepicq's fan be?" I started from my trance. The deuce take the fan, and the querist—but where is Miss Lepicq? She had just left the room—her carriage was stopping the way. I rushed to the landing-place, cleared the stairs with the celerity of a kangaroo, overturned a brace of footmen, and broke my shins over the pole of a sedan, arriving at the house-door just in time to see the last gleam of a kid slipper glide into the conceal-ment of a carriage, to hear the "Home!" of the footman, and to make the best of my way to my hotel, with a head-ache and a sprained ankle.

Inquiries were bootless; she left London, England, the world; for she shut herself up in a convent, Heaven knows why; and, as her epitaph might say, is remembered with regret by all who knew her—and by one who did not.

Perhaps I ought not to lament—perhaps I do not lament —that I saw no more of Adèle Lepicq. I might have been blind to beauties which all the world adored; I might have discovered imperfections of which no others dreamed. It is pleasant, when I find in all I meet some little admixture of human frailty, to look back to one object which appears still all divine; it is charming, when I am deserted by the fondest friends, betrayed by the dearest hopes, to cling to an imaginative pleasure from which I can expect no treason or desertion. I have flirted with some score of beauties with sufficiently great perseverance, and sufficiently poor success; I have been desperately in love more than once; but if all the rapture of my real passions were set in one scale of a balance, and the luxury of this ideal one were put into the other, I believe the madder weight of the two would preponderate. I remember that in the fervour of my last disappointment I wrote a very fine copy of verses to the same effect; and thus, or nearly thus, they ran—

> Many a beaming brow I've known,
>   And many a dazzling eye,
> And I've listened to many a melting tone
>   In magic fleeting by;
> And mine was never a heart of stone,
> And yet my heart hath given to none
>   The tribute of a sigh;
> For fancy's wild and witching mirth
> Was dearer than aught I found on earth;
> And the fairest forms I ever knew
> Were far less fair than—L'Inconnue!

> Many an eye that once was bright
>   Is dark to-day in gloom;
> Many a voice that once was light
>   Is silent in the tomb;
> Many a flower that once was dight
> In beauty's most entrancing might
>   Hath faded in its bloom;
> But she is still as fair and gay
> As if she had sprung to life to-day;
> A ceaseless tone and a deathless hue
> Wild Fancy hath given to—L'Inconnue!

Many an eye of piercing jet
  .Hath only gleamed to grieve me
Many a fairy form I've met,
  But none have wept to leave me ;
When all forsake, and all forget,
One pleasant dream shall haunt me yet,
  One hope shall not deceive me ;
For oh ! when all beside is past,
Fancy is found our friend at last,
And the faith is firm, and the love is true,
Which are vowed by the lips of—L'Inconnue !

THE INCONVENIENCE OF HAVING AN ELDER BROTHER.

I DO not care for the paternal acres. To say the truth, Halbert Hall never pleased me. As a child I detested the long dark avenues of stunted trees ; and the heavy melancholy stream of moaning water, and the long passages, with their doleful echoes, and their countless doors, and the vast chambers with all their pomp and pageantry of faded furniture and family portraits. I am happier here in Lincoln's Inn, though one floor is my palace and one lackey my establishment ; and I leave the Hall, without a sigh, to my elder brother.

I shall not die for the lack of ten thousand a year. I never longed to keep hounds, or an opera-dancer ; to give champagne dinners, or to represent a county ; to win at Doncaster, or to lose at *rouge et noir*. Your true Epicurean does not need great wealth ; I can afford to wear a tolerable coat, and drive an unexceptionable cabriolet ; to be seen sometimes at the Opera, and keep myself out of reach of the Bench ; to throw away a trifle at picquet, and cook a wild duck for my antagonist. These things content me ; and, except when some unusual temptation has awakened my appetite or some more than common loss, for a time, ruffled my philosophy, I would not readily exchange them for the rent-roll and the three per cents. of my elder brother.

As for the title, it is not to be mentioned seriously as the object of a reasonable man's ambition. In old times a belted lord had certain privileges and pastimes, which might make life pass pleasantly enough. It was interesting to war upon his equals; it was amusing to trample on his inferiors; there was some merriment in the demolition of an abbey; there was some excitement in the settlement of a succession. Nowadays, it is as well to be called Tom as my Lord, unless you have a mind to dine at the dullest tables, and make speeches to the drowsiest audience in the world. So I resign my chance of the peerage without reluctance; the more that the coronet must pass from the temples of its present apoplectic possessor over an artillery officer, a rural dean, and an attaché to an embassy, before it decorates the honoured brows of my elder brother.

But when I have resigned philosophically all longings after these distinctions and advantages, which would be mine if I could date my birth but a twelvemonth earlier—when I have congratulated myself that I am not bound, by any necessity or interest, to do battle for the privileges of the order or talk nonsense in support of the Game Laws—why am I to be crossed at every turning by some hateful memento of the inferiority to which my unlucky planets have doomed me? Why are smiles to grow colder, and conversation more constrained, at my approach? Why are my witticisms listened to with such imperturbable gravity? And why does Lady Montdragon look zero when I bow, and turn away to whisper "Viper!" in her daughter's ear?

Thus it has been from my infancy. My mother, to be sure, had the usual maternal peculiarities, and was always in our nursery squabbles the unfailing protectress of the party which was most immediately dependent upon her protection. But she died, poor lady, almost before I could be sensible how much I needed her alliance, leaving me to carry on the war unaided against an adversary whose auxiliaries were many and zealous, in the butler's pantry and the servants' hall, in the tenant's cottage and the keeper's lodge. I was as handsome as Frederic; but his dress was more carefully tended, and his ringlets more studiously arrayed. I was as ravenous as Frederic; but his acquaintance with the cellar was more close and his visits to the store-closet more frequent. I was the bolder rider, but my pony was as rough as a bear. I was the better shot, but my gun was as heavy as a blunderbuss. Both learnt the lesson, but the praise and the shilling were for him; both plundered the orchard, but the reproof and the correction were for me. And when our father, with an unwonted exertion of impartiality, sent us to the same school, and supplied us with the same means of extravagance, though my hexameter was as smooth and my laugh as hearty, my scholarship as sound and my pluck as indisputable as my brother's, he had more patrons and more friends than I had; and somehow or other, between Halbert major and Halbert minor there was a plaguy difference, though I scarcely yet suspected where it lay.

But I was soon able to discover of what materials the talisman was composed. My father broke his neck in a fox-chase, and my brother was master of the kennel and the stud; my uncle died of a late division, and my brother represented the borough. We came into the world, and began to jostle for places like the rest of its industrious citizens.

I met Lord Fortalice at a dinner-party. What could be more condescending than his lordship's manner, or more flattering than his expressions? He had heard of my renown at college; he was confident of my success in life; he knew a host of my connections; he had had the sincerest respect for my father, he could assure me the Duke of Merino entertained the highest opinion of my talents, and Lady Eleanor had pointed me out last week as a model to her son. But when at last his lordship hoped that my principles would allow me to support the Bill which was next week to be before Parliament, and understood from me that the interests of sixty-seven independent men were in my brother's hands, not mine, he gradually withdrew his civilities from me, and devoted himself thenceforth to the entertainment of a puny divine, who spoke in monosyllables, and took an appalling quantity of snuff.

I was introduced to Tom Manille at the Opera. He was charmed to make my acquaintance; he had been told of my good fortune at the Salon, and was aware what a favourite I had been with the Baronne de Lusignan. Did I want a servant? A friend of his was going to dismiss one who was worth all the Indies. Was I looking for a hunter? His cousin had one, which would suit my weight exactly. He would make my betting-book, he would superintend my cellar, he would take me to a *soirée chez Mademoiselle*, he would give me a special recommendation to his tailor. He must make me known to the Somerses—their cook was Ude's first pupil. Of course I should belong to the Club—his influence was omnipotent there. A few weeks elapsed; and Tom Manille was riding my brother's horses, and drinking my brother's chambertin. He always calls me "My dear fellow!" and never passes me without a most encouraging nod. But I have never dined with the Somerses, and last week I was blackballed at the Club.

I wrote a treatise on the state of the nation, and submitted it to an eminent publisher. He was wonderfully delighted with the work. The views were so sound, the arguments so convincing, the style so pure, the illustration so apposite. I began to look forward to an infinity of popularity and an eternity of fame; I dreamed of laurel wreaths; I calculated the profits of tenth editions. In imagination I was already the pilot of popular opinion, the setter-up and the putter-down of Cabinets. But when I struck out the magical M.P. from the proof-sheet of my title-page, my fall was immediate and disastrous. My language lost its elegance, and my subject its importance; and my pamphlet lies forgotten in the limbo of unpublished embryos, wanting only life, and willing to win immortality. I should have been the most influential writer of the day if I had not had an elder brother.

At Brighton I fell in love with Caroline Merton. She was an angel, of course; and it is not necessary to describe her more particularly. Her mother behaved to me with the greatest kindness ; she was a respectable old lady who wore a magnificent cap, and played casino while her daughter was waltzing. Caroline liked me, I am sure; for she discarded a dress because I disliked the colour, and insulted a colonel because I thought him a fool. I was in the seventh heaven for a fortnight ; I rode with her on the downs, and walked with her on the Chain Pier. I drew sketches for her scrap-book, and scribbled poetry in her album. I gave her the loveliest poodle that ever was washed with rose-water, and called out a corpulent gentleman for talking politics while she played. Caroline was a fairy of a thousand spells ; she danced like a mountain nymph and sang like a syren ; she made beautiful card-racks and knew Wordsworth by heart ; but to me her deepest fascination was her simplicity of feeling, her independence of every mercenary consideration, her scorn of Stars and Garters, her *penchant* for cottages and water-falls. I was already meditating what county she would choose for her retirement, and what furniture she would prefer for her boudoir, when she asked me, at an ill-omened fancy ball, who was that clumsy Turk, in the green turban and the saffron slippers. It was my elder brother. She did not start nor change colour ; well-taught beauties never do ; but she danced that night with the clumsy Turk in the green turban and the saffron slippers ; and when I made my next visit she was just sealing a note of invitation to him, and had lighted her taper with the prettiest verses I ever wrote in my life.

If your father was an alderman, you may nevertheless be voted *comme il faut ;* if your nose is as long as the spire of Strasburg, you may yet be considered good-looking ; if you have published a sermon, you may still be reputed a wit ; if you have picked a pocket, you may by-and-by be restored to society. But if you have an elder brother— migrate ! Go to Crim Tartary or to Cochin China—wash the Hottentot—convert the Hindoo ! At home you cannot escape the stigma that pursues you. You may have honesty, genius, industry—no matter. You are a "detri-mental" for all that.

Last summer I saw Scribe's amusing scenes, "Avant,

Pendant, et Après," at the Théâtre de Madame. In the
"Avant," when the Duchess of the old *régime,* after
bestowing upon her eldest son unearned military rank and
the richest *parti* in all France, was quietly dooming her
youngest born to live poor, unknown, and Chevalier of
Malta, a fine little fellow, who was sitting in the front row
before me, looked up at his father, and cried, "Mais nous
avons changé tout cela, nést ce pas, mon papa?"

Much of it is changed. But to change it all, we must
wait for a stranger revolution than that which has regene-
rated France.

TOUJOURS PERDRIX.

WE have all been occupied for a great many years in con-
sidering whether we ought to emancipate the Catholics from
their disabilities. Let us at last begin to think whether it
is not high time to emancipate ourselves from the discussion
of them. My respectable and Popish cousin, Arthur
M'Carmick, inhabits a charming *entresol* in the Rue St.
Honoré, where he copies Vernet and reads Delavigne, dreams
of Pauline Latour, and spends six hundred a year in the
greatest freedom imaginable; yet, because he is not yet
entitled to frank letters and address the Speaker's chair,
Arthur M'Carmick wants to be emancipated. I, whom fate
and a profession confine in my native country, am fettered
by the thraldom, and haunted by the grievance, at every
turn I take. In vain I fly from the doors of Parliament,
and make a circuit of five miles to avoid the very echo of
the county meeting; my friend in the club and my
mistress in the ball-room, the ballad-singer in the street and
the preacher in the pulpit, all combine to harass my nerves,
and weary my forbearance; even Dr. Somnolent wakes
occasionally after dinner, to indulge in a guttural murmur
concerning martyrdom and the Real Presence; and Sir

Roger, when the hounds are at fault, reins up at my side, and harks back to the Revolution of 1688. Our very servants wear our prejudices, as constantly as our cast-off clothes, and our tradesmen offer us their theories more punctually than their bills. Not a week ago my groom assured me that there was no reason to be alarmed, for the Pope lived a great way off ; and my barber on the same day hinted that he knew as much as most people, and that all he knew was this, that if ever the Catholics were uppermost they would play the old bear with the Church. I could not sleep that night for thinking of Ursa Major and the Beast in the Revelations. Yet I, because I may put on a silk gown whenever it shall please His Majesty to adorn me in such radiant attire, and because, some twenty years hence, I may have hope to be in the great council of the nation, the mouthpiece of some two or three dozen of independent individuals—I, forsooth, am to petition for no emancipation.

There are persons who cannot bear the uninterrupted ticking of a pendulum in their chamber. The sustained converse of a wife vexes many. I have heard of a prisoner who was driven mad by the continued plashing of water against the wall of his cell. Such things are lively illustrations of the disquiet I endure. It is not that I am thwarted in an argument or beat on a division ; it is not that I have a horror of innovation, or a hatred of intolerance ; you are welcome to trample upon my opinions, if you will not tread upon my toes. I will waltz with any fair Whig who has a tolerable ear and a pretty figure ; and I will gladly dine with any septuagenarian Tory who is liberal in his culinary system and puts no restrictions upon his cellar. The Question kills me : no matter in what garb or under what banner it come. Brunswick and Liberator, reasoner and declaimer, song and speech, pamphlet and sermon—I hate them all.

Look at that handsome young man who is so pleasantly settling himself at his table at the Travellers'. He spends two hours daily upon his curls, and the rings on his fingers would make manacles for a burglar ; surely he has no leisure for the affairs of the nation ? The waiter has just

disclosed to his view the *anguilles en matelotte*, and the
steward is setting down beside him the pint of Johannisberg.
And he only arrived yesterday from Versailles; it is impossible he can have been infected in less than four-and-
twenty hours. Alas! there is the *Courier* extended beside
his plate; and the dish grows cold, and the wine grows
warm, while Morrison sympathizes with the feelings of
the Home Secretary, or penetrates the mysteries of the
Attorney-General's philippic.

Watch Lady Lansquenet as she takes up her hand from
the whist-table. With what an ecstasy of delight does she
marshal the brocaded warriors who are the strength of her
battle; how indignantly does she thrust into their appointed
station the more ignoble combatants, who are distinguished,
like hackney-coaches, only by their number; how reveren-
tially does she draw towards her those three last lingering
cards, as if the magic alchemy of delay were of power to
transmute a spade into a club, or exalt a plebeian into a
prince. Then, with what an air of anxiety does she
observe the changes and chances of the contest; now
flushed with triumph, now palsied with alarm; and
bestowing alternately upon her adversary and her ally
equal shares of her impartial indignation. Lady Lansquenet is neither pretty nor young, nor musical nor
literary. She does not know a Raphael from a Teniers.
nor a scene by Shakespeare from a melody by Moore.
Yet to me she seems the most conversible person in the
room; for at least the Question is nothing to Lady
Lansquenet. One may ask her what her winnings have
been without fear. "I, have lost," says her ladyship,
"twenty points. I am seldom so unfortunate; but what
could I expect, you know—with a Popish partner!"

I will go and see Frederick Marston. He has been in
love for six weeks. In ordinary cases I shrink with unfeigned
horror from the conversation of a lover—barley-broth is not
more terrible to an alderman, nor metaphysics to a blockhead, nor argument to a wit. But now, in mere self-defence,
I will go and see Frederick Marston. He will talk of wood-
pigeons and wildernesses, of eyebrows and ringlets, of
sympathies and quadrilles, of "meet me by moonlight" and

the brightest eyes in the world. I will endure it all; for he will have no thought to waste upon the wickedness of the Duke of Wellington or the disfranchisement of Larry O'Shane. So I spoke in the bitterness of my heart; and, after a brief and painful struggle with a Treasury clerk in the Haymarket, and a narrow escape in Regent Street from the heavy artillery of a Somersetshire divine, I flung myself into my old schoolfellow's armchair, and awaited his raptures or his apprehensions, as patiently as the wrecked mariner awaits the lions or the savages, when he has escaped from the billow and the blast. "My dear fellow," said my unhappy friend, and pointed, as he spoke, to a letter which was lying open on the table, "I am the most miserable of fortune's playthings. It is but a week since every obstacle was removed. The dresses were bespoken; the ring was bought; the Dean had been applied to, and the lawyer was at work. I had written out ten copies of an advertisement, and sold Hambletonian for half his value. A plague on all uncles! Sir George has discovered 'an insuperable objection.' One may guess his meaning without comment."

"Upon my life, not I! Have you criticized his Correggio?"

"Never."

"Have you abused his claret?"

"Never."

"You have thinned his preserves, then?"

"I never carried a gun there!"

"Or slept while his chaplain was preaching?"

"I never sat in his pew."

A horrible foreboding came over me. I sat in silent anticipation of the blow which was to overwhelm me. "Oh, my dear friend," said Frederick after a long pause, "why was I born under so fatal a planet? And why did my second cousin sign that infernal petition?"

My father's ancient and valued friend, Martin Marston, Esq., of Marston Hall, has vegetated for forty years in his paternal estate in the West of England, proud and happy in the enjoyment of everything which makes the life of a country gentleman enviable. He is an upright magistrate,

a kind master, a merciful landlord, and a hearty friend. If
you believe his neighbours, he has not been guilty of a
fault for ten years, but when he forgave the butler who
plundered his plate-closet; nor uttered a complaint for
twenty, except when the gout drove him out of his saddle,
and compelled him to take refuge in the pony-chair. If
his son were not the readiest Grecian at Westminster, he
was nearly the best shot in the county; and if his daughters
had little interest in the civil dissensions of the King's
Theatre, and thought of Almack's much as a Metropolitan
thinks of Timbuctoo, they had nevertheless as much beauty
as one looks for in a partner, and quite as many accomplishments as one wants in a wife. Mr. Marston has always
been a Liberal politician, partly because his own studies and
connections have that way determined him, and partly
because an ancestor of his bore a command in the Parliamentary army at the battle of Edgehill. But his principles
never interfered with his comforts. He had always a knife
and fork for the vicar, a furious High Churchman; and
suffered his next neighbour, a violent Tory, to talk him to
sleep without resistance or remonstrance—in consequence
of which Dr. Gloss declared he had never found any man
so open to conviction, and Sir Walter vowed that old
Marston was the only Radical that ever listened to reason.

When I visited Marston Hall two months ago, on my
road to Penzance, matters were strangely altered in the
establishment. I found the old gentleman sitting in his
library with a huge bundle of printed placards before him,
and a quantity of scribbled paper lying on his table. The
County Meeting was in agitation; and Mr. Marston, to the
astonishment of every one, had determined to take the
field against bigotry and persecution. He was composing
a speech. Poachers were neglected, and turnip-stealers forgotten; his favourite songs echoed unheeded, and the urn
simmered in vain. He hunted authorities, he consulted
references, he hammered periods into shape, he strung
metaphors together like beads, he translated, he transcribed.
He was determined that, if the good folk of the West remained unenlightened, the fault should not rest upon his
shoulders. Every pursuit and amusement were at an end.

He had been planning a new line of road through part of his estate, but the labourers were now at a standstill ; and he had left off reading in the middle of the third volume of "The Disowned." I found that Sir Walter had not dined at his table for five weeks ; and when I talked of accompanying his party to the parish church on Sunday, Emily silenced me with a look, and whispered that her papa read the prayers at home now, for that Dr. Gloss was a detestable fanatic, who went about getting up petitions. Mr. Marston could talk about nothing but the Question, and the speech he meant to make upon it. "Talk of the dangers of Popery," he said, "why old Tom Sarney, who died the other day, was a Papist ; I hunted with him for ten years ; never saw a man ride with better judgment. When I had that horrid tumble at Fen Brook, if Tom Sarney had not been at my side my Protestant neck would not have been worth a whistle that day. Danger, forsooth ! They are Papists at Eastwood Park, you know ; and, if my son's word is to be credited, there is one pretty Catholic there who would save at least one heretic from the bonfire. My tenant Connel is a Papist ; never flinches at Lady-day and Michaelmas. Lady Dryburgh is a Papist, and Dr. Gloss says she keeps a Jesuit in her house. By George, sir, she may have a worse faith than I, but she contrived to give twice as many blankets to the poor last Christmas. And so I shall tell my friends from the hustings next week."

When I observed the report of the proceedings at the County Meeting in the newspaper a fortnight afterwards, I find only that Mr. Marston "spoke amidst considerable uproar." But I learn from private channels that his speech has been by no means thrown away. For it is quoted with much emphasis by his gamekeeper, and it occupies thirteen closely written pages in Emily's album.

"It is the best bat in the school. I call it Mercandotti, for its shape. Look at its face; run your hand over the plane. It is smoother than a looking-glass. I was a month suiting myself, and I chose it out of a hundred. I would not part with it for its weight in gold; and that exquisite knot! lovelier, to me, than a beauty's dimple. You may fancy how that drives. I hit a ball yesterday from this very spot to the wickets in the Upper Shooting Fields; six runs clear, and I scarcely touched it. Hodgson said it was not the first time that a ball had been wonderfully struck by Mercandotti! There is not such another piece of wood in England. Collyer would give his ears for it; and that would be a long price, as Golightly says. Do take it in your hand, Courtenay; but, plague on your clumsy knuckles! You know as much of a bat as a Hottentot of the longitude or a guinea-pig of the German flute!"

So spoke the Honourable Ernest Adolphus Volant, the *decus columenque* that day of his Dame's Eleven; proud of the red silk that girded his loins, and the white hose ,that decorated his ankles; proud of his undisputed prowess, and of his anticipated victory; but prouder far of the possession of this masterpiece of nature's and Thompson's workshop, than which no pearl was ever more precious, no phœnix more unique. As he spoke, a bail dropped. The Honourable Ernest Adolphus Volant walked smilingly to the vacant wicket. What elegance in his attitude! What ease in his motions! Keep that little colleger out of the way, for we shall have the ball walking this road presently. Three to one on Ragueneau's! Now! There was a moment's pause of anxious suspense. The long fag rubbed his hands, and drew up his shirt-sleeves; the wicket-keeper stooped expectantly over the bails; the bowler trotted leisurely up to the bowling crease, and off went the ball upon its successive errands; from the hand of the bowler to the

exquisite knot in the bat of the Honourable Ernest
Adolphus Volant, from the said exquisite knot to the
unerring fingers of the crouching Long Nips, and from those
fingers up into the blue firmament of heaven with the
velocity of a sky-rocket. What a mistake! How did he
manage it? His foot slipped, or the ball was twisted, or
the sun dazzled him. It could not be the fault of the bat;
it is the best bat in the school!

A week afterwards I met my talented and enthusiastic
friend crawling to absence through the playing-fields, as
tired as a posthorse, and as hot as a salamander, with
many applauding associates on his right and on his left,
who exhibited to him certain pencilled scrawls, on which he
gazed with flushed and feverish delight. He had kept his
wicket up two hours, and made a score of seventy-three.
"I may thank my bat for it," quoth he, shouldering it as
Hercules might have shouldered his club; "it is the best
bat in the school!" Alas for the instability of human
affections! The exquisite knot had been superseded. Mercandotti had been sold for half-price, and the Honourable
Ernest Adolphus Volant was again to be eloquent, and
again to be envied; he had still the best bat in the
school.

I believe I was a tolerably good-natured boy. I am sure
I was always willing to acquiesce in the estimation my
companions set upon their treasures, because they were
generally such that I felt myself a vastly inadequate judge of
their actual value. But the Honourable Ernest Adolphus
Volant was exorbitant in the frequency and variety of his
drafts upon my sympathy. He turned off five hockey-sticks
in a fortnight; and each in its turn was unrivalled. He
wore seven waistcoats in a week, and each for its brief day
was as single in its beauty as the rainbow. In May,
Milward's shoes were unequalled; in June, Ingalton's were
divine. He lounged in Poet's Walk over a duodecimo, and
it was the sweetest edition that ever went into a waistcoat-
pocket; he pored in his study over a folio, and there was
no other copy extant but Lord Spencer's and the mutilated
one at Heidelberg. At Easter there were portraits hanging
round his room; Titian never painted their equal. At

Michaelmas, landscapes had occupied their place; Claude
would have owned himself outdone. The colt they were
breaking for him in Leicestershire, the detonator he had
bespoken of Charles Moore, the fishing-rod which had
come from Bermuda, the flageolet he had won at the raffle
—they were all, for a short season, perfection; he had
always "the best bat in the school."

The same whimsical propensity followed him through life.
Four years after we had made our last voyage to Monkey
Island in "the best skiff that ever was built," I found him
exhibiting himself in Hyde Park on "the best horse that
ever was mounted." A minute was sufficient for the compliments of our reciprocal recognition, and the Honourable
Ernest Adolphus Volant launched out forthwith into a·
rhapsody on the merits of the proud animal he bestrode.
"Kremlin, got by Smolensko, out of my uncle's old mare.
Do you know anything of a horse? Look at his shoulder!
Upon my honour, it is a model for a sculptor. And feel
how he is ribbed up; not a pin loose here; knit together
like a ship's planks; trots fourteen miles an hour without
turning a hair, and carries fifteen stone up to any hounds in
England. I hate your smart dressy creatures, as slender as
a greyhound and as tender as a gazelle, that look as if they
had been stabled in drawing-rooms and taken their turn
with the poodle in my lady's lap. I like to have plenty of
bone under me. If this horse had been properly ridden,
Courtenay, he would have won the Hunters' Stakes at our
place in a canter. He has not a leg that is not worth a
hundred pounds. Seriously, I think there is not such
another horse in the kingdom."

But before a month had gone by, the Honourable Ernest
Adolphus Volant was ambling down the ride in a pair of
stirrups far more nearly approaching *terra firma* than those
in which his illustrious feet had been reclining while he
held forth on the excellences of Kremlin. "Oh yes," he
said, when I inquired after "the best horse in England,"
"Kremlin is a magnificent animal; but then, after all, his
proper place is with the hounds. One might as well wear
one's scarlet in a ball-room as ride Kremlin in the Park.
And so I have bought Mrs. Davenant's Bijou—and a perfect

bijou she is ; throws out her little legs like an opera-dancer, and tosses her head as if she knew that her neck is irresistible. You will not find such another mane and tail in all London. Mrs. Davenant's own maid used to put up both in papers every night of the week. She is quite a love!" And so the Honourable Ernest Adolphus Volant trotted off, on a smart dressy creature, as slender as a grey-hound and as tender as a gazelle, that looked as if it had been stabled in a drawing-room and taken a turn with the poodle in my lady's lap.

An analysis of the opinions of my eccentric friend would be an entertaining thing. "The best situation in town" has been found successively in nearly every street between the Regent's Park and St. James's Square; "the best carriage for a bachelor" has gone to-day on two wheels and to-morrow on four ; "the best servant in Christendom" has been turned off, within my own knowledge, for insolence, for intoxication, for riding his master's horse, and for riding his master's inexplicables ; and "the best fellow in the world" has been at various periods deep in philosophy and deep in debt—a frequenter of the Fives Court and a dancer of quadrilles—a Tory and a Republican—a prebendary and a Papist—a drawer of dry pleadings and a singer of sentimental serenades. If I had acted upon Volant's advice, I should have been to-day subscribing to every club and taking in every newspaper ; I should have been imbibing the fluids of nine wine merchants, and covering my outward man with the broadcloth of thirteen tailors.

It is a pity that Volant has been prevented by indolence, a doting mother, and four thousand a year, from applying his energies to the attainment of any professional distinc-tion. In a variety of courses he might have commanded success. A cause might have come into court stained and spotted with every conceivable infamy, with effrontery for its crest, falsehood for its arms, and perjuries for its supporters ; but if Volant had been charged with the ad-vocacy of it, his delighted eye would have winked at every deficiency, and slumbered at every fault ; in his sight weak-ness would have sprung up into strength, deformity would have faded into beauty, impossibility would have been sobered into fact. Every plaintiff, in his showing, would have been wronged irreparably ; every defendant would have been as unsullied as snow. His would have been the most irreproachable of declarations, his the most impregnable of pleas. The reporters might have tittered, the bar might have smiled, the bench might have shaken its heads; nothing would have persuaded him that he was beaten. He would have thought the battle won, when his lines were forced at all points ; he would have deemed the house secure, when the timbers were creaking under his feet. It would have been delicious, when his strongest objection had been overruled, when his clearest argument had been stopped, when his stoutest witness had broken down, to see him adjusting his gown with a self-satisfied air, and concluding with all the emphasis of anticipated triumph, " That is *my* case, my Lord ! "

Or if he had coveted senatorial fame, what a space would he have filled in the political hemisphere ! If he had introduced a Turnpike Bill, the House would have forgotten Emancipation for a time ; if he had moved the committal of a printer, Europe would have gazed as upon the arrest of a peer of the realm. The Minister he supported would have been the most virtuous of statesmen when both Houses had voted his impeachment; the gentlemen he represented would have been the most virtuous of constituents when they had sold him their voices at five per cent. over the market price.

Destiny ordered it otherwise. One day, in that sultry season of the year when fevers and flirtations come to their crisis, and matrimony and hydrophobia scare you at every corner, I happened to call at his rooms in Regent Street, at about that time in the afternoon which the fashionable world calls daybreak. He was sitting with his chocolate before him, habited only in his *robe de chambre ;* but the folds of that joyous drapery seemed to me composed in a more studied negligence than was their wont, and the dark curls upon his fine forehead were arranged in a more scrupulous disorder. I saw at a glance that some revolution was breaking out in the state of my poor friend's mind; and when I found a broken fan on the mantelpiece and a

withered rosebud on the sofa, Walker's Lexicon open on
the writing-table and an unfinished stanza reposing on the
toast-rack, I was no longer in doubt as to its nature; the
Honourable Ernest Adolphus Volant was seriously in
love.

It was not to be wondered at that his mistress was
the loveliest being of her sex, nor that he told me so
fourteen times in the following week. Her father was a
German prince, the proprietor of seven leagues of vineyard,
five ruined castles, and three hundred flocks of sheep. She
had light hair, blue eyes, and a profound knowledge of
metaphysics; she sang like a siren, and her name was
Adelinda.

I spent a few months abroad. When I returned, he was
married to the loveliest being of her sex, and had sent me
fifty notes to inform me of the fact and beseech me to
visit him at Volant Hall, with the requisite quantity of
sympathy and congratulation. I went, and was introduced
in form. Her father was a country clergyman, the proprietor of seven acres of glebe, five broken armchairs, and
three hundred manuscript discourses; she had dark hair,
black eyes, and a fond love of poetry; she danced like a
wood-nymph, and her name was Mary.

He has lived since his marriage a very quiet life, rarely
visiting the metropolis, and devoting his exertions most
indefatigably to the comfort of his tenantry and the
improvement of his estate. Volant Hall is deliciously
situated in the best county in England. If you go thither,
you must go prepared with the tone, or at least with the
countenance, of approbation and wonder. He gives you,
of course, mutton such as no other pasture fattens, and ale
such as no other cellar brews. The stream that runs
through his park supplies him with trout of unprecedented
beauty and delicacy; and he could detect a partridge that
had feasted in his woods amidst the bewildering confusion
of a Lord Mayor's banquet. You must look at his con-
servatory; no other was ever constructed on the same
principle. You must handle his plough; he himself has
obtained a patent for the invention. Everything, within
doors and without, has wherewithal to attract and astonish;

the melon and the magnolia, the stable and the dairy, the mounting of his mother's spectacles and the music of his wife's piano.   He has few pictures, but they are the masterpieces of the best masters.   He has only one statue, but he assures you that it is Canova's *chef-d'œuvre.*   The last time I was with him, he had a theme to descant upon which made his eloquence more than usually impassioned. An heir was just born to the Volant acres.   An ox was roasted, and a barrel pierced in every meadow ; the noise of fiddles was incessant for a week, and the expenditure of powder would have lasted a Lord High Admiral for a twelvemonth.   It was allowed by all the county that there never was so sweet a child as little Adolphus.

Among his acquaintance, who have generally little toleration for any foibles but their own, Volant is pretty generally voted a bore.

"Of course our pinery is not like Mr. Volant's," says Lady Framboise; "he is prating from morning to night of his fires and flues.   We have taken some pains, and we pay a ruinous sum to our gardener, but we never talk about it."

"The deuce take that fellow Volant," says Mr. Crayon, " does he fancy no one has a Correggio but himself?   I have one that cost me two thousand guineas, and I would not part with it for double the sum ; but I never talk about it."

" That boy Volant," says old Sir Andrew Chalkstone, "is so delighted to find himself the father of another boy, that, by Jove, he can speak of nothing else.   Now I have a little thing in a cradle, too ; a fine boy, they tell me, and vastly like his father, but I never talk about it."

Well, well ! let a man be obliging to his neighbours, and merciful to his tenants, an upright citizen and an affectionate friend, and there is˙one judge who will not condemn him for having " the best bat in the school ! "

PRINTED BY BALLANTYNE, HANSON AND CO.
LONDON AND EDINBURGH

GEORGE ROUTLEDGE & SONS' CATALOGUE.

NATURAL HISTORY—ZOOLOGY.

Routledge's Illustrated Natural History. By the Rev. J. G. Wood, M.A. With more than 1500 Illustrations by Coleman, Wolf, Harrison Weir, Wood, Zwecker, and others. Three Vols., super-royal, cloth, price £2 2s. The Volumes are also sold separately, viz. :—Mammalia, with 600 Illustrations, 14s. ; Birds, with 500 Illustrations, 14s. ; Reptiles Fishes, and Insects, 400 Illustrations, 14s.

Routledge's Illustrated History of Man. Being an Account of the Manners and Customs of the Uncivilised Races of Men. By the Rev. J. G. Wood, M.A., F.L.S. With more than 600 Original Illustrations by Zwecker, Danby, Angas, Handley, and others, engraved by the Brothers Dalziel. Vol. I., Africa, 14s.; Vol. II., Australia, New Zealand, Polynesia, America, Asia, and Ancient Europe, 14s. Two Vols., super-royal 8vo, cloth, 28s.

The Imperial Natural History. By the Rev. J. G. Wood. 1000 pages, with 500 Plates, super-royal 8vo, cloth, 15s.

An Illustrated Natural History. By the Rev. J. G. Wood. With 500 Illustrations by William Harvey, and 8 full-page Plates by Wolf and Harrison Weir. Post 8vo, cloth, gilt edges, 6s.

A Picture Natural History. Adapted for Young Readers. By the Rev. J. G. Wood. With 700 Illustrations by Wolf, Weir, &c. 4to, cloth, gilt edges, . 7s. 6d.

The Popular Natural History. By the Rev. J. G. Wood. With Hundreds of Illustrations, price 7s. 6d.

The Boy's Own Natural History. By the Rev. J. G. Wood. With 400 Illustrations, 3s. 6d. cloth,

Sketches and Anecdotes of Animal Life. By the Rev. J. G. Wood. Illustrated by Harrison Weir. Fcap. 8vo, cloth, 3s. 6d.

Animal Traits and Characteristics. By the Rev. J. G. Wood. Illustrated by H. Weir. Fcap., cloth, 3s. 6d.

The Poultry Book. By W. B. Tegetmeier, F.Z.S. Assisted by many Eminent Authorities. With 30 full-page Illustrations of the different Varieties, drawn from Life by Harrison Weir, and printed in Colours by Leighton Brothers ; and numerous Woodcuts. Imperial 8vo, half-bound, price 21s.

The Standard of Excellence in Exhibition Poultry. By W. B. Tegetmeier, F.Z.S. Fcap., cloth, 2s. 6d.

NATURAL HISTORY, *continued.*

Pigeons. By W. B. TEGETMEIER, F.Z.S., Assisted by many Eminent Fanciers. With 27 Coloured Plates, drawn from Life by HARRISON WEIR, and printed by LEIGHTON Brothers ; and numerous Woodcuts. Imperial 8vo, half-bound, 10s. 6d.

The Homing or Carrier Pigeon : Its History, Management, and Method of Training. By W. B. TEGETMEIER, F.Z.S. 1s. boards.

My Feathered Friends. Containing Anecdotes of Bird Life, more especially Eagles, Vultures, Hawks, Magpies, Rooks, Crows, Ravens, Parrots, Humming Birds, Ostriches, &c., &c. By the Rev. J. G. WOOD. With Illustrations by HARRISON WEIR. Cloth gilt, 3s. 6d.

British Birds' Eggs and Nests. By the Rev. J. C. ATKINSON. With Original Illustrations by W. S. COLEMAN, printed in Colours. Fcap., cloth, gilt edges, price 3s. 6d.

The Angler Naturalist. A Popular History of British Freshwater Fish. By H. CHOLMONDELEY PENNELL. Post 8vo, 3s. 6d.

British Conchology. A Familiar History of the MOLLUSCS of the British Isles. By G. B. SOWERBY. With 20 Pages of Coloured Plates, embracing 150 subjects. Cloth, 5s.

The Calendar of the Months. Giving an Account of the Plants, Birds, and Insects that may be expected each Month. With 100 Illustrations. Cloth gilt, 3s. 6d.; Cheap Edition, 2s.

White's Natural History of Selborne. New Edition. Edited by Rev. J. G. WOOD, with above 200 Illustrations by W. HARVEY. Fcap. 8vo, cloth, 3s. 6d.,

Dogs and their Ways. Illustrated by numerous Anecdotes from Authentic Sources. By the Rev. CHARLES WILLIAMS. With Illustrations. Fcap. 8vo, cloth, 3s. 6d.

Sagacity of Animals. With 60 Engravings by HARRISON WEIR. Small 4to, 3s. 6d.

The Young Naturalist. By Mrs. LOUDON. 16mo, cloth, Illustrated, 1s. 6d.

The Child's First Book of Natural History. By Miss BOND. With 100 Illustrations. 16mo, cloth, 1s. 6d.

The Common Objects of the Country. By the Rev. J. G. WOOD. With Illustrations by COLEMAN, containing 150 of the "Objects" beautifully printed in Colours. Cloth, gilt edges, price 3s. 6d.
Also a CHEAP EDITION, price 1s., in fancy boards, with Plain Plates.

Common British Beetles. By the Rev. J. G. WOOD, M.A. With Woodcuts and Twelve pages of Plates of all the Varieties, beautifully printed in Colours by EDMUND EVANS. Fcap. 8vo, cloth, gilt edges, price 3s. 6d.

Westwood's (Professor) British Butterflies and their Transformations. With numerous Illustrations, beautifully Coloured by Hand. Imperial 8vo, cloth, 12s. 6d.

Natural History, *continued.*

British Butterflies. Figures and Descriptions of every Native Species, with an Account of Butterfly Life. With 71 Coloured Figures of Butterflies, all of exact life-size, and 67 Figures of Caterpillars, Chrysalides, &c. By W. S. Coleman. Fcap., cloth gilt, price 3s. 6d.

*** A Cheap Edition, with plain Plates, fancy boards, price 1s.

The Common Moths of England. By the Rev. J. G. Wood, M.A. 12 Plates printed in Colours, comprising 100 objects. Cloth, gilt edges. 3s. 6d.

*** A Cheap Edition, with plain Plates, boards, 1s.

British Entomology. Containing a Familiar and Technical Description of the Insects most common to the localities of the British Isles. By Maria E. Catlow. With 16 pages of Coloured Plates. Cloth, 5s.

Popular Scripture Zoology. With Coloured Illustrations. By Maria E. Catlow. Cloth, 5s.

The Common Objects of the Sea-Shore. With Hints for the Aquarium. By the Rev. J. G. Wood. The Fine Edition, with the Illustrations by G. B. Sowerby, beautifully printed in Colours. Fcap. 8vo, cloth, gilt edges, 3s. 6d.

*** Also, price 1s., a Cheap Edition, with the Plates plain.

British Crustacea: A Familiar Account of their Classification and Habits. By Adam White, F.L.S. 20 Pages of Coloured Plates, embracing 120 subjects. Cloth, 5s.

The Fresh-Water and Salt-Water Aquarium. By the Rev. J. G. Wood, M.A. With 11 Coloured Plates, containing 126 Objects. Cloth, 3s. 6d.

A Cheap Edition, with plain Plates, boards, 1s.

The Aquarium of Marine and Fresh-Water Animals and Plants. By G. B. Sowerby, F.L.S. With 20 Pages of Coloured Plates, embracing 120 subjects. Cloth, 5s.

FLOWERS, PLANTS, AND GARDENING.

Gardening at a Glance. By George Glenny. With Illustrations. Fcap. 8vo, gilt edges, 3s. 6d.

Roses, and How to Grow Them. By J. D. Prior. Coloured Plates. Cloth gilt, 3s. 6d.

*** A Cheap Edition, with plain Plates, fancy boards, 1s. 6d.

Garden Botany. Containing a Familiar and Scientific Description of most of the Hardy and Half-hardy Plants introduced into the Flower Garden. By Agnes Catlow. 20 Pages of Coloured Plates, embracing 67 Illustrations. 5s.

FLOWERS, PLANTS, AND GARDENING, *continued.*

The Kitchen and Flower Garden; or, The Culture in the open ground of Roots, Vegetables, Herbs, and Fruits, and of Bulbous, Tuberous, Fibrous, Rooted, and Shrubby Flowers. By EUGENE SEBASTIAN DELA-MER. Fcap., cloth, gilt edges, price 3s. 6d.
THE KITCHEN GARDEN, separate, 1s.
THE FLOWER GARDEN, separate, 1s.

The Cottage Garden. How to Lay it out, and Cultivate it to Advantage. By ANDREW MEIKLE. Boards, 1s.

Window Gardening, for Town and Country. Compiled chiefly for the use of the Working Classes. By ANDREW MEIKLE. Boards, 1s.

Greenhouse Botany. Containing a Familiar and Technical Description of the Exotic Plants introduced into the Greenhouse. By AGNES CATLOW. With 20 Pages of Coloured Illustrations. 5s.

Wild Flowers. How to See and How to Gather them. With Remarks on the Economical and Medicinal Uses of our Native Plants. By SPENCER THOMSON, M.D. A New Edition, entirely Revised, with 172 Woodcuts, and 8 large Coloured Illustrations by NOEL HUMPHREYS. Fcap. 8vo, price 3s. 6d., cloth, gilt edges.
** Also, price 2s. in boards, a CHEAP EDITION, with plain Plates.

Haunts of Wild Flowers. By ANNE PRATT. Coloured Plates. Cloth, gilt edges, 3s. 6d.
** Plain Plates, boards, 2s.

Common Wayside Flowers. By THOMAS MILLER. With Coloured Illustrations by BIRKET FOSTER. 4to, cloth gilt, 10s. 6d.

British Ferns and the Allied Plants. Comprising the Club-Mosses, Pepperworts, and Horsetails. By THOMAS MOORE, F.L.S. With 20 Pages of Coloured Illustrations, embracing 51 subjects. Cloth, 5s.

Our Woodlands, Heaths, and Hedges. A Popular Description of Trees, Shrubs, Wild Fruits, &c., with Notices of their Insect Inhabitants. By W. S. COLEMAN, M.E.S.L. With 41 Illustrations printed in Colours on Eight Plates. Fcap., price 3s. 6d., cloth, gilt edges.
** A CHEAP EDITION, with plain Plates, fancy boards, 1s.

British Ferns and their Allies. Comprising the Club-Mosses, Pepperworts, and Horsetails. By THOMAS MOORE. With 40 Illustrations by W. S. COLEMAN, beautifully printed in Colours. Fcap. 8vo, cloth, gilt edges, 3s. 6d.
** A CHEAP EDITION, with Coloured Plates, price 1s., fancy boards.

Plants of the World; or, A Botanical Excursion Round the World. By E. M. C. Edited by CHARLES DAUBENY, M.D., F.R.S., &c. With 20 Pages of Coloured Plates of Scenery. Cloth, 5s.

Palms and their Allies. Containing a Familiar Account of their Structure, Distribution, History, Properties, and Uses; and a complete List of all the species introduced into our Gardens. By BERTHOLD SEEMANN, Ph.D., M.A., F.L.S. With 20 Pages of Coloured Illustrations, embracing many varieties. Cloth, 5s.

FLOWERS, PLANTS, AND GARDENING, *continued*.

Profitable Plants : A Description of the Botanical and Commercial Characters of the principal Articles of Vegetable Origin, used for Food, Clothing, Tanning, Dyeing, Building, Medicine, Perfumery, &c. By THOMAS C. ARCHER, Collector for the Department of Applied Botany in the Crystal Palace, Sydenham. With 20 Pages of Coloured Illustrations, embracing 106 Plates. Cloth, 5*s*.

The Language of Flowers. By the Rev. R. TYAS. With Coloured Plates by KRONHEIM. 4to, 7*s*. 6*d*.

Language of Flowers. Compiled and Edited by Mrs. L. BURKE. Cloth elegant, 2*s*. 6*d*.

₄ CHEAPER BOOKS, 1*s*. and 6*d*.

SCIENCE.

Discoveries and Inventions of the Nineteenth Century. By ROBERT ROUTLEDGE, B.Sc. and F.C.S. With many Illustrations, and a beautiful Coloured Plate, 7*s*. 6*d*.

Science in Sport made Philosophy in Earnest. By ROBERT ROUTLEDGE. Post 8vo, cloth, gilt edges, 3*s*. 6*d*.

The Boys' Book of Science. Including the Successful Performance of Scientific Experiments. 470 Engravings. By Professor PEPPER, late of the Polytechnic. Cloth, gilt edges, 5*s*.

The Book of Metals. Including Personal Narratives of Visits to Coal, Lead, Copper, and Tin Mines; with a large number of interesting Experiments. 300 Illustrations. By Professor PEPPER, late of the Polytechnic. Post 8vo, cloth, gilt edges, 5*s*.

The Microscope : Its History, Construction, and Application. Being a Familiar Introduction to the Use of the Instrument, and the Study of Microscopical Science. By JABEZ HOGG, F.L.S., F.R.M.S. With upwards of 500 Engravings and Coloured Illustrations by TUFFEN WEST. Eighth Edition, crown 8vo, cloth, 7*s*. 6*d*.

The Common Objects of the Microscope. By the Rev. J. G. WOOD. With Twelve Pages of Plates by TUFFEN WEST, embracing upwards of 400 Objects. The Illustrations printed in Colours. Fcap. 8vo, 3*s*. 6*d*., cloth, gilt edges.
₄ A CHEAP EDITION, with Plain Plates, 1*s*., fancy boards.

The Orbs of Heaven ; or, The Planetary and Stellar Worlds. A Popular Exposition of the great Discoveries and Theories of Modern Astronomy. By O. M. MITCHELL. With numerous Illustrations. Crown 8vo, 2*s*. 6*d*.

Popular Astronomy ; or, The Sun, Planet, Satellites, and Comets. With Illustrations of their Telescopic Appearance. By O. M. MITCHELL. 2*s*. 6*d*.

The Story of the Peasant-Boy Philosopher. Founded on the Early Life of FERGUSON, the Astronomer. By HENRY MAYHEW. Illustrated. Cloth gilt, 3*s*. 6*d*.

SCIENCE, *continued*

The Wonders of Science; or, The Story of Young HUMPHREY DAVY, the Cornish Apothecary's Boy, who taught Himself Natural Philosophy. By HENRY MAYHEW. Illustrated. Cloth gilt, 3s. 6d.

The Book of Trades, and the Tools used in Them. By One of the Authors of " England's Workshops." With numerous Illustrations. Small 4to, cloth, gilt edges, 3s. 6d.

Wonderful Inventions, from the Mariner's Compass to the Electric Telegraph Cable. By JOHN TIMBS. Illustrated. Post 8vo, 5s.

A Manual of Fret-Cutting and Wood-Carving. By Sir THOMAS SEATON, K.C.B. Crown 8vo, cloth, 1s.

The Laws of Contrast of Colours, and their Application to the Arts. New Edition, with an important Section on Army Clothing. By M. E. CHEVREUL. Translated by JOHN SPANTON. With Coloured Illustrations. Crown 8vo, 3s 6d. cloth gilt.

Geology for the Million. By MARGARET PLUES. Edited by EDWARD WOOD, F.G.S. With 80 Illustrations. Fcap., picture boards, 1s.

A Manual of Weather-casts and Storm Prognostics on Land and Sea; or, The Signs whereby to judge of Coming Weather. Adapted for all Countries. By ANDREW STEINMETZ. Boards, 1s.

Scientific Amusements. Edited by Professor PEPPER. 100 Woodcuts. 1s., boards ; 1s. 6d., cloth gilt.

Electric Lighting. Translated from the French of Le Comte Th. du Moncel. By ROBERT ROUTLEDGE, B.Sc. (Lond.), F.C.S. Crown 8vo, cloth, 2s. 6d.

HISTORY.

THE HISTORICAL WORKS OF WM. H. PRESCOTT.

The History of the Reign of Ferdinand and Isabella the Catholic of Spain. By WILLIAM H. PRESCOTT. With Steel Portraits. Two Vols. 8vo, cloth, price 10s.

 Do.   Do.   Three Vols. post 8vo, cloth, 10s. 6d.
 Do.   Do.   One Vol. crown 8vo, cloth, 3s. 6d.

History of the Conquest of Mexico. With a Preliminary View of the Ancient Mexican Civilisation, and the Life of the Conqueror, FERNANDO CORTES. By WILLIAM H. PRESCOTT. With Portraits on Steel. Two Vols. 8vo, cloth, 10s.

 Do.   Do.   Three Vols. post 8vo, cloth, 10s. 6d.
 Do.   Do.   One Vol. crown 8vo, cloth, 3s. 6d.

History of the Conquest of Peru. With a Preliminary View of the Civilisation of the Incas. By WILLIAM H. PRESCOTT. With Steel Portraits. Two Vols. 8vo, cloth, 10s.

 Do.   Do.   Three Vols. post 8vo, cloth, 10s. 6d.
 Do.   Do.   One Vol. crown 8vo, cloth, 3s. 6d.

ROUTLEDGE'S
POCKET LIBRARY.

In MONTHLY VOLUMES, Cut or Uncut Edges, 1s. ;
Uncut Edges, with Gilt Tops, 1s. 6d. ; or Paste Grain, 2s. 6d. each.

"A series of beautiful little books, tastefully bound."—TIMES.
"Deserves warm praise for the taste shown in its production. The 'Library' ought to be very popular."—ATHENÆUM.
"Beautifully printed and tastefully bound."—SATURDAY REVIEW.
"Choice and elegant."—DAILY NEWS.
"Routledge's PERFECT Pocket Library."—PUNCH.

VOLUMES ALREADY ISSUED :

Bret Harte's Poems.
Thackeray's Paris Sketch Book.
Hood's Comic Poems.
Dickens's Christmas Carol.
Poems by Oliver Wendell Holmes.
Washington Irving's Sketch Book.
Macaulay's Lays of Ancient Rome.
Goldsmith's Vicar of Wakefield.
Hood's Serious Poems.
The Coming Race, by Lord Lytton.
The Biglow Papers, by J. R. Lowell.
Manon Lescaut, by the Abbé Prevost.
The Song of Hiawatha, by H. W. Longfellow
Sterne's Sentimental Journey.
Dickens's The Chimes.
Moore's Irish Melodies.
Fifty "Bab" Ballads, by W. S. Gilbert.
Poems, by Elizabeth Barrett Browning.
The Luck of Roaring Camp, by Bret Harte.
Poems by Edgar A. Poe.
Milton's Paradise Lost.
Scott's Lady of the Lake.
Campbell's Poetical Works.
Lord Byron's Werner.
Humour, Wit, and Wisdom.
Longfellow's Hyperion.

GEORGE ROUTLEDGE AND SONS,
BROADWAY LUDGATE HILL, LONDON, E.C

ROUTLEDGE'S WORLD LIBRARY.

Edited by the Rev. H. R. HAWEIS, M.A.

EACH VOLUME **3d.**, 160 pages, Paper Cover ; or in Cloth, 6*d*

LIST OF THE SERIES :

Goethe's Faust. Translated by JOHN ANSTER, LL.D.
Life of Lord Nelson.
Goldsmith's Plays and Poems.
Memoirs of Baron Trenck,
White's Natural History of Selborne.
Captain Cook's Third and Last Voyage.
Longfellow's Popular Poems.
Life of the Duke of Wellington.
Gulliver's Travels.
De Foe's Journal of the Plague.
Æsop's Fables.
British Birds' Eggs and Nests.
The Mutiny of the "Bounty."
Lamb's Tales from Shakespeare.
O. W. Holmes' Professor at the Breakfast Table.
Chinese Gordon.
Addison's Spectator (Selections).
Travels of Dr. Livingstone.
Comic Poets of the Nineteenth Century.
Poe's Tales of Mystery.
Mrs. Rundell's Cookery—Meats.
     Ditto   Ditto   Sweets.
Common Objects of the Seashore.
     Ditto   Ditto   Country.
Frankenstein. By Mrs. SHELLEY.
Henry Ward Beecher in the Pulpit.
Essay-Gems of Emerson.
Napoleon Buonaparte.
Old Ballads.
Pet. By the Rev. H. R. HAWEIS, M.A.
Select Poems.
The Siege of Jerusalem. By JOSEPHUS.
Gems of Byron.
Dickens' Christmas Carol and the Chimes.
Bret Harte's Poems.
Tales from Chaucer. Mrs HAWEIS.
The Innocents Abroad. By MARK TWAIN.
The New Pilgrim's Progress. By MARK TWAIN.
Essays of Elia. By CHARLES LAMB.
Life of Queen Victoria.

GEORGE ROUTLEDGE AND SONS.

ROUTLEDGE'S EXCELSIOR SERIES

OF STANDARD AUTHORS,

Without Abridgment, Crown 8vo, 2s. each, in cloth.

1 The Wide, Wide World, by Miss Wetherell.
2 Melbourne House, by Miss Wetherell.
3 The Lamplighter, by Miss Cummins.
4 Stepping Heavenward, and Aunt Jane's Hero, by E. Prentiss.
5 Queechy, by Miss Wetherell.
6 Ellen Montgomery's Bookshelf, by Miss Wetherell.
7 The Two School Girls, and other Tales, illustrating the Beatitudes, by Miss Wetherell.
8 Helen, by Maria Edgeworth.
9 The Old Helmet, by Miss Wetherell.
10 Mabel Vaughan, by Miss Cummins.
11 The Glen Luna Family, or Speculation, by Miss Wetherell.
12 The Word, or Walks from Eden, by Miss Wetherell.
13 Alone, by Marion Harland.
14 The Lofty and Lowly, by Miss M'Intosh.
15 Prince of the House of David, by Rev. J. H. Ingraham.
16 Uncle Tom's Cabin, by Mrs. Stowe, with a Preface by the Earl of Carlisle
17 Longfellow's Poetical Works, 726 pages, with Portrait.
18 Burns's Poetical Works, with Memoir by Willmott.
19 Moore's Poetical Works, with Memoir by Howitt.
20 Byron's Poetical Works, Selections from Don Juan.
21 Pope's Poetical Works, Edited by the Rev. H. F. Cary, with a Memoir
22 Wise Sayings of the Great and Good, with Classified Index of Subjects
23 Lover's Poetical Works.
24 Bret Harte's Poems.
25 Mrs. Hemans' Poetical Works.
26 Coleridge's Poetical Works, with Memoir by W. B. Scott.
27 Dodd's Beauties of Shakspeare.
28 Hood's Poetical Works, Serious and Comic, 456 pages.
29 The Book of Familiar Quotations, from the Best Authors.
30 Shelley's Poetical Works, with Memoir ky W. B. Scott.
31 Keats' Poetical Works, with Memoir by W. B. Scott.
32 Shakspere Gems. Extracts, specially designed for Youth.
33 The Book of Humour, Wit, and Wisdom, a Manual of Table Talk.
34 E. A. Poe's Poetical Works, with Memoir by R. H. Stoddard.
35 L. E. L., The Poetical Works of (Letitia Elizabeth Landon). With Memoir by W. B. Scott.
37 Sir Walter Scott's Poetical Works, with Memoir.
38 Shakspere, complete, with Poems and Sonnets, edited by Charles Knight.
39 Cowper's Poetical Works.
40 Milton's Poetical Works, from the Text of Dr. Newton.
41 Sacred Poems, Devotional and Moral.
42 Sydney Smith's Essays, from the *Edinburgh Review*.
43 Choice Poems and Lyrics, from 130 Poets.

[*continued*.

www.ingramcontent.com/pod-product-compliance
Lightning Source LLC
Chambersburg PA
CBHW020900020726
47497CB00005B/1500